OF

FANGS

AND

SHADOWS

JESSICA J AYALA

To the introvert who prefers reading instead of talking to people

And to mi amor, te amo

PLAYLIST

"Everything Black"—Unlike Pluto
"The Hate Inside"—Tommee Proffitt, Sam Tinnesz
"Behind the Mask"—Ivy & Gold
"Nightmare"—UNDREAM, Neoni
"Song of the Man Who Never Gave Up"—Eternal Eclipse
"Charges from the Sky"—Joseph William Morgan
"Less Alone"—Eternal Eclipse
"Soul Battles"—City & Vine
"Can't Help Falling In Love (LIGHT)"—Tommee Proffit, brooke
"War (Epic Trailer Version)"—J2, Maddi Lasker
"With Arms Wide Open"—Tommee Proffit, Nicole Serrano
"And A Legend You Shall Be"—ScoreHero

A Note To The Reader

While this story is not formally a dark fantasy romance, it does explore darker themes of trauma and loss. There are sexually descriptive scenes with a mild kink scenario.

The characters in this book are not knights in shining armor, nor are they stereotypical heroes. They are morally grey warriors who undergo their own experiences of healing and growth. Reader discretion is advised. I trust that you will be mindful of your own triggers and limitations.

WOLF AND FLAME

The people
who consider you weak
have not yet noticed
the wolf hiding
behind your eyes,
nor the flames
inside your soul.

Let them think
you are weak
and do what
wolves and fire
do best.

Surprise them
when they least expect it.

Nikita Gill

PROLOGUE

The deep gold pommel of the god of war's sword winked under the undying light of Olympus. An endless clash between dusk and dawn hung above the golden plains. Mountains with a height beyond reason speared through the pale clouds. Rivers of crystalline blue cut through the tall grass. This place would be the resting place of the gods' creations. Future creations. He felt the shift in the aether, the fifth element composed of the essence that divided the realms. That divided him from the mortal realm he and his brothers and sisters had created. Where his mortal love meandered, heavy with life in her belly. *His* descendants. Twins. He knew it and he couldn't suppress the excitement about sharing the news with her.

The warm breath of Olympus swept a gentle, invisible hand through his brown curls. The god of war focused his gaze back to the war room, where the creature was bound in chains. Obsidian horns curled like that of a ram, a body made of dark, leathery hide. Crescent-shaped eyes that leered, and lips that spat at the floor of the god's feet.

"You betrayed me," the daemon sneered.

The god of war refused to show the turmoil that burned in his chest. The heartbreak. This daemon had been one of them. A god in the making. Thrived in the mortal land with his kind, but it was a mistake. Daemons didn't belong in that realm. No, they had been sent to another, a better one, where they could thrive among others like them.

The one bound to the floor knew it but still refused to join his kind. Began to call himself the daemon king. The god of war could've mocked him but refrained. For whatever reason the daemon had become obsessed with the mortal realm. Had become arrogant, corrupt, and entitled. He had rallied followers—armies. The realm was too young for such matters. The gods had to intervene before the mortal land could even begin. Now the daemon would be an outcast, his name forgotten by the demand of the gods and goddesses. His armies banished along with him.

"Bold statement seeing as you betrayed your own kind," the god surmised, a look of boredom drawn over the sculpted planes of his face. "You want to overthrow the mortal lands when they are not yours to rule."

The daemon shook with rage. "They are bound to destroy themselves regardless. Why not let me take control? Why not change the course of the mortals' fates?"

The god of war was silent for a breath. "That is not your decision to make. They are to choose for themselves."

"Mars."

Void of the previous anger, the daemon's voice sounded almost desperate. Mars closed his eyes against the sound, unable to look at the creature who could've been part of something wondrous. Now the Fates were rescripting, he could sense it, and it disturbed him.

When Mars opened his eyes, embers of his power flared. White, like moonlight. "No one will know your name . . ."

The daemon yanked against the binds. "No—"

"You will be cast out into a prison realm."

Chains wailed. "Mars, you can't."

"I no longer know you. The gods and goddesses of the cultures no longer see you." Mars' eyes lowered, meeting the hatred that burned in the exiled daemon's. "You could've been so much more."

The god raised his palm. The creature shook, muscles straining against the aether-laced chains. He knew what was to come. Behind him, a light split. Pulling at the seams of the realms, opening to the prison land. Silvery light yanked the daemon, ripping him from the chains and into the chasm. His roars echoed even after the last of the light sealed the realms again.

Mars released a sigh, laden with an odd taste of sadness. What happened with the creature was disappointing, but that wasn't what concerned him. From here on, everything that occurred would be out of his godly hands. Rules of nature bound him and those of his kind. He hoped what was done was enough. It had to be.

He strode into the open courtyard. Torches of aether flickered along the pillars, soft shadows dancing, guiding the god down the marble steps all the way down to the golden plains. Jupiter and his other siblings were waiting. He didn't want to see them, didn't care to. There was someone else waiting for him. Someone who meant more to him than all of Olympus.

In a blaze of light, Mars found himself in the woods. The air in the mortal realm was heavier, not as light and fresh as that of Olympus. There were no grand mountains here, no sky of dusk and dawn. However, none of that celestial beauty compared to when he was with her. He would gladly leave it all behind if he had to, for her.

A woman was bent over the riverbank, her gown of silk and pale moonlight. Curls rained over her head down to her waistline. Entwined and beaded along a thin band of gold were white blossoms that crowned her head. Her body relaxed at sensing his presence. She always knew when it was him, and the thought seared through his chest with a beautiful hiss of heat.

Mars strode toward her, an arm wrapping around her waist. He relished how her body melded against his chest. His fingers trailed a line down her neck, and his lips followed.

"Rhea," he breathed.

The princess smiled. "Mars."

"I've missed you." His hand rounded over the swell of her belly. "And them."

Rhea's round, brown eyes widened and glistened. "Them?"

He smiled. "Twins. Boys."

Rhea sighed happily, resting a hand over his as they felt the warmth of their children stir underneath her skin. "Though it is a beautiful thing to bring life into this world, it's utter torture."

Mars barked a laugh, the sound deep and rustic like ancient wood. "It is a power only females have. It may be barbaric, but it reveals their strength."

Rhea's lips turned sly, humor kissing the corners of her mouth. "I didn't need pregnancy to tell me that."

Mars grinned and pressed his lips to her head. "No, you didn't."

"The king will know soon." Concern knitted at her brow.

The god froze. He had been battling this pestilence plaguing his thoughts, had shoved it down, locked it away. It had been haunting him since the moment Rhea became pregnant, and now it flared through his godly veins. It dimmed the color of his aether, pulled at his chest to the point he tasted something bitter on his tongue. This was foreign to him; never in his entire existence had he experienced fear. The god was afraid for the human he had fallen in love with.

His arms slid up to her chest, holding her tighter as if that could protect her from what fate had written for them. "I know we have a plan and we've discussed it many times, but I hate that I can't intervene. Every part of me screams to do something."

Rhea angled her head to look up at him. "This is what needs to be done. Creatures of wonder already stalk these lands. You and I are leaving a legacy. Our sons will begin a new lineage, and the wolves will leave our imprint throughout the millennia."

Mars observed the woman. How queenly she was and would never be. At least not in this mortal realm. He would make her a goddess and wander the golden plains with her forever.

He pressed his lips against hers. The taste of cinnamon and apple. "You are my glory."

Rhea sighed against his mouth, and they held each other under the eye of the moonlight. The waters rushed gently at their feet and the trees witnessed the love between a god and a mortal as the Fates shifted their threads of the future. Their nightly fingers, freckled with stars and constellations, weaved the multiple strands of fate, curious as to what would unfold.

The creature bowed his head. His aether, ancient, forged by the birth of the sun and its stars, coursed through his veins, bleeding into the cursed ground. His armies stirred behind, a shifting of wings, and a gnashing of teeth. Yes. His time would come. Crescent eyes, red like the blood of a descending sun, glared at where the seams of the realms once flared. They had removed him. To punish him. Robbed him of his kind and the power that was rightfully his. It may not be for thousands of years, but the plot of his revenge would taste so sweet he was willing to wait. By his ancient aether, he would influence the mortals that plagued his land. Spite those who banished him. Gods and the Fates be damned.

PART 1

THE LONE WOLF

ONE

Remus

Smoke curled its dusted fingers below the sea of stars. Night had thrown a starred cloak over the mortal land, a deep purple light caressing the mountains. The sun had long bled the last of its golden rays, and the elegance of the night did little to pull my attention from the carnage ahead. The blood soddened the ground underneath my paws. Black and red seeped between my ebony claws. Remnants of the latest daemon attack had left this town desolated. Roofs were caved in, chunks of red tile and pale limestone littered the roads. Bodies were whittled into ribbons. I had become so accustomed to gore I could no longer hurl at the sight and stench of it.

Scattered fires were the only forms of light, making the trees look like tall, lonely guards, sore witnesses to the death that resided here. This had not been my intended destination. I had been hunting, heading to a city with a harbor where another life would meet the end of my fangs, when the stark scent of daemons had lured me there instead, like a fucking fish to a hook.

The night called to me as it would to any of my kind. Darkness caressed through the soft, dark furs of my wolf form. My ears twitched, straining to catch sounds of life. The sickly, sweet smell of rendered flesh tugged me toward a house. The entire rooftop had been obliterated, and red tiles filled what would have been the living space.

I prowled closer, the fine hairs on my neck bristling. My voice curled between my fangs. Deep and rumbling like the quaking of the ground. *"I hear you, you best come out now."*

There was a scuffle and the shattering of a tile. Dust popped into a thin plume, and a small head emerged from the debris. I immediately closed my jaws. It was a young boy, staring at me with wide eyes. He balked and, with a frightened squeak, ducked low behind part of the crumbled wall while still keeping his eyes on me. He watched me for a few moments, and once he'd realized I would be no threat to him, he slowly rose.

"I can't find *Mater*," he stuttered, stumbling out of the broken tiles. Cuts and bruises covered his flesh. He couldn't have been more than six years of age.

The little boy wobbled towards me. "Are you Rome's wolfie? Mater told me stories."

I was not too sure about the name 'Rome's wolfie.' The mention of the Roman Pack prodded at my senses in a way I didn't want to acknowledge. The child was familiar with our kind, which was of no surprise. The wolves were proclaimed sons of war. Revered and admired by all.

"Not quite, little one." I lowered my snout, releasing a breath that tousled the hair on his head. *"Can you tell me what happened here?"*

Tears began to swell in his eyes. "Mater started screaming. She told me to hide. I—I heard them. Daemons broke through up there." His small finger pointed to the nonexistent roof. "But then it got quiet. And I can't find Mater."

Unease prickled down my spine. My eyes coasted over the debris. I couldn't sense another heartbeat. Dark red stained what was once the hall, its entrance blocked with broken tiles, and led into another room. Nostrils flaring, I caught that sickly-sweet smell of death. It was also human. I could only assume that it was the boy's Mater. Thank the gods it was too dark for his little human eyes to see. A hiss caused the little boy to jump. I swept a leg in front of him, gently guiding him to stand behind me.

The little boy whimpered, on the verge of tears, and I could feel his little hands gripping my fur. I glanced back at him. *"A lesson for you. Either you control your fear, or your fear will control you."*

The child nodded, the skin between his brows pinched with determination. Small fingers clenched into tiny fists. There was another hiss and a snapping of teeth, and I twisted my head in the direction of the sound. A black claw wrapped around the corner of the hallway wall, hovering above the tiles.

It was a daemon, its head similar to a snake's skull. Horns like that of an antelope sticking out from the back of its head. Its skin was dark and leathery, a tough but penetrable hide. In the center of the skull face, crescent-shaped eyes, red as a dying sun, stared hungrily at me.

The daemon hissed again, revealing rows of razor teeth. A forked tongue flicked between four sharp canines. It suddenly lunged from its corner. I snarled, diving toward the daemon, fangs finding purchase in the space between its shoulders and neck. The creature screamed, the sound of angry winter winds. It lashed out a claw against my muzzle, causing me to drop it. As soon as it hit the ground, it scrambled for the boy. Shit. The child screamed. I pounced again on the daemon, my teeth snatching one of its hind legs and tossing it back onto the pile of debris. I lunged after it, fangs meeting leathery skin. The liquid warmth of its blood ran down the furs of my throat.

The creature squirmed between my jaws. I tightened my grip until I heard a loud *snap*. I dropped the body and turned to see the boy's eyes grow wide at the daemon's motionless figure.

"Is it dead?" he asked.

I nodded, running my tongue over my muzzle. *"I'm taking you to the next town. You will be safe there."*

"Will Mater be there?"

I stilled. How did one tell a child that his mother had been brutally murdered by a daemon? That it had sunk its teeth into her flesh, eating her alive. The child didn't deserve this. No one deserved this. Life had become so cruel.

"Little one, you must promise me that no matter what, you will be strong." I waded through the debris and out onto the road. The child followed. Light flared, and the aether that wolves were born with burned

sweetly as my skin shifted. I stood before the child in my human body. Clothes still intact, the deep brown fighting leathers and ivory cloth melded against the hard lines of my chest and legs.

The boy watched the transition in awe. I bent to retrieve him, his small arms reaching out just as I swept him into my arms.

"Promise?" I pressed.

Emotion toiled beneath his bruised gaze. He only nodded, tucking his face into the space between my neck and shoulder, whispering, "I promise."

It didn't take long to reach the neighboring town. Walls of wood reached into the nightly sky, surrounding structures of stone and brick within. Red tiled rooftops and torchlights dotted the land that rounded upon a hill. I could hear, in the distance, the snarls of the daemons feasting on their kills. They were becoming bold. The daemons hardly ever ventured this inland, usually keeping to the distant hills and mountain ranges.

Crowds of humans and satyrs were crossing the entrance. Some with wagons filled with belongings, others with nothing but the dirt-stained clothing on their backs. All held a defeated look in their eyes. This had become a way of life. Live under your roof knowing that one night a daemon horde may shatter everything you hold dear. All of this graciously provided by the Order.

The Order. Even their godsdamn name brought a bitter taste in my mouth. The subject of my personal hunt.

Many of the people here were seeking refuge. I weaved through the crowd, curious eyes following me like a plague. Some gazes flickered with recognition, others with the usual light of admiration. There were those who believed that as a wolf of Rome, I would be ceaselessly loyal to them, and there were those who heard the whispers and presumed to know who I was. Those who judged me. Rumors managed to travel to even the farthest corners of Rome. But I didn't care what they thought or believed. I didn't care what anyone thought.

After asking a few bystanders for assistance, I was told about a little villa being used as a shelter where all the lost children were gathered.

I followed the small crowd to the villa underneath a small grove of blossom trees, off to the side of a pasture.

A soft column of moonlight beamed upon the growing crowd. Parents cried out as they were reunited with their children. The little hooves of the satyr children clopped on the ground as they rushed into their parents' embrace. I wished there could be a similar ending for the little one in my arms, although the recollection of his slaughtered Mater brought a sense of anguish for what his future held.

A tall woman stood at the open door. As I approached, more shouts and cries of children exploded from behind her. She almost stumbled back at the sight of me.

"Never in my years did I think I would see one of your kind at my doorstep." Her voice was like gravel. She tilted her head, eyes narrowing.

Before I could respond, the little boy lifted his head. His eyes were puffy and red from crying almost the entire way. The woman's eyes softened and then looked up at me.

"I found him," I said.

Her eyes darted to the group of parents and looked back at me questioningly. I shook my head. She opened her arms beckoning to the boy. He shrank back into my hold.

I pulled back, forcing him to meet my eye. "She will take good care of you. Remember what you promised?"

The boy stared at me, and something in my chest twisted. I didn't want to leave him, but I couldn't bring him along. My life was no place for a child. Too dangerous and unpredictable.

The boy nodded. "I promise."

The woman took him in her arms. As she propped him on her hip, she looked at me with curiosity. "You're him, aren't you? The Lone Wolf?"

Years ago, I would've winced at the sound of the name. Now it fell with a thud, and it didn't sway me. I didn't answer the question while I took a step back, one last look at the boy. "Thank you."

As I turned around to face the dirt road leading to the harbor city, where my prey unknowingly waited, I could hear the small voice call out to me.

"Bye, wolfie."

TWO

Diane

Battle was my mantle. Promises of death poised in every breath. Aether stirred in my blood, its humming a delicious thrill as my fingers itched to wrap around the handle of my dagger. I was a wolf among snakes.

I dragged my gaze from the cup of dark wine in front of me to the politicians and businessmen at the opposite side of the room. They drained their drinks, their hands plastered around the waists of the females that entertained them. They slouched in their seats, tunics stretching along their spread thighs. I fought the urge to roll my eyes.

Glasses clinked and slurred shouts followed. Females danced throughout the courtyard, ember light from the torches along the walls kissing the thin lace that hugged their breasts and hips. Legs wrapped around males' waists as the females dipped their heads in sultry laughter. Fingers trailed, lips parted, eyes sharp and confident. Heat pinked my cheeks at their movements. There was a sense of confidence and brilliant manipulation in their flirtation. I admired it.

It wasn't the wine or the erotic dancers or the strong smell of arousal in the air that caused the grinding in my teeth. No, it was the overly smug disdain and excessive pomposity of the wealthy patrons. They partied and feasted, uncaring of what others were going through. Perhaps it was unfair of me to draw these conclusions—not all wealthy were ignorant of the harsh realities surrounding them—but my heart pulled for those in less fortunate circumstances. It was why I was here: to put an end to the nightmares caused by the Order and provide an opportunity to rebuild.

"Last tip I received was concerning a particular scholar." I cast a sidelong glance to the woman who sat at my table. "Care to elaborate?"

The woman's bright eyes tracked the movements of her employees entertaining the men. "The name is Oeneus." Her voice held a rasp. It was deep and lovely, almost falling into a purr. "My girls have heard that he has a study inside the city's library. Apparently he has been making appearances in court, appealing to withdraw the support of housing refugees. Some public groups adore him, but other politicians are not too fond of him."

Wine slipped between my lips, down my throat. Sweet like berries. "Your staff is clever and crafty."

Pride lit her eyes. "My women can drag truth from anyone's lips. I am glad you came to us with this opportunity, albeit a temporary one."

My eyes roamed the grand villa. It was a higher-end establishment. Marble and white pillars composed the floors and bordered the walls. A fountain sat in the center of the inner courtyard. Petals floated in the pool at the feet of carved statues of sirens. How fitting. Music lured those within its reach. Bodies grinded and tongues clashed in the dark corners. Others lounged on velvet settees as they plucked fruit from silver platters. I needed more wine.

I slipped out a leather pouch from within the folds of the blood-red fabrics of my dress and placed it on the table. The slit of my gown parted, revealing the glinting steel of the dagger at my thigh.

The woman eyed the weapon, and her painted lips spread into a cruel smile. "Always a pleasure to be working with a female who knows her way around a blade."

I smirked as I slid the pouch toward her, a faint jingle from the coins inside. "It's entertaining to say the least."

Her eyebrows rose, lips twisting in amusement. "I hope the wolves succeed in eradicating the Order. Daemons have been feasting on us for far too long."

All too true, and the damage was extensive. The daemons' existence was affecting the towns that produced food and supplies.

Consequently, there were limited resources for all Olympians' races. There were various Olympians living in this Roman region—minotaur, satyrs, harpies, chimeras, griffins, sirens, and gods know what else that hadn't been discovered yet, and all had been equally affected by the attacks. In order to have the slightest chance against the daemons, the mortal realm needed to be unified. Alliances and partnerships were made between the Olympians. Satyrs had been aligned with the human Roman armies for years. Similarly, the harpies had long been united with the Roman wolves. It had been a positive yet slow start, but it had proven not to be enough against the attacks. More was needed, and the answer to our survival had yet to be found.

In addition, the presence of the daemons brought conversations about whether the aether of our realm had been manipulated, abused into opening gateways to other realms. Thank the gods and goddesses that the she-wolves had been born with the ability to use aether at will. A powerful force of nature that could be weaponized. All Olympians, including the humans, were made of aether in essence, but none could control it as she-wolves could. It had also been said that the very soil was coarse with aether.

Among all of this, it was believed that behind the raids of the daemons and the abuse of aether was the Order. A group of power-deranged fanatics who claimed that the Ram, the nameless daemon king, had been wronged by the gods, and would rise once more. The creature was a victim, seeking vengeance for all the years of unjustified suffering, or such was their belief. I was unsure why anyone cared to believe such stories, but Rome had been expending resources and soldiers in battling daemons for years, since the first horde had entered our world.

Since the death of our previous Alpha.

A faint crack crawled along the wine glass from underneath my fingers. I placed the glass down on the table and stood.

"Duty calls. Let's hope our paths do not cross again." I winked.

The woman laughed and raised a glass. "Best of luck, she-wolf."

I waded between the tables and settees, the crowd thinning the further I went. As I rounded a column near the edge of the room, a male brushed against my shoulder. His lips curled, revealing yellow teeth, and sluggish eyes ran down my body.

He made an approving sound. "Pretty thing."

The world seemed to slow as I registered his words. "Excuse me?"

The human man reeked of alcohol. And continued to stare at my body. "How about we take these festivities somewhere more private? I would pay double to have a moment with you, precious."

Dear gods, he thought I was from the hired brothel. And did he just call me 'precious'? Surely I misheard him. Before I had a chance to respond, he raised his hand as if to smack my ass. I remained still, impassive as aether rose and stretched into the space between us. My power halted his movement. Invisible tendrils of thrumming energy curled around his neck, cutting the air from his throat. His eyes bulged once he realized what I was.

"My apologies . . . she-wolf . . ." The words were garbled between his purpling lips.

I leaned in. Death skirted around his fate, and he seemed to realize it. "Whether a she-wolf or not, you would do well to remember to never lay a hand on a woman without her fucking approval. Do you hear me?"

After a nod from him, I withdrew my aether. He stumbled back, gasping for air, and ducked toward the more crowded area of the banquet hall. I turned as a shadow rose from the corner.

"Marcus." I greeted him with a warm smile.

A tall, lithe Roman warrior dipped into the firelight. Brown curls framed his beautiful olive-toned face, and a handsomely wicked smile split his shadowed expression. "I knew you were going to put him in his place."

I inspected my nails. "He deserved more than that."

Marcus's eyes, like ice and water, observed me. His lips fought a smile. "I wonder how he didn't realize you were a she-wolf. All of the she-wolves have this power and energy surrounding them. Not to mention their attitude."

I snorted at that. Marcus and I had been friends for as long as I could remember. At one point, we had even been lovers. He had been my first. Countless heated nights spent under the stars. This had stopped some years back, but we would always remain friends. Such dear, innocent memories. It almost brought a small smile to my lips. Almost.

I folded my arms, sweeping the gentle black waves of my hair over my shoulder. Constant training over the years had carved the dips and edges of my body. Muscles flexed and tightened when I moved my arms and legs. Strength lined my abdomen, but I still had the generous curves of my breasts and hips. And being a warrior she-wolf, I had required more rigorous training than the others.

As wolves, we bore the blood of the god of war. The essence of his aether in our veins. While the males had the ability to shift, she-wolves couldn't. We had the ability to will the essence of aether, an immense honor among the Pack. But not all she-wolves were warriors. Some decided to pursue other professions instead and usually tended to be healers or scholars of sorts. That livelihood was simply not in my taste. My childhood had been built upon the sword and the fist. Aether may reside in our blood, but battle was my air.

"Where are the others?" I asked.

"I'm here," a deep voice droned from behind me.

Atticus strolled toward us with a grim look on his face. A lean, athletic frame, his tawny-colored skin taut with irritation.

"Remind me, why are we here again?" he grumbled, running a hand over his shorn head, the muscles of his large arms straining against his tunic.

I grunted in agreement. "Can we go now?"

Marcus gave us a dry look. "We were invited here by the city's governor to honor our presence in their city. Did our hired help bring any news?"

I grinned, arching an eyebrow. "It seems that our anonymous tip about Oeneus may be accurate. He may be in bed with the Order. His study is inside the library. We need to search his office and see if there is anything that could be useful to us before killing him."

Atticus breathed a chuckle. "You talk of killing like you talk of the weather."

I winked at that.

A pair of females twirled by, swaying their asses and calling out to Atticus. He politely shook his head and turned away with a frown. "I may have heard something of use. It seems many of the market traders have been reporting cloaked beings, walking the harbor at night. Assuming these robed figures were human. Where they go, no one knows."

Marcus nodded, his eyes scanning the villa. "Interesting. We may have to increase our nightly patrols, see if what these people claim is true."

I glanced around. "Where are Drusus and Cato?"

Marcus jerked his chin toward the hallways at the back of the establishment. A high-pitched squealing could be heard from the back rooms. Drusus and Cato appeared just then, both with human and satyr females on either side—gods knew what they'd been doing. My jaw almost dropped. I had seen this show countless times but was yet to be accustomed to it. Atticus chuckled, and Marcus's lips thinned to a line, though there was a hint of amusement in his eyes. I fought a smile, my chest pulling at the fact I was surrounded by my brothers in arms. My pack. We watched as the remainder of our group emerged.

Drusus was broad-shouldered with short dark hair that tended to drift over his brow and curl at the nape of his neck, sun-kissed olive skin, and coal-dark eyes. Cato was just as muscular as Drusus but leaner, with a back carved in the shape of an arrowhead. He had wild, dark brown hair that had once been shaved at the sides and was now growing out. Ink painted their arms and chests—flames, claw marks, depictions of the god of war, whorls, and other various designs.

The other two males of my pack also sported ink. Atticus's lithe body was entirely covered from legs to neck, while Marcus had ink stretching along his back and around his torso.

Unlike the human Romans, the wolves took a sense of pride in their tattoos. A symbol unique to the wolf culture, a way of saying that the wolves may work the roads and lands of Roman territory, but they were their own masters. We had our own rules, traditions, and culture. I, too, had a few designs inked on my skin when I graduated from the Academy: a crescent moon and stars around a thin blade etched down the valley of my back, as well as a laurel crown wrapped around my right bicep.

Even though Drusus and Cato were constant flirts, I had never met more respectful males. The women giggled, all casting doe eyes at the wolves they were fawning over. We had hired the women to feed us information, but it looked as though they were enjoying this job a little too much. I fought the urge to hurl.

"Well, we must thank you ladies for the wonderful evening. We will have to return sometime," Cato said to them.

One female ran her fingers down Drusus's large, inked arm. "Are you sure you don't want to stay?"

He looked at the female, his dark hair flopping over his brow and revealing brilliant teeth. The sight would have any female swooning. Thank the gods I was immune to it. "We are humbled by the offer, but I'm afraid our little sister here needs our attention."

Gods.

All the females looked toward me and gave me knowing smiles. I wanted to roll my eyes, but my lips twisted into a tight smile.

"Big brother, how I missed you," I ground out.

A smirk grew on Drusus's face as he sensed the venom in my tone. Drusus and Cato wiggled out of the females' grasps despite their squeaky protests. The males looped their arms through mine and hauled me toward a table in the far corner. Atticus and Marcus trailed after us.

I shoved them away as I sat in my chair. "Must you have females obsessing over you every godsdamn city we visit?"

Cato shrugged. A grin pulled at his lips. "We can't help it. And it was you who arranged for us to work with them, you know."

"Besides," Drusus exclaimed, eyes gleaming, "we didn't sleep with them. But we sure enjoyed watching *them* have fun with each other."

I choked on air as Marcus sighed. "Did either of you manage to find any more information?"

Cato's expression turned serious. "Further confirmation on suspicious behavior regarding Oeneus. Apparently, another scholar who works with him was one of the women's *clients* and claimed that Oeneus has a secret room in his study. That he disappears and doesn't return for hours."

Atticus leaned back in his seat, running a hand over his jaw. "It looks like you're right, Diane. We should start by investigating Oeneus's study room."

Marcus grunted in agreement. "We will tomorrow night." His eyes flashed. "Governor. Incoming."

We relaxed in our seats. Drusus and Cato tossed banter as the governor, Thaddeus, approached our table. A guard followed him like a shadow, and I briefly wondered why. Governors were hardly ever heavily guarded, especially in festive settings such as these, but perhaps Thaddeus was paranoid.

He was a lean man with dark-blond hair and a yellow beard and pale skin from lack of sun. I would bet all the blades on my attire that this male's hands were soft and had never known the true work of a soldier. He bore a white tunic where the shoulders were clasped in purple linings. A bronze broach in the shape of a leaf was tucked to the side of his hair.

The Governor spread his arms. "Welcome, wolves. I give my warm thanks for accepting my invitation. I hope the festivities are to your liking."

Marcus bowed, an arm over his chest, and we mirrored the movement. The curls on Marcus's head bounced as he looked up, flashing a bright smile, more teeth than anything. "The honor is ours, governor. It's been . . . exquisite."

Thaddeus smiled. "I'm glad to hear it. I hoped that I may steal some of your time tomorrow. I would like to discuss the most recent daemon attack."

I perked in my seat. "Where was the attack?"

He slid eyes to me as if he had just noticed I was there. By the love of gods. "In the small settlement near our neighboring city from the northside."

Something flashed across Drusus's dark eyes, but he blinked it away and began to stand. "Excuse me, I must be off. Farewell, governor. Wolves, I will see you at the inn."

In every city we visited, at least once during our stay, Drusus would disappear and wander the streets at night. He never elaborated why, and we respected his privacy and need for solitude. However, as Drusus sauntered out of the villa, I had a lingering sensation that something was wrong.

I exchanged a look with Marcus and left the table.

I followed Drusus's shadow from a distance, leaving the villa into the quiet darkness of the city. Dirt coasted my sandals, snagging onto the leather straps that crisscrossed my calves. Aether purred underneath my skin, my gown sweeping at my feet like a whisper. The blade clasped at my thigh kissed my skin.

Something told me to be vigilant. Reminding me that I was not only a wolf among snakes but that there were even more malicious creatures waiting in the dark.

THREE

Remus

Market sellers had begun to dismantle their stalls and the throngs of citizens were gradually thinning. Underneath the orange painted sky, the ocean's surface shimmered with shards of light. The salty air sent a sense of nostalgia through my body. I always preferred being near the sea. The scent of the salted waters brought blissful memories with it.

Many years before, I had traveled across those deep waters to a land full of sand and various kinds of wondrous aether. Those weren't exactly delightful recollections, but they still brought a sense of familiarity. Of home, even. Funny. Battle scars and haunted nights had become the only memories of what home meant to me.

Not now, Remus. Enough with the self-pity. It will find you when you're trying to sleep anyway.

I twisted and turned between the stalls. Cooked meat and herbs filled the air, making me salivate. My fingers reached for the sword that was strapped over my back. I felt my shoulders relax as I lightly touched the pommel. It was the one thing I cherished since my punishment as the Lone Wolf began. Not just any sword, but my pater's. There was nothing special to the blade. It hadn't even been meant for me but, for whatever reason, I couldn't seem to part with it.

Even though it was near the market's closing time, it didn't stop sellers from trying to make a last-minute bargain. Instead of trading coins for trinkets, I bargained for information. For what felt like hours, I questioned people but didn't obtain fruitful results.

Flipping the bronze coin in-between my fingers, I eyed a wrinkled woman ahead of me. "Any news of interest amidst your trading days?"

The woman's grayed hair sprawled over her brown face. Hazel eyes peered up at me. I flicked the coin to her, and she caught it with ease.

Her eyes slid back to me. "With that handsome face, I'm willing to tell you anything you want." She winked, and a raspy chuckle hummed between her closed lips.

The corner of my lips tipped up. "You flatter me. I'm looking to see if there has been any sort of particular . . . dealings."

The woman smacked her lips. "If you mean illegal, then take your pick. There are always dark dealings in our business, boy. It depends on what kind of business you speak of."

"Anything of the aether sort?" I lowered my voice.

A shadow danced across her wrinkled gaze. "Aye, there may be something. Over these past months, in the darkest hours after the market clears, I've seen cloaked figures gather at the harbor. They think I don't see, but I do." She shook a gnarled finger at those last words.

"What do these figures do?"

"They meet—a whole lot of them. They whisper. Then they walk. Well, *float* seems more appropriate. They look like ghosts in their black hoods. They drift through the city toward the temple. Where they go after that, I know not—but the energy around them, it is something nasty."

"Can you tell who these people might be?"

She paused, raising her finger once more. "I may need a little more convincing, boy."

I pulled out another coin, a grin pulling at my lips. "You are a conniving woman."

The old trader snickered as she plucked the coin from my palm. "To answer your question, it's hard to say, it could be anyone under those cloaks. One night they were close enough I could hear them speaking. I recognized their voices, their stature, and the way they moved. I'm afraid to assume the worst."

I leaned in, placing my palms on the wooden table between us. "Why would they meet so close to peering eyes and ears such as yours?"

"You see, it was dark, and I'm a little old lady who happened to be huddled next to her packed wagon after a long day. Anyone who thinks highly of their status wouldn't even notice someone like me." Her throat bobbed slightly. "Now, you didn't hear it from me, but don't trust anyone on these streets, especially the priests."

Dusk waned, and the darkness welcomed me as I waited on a rooftop belonging to a business of a sort. No one had been in, and the buildings were easy to scale. An eeriness coasted over the empty streets. A stray dog skittered between the city's crevices. Only the moon and the sound of waves as my company.

With my arms crossed, I gazed at the dimming torchlight that still burned underneath the city temple's towering entrance. Petals were scattered over the marble steps, the light of the flames painting them gold. White pillars gleamed a pale blue against the moonlight.

Ironic that I was to meet here, given what the old woman at the market had told me. Her words had lingered over my shoulders since this evening.

Don't trust anyone on these streets, especially the priests.

What had she meant by that? Could it be possible—

"I am hoping one of these days we can actually meet at a place that serves food . . . or wine." The deep voice sounded behind me, and I felt a smirk begin to draw over my lips.

"Don't tell me you're hungry?" I asked.

Drusus stepped from the pool of darkness, a scowl already plastered on his face. "I'm always hungry."

"You know how it works. Every city, we meet at its temple. It's easier that way." I stepped forward, stretching out an arm.

Drusus jumped a step and wrapped me in an embrace. It took me a moment to relax into the touch. I spent my days alone, and although I was not opposed to the isolation, at times I found myself forgetting what human touch felt like. Drusus never failed to remind me. He was the closest thing I had to home. There was no blood relation, but he was still my brother.

Pulling away, Drusus lightly punched my arm. "I've missed you, brother. I heard of the little town that was decimated by the daemons. I knew you were coming from that direction, so it had me worried."

I waved a hand. "No need to worry about me. The attack had stopped before I arrived, but I did find an orphan in the ruins of a house."

Warmth lit his coal black eyes. "And you, being the gentle giant you are, made sure the child was safe."

I rolled my eyes. "Of course I did."

Drusus grinned and beckoned toward the sleeping streets. "I have a feeling this city is overrun by the Order."

"It would make sense. It's a harbor city, filled with resources and opportunity to travel easily." I leaned against the railing, my gaze on the temple. "What do you have for me?"

Drusus's gaze darkened as his eyes followed the dust that coiled over the ground like a nest of snakes. "Oeneus is suspected to be part of the Order, or at least a fervent follower. His study room in the libraries would be the ideal place to start investigating."

I listened as he provided me with additional details pertaining to this Oeneus. The fire's shadows danced along the sacred walls.

My hands braced over the rooftop's edge, and I gave Drusus a sidelong glance with a wicked grin. "Are you coming?"

Drusus snorted. "Like I would let you have all the fun."

I flew over the edge, my knee cracking the ground. Drusus followed suit, rolling to his feet. We stayed close to the dark walls of the buildings, passing limestone buildings and bending roads until the library emerged.

"Stay in your human form," I ordered.

Drusus growled in irritation. "Fuck you, I know what I'm doing."

I chuckled. "I had to make sure."

We edged toward the windows and easily slipped inside. My boots almost slid on the marble ground. My eyes adjusted quickly to the dark, the wolf sight naturally seeping in. The crimson columns filled the hallways, leading to rooms drenched with literature.

"How do we know which office is his?" Drusus whispered. His nostrils flared in search of a scent.

I straightened, looking toward the dark hallway. "We will know."

Silence followed our feet. Predators. Always hunting. Though Drusus was more than that. He was a warrior, part of the Pack. What was I?

Disgrace.

Exile.

Lone Wolf.

Ember light bled underneath a closed door, the only one that was lit within the dark library. Call it instinct, but I had a sense we were heading in the right direction. There was no indication of life behind the door. I pushed it open and stepped into a small study. The space was crammed with shelves and scrolls. I sauntered towards the desk in the center and started rummaging through the papers on it. It didn't take long to find Oeneus's name inked upon the parchment. Too good to be true.

Drusus had been searching the shelves for a short time when he growled quietly. "There's nothing here."

Without lifting my gaze from the table, I pointed at the wall. "Check there."

Excitement lit Drusus's voice. "Now that's more like it. How did you figure it out?"

I finally looked up, giving Drusus a dry look. "You're a fucking wolf, you should've heard the air on the other side."

He tossed me a vulgar gesture before placing his hands on the wall. Inhaling deeply, Drusus thrusted a fist into the limestone. Chunks exploded as he punched the wall again until a hiss of air escaped from the hole created. Drusus lifted his leg and kicked the makeshift door, the stones raining into the dark abyss.

He clapped the dust from his hands. "Well, it wasn't gracefully done but it'll do."

I stepped into the dark tunnel, unsheathing my sword. The steel sang, and I relished in the sound. "Doesn't matter, he's a dead man anyway."

I was unsure if Oeneus would be here, if he was even a member of the Order. A part of me hoped he was. Craved it, even.

There was something else lurking within these walls, heavy and dark, its whispers trailing around my shoulders. The hairs on the nape of my neck rose. I looked to Drusus, and he nodded at the question he read in my eyes. He had felt it too. This wasn't the aether we knew.

The hallway was narrow and opened into a small room. Oeneus was nowhere to be seen.

On one wall was a shelf filled with scrolls. I grabbed a piece of parchment and scanned the inscriptions on it. My stomach dropped. Drusus had not been wrong. Oeneus was not a simple scholar.

These scrolls were years' worth of aether studies, specifically on how to manipulate it and introduce beings into the mortal realm. How to introduce daemons into it. In some of the other scrolls, there were etchings of the daemons and passages on how to cut an opening into our world. Many of these writings were . . . foreboding. Ancient rituals and chants—it was all so twisted it brought an icy chill down my spine.

These inscriptions didn't mean much to me, though I knew enough about cult like practices to recognize what they were. Fuck. Had the Order been harboring knowledge on how to abuse the natural order of our realm? Based on this tunnel stacked with scrolls, that wouldn't be a far-fetched assumption. Why the Order would be collecting such literature, I wasn't sure. To attack Rome? Summon more daemons? And for how long?

"Oh, gods," Drusus whispered, dread in his voice, pulling my attention away.

He passed me a sheet of paper, and my blood chilled at what I saw. Suddenly all my previous theories and thoughts withered like a damn weed. *No.*

Curved horns and crescent eyes. The skull of a ram. An all too similar image forced its way from the depth of my memory, something I thought I had freed myself from.

It felt as if someone had squeezed the air from my lungs. I now knew what the Order was plotting, and I couldn't help but feel help-less. Maybe a little afraid.

Godsdamn, when was the last time I had felt like this? No, I re-membered exactly when. My consciousness slipped back to that night, all those years ago . . .

The paper bunched in the tight grip of my hand. Knuckles turned bone white. My teeth grinded harshly to the point of pain. *After all this time. I thought it was done.*

"Are you okay?" Drusus stepped closer. A franticness crept into his tone, and I immediately fought back the burning anger in my chest.

"Yes," I managed to say.

Drusus eyed me warily. He knew me well enough. "Bullshit. You acted like you just saw a ghost. What's wrong?"

The image of the Ram flared in my thoughts, and I swallowed thick emotion. I couldn't delve into the unease brewing inside me; Drusus didn't need another burden of mine to shoulder. "I think you were right. There are more of the Order here. After we find this Oeneus, I am going to stay to hunt the others."

Drusus made a sound, a genuine look of surprise revealed under-neath the shadows of the torchlight. "You plan to stay longer? That isn't how we normally do this."

I had to agree. Throughout the years, since I had become the Lone Wolf, I had been hunting the Order. Slitting their throats as they slept alongside their wives, sweeping them off the dark streets only so they could be gutted in the alleyways. My hands were coated with their blood. Bodies had fallen lifeless from my calloused hands, to bleed and rot as if they were nothing. After everything the Order had done to me, this was a mere scratch at the surface of what they deserved.

Drusus understood my bloodthirsty need. The unquenchable fires that only burned brighter with each kill.

My friend had extended his hand to me in my darkest moment and helped arrange ways to satiate the twisted desires of my heart. As he worked alongside the Pack, I would do my own tracking. We would feed each other information and meet at night, where Drusus would witness the execution of my own justice.

My brother served the Pack fervidly. I had argued with Drusus when he first propositioned to help me. He was loyal to the Pack and understandably so. It was his home. They were his people. That was something I didn't want to get in the way of, but Drusus had fought me on the notion. Somehow he managed to uphold his duties to the Pack and support me at the same time.

I was now at a fork in the road. Under our usual arrangement, I would kill those of the Order and leave. To the next city. To keep hunting.

The image of the Ram returned. A deep rumble grew in my chest. This changed everything. Godsdamn it.

I cleared my throat. "I need to know where that tunnel leads. There are more of the Order here, and I intend to find them."

Drusus watched me a moment, his dark eyes piercing deeper into my soul, but then he sighed. Drusus wouldn't push me; he knew I would open up to him when I was ready. It was something I had always appreciated from him. Deeply. "Sometimes I wish we didn't have this damn arrangement. And I understand you had your reasons, but I also wished you never left the Pack. Your pater would never have wanted that."

The mention of my pater sent a bitter taste down my throat, determined to poison the air in my lungs. Inevitably, the thought of him threw me back into my worst nightmare. Where I could still feel my sister, lifeless and cold in my arms. Grief tore at my heart, ripping at the seams. My fists clenched so tightly I could've drawn blood, my breathing turning rampant. Drusus didn't blink. He took a step as if ready to pull me into an embrace.

"Easy," he soothed.

Drusus had been there that night. Had seen me on my knees. Witnessed the misery etched on my face. But he was still not aware of the full story or of what had occurred shortly after my sister's death.

A softness cascaded over Drusus's gaze. "It's been almost eight years, Remus. It wasn't your fault. You need to move on."

No, I couldn't.

Drusus hesitated. "Helena wouldn't want you like this."

Helena. My twin sister. Stoic, fierce. A true Daughter of Mars and loved by her she-wolves. Our pater had had a special fondness for her. Preferred her, something I had never been bitter over. If anything, I was grateful for it. It had spared her from the darker sides of our pater.

I turned suddenly, hand flying to my sword. *Someone had followed us.* The cold sting of steel pressed into my neck. I narrowed my gaze on the female holding the sword against my throat as she stepped further into the amber light.

Eyes of a gilded brown that reminded me of the continent filled with sands that glowed gold underneath the sun. Dark hair that shone and danced over her shoulders. Roman armor melded to the curves of her hips and breasts, and to the muscles lining her body. Aether strummed from her. Its invisible threads brushed against my skin. My lips curled in a snarl.

Drusus groaned. "Diane, I can explain, but please don't kill my brother."

FOUR

Diane

I knew the male. Well, I knew *of* him. The stories surrounding the Lone Wolf were infamous, a favored topic of gossip. It was hardly a secret in the Pack. A shroud of shame and tragedy surrounded his name.

Remus.

Namesake of one of the Fathers of the Wolves, the founders of Rome, Romulus and Remus. The twin demigods raised under the Mother Wolf.

My blade still at his neck, I took a moment to observe the Lone Wolf.

Midnight hair reached his shoulders, thick locks that hung loosely against the planes of his cheekbones. A firm jaw dusted with a faint stubble. Straight nose and full lips. A pale scar ran down the corner of his right brow. His skin was a deep olive, no doubt from constant exposure to the sun. Dark ink, blossoms and leaves, peeked from underneath his fighting leathers, stretching from his left clavicle to the end of his left arm. There were also some symbols etched over his knuckles. The figures looked vaguely familiar.

And his eyes—green like jade. Orange surrounded the pupils like wildflowers. He was beautiful. From his features, he hailed from the Mediterranean isles.

The Lone Wolf still glared at me. "And I thought we were alone, Drusus."

His deep voice shuddered down my spine. It was dark and alluring, rolling from his lips. I lifted my chin higher. "It's embarrassing, really. Neither of you sensed or saw me following you. So much for being the 'almighty wolves of Rome.'"

Remus's eyes dilated at the sound of my voice. His lips curved. "I see you now."

The intensity of his stare almost made my legs buckle. Almost made me drop my weapon and bend the knee.

I smirked. "Drusus, please explain yourself before I skewer the Lone Wolf."

When I'd seen Drusus leap into the arms of the male, I had almost exposed myself. I had wanted to wrench him away from the Lone Wolf. There was a poison to the title, and we were forbidden to interact with anyone deemed as such. I didn't understand why Drusus was meeting with him. They had conversed, laughed, as if they had known each other for years.

We were supposed to be making strides in eradicating the Order. Not have the Lone Wolf—the *fucking* Lone Wolf—interfering with our efforts.

Drusus edged closer. "Diane, please. I know him. Remus is my brother by battle and bond. There is no need to trouble yourself with him, so put the blade down."

His voice sidled closely to panic. Realization dawned. "You've been lying to us," I murmured. Remus's eyes narrowed as I spoke. "I heard everything. Your *arrangement*. Every city, you disappear, Drusus. We always respected your privacy, assuming it was a coping mechanism of sorts from all the years of battle you've endured. Gods know Marcus and the others have their own dark memories. But you've been meeting with *him*, the wolf who abandoned his Pack."

Remus growled, daring a step toward me. I dug the tip of my sword into his throat. A bead of red trickled down. "You don't know anything about me," he snapped.

The tightness in my gaze smoothed. "I know all I need to know." His green eyes flared, but he said nothing.

Drusus stepped in front of me. The blade just inches from his shoulder. "We can find Oeneus together. Remus knows about the investigation and can help. I'm not going to turn him away, so just let this go, Diane. Please."

The last of his words dipped into a plea and chipped away at something in my chest. Not once had Drusus confronted me like this. I had never heard him be so passionate. It seemed to have the same effect on the Lone Wolf, as his eyes flashed to Drusus. It was fleeting, but I could've sworn I saw something within the depths of his eyes. Something tortured.

My grip on the sword trembled. Not with fear but with frustration. Fates be damned.

I groaned and pulled my blade back, and Drusus stepped aside, looking relieved. "The Lone Wolf can go, but the *Pack* will take it from here."

Remus growled. The deep sound trembled through my bones as he stepped closer. His long legs swallowed the space between us, and the breadth of his chest almost knocked me back. He stood close enough for me to taste the ocean and cedar from his skin. I raised my chin even higher to meet his sweltering gaze. Anger. Hatred. It rolled from his thick shoulders in waves.

His green eyes seemed to burn brighter. Voice like molten steel and fire. "This kill is mine. I am owed it more than you and certainly more than the Pack."

"Intriguing," I purred. "I don't care."

Remus smirked, and I found myself becoming irritated at the smug look. "I'm not going anywhere, she-wolf. If you want me to leave . . . you'll have to *make* me."

Drusus groaned, but I only smiled. Without raising my hands, I pulled on my aether. The air trembled and roiled as it caught Remus in its snare. The Lone Wolf's grin seemed to widen as the aether pressed against him, sending him back a few meters. His boots slid over the ground until he took a step toward me. And another. It was slow and methodical, muscles straining in his neck and arms, but he continued to push against the aether. I found myself taking a step back, and

I didn't like it. It was impressive, I begrudged; hardly anyone could simply push through the forces of the she-wolf.

I inspected my nails. "You expect me to care about what the Lone Wolf wants? You are a deserter. A coward."

"Diane," Drusus warned. "Stop. Both of you."

"At least I am not a prideful soldier, blindly following every order, oblivious to the bullshit in front of them," Remus taunted.

My restraint snapped. I willed the aether. It lurched from under Remus, knocking him off his feet and onto his back. I charged after him, landing with one knee on Remus's abdomen and the other planted on the ground beside him, holding me up, my dagger pressed to his neck. My aether hummed angrily as I gritted my teeth.

"We are warriors, I hissed. "Loyalty is what makes the Pack brings us together as one. You knew what that meant once."

Remus didn't struggle. He stared with an intensity that challenged me. Something I was not used to but was also oddly exciting. Shadows danced over his brow, and I only then noticed the hardness of his body underneath me. The strength of his chest and waist. We weren't touching, but I could still feel the heat of his skin seeping from his fighting leathers.

I could see the thoughts churning in his head until suddenly the world spun, and he was on top of me. I groaned at the impact. His hands pinned my wrists at either side of my head.

Stray strands of his hair fell forward and brushed my cheeks. Remus grinned a dark smile. "I am only loyal to myself and Drusus."

"That's enough." Drusus shoved Remus off me. He helped me to my feet and planted himself between us, glaring at Remus. A deep rumble ran through his chest. "Push her again, Remus, and so help me, I will gut you myself. I am calling a truce. Only for tonight."

Remus eyed me and huffed. His bright eyes flickered to Drusus, and whatever he saw had him dropping his shoulders. "So long as the warrior she-wolf doesn't try to stab me."

Warrior she-wolf. I narrowed my gaze, sheathing the dagger. "Don't give me reason to."

"I never did," he grounded out. That only stoked the frustration within me.

Drusus sighed. "I will take this as progress to a civil conversation. Tomorrow we can resume drawing the line between Pack and Lone Wolf."

"More like drawing lines in the sand," I muttered.

Drusus glanced at me, hurt flashing in his dark eyes. He plucked a torch from the wall. "Someone lit this not too long ago. Let's check where this tunnel leads."

His broad frame slipped into the tunnel that continued from the spare room. He was right. There was a faint scent of musky wood, and I knew it was human. Remus paused to let me walk ahead of him. He may be a cocky bastard. He may be the Lone Wolf. But at least he had some manners. Only some.

We trod carefully between the stone walls. The cool air bit at my skin and chills ran down my spine. If Oeneus had access to these underground tunnels, then it was highly probable he'd been working with the Order.

Hallways split into more passageways as we walked, but we remained on the main path. We had been in silence for several minutes. Drusus's shoulders were bunched, Remus was deathly quiet, and I was brimming with questions.

"How long have you been working with the Lone Wolf?" I asked Drusus. "Do you not trust us?"

Drusus's coal-black eyes kept to the darkness ahead. His eyes were actually brown, but the deepness of the color made them look black at times. "It's not that I don't trust you and the others. Well, maybe partly. I know you all care for me and mean well, but I also care for Remus. I will always be there for him as I will be there for you. Tradition wants me to choose, but I refuse to do so. The world is not always so black and white."

His words strung a chord within me. I always believed myself to be open-minded. There was nothing wrong with tradition, but this piece of the wolf culture pertaining to the Lone Wolf meant he was an utter outcast. A Lone Wolf would be shamed, ignored, and unable to marry another wolf. A part of me felt this level of punishment was a bit excessive. To what degree did an individual truly deserve the full extent of this punishment?

"But he abandoned his duties," I wondered aloud. "They say he left when—"

Drusus jerked his head toward me, his eyes ablaze. "Those stories were conjured up by rumors. The truth of why he left is not so simple. Why are you judging a situation if you aren't aware of all the facts?"

I blinked. Godsdamn it. I threw a look at Remus, who watched us impassively. "Drusus says the world is not so black and white, and I agree. Help me understand why you became the Lone Wolf, then."

Remus stared at me, but his gaze wasn't full of fire and anger this time. It was cold and empty. As if a mask had clicked into place, hiding whatever was battling within that violent mind.

"I left the Pack because I didn't want anything to do with it anymore." His voice was sharp and biting, like ice.

Drusus flinched but said nothing. I waited for more elaboration but when none came, I decided to drop the topic. For whatever reason, I knew he didn't want to say his truth.

Shame burned my cheeks. I hardly knew this wolf, yet I expected him to reveal the most vulnerable parts of him. An apology crept along my tongue but never passed my lips.

The air seemed to thicken the deeper we walked. The aether in my blood thrummed in agitation. I realized that it was not the air but a different sensation that licked and crawled up my skin. I rolled my shoulders, unsure what to make of it. It felt a lot like aether. Steel winked in the firelight as Remus and Drusus raised their swords.

Drusus glanced over his shoulder at Remus. "You feel that too?"

Remus nodded. He ran a hand through his hair, the locks brushing his shoulders. "This aether is not of our world. It is old and angry."

We prowled deeper until the hall led into a small clearing where other tunnels began.

Darkness suddenly fell over the space. I yelped as a column of heavy energy knocked us all to the ground. Drusus grabbed my wrist and tugged me to his side. Remus had already pulled himself into a crouch, angling his body in front of us. I glanced around. We were surrounded by shadows, and by the way my power was responding, I knew it was another form of aether. It spiraled around us like a dark current. It wasn't as black as the night. It didn't hold that kind of serenity. This was oblivion, obsidian like bottomless pits.

The plumes withdrew, skittering over the ground and trailing over my skin like talons. I gritted my teeth against the discomfort.

A male stepped into the clearing. He was tall and held a wicked grin. I recognized him from the portrait I had received from the anonymous tip. Oeneus. He had known we suspected him.

"Wolves," he drawled with outstretched arms. "You've been looking for me?"

"Oeneus," Remus spat out as if the name was a bad taste in his mouth.

My eyes widened as I remembered the unnatural darkness and the feel of it along my body. "I did not know that those of the Order could control aether."

Oeneus grinned even wider. Shadows snaked along his arms. "It's temporary power. I am just like you now, she-wolf. If anything, I am better."

I snarled, pulling myself to my feet. The next moment I was slamming Oeneus to the wall at the other end of the clearing. My forearm dug into his neck as my aether plastered him to the stone.

"If I allowed it," I murmured, "my aether could snap your bones right here. Shall I show you?"

I heard a sharp inhale and glanced over my shoulder. Remus. A dangerous hunger, like bloodlust, shone in his luminous gaze. His eyes crawled up my body to where I held Oeneus. Those full lips curled into a smirk.

"Don't antagonize a she-wolf, human." His voice was coated with darkness.

I looked back at the human. My aether flared, and I could hear the faint snap of Oeneus's ribs cracking. His shouts almost drowned out my next words. "We received a tip that you've been making your way into court. Intercepting correspondence aimed to help the refugee efforts. You *want* the daemon attacks to continue happening. Why?"

I felt the shudder of my power underneath my palm. My brow pinched as I met the male's bloodless smile. There was a cruel light in his eyes, but it looked unnatural. I felt . . . exposed. Like I was being watched by someone else, not the human looking directly at me.

He revealed bloodied teeth. "Because my king commanded it. He promised a life free of pain and feeling."

A shadow flickered over his gaze before the dark tendrils broke my hold and threw me against the opposite wall. Pain blared up my spine.

Drusus shouted, his hands suddenly there helping me up, but I could only see Remus's large frame dash between me and the human. Oeneus's aether lashed at Remus like a whip. The flash of steel from the wolf's sword sparked against the thrumming energy as Remus twisted and turned, stalking closer to Oeneus.

Power reverberated the very air. Remus's movements stopped just before the teeth of his blade could meet Oeneus's chest. His eyes turned distant as if he were peering through a window.

I shouted his name, but he didn't respond, as if he couldn't hear me. I could feel Oeneus's power coaxing me, promising a life without pain. I imagined the same thing was happening to Remus. His brow furrowed as his grip on his sword tightened, as if he were fighting whatever was controlling him. I could see the tip of the blade pressing against the force of the shadows. At any other point, I would've appreciated the Lone Wolf's sheer strength of will.

Drusus lunged toward the human, swinging his sword in a beautiful arc. He managed to slash Oeneus's chest just before shadows unfurled from the human, pushing Drusus back. Oeneus pivoted, raising a blade of his own to clash against Drusus's, breaking the influence on Remus in the process.

Remus blinked out of the trance. The darkness of the cave seemed to embrace him as he charged at Oeneus like a creature of the night. For a human, Oeneus was lightning quick on his feet. He danced between the two wolves, crossing blades and dodging attacks. He willed the shadowed aether to collide with Drusus's sword while he was locked against Remus's.

Oeneus smiled coldly at Remus. "You wolves seem surprised. I am human yet I can easily fight against two of you. Imagine what a whole army of us could do."

Remus snarled. The muscles of his arms strained as he pushed against Oeneus. The aether thickened, pushing against Drusus with more force.

Drusus shouted, "Anytime now, Diane."

Streams of energy rushed from me, cracking the air like lightning, intercepting the aether. It was enough distraction for Remus to twist the handle of his sword and free himself from Oeneus. Steel sank into flesh. Remus grasped the back of Oeneus's head and drove the sword deeper. Blood bubbled from the human's lips.

The Lone Wolf leaned toward the dying man's ear. "Fuck. You."

The corners of Oeneus's lips remained tilted as his eyes dimmed. His large body slumped into a growing pool of blood. Remus stumbled, his chest heaving up and down until his eyes met mine.

"I told you," Remus rumbled after a moment. He wiped the blood from his blade. "That kill was mine."

FIVE

Remus

The night was like all the other nights. Quiet. Solemn. Lonely.

I had returned to the rooftop facing the temple. I rested my muzzle on my paws. Stars gleamed peacefully above me. The cool ocean air swept through my fur. There was solace to sleeping like this. I hardly ever slept in my human body these days.

My eyes closed, but I knew sleep was far from me. The thoughts couldn't be silenced.

Oeneus was dead. Another of the Order wiped from this world and yet the emptiness in my chest hadn't filled. The anger and agony that constantly writhed in my heart had still not been silenced.

I had wanted to continue exploring the tunnels. If Oeneus had been there, then where did he come from? Drusus would've been inclined to join, but with the discovery of the Order being able to control aether, he had felt obligated to report to the others. I hadn't opposed it. It was unnerving and meant that the Order was becoming stronger. How far did their power extend?

That was not the only thing warring with my mind.

Honey brown skin and ebony hair. Eyes that were a melted gold, sparking with rebellion and fervor. Skin that smelled of wild blossoms. That wit and smart mouth. I was ... enticed. I had found myself feeling intrigued at being the cause of her fire and was curious to see more.

When we had finally left the tunnels, Diane had raised a firm finger telling me to keep my distance. "This matter is officially Pack business, and your *arrangement* with Drusus needs to come to an end. I don't know you, and I don't trust you. We will handle the Order from here on."

A silent conversation had passed between Drusus and me at that. He knew I wasn't going to leave. He knew I would venture those tunnels in hopes of finding more evidence of the Order. And we would continue what we had been doing for the past eight years.

Drusus's departing words still echoed in the lonely corners of my thoughts. "You are my Pack, Remus. I don't care what the Lone Wolf means." It had cracked something within my chest. Cleaving deeper within my bones. "I want you home."

I hadn't answered. I'd only watched as my brother disappeared with the beautiful she-wolf at his side. Leaving me to my own darkness.

My heart began to thrash as the events of tonight wore thin and were replaced by the same hauntings that always found me at night.

The memories. The night I lost everything. Helena's body in my arms. Cold and stiff. My chest heaved but no tears came. The last time I had known tears had been that night. I could still feel the blood roaring in my ears when my cries had shattered the sky, agony spearing the stars and the realm of the gods. My pater . . .

It was my fault. Mine. Mine. Mine.

Guilt kept my mind restless until exhaustion, both physical and emotional, finally strangled me to the depths of slumber. I didn't deserve to sleep peacefully, anyway.

The last desperate thought clung to me as the depths swallowed me. Drusus was right about one thing. Helena would not have wanted me like this.

Shit, Helena. I would rather I had died and you had lived. I would rather you had been the one to kill me than I kill you.

SIX

Diane

Sweat was already beginning to bead underneath my armor. The bronze of the breastplate had warmed, and the leather straps from the tunic rustled gently over my legs. My fingers brushed the hilt of the dagger at my thigh and traveled up to the sword strapped to my back.

Towering pillars of ivory and grey stone glinted under the late morning sun. The columns stretched through the main courtyard of the grand villa as pools of water ran on either side of the main pathway. Petals and leaves floated carelessly on the water's surface. Human and satyr soldiers strolled through the yard and the deep red halls. It was highly guarded, even for the home of a politician.

My brothers sauntered alongside me, Marcus taking the lead toward Thaddeus's meeting room. Deep red cloaks were clasped over our shoulders, cascading down our backs like bloody waterfalls. Drusus and Cato were on either side of me while Atticus drifted to the back.

I cast a glance at Drusus. A faint purple bloomed underneath his eyes. We hadn't spoken since last night, and it was unlike us.

"Are you alright?" I asked.

Soft beams of light slipped through the open spaces of the villa's ceiling and crowned his handsome face. He grabbed my arm and pulled me, so we were at the back of the group.

"Why haven't you told them?" Drusus's voice dropped low enough the others couldn't catch it.

The skin between my brows creased. "What made you think I would go skipping to Marcus to spill all your secrets? I may be wary of your friend, but I am not an ass. I can tell you care for him."

It was true. I may not have known Remus or what had made him become the Lone Wolf but I would keep Drusus's secret, out of my love for him. He was my family just as much as I was his.

His lips quirked into a small smile. "I shouldn't have doubted you."

I flashed my teeth and bumped his shoulder. "You might be surprised, if you give them a chance. Except for Marcus." I laughed.

Drusus grinned. "That's true. Marcus is going to throw a fit."

"What are you two whispering about?" Cato looked over his shoulder. His wild hair looked even more mussy than when he'd woken. "I want to be included."

Atticus rolled his eyes. "You always want to be included."

I smiled. It was always easy when around them. "Last night, Drusus and I ended up taking a nightly stroll through town."

"That's unexciting. I was hoping for a scandal of a story." Cato snickered.

A brow arched as I shot an amused look at Drusus, who only scowled back. Marcus looked over his shoulder at us, his blue eyes narrowing slightly, but continued walking. Yes, I would let Drusus handle that conversation.

The meeting room opened to reveal high ceilings. Tall windows splashed light onto the marble floor, and gold lined the walls. Lavish emerald-green cushions and settees filled the far corner of the room, sitting upon a large dark rug.

Governor Thaddeus was lounging on one of the settees. His pale eyes tracked our movements as he picked grapes from a silver platter. My lips twisted in disgust.

The human soldier who had opened the doors bowed. "The wolf warriors have arrived, led by Marcus of Rome."

Marcus nodded in greeting. He was not one to bow to males with pretty titles. None of us were. "You wished to discuss the recent daemon attack?"

Thaddeus nodded, a gleam in his eyes. "Eager to get to business, aren't you?" He clapped his hands. "I appreciate that, Marcus. I was hoping Oeneus would turn up as well. He's been a growing advisor of sorts and has given me helpful insight in the past, but we can begin without him."

The governor stood and began to pace the room, hands clasped behind his back. "As you have been made aware, the neighboring town was overrun by daemons. Many of the people are searching for refuge and the other towns do not have enough space. My city has officially extended an offer to house many of the escapees. The priests are leading the relief efforts and have asked for your support. It may be helpful for my men to have the expertise of the wolves at their disposal."

Marcus slowly looked to Drusus and me at the mention of Oeneus, and we almost shrank under his scrutiny. An innocent grin played at my lips. *Apologies, Marcus, but Oeneus is currently lying dead in a network of underground tunnels.*

Marcus's jaw ticked and he turned back to the governor. "We are currently here with orders on behalf of the Pack, but we'll support the relief efforts when possible."

Thaddeus's lips seemed to tighten but he quickly plastered on a wide grin. "That is good. If I may inquire, as it is my city you are visiting, what sort of business are you here for?"

Nothing betrayed the stone-clad seriousness on Marcus's face. "We are here to monitor the increase of daemon attacks, so it seems we have a similar objective."

The half-truth slipped so easily. Marcus was undeniably calculating in every decision he made. It was what made him a brilliant leader of our small group. The wolves could not blatantly announce that we were hunting the Order. It had been revealed over the years that many politicians and those running the businesses of Rome had succumbed to the Order's tempting promise of power and control.

Thaddeus held Marcus's gaze. "Reports state that the cause of that little town's annihilation was due to the people rioting. I suspect that the daemons were attracted to the violence that was sparked in that town. Fanatics of the Order tend to be boisterous and the root cause of many riots. The people did nothing about the commotion and faced the consequences. Now, for the safety of my city, I have increased the soldier patrols in the hopes of stopping any rebellion before it starts."

A flare of irritation crawled up my cheeks. Marcus tensed as I reached his side. "If I may, Thaddeus, it is naive to blame the innocents for the riots and the daemon attack."

Marcus shot me a warning look. The governor raised an eyebrow, his gaze slowly meeting mine.

His voice turned cold. "When people are desperate, they do desperate things. Are you accusing my reports of being dishonest?"

Growls echoed behind me. In *my* defense. It took everything to suppress a sigh of disappointment. What a sensitive male. Before I could respond, Marcus interjected. "Apologies, governor. Diane is a fervid fighter for those who cannot fight for themselves . . . as we all are."

It almost felt like Marcus had posed it as a question directed to the governor.

Thaddeus held still for a moment before responding with a simple, "Indeed, we are." Prick.

Marcus's blue eyes turned to ice as he stared me down. I raised my chin and reluctantly stepped back. Cato appeared behind me and placed a reassuring hand on my back.

Thaddeus's cold gaze lingered on me. A heaviness brushed against my senses, an invisible hand running its knuckles down my cheek. My eyes widened at the sensation. I thought I saw the governor grin slightly before sliding his eyes back to Marcus.

I wasn't quite sure what to make of the sensation, but I didn't like it. The hairs on my neck rose, and I narrowed my eyes, lips curling.

The male guard next to the governor twitched at my reaction, assuming it to be of disrespect. To be honest, I didn't really care what he thought. I eyed the soldier, fingers trailing to the pommel of my sword. The soldier stiffened.

Atticus's deep voice drawled behind me. "Don't expect me to save you if she attacks."

Drusus grunted his approval, echoed by Cato's snicker. The soldier only paled and took a step back.

Thaddeus was still rambling. "The priests will be grateful for your assistance. They said having the presence of Rome's wolves would act as a beacon of hope and security to the people."

The soft light that splashed the ground extended, running a gentle hand along Marcus's face. The light in his blue eyes sparked. "We fight for the people. It is what we always do."

<hr/>

Masses of people and satyrs meandered along the forest trail toward the city. Trees loomed over the crowd of refugees like watchful guards. Clouds of flocks whirled above with their endless chittering. The smell of sweat and urine hung faintly in the air. Oxen and horses pulled wagons carrying children and the elderly. A heavy sadness clung to the refugees like a sickness. My heart twisted at the sight.

The governor was a fool to say that it was the people's fault for the daemon attack. The notion was absurd. He believed their lack of action in addressing the riots was what led to their settlement's demise. If only these individuals in power took a moment to see how the common folk were faring. It was obvious the citizens didn't have the resources or the support to face the riot issues. I couldn't fathom how some leaders could fail their people so. How they could disregard the lives of others. If only they understood that every individual, no matter their social status, plays a vital role in the longevity of an ecosystem. There is success when opportunities are made available to everyone. It may be a difficult path but since when did anything worthwhile come without obstacles? Such thoughts were a fantasy. Some in power may very well not care to understand.

Yes, the Roman Pack were focused on eradicating the daemons and ultimately the Order. But the wolves would never stop supporting the less fortunate. It was one of the many reasons why I loved doing this. Being in the field, among the citizens, where I could actively make a difference. A sense of purpose that kindled my soul. Something the governor would not be able to understand.

I watched from atop the gate walls, monitoring the expanse, Cato beside me in his wolf form. The gate wall was wide enough for his large frame; the wolves were practically the size of horses. His fur was a beautiful dove-gray that seemed to shimmer underneath the beams of light, his muscular body shading me from the heat.

Marcus and Drusus were below speaking with the priests, ensuring proper arrangements would be made for the people.

Many of the priests were thin and seemingly frail. There was a variety of dark and ivory skin. Their garments consisted of pale togas and leather sandals.

Human and satyr soldiers stood alongside the city's entrance ready to support the incoming crowds.

Atticus appeared beside us, still in his human form, stretching his arms. The muscles under his skin flexed and tightened. He tilted his head toward me, hazel eyes glinting wickedly, a grin curling over his sensual lips.

"What are you doing?" I asked.

Atticus bared his teeth. Canines began to sharpen. "Lightening the mood. Watch this."

He dove from the roof, his body slipping into ripples of light and aether. A beige colored wolf with glacier eyes landed on the ground below. The crowd gasped and murmured in awe as Atticus padded to a wagon where a group of children were huddled. He dipped his large head, letting the curious little hands run over his snout.

Marcus started jogging toward the evacuees and exploded into a brown wolf, strutting between the lines of people. His deep voice murmured consolations and directions of where they should go when they entered the city. Drusus soon followed, his wolf a dark gray like rolling thunderclouds.

Something seemed to ignite in the people's gazes at the sight of the wolves among them. Hope.

Cato snorted. His jaws unmoving, the sound of his voice resounded in the space between us. "*Showoffs, all of them.*"

We eventually made our way to the crowd. The wolves began helping pull wagons with their teeth. The mood lightened, and conversations began to take life.

A woman was struggling, trying to pull a cart filled to the brim with blankets and other belongings. A little girl sat at the head of it.

Dirt caked her little head, and exhaustion resided in her eyes. I quickly took the handles of the cart from the woman.

"Let me," I said.

The woman flushed. "Thank you kindly, she-wolf."

The little girl watched me with wide eyes as I hauled the cart effortlessly. "How are you pulling this thing so easily?"

The woman looked back, smiling. "She's a she-wolf, Emilia."

I could feel Emilia's eyes on my back. Wonder drenched her words. "You're so strong."

A smile touched my lips. "As are you."

Minutes blended into hours. Inns and open villas were made available to the refugees. Many families, both human and satyr, managed to find room. Soldiers passed food and water. The priests' frail figures hovered at the city entrance preaching to those who wished to listen.

Dusk came and stars slowly emerged with the darkening sky. I had just finished assisting a satyr family when a wrinkly hand patted my arm. One of the priests looked at me with a toothless smile.

"These people have lost everything, and it is good to know our city can offer them a new beginning. We wish to thank you wolves, please join us at the temple."

Marcus and the others—now in their human forms—were being led by the other priests. The thinning crowds gradually revealed the temple's entrance. I shot a silent prayer that whatever occurred next would be a step closer to freeing our lands from hungry, wicked teeth.

SEVEN

Diane

The god of gods stood at the heart of the temple. Jupiter's marble eyes stared down at those who entered the temple, his stone brow pinched in eternal determination and grace. Gold lined the ivory walls surrounding the statue. Vines and garlands were draped at the god's feet and along the various rails in the temple. The smell of burning incense and sage was strong. I wrinkled my nose. Temples were to be a place of sanctity and peace. Then why was I feeling the urge to run?

The head priest faced us just as the other priests closed the temple doors, locking us in. "We are so glad that you received our message."

Marcus stood ahead of us, turning his body as if in an attempt to protect us. The veins on his muscled arms tightened. He must've felt the same sense of warning as I did. "What message?"

The priest opened his arms. "Might as well let you in on our scheme. We sent the anonymous tip and planted Oeneus's name in order to bring the wolves to our doors. He was in on it, but seeing as he never returned to us, we have to assume the poor fool is dead. No matter though, we have what we need."

Aether stirred the chords of the air. It rifted and trembled. The same heaviness from last night. Remus's words about the foreign aether echoed in my head. *Old and angry.*

Drusus and Cato edged closer on either side of me. Atticus flanked Marcus.

"I don't think the priests are good people," Drusus murmured.

I scoffed quietly. "No, really?"

A growl seeped from between Marcus's clenched teeth. "Why bring us here?"

The head priest spoke again. The same bloodless smile Oeneus had. "We listened to the call. The voice beyond the veil. Generations of plotting, and finally we have managed to break the boundaries of our mortal realm. Incredible power is now within our reach with the blood of wolves. Blessed by the god of war's aether. The key to our king."

Something whistled through the air. Atticus struck his arm out, his sword a flash of silver in his hand. A black spear shattered into pieces and wisps of dark smoke at his feet.

Atticus slowly looked to the priest who had cast the orther, his hazel eyes lit with a devilish excitement to draw blood. "Try again, old man."

Shadows exploded. The world plunged into darkness. I swung my sword, and it clashed against a blade of aether. I thrust a palm out and struck a priest, sweeping the blankets of shadow from my view. His bones snapped, blood gushing from his eyes and ears. Drusus and Cato circled me, cutting off the conjured blades of aether. I had never seen this type of aether at work.

Clouds of darkness twisted, and daemons stepped out from the plumes. Had the priests summoned them into our realm? No, that couldn't be possible. Could it?

The skull-faced creatures hissed. Saliva dripped from their razor teeth; red eyes flared in hunger. My brothers shifted into their wolf forms. The heat from their bodies pressed at my skin as my aether thrummed with excitement.

Somewhere in the temple, within the crevices of its walls, thunder rolled against the limestone. The strength and anger of it made even the statue of Jupiter tremble.

But it wasn't thunder, I realized. It was the sound of an animal roaring. From behind the daemons, rocks exploded from the temple's walls. My brothers and I ducked as the debris crashed against the wall behind us, tables and chairs battered into splinters. The daemons shrieked, readying to pounce on the new threat, but were halted by the hand of the head priest.

Within the dust and darkness, green eyes gleamed. A black wolf emerged, fangs bared into a snarl, the sound like a rolling storm just before the crack of thunder. Large paws scraped the marble ground. Muscles flexed on its back as the black wolf prowled.

There was something in how it moved. In the power that echoed within every step. I knew it was Remus. The Lone Wolf had come.

Looking toward the gaping hole he had left in his wake, I noticed steps leading into a tunnel. The godsdamn Lone Wolf had ventured further into the tunnels and it had led *here*. To the temple. I had told Remus to stay away and not explore them but in that bleeding moment I was utterly grateful for his stubbornness.

The priests remained eerily still even with Remus's explosive entrance. Not even a blink. It was unnatural. Instead, the head priest's face lit with intrigue. "Now this is a surprise. How lovely of the Lone Wolf to join us. Oh, you didn't think I wouldn't remember the son of the late Alpha Anthony."

Remus grimaced at the sound of his pater's name. Anthony, one of the most revered Alphas, had been killed in battle against the Order and its daemons. His body had been burned so brutally by the fires caused by the attack that it was almost unrecognizable. Anthony's demise had followed shortly after the death of his daughter. It was said that the Alpha's heart was heavy with sorrow and that heartbreak led to his own end.

I couldn't fathom the amount of heartache of losing your whole family. Was that why Remus had left the Pack?

Marcus and Atticus narrowed their gazes on Remus, their pearl white fangs gleaming. But they turned their attention back to the priests. Yes, we would deal with the Lone Wolf later. Drusus, however, angled his body protectively in front of Remus. Another testimony to their bond.

The head priest shouted a command and the daemons charged. The trills of their screams iced my blood. Remus lunged toward them. He sank his fangs into a daemon's neck and twisted the body into a horrific angle. Drusus was at his side, his claws finding purchase in another daemon as his teeth ripped its throat apart. Black gore splattered along the walls and floor, echoed by the sound of ripped flesh.

Aether tore from my skin. Power connected with the oncoming daemons. A relentless force of energy. Their skulled faces cracked, and blood spilled onto the temple ground. I shouted as a daemon pounced on me, its claws digging into my fighting leathers. I fell onto one knee. I quickly unhitched my dagger and jammed it up the daemon's neck. By now, I was beginning to feel my power waning.

The daemons pulled away as shrouds of dark clouds gathered across the floor. Dark plumes fell from the priest's hands, twisting and turning, clawing their way through the wolves' nostrils and mouths.

Drusus's chest heaved for air, his eyes rolling until he collapsed. Remus reached for him, clawed the ground, and roared curses at the priests. Marcus and Atticus struggled against the onslaught of the priests' aether. Their paws dug out chunks of stone from the ground as Marcus lunged, snapping his jaws around another priest's throat. The man's screams ended in a crunch of bone. Marcus dropped the body, staggering until he finally fell.

I screamed, forcing the extent of my energy, the essence within me, to do *more*. Unseen forces that I willed forward crashed against the plumes of darkness. The wolves were down, but I could still help them.

Deep inside me, something stirred. *Shit.* It had been years since I'd felt it, remaining dormant after constant practice in shutting it away. The energy shifted. Like an animal rising from sleep, I felt the timbre of its power unfurl from the core of my soul—

Pain shot through my arm, cutting the connection. A daemon had slid away from the havoc, sparks flying and claws skidding on the ground as the creature continued its charge. I didn't react fast enough. Its teeth sank into my arm and pulled me to the ground. My chin slammed onto stone. Another daemon came at my leg, tearing at the skin.

My screams echoed in the temple. And Remus roared in response. He was the only one left. Had resisted the urge to fall. White hot flares of pain caused my eyelids to flutter. Wetness pooled where the daemons held me. *Stay awake. Stay awake. Stay awake.*

Darkness seeped through the corners of my sight, and the last thing I saw was a black wolf tearing through the folds of the priests' aether.

Gleaming fangs. A piercing roar.

It wasn't long before I regained consciousness, a dull throb beating at my temples. Blurs of chains and lolling tongues. Masked figures. The echo of a wolf's roar.

Pain seared through me but I bit my tongue till I tasted copper. The gashes on my arm and leg were sensitive, even though the power in my blood was already healing the wounds. I stilled, sensing my surroundings. I was not alone. My fingers grabbed at the loose dirt as I rolled over and crawled on my arms. Torches lit the space. Lights flickered dimly as my vision had yet to clear, but I slowly made my way toward them. I needed to make sense of where I was. My hands met something hard, and I realized it was iron.

Iron bars. I blinked several times to see walls made of rock and stone. I swore under my breath. I was in the underground tunnels.

The faint sounds of heavy breathing had me twisting my head, looking around the makeshift cell room. The priests must have been using the network the entire time. We had been fools to believe that we were making a difference in eradicating the Order. They had baited us.

Marcus, Atticus, and Cato were chained to the walls. Still in their wolf forms, iron chains were coiled around their thick necks and legs. They were sprawled on their sides, tongues lolling between their teeth. Remus and Drusus were nowhere to be seen. I had to ignore the roaring fear in my chest as I turned my attention toward the sound of voices.

Two figures clad in dark robes and hoods hovered at the cell's entrance.

"Are we to attend the summoning?" one of them asked.

The other merely shook his head. "We are to wait. The wolves are a welcoming gift for the king."

I grasped the iron bars and bit back my cries of pain, hauling myself to my feet. I listened to the quiet drums of my aether. The she-wolf power. It hungered for chaos. The muscles at my biceps clenched as I prepared to pull.

The robed figures turned abruptly as they finally noticed me. My jaw clenched, yanking the iron apart enough to fit through. Without lifting a hand, I hurled the invisible threads of my strength toward the humans. They froze in place, their eyes bulging and skin purpling. The pressure from my power was too much, and it didn't take long for the life to be choked out of them.

I grabbed my weapons from the cave wall, strapping and hitching the blades at my armor before running to Marcus's side.

A hiss seeped between my clenched teeth as I observed the chains. The bondages were latched so tight they were drawing blood. My hands ran over Marcus's brown fur as he slowly opened an eye.

"It's going to be fine," I said. "This will only take a moment."

I tried to curl my fingers around the chain. I swore under my breath as I continued to fidget around iron until I had enough of a grip. I squeezed the metal as much as I could until it snapped loose. Marcus heaved as the chains fell to the ground, and I continued snapping the binds from his paws. He turned his large head to me, gently pressing his muzzle to my arm.

"Your power never ceases to amaze me," he rasped.

It was no secret that my aether was of a higher strength than the average she-wolf. Something I'd been told to thank the gods for. And while I was indeed grateful, I never allowed myself to fully test the limits of my power. It may have stemmed from fear—I wasn't sure of what—but I couldn't dwell on that now.

I smiled, tapping Marcus's snout before scrambling toward Atticus. His beautiful beige fur was matted with blood, much of it not his own. I broke his chains, and a little dog-like whine escaped him. Once I released Cato from his binds, he shook his mane and stood, towering above my head.

"Where are Drusus and Remus?" I asked, getting to my feet.

Marcus sauntered toward the cell's entrance, jerking his head to the adjacent hallway. *"They took them. They kept talking about summoning their king and, for whatever reason, they wanted Remus and Drusus."*

Blood drained from my face. "Before we met with the governor, Drusus had mentioned something yesterday. The Ram, I think. Do you remember the story?"

Cato swore. *"About the daemon who betrayed the gods and goddesses, banished to a prison realm, never to be remembered? Why yes, I know the story."*

"That can't be good," Atticus rumbled.

Marcus shook his head. *"The priests took a keen interest in the Lone Wolf. Which, by the way, serves the question: what the bleeding skies was he doing there?"*

He shot the accusation at me. My stomach flipped, and a metallic taste formed in my mouth. Before I could manage to find the words, the walls began to shake. My senses roared at the immense amount of foreign aether. A blood-curdling scream pierced the air, and my heart plummeted as I recognized the sound.

Drusus.

EIGHT

Remus

F*uck.*

    This shouldn't have surprised me. The old woman in the market had even told me. I wanted to find solid evidence before telling Drusus. And I had been too damn slow. I should've warned the wolves, pushed away my pride.

I had been searching through textbooks in the library earlier that day, hoping to find more information on the Ram, or even regarding the aether of the gods. Something. But it seemed as though the Order had taken away anything useful. Thankfully no one had ventured into Oeneus's office, and I had been able to sneak back in. I knew the fiery she-wolf would have my balls if she saw me here. She would've raised her blade to me, perhaps willed her aether to push me against a wall. Gods. There was no reason for me to be thinking of her. But why did that little fantasy intrigue me? Oh, yes. I knew why. Because it had been too damn long since I'd slept with someone. I normally wouldn't entertain myself that way. When I had first become the Lone Wolf I may have indulged myself, trying to find a distraction from my guilt and sorrow by fucking strangers. But the pain was always there. Waiting for me. There came a point where I could no longer divert myself from the agony and I let myself wallow in it. I deserved it anyway. I always reminded myself of that.

I had ventured into those underground tunnels, following the path we had taken the night before. I passed Oeneus's body, inspecting his robes but finding nothing of use. The dark, heavy sensation from his aether was no longer there. It had left as soon as Oeneus had drawn his last breath. I had continued further down the path only to find steps leading up a narrow passageway to a stone door. I had heard a shout, the sound of metal clanging, and the feeling of that foreign power returning. I had thought of Drusus and panicked. No rational thought had existed as I'd burst into my wolf form and charged through the stone door.

And now here I was. Somewhere.

When my eyes opened, I first noticed the lack of chains and cell bars. I was no longer in my wolf form, laying on the cold ground. There were torches along the rocky walls. It looked like I was in an underground room of sorts. The Order must've been using this place all along. Something stirred beside me, and I was relieved to see it was Drusus—in his human body—waking up and running a hand over his face. Like the warrior he was trained to be, Drusus froze. Still as death as he listened to his surroundings.

"I'm here." My throat was dry and rough.

Muscles strained underneath Drusus's fighting leathers as he pulled himself upright. His shoulders seemed to loosen upon seeing me, his dark hair plastered to his brow with sweat. "What is happening?"

A cloaked figure, similar to the one we saw the night of Oeneus's death, stepped out of a dark corner. The hood was drawn, and a mask covered the entirety of their face. It glistened a dull copper, shaped into the skull of a snake, the face of the daemons.

"Our efforts have not been in vain." I recognized the voice as belonging to one of the priests.

I slowly got to my feet, Drusus following my lead. The ground seemed to waver as I fought through the sluggish sensations. "Why cloak yourself when we know who you are?"

The priest didn't respond. Chants and murmurings echoed within the tunnel walls. I could see the forms of other robed figures emerging from the dark corners, as if they'd been there the entire time. Aether riled from their words. This looked too familiar . . .

"It will either be death or a life of servitude," the priest finally said. "You decide."

Drusus snarled as another cloaked figure moved from where the priest stood. This one was different from the others. Tall with a muscled build. From the wide, broad frame, I could tell it was a male. He wore a sleek mask in the shape of a wolf, the ends of it curved into the horns of an antelope. Also very much like the daemons. The wolf-masked male remained silent, but it felt as though he was watching me.

The priest withdrew a wicked dagger from his robe and offered it to the male. "It's almost poetic, no? To use the Alpha's son to summon our king."

With a subtle flick of his wrist, the priest sent a rippling pulse of energy toward us. Drusus crashed against the rock wall with a shout of pain. Red crept from the corners of my eyes until I was blinded by it. I roared, rushing the priest, unsheathing my sword. If they wanted something poetic, I would be sure to let my blade sing a song worthy of an encore.

Pain jammed into my chest, and my limbs buckled. The priests' chanting grew louder and the foreign aether hummed. Drusus's body flew against the cave wall once more. Twice. He swayed onto his feet, blood dripping down his inked arms.

Rage strangled my heart as I whipped around to the wolf-masked male. "What do you want from me?"

Silence. He raised the blade, but it was the priest's voice I heard. "Give us your blood."

Drusus was holding himself up against the cave wall. "No!"

Another wave of aether, like a black serpent, wrapped around his neck as it forced him to his knees. His breath ensnared, the muscles of his neck worked as the skin on his face began to purple.

"Lone Wolf," the priest taunted. "Your blood."

My feet were already moving. We were warriors. Wolves. We understood the meaning of sacrifice and what it meant to step into battle. All that meant nothing when I saw Drusus under the Order's mercy.

"Stop! Take whatever you want from me, just let him fucking breathe."

The binds loosened enough for Drusus to gasp for air. The silent male extended a gloved hand and made a slit in my palm with the dagger. The hairs at the nape of my neck rose as the sensation returned, heavy like molasses. Bitter. To the point where it was difficult to swallow. The male raised his fingers and beads of my blood dripped from the silver blade. He suddenly latched a gloved hand on the cut of my palm. I hissed at the contact and choked on the energy that surged from me.

A burning sensation ran through my body, quickly going rampant. Whatever aether resided in my wolf blood was now being manipulated and channeled.

My body jerked, and I fell to my knees, the wolf-masked male still gripping my hand. Power was pulled from me as it bled through the Order's aether. Coils of their darkness, beaded with my blood, seeped from our joined hands into the blade he was holding; the silver vibrated as he swiped the blade at the air behind him.

A shard of light cracked in the dagger's wake. A chasm of aether unfolded before me. As if it had inhaled the energy of my godsgiven blood, it became tethered to me, and I couldn't fight the onslaught.

Drusus's blood-curdling cries pierced through me just as pain overtook my senses. The wolf-masked male let go of my hand, and I dropped to the ground, thrashing from side to side as if my blood was boiling. My screams wrung into roars. Animal. Raw.

Soft fingers caressed the corners of my mind. *To live without pain,* the ancient power seemed to say. I tasted that freedom like crisp air, and I craved it. The dark expanded, grasping onto my own aether, trying to suffocate it. My body convulsed, and my mind began to fall.

A forest. Dark and malignant. Branches reaching like old, gnarled fingers. In a clearing, under a beam of moonlight, a female. Long midnight hair. Olive skin. The frame of her form painstakingly familiar.

My voice broke. "Helena?"

My twin sister didn't move, her back to me, face tilted to face the moon. I remembered this. But was it a memory or a distorted reality? Some trickery of the Order? Perhaps they were taunting me. Using my sister as a means of making me give in to their power. I almost laughed. They would have to try harder.

My sister was bathed in the moonlight for a moment longer, but in a blink of an eye, there stood a daemon. Crescent eyes on me, it lunged. Teeth snapped at the small space before my face. Scraped the skin on my nose. My feet tried to kick at the creature but it felt as if I were under water.

I cried out to the depths of this void. Searching, scratching for any sliver of strength. The shadows danced throughout my mind, threatening to overwhelm me. I couldn't control aether like the she-wolves but I called out anyway. Wolves were made of aether; that had to mean something, and I refused to die tonight. I was not done with the mortal realm yet.

Somewhere, a deep essence answered. Powerful, like the shaking of stars and the splitting of seas. I could've sworn I heard a male's voice in the distance. The void silenced for a breath.

An explosion of light. Tearing through the wood, barreling against the heavy forces against my mind. I was sure I screamed as the light ripped me from the madness.

I held onto it—the light.

Drusus's shouting and roars snapped me awake. I found myself curled on the cold ground.

"What did you do?" Drusus snarled at the Order, shadows still holding him down on his knees. Sweat and blood trickling along his skin. "I'm going to fucking kill you!"

The shard of light the wolf-masked male had created was still suspended in the air. Even now, energy was being seeped out of me, though the wolf-masked male wasn't touching me. It was too much. Overwhelming.

Claws, the size of a man's hand, appeared from the bright slit in the air. An angry roar bellowed as the realm's opening was peeled open. Jagged, pale lines, like lightning, splintered further in the air the more the portal expanded. A clawed foot stepped from the crackling light. Curved and rounded horns. A broad chest, the skin gray and tough. A face made of bone, in the shape of a ram's skull. Glowing red eyes, like dying suns, the shape of crescent moons.

The images hadn't done the Ram justice.

Ice ran through my blood. Drusus's face paled to a deathly white. The masked male slowly bowed as the priests went to their knees, pressing their brows on the ground. The daemon king made real.

Gods, this could not be happening.

The entryway suddenly closed and I collapsed as the connection broke. The Ram lifted its head and inhaled deeply. Then those terrifying crescent eyes found mine. Horns tilted as it observed me.

Its voice was deep and world-shaking. It was godlike anger and the clashing of stars combined. "I've been watching this realm for millennia. Through the eyes of my followers, I see all. And out of all the creatures I've seen across this plane, I remember you. You were the one to open the realm for me. Mind on the verge of breaking but you survived. Not unscathed it seems—there is something riling inside you. Shall we put it to the test?"

My body began to shake. *He remembered me?* What did that mean? My thoughts rushed to that night. Flashes of teeth and gnarled trees. No, it couldn't mean—

Fingers of smoke suddenly conjured a black blade. It was thin, narrow, and utterly sharp. The Ram held my gaze as he flicked it away. The world slowed, the sound of pierced flesh roaring in my ears. Drusus lurched forward, the dagger now wedged between his ribs. And Drusus fell.

"NO!"

The Ram raised a clawed hand and sent another.

I was unleashed.

Flames the color of the moon, like silver gems, ignited along my skin. Amplifying and swallowing me whole. This fire didn't burn. It sang to me. Melding with the essence of who I was. It was a moment of complete understanding, as if I knew the words to the song and simply followed its melody.

With unnatural speed, I landed in the space between the oncoming blade and Drusus. The white flames turned the weapon into coal-colored embers.

The Ram hummed as if intrigued. "So, it seems the gods found a way."

The fires grew wilder. An older energy, something unfathomable, unveiled an image in my mind's eye. A land of golden plains, a sky of dusk and dawn, towering mountains that had no end. The image disappeared quickly, and the power was relentless, shoving every conscious thought down and down until I lost sense of everything around me. The Ram's words fell on empty ears. I didn't think—*couldn't* think. Sending rivers of flames away from me, I managed to hit the cave walls and take out some members of the Order. Every godsdamn sliver of this power unraveled something within me.

From all the impacts, the cave walls began to shake viciously, and rocks crumbled. As quickly as they came, the bright flames dissipated from my skin. My knees buckled, and I fought to stay upright, gasping for breath. I almost missed the chaos surrounding me as the Order began to flee.

Only to suddenly find themselves at the mercy of Diane and the wolves.

With a swipe of her arm, Diane's aether snapped bones and popped blood vessels. The wolves launched into the air, fangs crunching bone.

I turned to the Ram, unsheathed sword in hand, angry power pushing against me, and my boots slid. The daemon king ran a finger through the air, and a spear of aether shot out, grazing my side.

As I was about to move, the she-wolf appeared, beating me to the Ram. Her lips twisted in a war cry as she raised her blade, black hair flipping wildly, golden eyes gleaming like a pair of suns. She was a goddess of the Underworld. Flames flared along my arms at the sight.

The Ram swung its clawed hand, dipped in shadow, and wrapped it around Diane's neck. Her shouts were cut short as the daemon king lifted her high enough that her feet dangled above the ground and drew her closer to its hungry crescent eyes.

"Diane!" I ignored the splitting pain at my side. A visceral need to reach her overcame me.

The Ram tilted its head to observe her, much the same way it had done with me, as Diane clawed at its grasp. "Curious. I feel something from your essence. My power speaks to you."

There was a space of silence before Diane's eyes widened, the brightness in them dimming as her gaze turned distant. My heart slammed against my ribs. Shadows whipped out from the Ram and clung to her.

A shout tore from my throat. "Diane, don't let him in!"

The Ram's grasp suddenly loosened, as if Diane's body had burned it. She slipped between its claws, falling limp to the ground. The Ram didn't move as I crawled toward her and took her body in my arms. I pressed my fingers against her neck, and sighed as I felt her pulse. I may not have been a member of the Pack but it wouldn't have boded well for me if one of them died tonight.

Diane's eyes fluttered open.

I was breathing heavily, relieved to see the fire return to her eyes. I couldn't help the remark that left me. "Aren't you glad I stayed?"

Diane's lips twitched. "I'm glad to see you can crack jokes at a time like this."

The Ram clenched its hand, snarling at the she-wolf in my arms. "Death. You are death."

I tightened my arms around Diane as her face paled. The wolf-masked male followed the daemon king's shadow. He unsheathed a sword, digging the tip into the ground and resting his hands atop the pommel, as he waited for orders.

"Curious, indeed," the Ram repeated. "This mortal realm has changed. Oh, the things I may be able to command with the power I see before me."

Still holding Diane's body, I leaned over her, shielding her from the Ram's sight. "Touch her again and I will kill you."

"What humor you have, wolf." Black tendrils of smoke billowed viciously around the daemon king. "You have killed many, haven't you? Imagine the devastation that can be done by your hand."

I grinded my teeth at the Ram's invitation. The masked male stood firmly at its side until the head priest with the copper mask appeared beside him.

"Let us be gone," the priest snickered. The male said nothing as he lowered his gaze to the priest. Then the priest's mouth dropped.

"You can't!" he begged, his frail hands reaching for him only to be brushed off. "I have served you! Brought the wolves to you as you wished!"

The male spun, grabbing the priest by the nape of his tunic. He pulled the priest forward, speaking too low for me to hear. Whatever was said caused the priest to growl. "You bastard, you can't leave me here! Leave the others but not me! That is not what I—"

"End it," the Ram commanded.

A slash of a sword, and the priest was removed from his head. The copper of the wolf-mask winked wickedly, the priest's blood skimming down the blade, as dark clouds swept the male and the Ram from the cave.

The voice of the Ram was the last thing to be heard, echoing like a cold winter wind. Like a fucking parting gift. "Save your strength, both of you. We will see each other again, and I look forward to having you at my side. You are both *mine.*"

I despised how his departing words caused my spine to shiver. Diane was stiff in my arms, and I assumed she was reeling just as much as I was.

The Ram had left its followers for our killing, the chaos of the bloodshed still continuing at the other end of the cave. The wolves were relentless, throwing Order members around like rag dolls.

Diane's hands pushed at my chest. "Where's Drusus?"

I looked around and saw him sprawled on the ground just a few meters behind us. His body was laying in an awkward angle, but there was some slight movement from his chest. I swore under my breath as I reached him.

"Drusus," I urged.

"I'm here," he rasped.

I hooked an arm under his shoulder and pulled him up. Rocks began to fall from the ceiling. Cracks crawled along the walls. Marcus's brown wolf was at one of the entrances. "*Everything is going to collapse!*"

Atticus and Cato quickly made their way to Marcus, while Diane had managed to pick a fight with another one of the Order despite the walls threatening to cave in on us. I pulled Drusus along toward the exit, but my eyes couldn't stray from Diane as she brought the cloaked figure to the ground with a boot to their chest.

She flipped the mask off and bared her teeth. "I knew I recognized that scent." At her feet was the governor, Thaddeus.

"Why?" Diane demanded. "Why sell your soul to a monster?"

The governor only grinned, revealing bloodied teeth. "For a life without pain. Even now as I serve my king I do not feel pain. Death is temporary for those who pledge their loyalty. Those who deny our king's call will fall, like this very city."

He laughed a soulless sound as his eyes slowly raised to the ceiling of the cave. The evacuees. I recalled seeing lines of citizens filing through the gates, and I'd heard they arrived from the same desolated town I had come across. My thoughts had briefly gone to the boy I'd saved, and I wondered if he was among those people. And if something was happening above ground now . . .

Diane must've followed the same thought. She gaped, the blade in her hand trembling. "You godsdamn traitor."

A flash of silver, Marcus shouting her name. Her blade struck a clean cut along the governor's throat. Blood sprayed, stray spots finding Diane's neck and arms. The other wolves seemed speechless, but an approving growl rumbled through my chest. The she-wolf had a violent bite.

A rock fell from the ceiling, snapping us all from our stupor. Marcus began shouting orders and turned to the exit.

Unbridled fury burned in Diane's eyes as she made her way to follow us out.

We finally reached the surface just as the cave collapsed, the temple following suit. I practically threw Drusus away from me to avoid the pillars crashing at our heels.

Dust brushed at my hands and knees as I brought myself to my feet and lifted my gaze. Only to see the harbor city in flames, at the utter mercy of daemons.

NINE

Diane

Battle was my mantle. Death poised in my every breath.

It was a sort of mantra I repeated to myself, but it seemed ridiculous in that moment. Death clearly had other plans.

Daemons tore through the limestone, slabs of brick tumbling as they hauled families from their homes, Roman soldiers already in the fray. Torches fell and sparse flames were beginning to eat at the structures.

Marcus brushed past me. His white fangs dripped with saliva, hairs bristled like daggers. His yellow eyes landed on Drusus, who was gripping the wound at his side, blood spilling between his fingers. Marcus's nostrils flared, a rumble in his chest.

After a beat, as the screams continued to echo through the city, Marcus's glowing eyes touched everyone except Remus. His voice the force of thunder. *"You know what to do."*

My feet were already moving. The heavy presence of my wolf brothers anchored me. I didn't look back to see what the Lone Wolf would do. Or to see Drusus's current state. I was afraid if I looked back upon my brother, the looming force inside me would reawaken. I didn't—couldn't—trust it. Nor did I want to think about the aether Remus had summoned. Adrenaline pumped through me, dousing me in a frenzy to draw blood.

Power rippled from my fingertips with the force of a raging

chariot, daemons crumpling on impact. Others managed to cling to their last breaths, limbs in awkward angles as their maws tried to find purchase, only for my sword to sink its silvery teeth into their leathery hides.

I made a sharp turn to the harbor and stumbled upon a daemon dragging a male by the ankle. Sprinting, I swung my hand, an exhilarating pulse gliding above the ground and spewing chunks of rock and dirt. The force threw the daemon off the human. The creature shook its skull face, crouching.

Daemon blood, thick and dark, glistened on my silver blade under the fire red sky. "Come for it, beast," I growled.

The creature launched into the air, and I kicked off of the ground. My blade sunk into its chest as the daemon's claw gouged my forearm, ripping the leather bracer. A cry was wrenched from my lips. I landed, and yanked the sword from the lifeless daemon. The human male was still on the ground, his face pale with fear.

"She-wolf," he breathed.

I nodded as I helped him up, then whipped the dagger from my thigh strap and placed it in his hands. I jerked my chin to the other people who had been huddled in the dark corners. "Take as many families as you can and run. Go to the boats. Daemons can't swim."

He nodded, twisting around as he began to shout for others to follow. I spotted Cato bolting through a villa, emerging with a dead daemon in his jaws. Atticus lunged over the rooftops, daemons falling lifeless in his wake.

I cleared a horde of daemons, finding myself on a lonely road of abandoned townhomes. Bright, silvery light beamed through the cracks of a shattered door. My hands slid over the bloodied walls as I pushed the door open with the tip of my boot.

I had seen the flashes of Remus's power in the underground tunnel. It had been fleeting, and I wasn't even sure I fully believed it. But witnessing the same silvery flames now . . . they were pure energy. Each lick of white fire caressed his fur. Smoke curled from between his fangs.

The black wolf's head was hunched over, at his paws a small figure.

My eyes drifted around the room noticing the lifeless daemons that surrounded him. I looked back at the small figure. A boy. Remus's eyes stayed on him, a twisted look of sadness and anger settling in the wolf's eyes. The Lone Wolf lifted his muzzle and released a howl that cracked the walls and threatened to lance hearts. Fire the color of the moon embraced him even more.

Remus could've been the god of war himself. The flames crowned him, bowed to him.

His snout gently touched the small body, and white flames slowly engulfed the boy's form, leaving him a torch of silver in the dark.

I took a step toward the Lone Wolf. Unsure whether this child had meant something to him, I hesitated before my voice cut through the suddenly thick silence. "I'm sorry."

The Lone Wolf didn't turn to me, but his ears flickered at the sound of my voice. Without responding, the black wolf padded out of the home. Silver still alight, the heat pulsed at my skin and my aether responded to the deep thrums of power that echoed from the wolf. I followed, and we silently tracked the remaining daemons. Side by side. Lone Wolf and she-wolf.

We scaled the walls and came across the daemons on the rooftops. Remus fought tooth and claw. The sleek white fire followed his wrath, striking daemons like bolts of lightning. I was all too stunned at the sight, at the reality before me. This was not supposed to be possible, and yet, a wolf was controlling aether. And not just any aether it seemed.

Perhaps it was the adrenaline, or the mere fact that a daemon had somehow managed to escape Remus's rage, but I snapped out of my stupor and flung myself into the battle. Sword and aether worked in tandem, a swing of the blade and a force of unseen power. Daemons began to fall, and it wasn't long before only the Lone Wolf and I remained.

Remus loomed over his killings, and the bright fires slowly faded. The black wolf finally looked at me, a wildness raging in his wolf green eyes before they rolled back and he dropped unconscious.

"No," I gasped. I ran my hands over the thick fur of his back until I felt the slight rise and fall of his breathing.

I jerked my head to the cracking of tile. Ebony claws curled around the edges of the rooftop and a daemon bounded over the edge. And another. Another. An entire band of daemons had begun to circle us.

Grabbing a piece of debris, I chucked it at them. "Haven't you done enough?"

I crouched in front of Remus's body. The deep power that had awoken in the cave—unlike my she-wolf aether—was stirring again. It drummed in my veins. This sensation was something . . . ungodly. My breaths quickened as the power slowly emerged.

I watched in horror as black tendrils seeped from my skin, waves of shadow crawling to the daemons. The creatures bristled and the dark waves forced their way through their mouths and eyes, suffocating them from the inside. Horrible shrieking rattled the air, but the power leaving me felt *good*.

Terror gripped me at the realization. I reeled the shadows back, sealing the atrocity away.

Some of the daemons still lived, the broken bone of their jaws snapping with an abnormal clacking. A daemon lunged, and I braced for impact just as I heard a deep drum of *wings*. I fell back, almost landing on Remus, when a figure landed in front of me. Large wings of a shimmering rose gold covered my view of the bloodshed, the screeches and snarls soon silenced.

A harpy turned to face me. She was tall and dark-skinned with shorn hair. A hooped ring pierced her nose, and ink curled around both of her muscled biceps.

Releasing a trembling breath, I managed an exhausted grin. "I was beginning to think you'd never show up, Laelia."

The harpy smirked, twisting her blades across her back. "You look like shit."

I could only sigh in relief as the loud war cries from her winged sisters sounded above.

Ten

Remus

Eight years. It had been eight years since I'd last come across the Pack. I usually kept my distance despite my interactions with Drusus. It didn't prevent crossing paths with the wolves every now and then throughout my travels, but those interactions were always fleeting. To think I would be back within their grasp. I knew I would not be returning to my days of isolation anytime soon.

The events from last night returned to my thoughts with a vengeance. The muscles in my body screamed as I pulled myself up and leaned against the wood of a bedframe, a groan slipping through my lips. At some point throughout the night, I had shifted back to my human form. Someone had brought me to this bed, changed me, and tended to my wounds. Bandages and ointment covered the gouges at my shoulders and back. Minor injuries.

The aether in our blood helped with healing, which also extended the lifespan of the average wolf, stalled aging. We could live beyond a hundred years. Death still made her visit, eventually.

The bedsheets were smooth under my palms as I took in the room. A single table sat near the foot of the bed, a lone pitcher atop it. Pieces of the walls were missing. The jagged lines of claw and teeth along them meant daemons had been through here. Wherever here was. I strained to hear anything outside the room, but there was a thick silence other than the occasional sound of beating wings.

My stomach lurched, and a pang hit deep within my chest.

The boy. The same child I had saved from the small, forsaken town. He was supposed to be safe. I thought—my hands tightened to fists, the dry skin at my knuckles split open and red. The boy had survived the first attack only to die at the next one. He was already dead when I'd found him. His body was wedged underneath the debris before I pulled him out. The only twisted satisfaction was that the daemons hadn't killed him, hadn't torn his skin off. For that I was grateful. I only hoped he had found his mater in the golden plains.

I wondered if the gods and goddesses had watched the horror unfold last night. If they grieved or even cared. If there was a reason why they had left us to deal with a hatred that dated back several hundred millennia. A resentment originally against the gods themselves that was now directed at the mortals.

My thoughts began to stray. The Ram. A wolf mask. Bright flames. Drusus—I flinched, my teeth grinding against the pain. *Drusus.* I remembered leaving him in an abandoned stable, begging the skies that no daemons would find him. I had to go and check on him, I had to see if he was still ali—

The door opened and a wild scent of blossoms whisked through it. Diane's long hair was pulled over her shoulders, scrapes and bruises covered her legs, muscles taut with exhaustion. She wore a pale tunic, her bloodstained armor out of sight.

In her hands was a bowl and a rag draped over her bandaged forearm. My eyes narrowed on the wound, at the red that stained the cloth.

She arched a dark brow, golden eyes fixated on me. "About time." Her voice like smoke and iron. Soft yet dominating.

"Drusus," I grounded. My throat was so dry, it hurt to speak. "Where is he?"

"He's alive." She strode to the table and poured water from a pitcher into the bowl. She then shoved it in my hands and tossed me the rag. "Drink and wash up. Your face needs it."

Grunting, I brought the bowl to my lips. Water cracked the roughness on my tongue and throat. When I had drunk it dry, Diane brought the vase to refill it. I used the water to wash the dirt from my face and took the rag she offered. Afterward, I finally looked up to see Diane's scrutinizing gaze.

"Are you going to tell me what became of my brother?" I snapped.

Diane's eyes narrowed further. "Drusus has lost a lot of blood. He needs to be seen by our healers, and soon."

I inhaled sharply, flinching at the pull of a sensitive muscle at my side. "What happened?"

"The harpies saved us. After the daemons were cleared from the city, Cato carried you to this inn. He helped me undress you and tend to your wounds."

"And how did the harpies come to our aid?" I asked.

The scent of blossoms grew thicker as Diane sat on the edge of the bed. "We had sent word for additional reinforcements to assist with the relocation of the people—and good thing we did, too."

She extended a hand, gesturing toward my bandaged shoulder with a questioning look, as if asking for permission. I nodded. Her fingers gently peeled off the bandages. A hiss escaped my teeth as cloth pulled at the skin. A sweet scent of honey and something icy, like mint, touched my nose.

Diane leaned closer, inspecting the gashes. My gaze went to the skin pinched at her brows, trailed down to thick eyelashes that swept above her cheekbones. Her lips were curved and full, pursed as she examined the wound. Those bright eyes flitted up, meeting mine.

My mask fell into place as my expression smoothed out into cold indifference. Diane's gaze lingered on me, as if she was trying to pull the thoughts from my head. She cleared her throat, plastering the cloth back over my wounds.

I gently grabbed her wrist before she could pull away. "Your arm."

Diane shook her head "It's nothing serious. But I do have to . . . thank you for helping us last night."

My lips twitched. "I'm sure that was hard for you to say."

She rolled her eyes. "You're an ass. How are you feeling, though?"

I shrugged. "I've dealt with worse."

She searched my gaze as if curious about what else I had gone through. My story was full of scars, but she didn't have to know that.

A thought suddenly occurred. "I saw what you did."

Diane stilled, pulling her hand away. Her golden gaze darkened enough to wreak havoc. "I don't know what you mean."

I didn't respond immediately. I ran the pad of my thumb over my lip, thoughtfully. Her eyes tracked my movement.

The previous night, I had been lost to the chaos. A servant to my own bloodlust. It had been blinding, overriding all senses until every stream of energy and strength had left me. But I still saw. Just before the dark overwhelmed me completely, I saw Diane. The ferocious she-wolf had crouched in front of me, protecting me, and shadowed aether had escaped from her. I remember feeling a sense of wonder before I was fully gone.

That she-wolf stood before me now. A vibration strummed the air like a musician's fingers on the strings of an instrument. Unseen stems of aether caused the hairs on the nape of my neck to rise. My body tensed, an animal growl rumbling in my chest.

"Doesn't seem like you don't know," I observed. "I was conscious enough to see you will the shadows last night. And I know that wasn't the aether of a she-wolf. Care to elaborate on what it was?"

Diane took a step away from the bed. "We are not close enough for me to confide in you, Lone Wolf."

Humor touched my lips. I flung the sheets off me, placing my feet on the cool floor, and stood. I towered over the she-wolf, making her seem smaller than she really was. Her eyes roamed my body before her gaze went back up to mine.

I noticed the tattoo of a laurel wreath around her bicep. I was intrigued by what other artwork could be found on this she-wolf's skin. She tucked a strand of hair behind an ear, revealing turquoise ear cuffs that wrapped around the cartilage.

I dipped my head toward hers, my lips near enough to take a sip of the blossoms and light brown skin. "We'll see about that, lotus."

The words were simple, but they dripped with promise. She felt it. I saw it in the parting of her lips before she smothered it with a smirk and began to turn from me. "Don't flatter yourself, male." She faltered a step, head cocking in question. "Did you just call me 'lotus'?"

"Well, I could call you prickly cactus. That is more accurate for you."

Her lips threatened to smile. "Out of all the flowers, why choose something from Egypt?"

I straightened. "The lotus is very common there." I gestured to the ear cuffs. "And I recognize that to be of Egyptian making. Does the place have significance to you?"

Diane blinked a few times. "Yes, I am part Egyptian. My mater was born there. But how—"

"It's also your eyes," I mused. "They remind me of the pyramids, the sun setting behind them, sands cast in a golden glow."

Diane didn't respond at first. Her eyes seemed to brighten the longer she stared. The sharp, calculating look softened. Slowly, her gaze trailed over the ink on my arm and chest. As if my secrets were hidden there among the blossoms and leaves that covered my skin. Lotus was curious about me, and I found that I liked having her eyes on me.

The sudden sound of her voice shot a blaze down my spine. "I'm assuming you've been there."

"Once," I said stiffly.

"I've never been. What was it like?"

I let the question drop into a pit of silence. A vast, bottomless pit. I refused to go there. A continent with golden teeth and sand. I clasped the memory away before I could venture further.

Diane watched me a moment, letting the topic drop. She jerked a chin to the fresh tunic hanging over the bed. "Change. I'll take you to Drusus."

She was almost at the door when I spoke up. "We will talk about those shadows of yours, she-wolf."

Diane's expression smoothed. No evidence that my previous words had gotten to her as she closed the door behind her.

When I had changed into fresh clothes, I followed a silent she-wolf to a room further down the hall. My gut twisted as the door opened. Drusus was in his human form, sprawled on a narrow bed. Bandages were wrapped around his waist and over his chest. A paleness had drained him of his sun-kissed olive skin. Beads of sweat dotted his brow, the copper tang of blood thick in the air.

My fists tightened, nails digging crescents into my palms.

Diane went down on one knee, placing a hand over Drusus's brow. The crease between her brow softened. "Drusus, how are you faring?"

Drusus shifted. His eyes immediately found me. Somehow those dark eyes seemed to have paled. Dimmed.

The corners of his lips curved up weakly. "Brother."

A small smile touched Diane's lips. She ran a hand through his hair once more before standing. "Meet the rest of us outside when you're done, Remus. We have a lot to discuss." She brushed past, the scent of blossoms leaving with her.

I crept to the edge of the bed, guilt suddenly surging through me. "Gods, Drusus. I'm so sorry. I fucking did this to you. The choices I made brought you here."

Drusus clenched his teeth. Most likely due to the pain. "No. I made my decision, too, don't forget that." There was a pause and he grimaced. "Remus, if something were to happen to me I beg that you do not forsake yourself. Do not lose yourself more than you already have. You have to promise me that."

The words stung a bit more than I thought they would. I looked away as I responded quietly. "You're all I have."

Drusus eyed me for a moment and I quickly added. "We should not be talking about how I feel when you're the one who is injured."

His face softened before he released a ragged breath. "Remus, what they did to you . . . I have never been more terrified in my life. For a moment, I thought they had killed you."

"Death hasn't claimed me yet," I replied.

Drusus shook his head, a large hand running weakly over his mouth. "It's unheard of. A wolf controlling aether, in the form of fire."

I stared at my hands. At the calluses that roughened my palms. "The Order fucking used me. Somehow channeled the aether in my godsgiven blood to create a split between realms. How is that even possible?"

Drusus began to chew on his lip. "The world is made of aether.

And with enough raw power, it would seem plausible that this aether could peel the veils between worlds. Fucking fates, that doesn't seem real. You know the Pack is not going to let you go. They're going to want answers."

I sighed. "I saw it coming."

He looked at me with regret. "There is limited choice in war."

I lifted my eyes to the ceiling, cursing under my breath.

"You're coming home, Remus." I could hear the ember of hope in Drusus's voice.

There was a reason I was being amenable to returning to the Pack. Ever since that night in the tunnels, encountering the Ram, I knew I would have to. I needed them, their resources. I would need access to whatever they would use to get closer to the Ram. It was a transaction of means. The Pack was going to use me for my power, that I was sure, and I would use them in return.

No one else knew the burden of knowledge I carried. And I intended to see my vengeance through.

So I said the only thing I could say. "It's not home, brother. Not for me."

The main floor of the inn was wrecked. Chairs and tables had been tossed and splintered. I steered myself toward the kitchen. Diane hadn't said anything about not eating before speaking to the wolves. I spotted the pantry but found someone already rummaging through it.

A broad back faced me as the male reached into the shelves. The wolf—though he was in his human form I could still sense he was a wolf—stiffened and turned to me. Wild hair and light brown eyes met mine. A chunk of bread wedged between his teeth. The male eyed me, slowly ripping the piece of bread.

As he chewed, he arched an eyebrow. "Fancy some?"

Not knowing what else to say, I only nodded. He grunted and turned back to the shelves, pulled out a basket of loaves, and tossed one to me.

"They're a bit dusty from the attack, but food is food. And . . ."

The wolf bent to another shelf, slid a crate forward and yanked out a tall bottle of dark wine. "Darling here also survived the wreckage. Hello, beautiful."

He planted a kiss on the bottle, eyes moving to me. "I don't give a shit if it's the morning. Have a drink with me."

The wolf ambled out of the pantry. I watched silently, chewing on the loaf, as he appeared with two cups and began to pour the wine.

"The name's Cato. Are you always this quiet?" he asked, offering the cup.

I stared at the cup for a moment before meeting Cato's measured stare. "Why are you—"

"So kind and incredibly handsome?" he interjected.

I let the silence swallow the space between us. Cato eventually sighed and placed the wine cup down. Palms splayed on the table between us, he leaned forward. "I know what's *supposed* to happen when one becomes the Lone Wolf. We are supposed to shun you and you are supposed to avoid us."

I waited, the words falling with a thud. The years of exile must have hardened even the furthest corners of my heart.

Cato continued. "But you helped us. You could've walked away, even though that would've made you a terrible person, but you still could've left. Me? I don't give a damn about titles. Much like Drusus, I care about the quality of the individual's character. So far, I don't see a reason to shun you." His fingers slid the wine glass to me. "I swear to the gods, you better drink. You look like you need it."

I swiped the cup from the table, irritated by the victorious gleam in his eyes. The slight burn was more than welcome, though. "You are different from most wolves, too. They usually avoid me like the plague." I paused. "You know of Drusus's friendship with me."

Cato wiped his mouth with the back of his hand. "Yes. Diane told us after Marcus practically interrogated her. How I see it, you must already be having a difficult time after leaving the Pack. Why make it worse?"

The thought of Diane withholding Drusus's secret was a surprise. I didn't like how my chest swelled with a sense of . . . gratitude and awe. I continued to eat and drink in silence. Cato continued to watch me; the stares I'd been receiving were becoming tedious.

I sighed. "Is there something you want to say?"

"You simply left the Pack," he asked. The tone crept almost into a question.

My eyes narrowed slightly as I snatched the wine bottle, pouring myself another drink. "Something like that."

A hint of a smile appeared over Cato's lips. "I think I might like you, Remus."

He took the tall wine bottle from me and strolled toward the inn's main door. "I guess we should meet with the others and get this conversation over with." He motioned for me to follow. "Listen, Marcus leads our group. He is strong, and one of the better ones. However, he can be a bit overly protective of us. He may not be as welcoming to the idea of the Lone Wolf as I am, but I ask that you respect him. He's my brother just as much as Drusus. I will always defend them."

The underlying threat didn't pull a reaction from me. If anything, it caused me to respect the wolf. And Cato had not once directly called me Lone Wolf.

Morning light greeted us. Its soft warmth pressed over my cheeks, I closed my eyes to savor it. When I opened my eyes, they landed upon black hair and golden skin. The she-wolf was speaking to a harpy. Wings the color of rose-gold were folded over the harpy's back. Armor and leather was strapped to her dark-skinned body, dual blades crossed on her back, nestled between the wings.

The harpies were primarily females; males were rare, but were enough to support the continuing growth of their population. I knew they lived on the same grounds of the Pack.

The harpy's sharp eyes darted to me, her lips breaking into a sly smile. "I see you gawking, wolf. You can come closer, I don't bite."

My mouth drew into a smirk as I sauntered forward. "What if I asked you to?"

Cato snickered behind me as Diane scoffed, her arms crossing. The harpy's lips twitched, amusement glinting in her brown eyes. "Unfortunately for you, I prefer those without cocks."

"That is certainly unfortunate for me," I winked.

Cato clasped a hand on my shoulder. "That's Laelia. I had the biggest crush on her for the longest time."

Diane made another noise, her eyes throwing daggers at me and Cato. "What is this? Are you both friends now?"

Cato moved his arm to wrap it around my shoulder as he tilted the wine bottle to his lips. "The best of friends, Diane. Don't you forget it."

I pulled away from Cato's grasp, groaning internally. Laelia nodded to me. "Son of the late Alpha. If circumstances were different, I would even say it is an honor."

"Likewise."

Diane gestured to Laelia as she spoke to Cato and me. "Laelia leads a battalion of harpy warriors. They are helping tend to the wounded and retrieve anyone lost in the rubble."

Another deeper voice interjected. "And it's all thanks to Diane's intuition to call on the harpies's aid."

It was a male with brown curly hair and ice blue eyes. The power and authority that glided with each pace his long legs drew had me assuming he was the infamous Marcus. Another male with tawny skin was at his side.

"Marcus," Cato confirmed. "How was it this morning?"

Marcus ran a hand through his hair, icy gaze drifting to the city roads. The other male didn't even try to hide the fact that he was eyeing me. Crossing his arms, he didn't balk when I met his leveled stare. Tattoos decorated him, from his neck to the ends of his arms, and I wouldn't be surprised if they covered the rest of him.

My gaze coasted the remnants of the city behind Marcus and the silent male. Debris piled the streets and smoke coiled the air. Citizens could be seen wandering through the buildings. The faint wails and cries muffled at this distance.

"Terrible," Marcus responded grimly, motioning to the male beside him. "Atticus and I managed to help the harbor side of the city, which took the most damage. Now, we face the matter of how to support these people in the meantime until the city can be rebuilt. And what of your efforts?"

Diane snatched the wine bottle from Cato's hand and pressed her lips to the rim. Cato gaped at Diane for a moment before facing Marcus. "I gathered the remaining Roman soldiers earlier this morning. Thankfully, they didn't suffer too many losses, but their spirits are drained. They thought they were working for a governor who had the people's interest as a priority. I have sent the soldiers to move the people who lost their homes to any homes and buildings still standing."

Laelia's velvet voice followed. "I've already sent one of my own to call for more human soldier reinforcements. The additional dispatches should be here by tomorrow."

Marcus was nodding, his long fingers tapping over his mouth. "Good, thank you both."

His blue eyes slammed into mine; the ice-blue burned brighter. I fought the urge to bare my teeth. "It looks like our paths have collided, Lone Wolf. Diane told me of your personal hunt for the Order with Drusus's aid. That is a conversation Drusus and I will have. I have no qualms with you killing off the Order on your own time, but I certainly have issues with betrayal and lying."

Now I did bare my teeth. "I tried not to involve him. Drusus did what he wanted to do, and you should know he is no traitor. He loves the Pack."

Marcus raised a hand, taking a step forward, authority in his every movement. A salted breeze swept through the thick curls on his head. "I know he does, but he also lied to me." I spotted a sting of betrayal flickering in his eyes.

But I couldn't fight the growl that escaped my lips. "Nothing will happen to Drusus. The Pack won't cast him out. And you will make sure of it. Otherwise, I will come for you."

Marcus's lips curled in anger. "You should've thought of that before remaining in contact with him. You were only thinking of yourself, with no regard to what could happen to Drusus."

Before I could react, I felt the firm grip of Cato's hand on my shoulder. His low voice rumbled near my ear. "Stand down, Remus. I just drank wine and I'd rather not throw it up to fight you."

I wanted to pommel the smug look off Marcus's too-symmetrical face. How he had insinuated that I didn't care for Drusus's well-being sent me into a whirl of fury and guilt. I could've hunted the Order on my own. Perhaps a part of me simply enjoyed having my brother's presence through it all.

Marcus folded his arms. He was practically the same height as me. "I will do what I can to help Drusus. You're not the only one who cares for him, Lone Wolf."

Diane rolled her eyes. "If we are done here, there are more pressing matters to discuss."

Marcus slid his icy gaze to her. She returned the stare with a look of boredom. He eventually sighed. A small crack, revealing the disappointment and exhaustion the male truly felt.

"The Order was planning this capture all along." He ran a hand through his curls. "They used Oeneus to draw us in and then took the blood of the Lone Wolf."

"I don't think they intended it to be me. I just happened to be in the wrong place at the wrong time," I responded.

Marcus grunted, that cold gaze returning to me at the sound of my voice. "Thanks for killing Oeneus by the way. It's not like it was official Pack business to begin with," he responded dryly. When I mocked a salute with two fingers at my brow, his jaw clenched so tightly I could almost hear the grinding of his teeth.

"I am unsure if you're caught up with current news," Marcus pressed on. "But with Rome's growing tension with Egypt, this was perfect timing for the Order to summon the exiled daemon king."

Since the assassination of Gaius Julius Caesar, there had been murmurs of war. A perfect moment for the Order to attack.

Egypt possessed aether and creatures of their own, jackal-shapeshifters who resembled their god of the dead, Anubis. These shapeshifters had terrifying power similar to the wolves.

"That's unsettling," Diane murmured. "So what is the plan?"

"The plan," Marcus emphasized by jerking a chin in my direction, "is to bring Remus back to the Pack. Caius will need to know what happened here."

I stilled.

Caius. The current Alpha.

My stomach roiled as the name brought an acidic taste to my mouth. *Shit, Helena. You should be here.* Caius, the one who had taken the burden of being the Alpha from me. The last person of the Pack I had turned my back on.

My lips thinned. "So be it." Marcus held our gazes as he spoke to the male called Atticus. "Please bring Drusus out here. Laelia is going to be taking him to the Pack haven."

Cato sighed, batting his eyes to Laelia. "How's Meredith? It's been a while since I've seen her."

Atticus's voice rose as he strode toward the inn. "Oh gods."

Laelia shook her head, lips twisting in amusement. "She's at the Pack haven. I can give her your regards."

Cato winked. "Let Meredith know her favorite wolf misses her."

I internally rolled my eyes. It wasn't long before Cato and Atticus hauled Drusus from the inn. Drusus looked at me from underneath the curtain of his damp hair, the corners of his chapped lips turning into a weak grin. The wolves released him so he could crawl atop the harpy's back, resting comfortably between her wings, the hilt of her sword peeking beside his head.

Diane wrapped a thin blanket around Drusus's shoulders, tucking it underneath his arms. "You better be alive when we get there," she snapped.

"Yes, mother," Drusus drawled, batting Diane's fingers away.

Laelia straightened, arms secured around Drusus's legs to hold him, unfazed by the weight of the grown male upon her back. She angled her head to the side. "You okay back there?"

Drusus's head rested on her shoulder, his eyelids already fluttering shut. A sigh pulled from his nostrils. "All I know is Cato is obscenely jealous that I am on top of you, and I see that as a victory."

Cato snorted and folded his arms, a grin pulling at his lips. Laelia chuckled, her hands reaching to embrace Diane's. The two female warriors pressed their foreheads together.

The harpy's wings unfurled, sunlight bouncing off them, shards of rose-gold light cascading across Diane's cheeks.

Diane smiled warmly. "Travel safely, sister."

Laelia saluted before thrusting into the sky, her powerful form joining the soaring battalion of harpies.

I watched as Drusus disappeared beyond the clouds. Apparently, we would stay one more night before we began the journey back to the city. The city I had avoided all these years. The place that had once been my home, but now only fostered haunted memories.

The city of Rome.

ELEVEN

Diane

My eyes strained to the cup in my hands, the flickering of the candles trying and failing to catch my attention. Deep hunger resided within me. Like coiled beasts, the shadows nudged against my conscience. They had tasted freedom and now yearned for it again.

Ancient threads of aether had laced through my heart and mind when I had met the endless gaze of the Ram, red eyes burning a hole through me as large claws gripped my neck. I had been plunged into darkness, offered a peek into the Ram's desires.

Bones and death. Blood-caked ground exhaling billows of smoke. Cities destroyed. The dead strewn about as daemons feasted on their flesh. Minotaurs, satyrs, harpies, and humans alike—all of Rome wiped out of existence. The Ram standing among the carnage as a king of its dominion. I had stood alongside it, stalking among the dead, eyes drawn ahead, undeterred by the lifeless wolves at my feet.

Spools of darkness suddenly burst from my hands. Shadows darted forward like dogs into the abyss of death. My wrists were bound in dark chains.

And then a string of light emerged beside me.

My face slowly turned to see Remus lit in moon-white flames. His green eyes stolen of life and light, as his aether spilled onto the ground and burned the earth. Darkness mixed with blinding fire.

My power speaks to you.

Humming. A deep, relentless sound that drowned the world out as I went back to staring into the cup in my hand. It was night, the starlight barely strong enough to pour through the window, and the water in the cup looked a lot like blood.

Death. Death. Death.

Black seeped down the veins of my wrists.

"Are you okay?"

My eyes snapped up to Marcus. The humming stopped as I returned to the present, clear of the numbness I was falling into. I quickly looked at my wrists. No black veins. No shadows. I rubbed my eyes and drank.

It had been a tiring day. With the support of the remaining Roman soldiers in the city, we had escorted the people who'd lost their homes to any building that could temporarily house them. The citizens had come together. People offered their villas, remaining food and clothes to those in need. Exhaustion quaked my muscles and thoughts, but it had been invigorating to see the progress.

"What's bothering you?" Marcus asked again, his brow furrowing.

I was slumped against a barrel, my legs stretched out lazily, my brothers around me, eating and chatting.

I nodded absentmindedly. "Nothing. I'm fine."

He drew a spoonful of broth to his lips. Broth and slices of cooked chicken, a generous token of appreciation from a Roman citizen. "You fought the Ram. I didn't see much but I saw you taking the daemon king head on. Don't be reckless, Diane."

I scoffed. "I saw an opportunity." I plucked a slice of chicken from his bowl and tossed it in my mouth. "And I took it."

Marcus shook his head and dropped the topic. I was never one to shy away from a fight and neither was he. He knew he would've done the same.

Cato folded an arm behind his head. His eyes steadied on Marcus. "Good thing Remus was there to help her."

Marcus's nose scrunched, as if he'd smelled something unpleasant. "How convenient."

"You're suspicious of him," Cato observed.

"Of course. The Lone Wolf and the Order appearing all within the same night? I can't say the thought didn't cross my mind."

Atticus shifted, unsheathing a dagger. My hand mindlessly trailed to the empty strap at my thigh. Though I did not regret my decision to give my dagger to the human, I missed the blade.

Atticus began to twiddle the thin sheet of steel between his fingers. "Until proven otherwise, the Lone Wolf is innocent, and he has been useful. Also, you can't get rid of him, Marcus, so I would stop any devious plans for the moment."

Curiosity bloomed over my tongue. "Did any of you know him when he was in the Pack?"

Marcus took another sip of broth. "Drusus was the only one who managed to get close to the brooding bastard. I never bothered to know him, past the formalities. The Lone Wolf was always among the Alpha's inner circle. Him and his sister."

"You'd never met before?" Cato asked me.

I shook my head. "I was still in the Academy at the time. I'm younger than you old wolves, albeit stronger."

Cato grumbled. "You're twenty-six, not that much younger than the rest of us."

Marcus snorted, a playful smile at his lips. The Academy was a place designed for she-wolves and other females to learn the ways of the sword, as well as medicine. Helena, Remus's sister, was older than me and hadn't been in my class. When she died, Remus had left, and it wasn't long before his pater had died as well.

The Fallen She-Wolf, we called her. How she died had never been confirmed. Mystery unsolved. The older she-wolves started celebrating Helena's life by spending a week at a large estate hidden among the hills. By then, I had graduated from the Academy and joined the memorial celebrations. It was supposed to be a week-long hunt, though it primarily consisted of drinking, sparring, and fucking. Which I wasn't opposed to. Apparently, Helena wouldn't have been opposed either. The she-wolves who knew her said that Helena would have roared with laughter and joy at how we were celebrating her memory.

I remembered returning home feeling warm and fuzzy with a

satisfying ache between my legs. I may or may not have enjoyed a few human males. All at the same time.

A faint memory flickered. I *had* seen Remus before, I realized. It was during Helena's funeral procession. I don't know how I could have forgotten his large, formidable presence. His expression had been etched in deep sorrow, a black cloak flowing behind him like a mast to a ship. Remus had kept his head bowed as the Pack lowered his twin sister into the sarcophagus.

Atticus flipped the dagger. The pointed tip punctured the floor with a loud thud. "Now that the Lone Wolf controls aether, we shall see how the cards play for us."

My brothers continued to talk, and I drowned in the murmurs of their conversation. My gaze snagged on the dirt and blood that caked my fingernails. How the Lone Wolf had managed to find the ability to control aether was beyond me. Could this be the answer to ridding our realm of the daemons? I couldn't deny that there was something about him that was . . . captivating. Fuck's sake. *No, Diane.* Not captivating. I was just curious. Nothing more. I was only curious as to who the Lone Wolf was. How his story had brought him here, how his path had crossed with the Pack's.

He had helped us today. Without uttering more than a handful of words, Remus had gathered the dead and helped the refugees. There were whispers of how the Lone Wolf had arrived as a warrior in a torrent of fiery light. It had been enough to cause Marcus to grate his teeth.

A heavy presence stepped down the stairs. The smell of cedar and ocean brushed at my senses.

Dim light lined his broad shoulders and thick thighs. The Lone Wolf stalked forward with lethal quiet as his gaze swept over the others before settling on me. Refusing to be the first to look away, I held his stare. It held indifference, but his eyes seemed to burn a brighter green the longer we clashed in that silent war.

Chills began to trickle down my neck, and I was close to squirming under the intensity. There was the faintest curl of his lip before it disappeared, and Remus exited the inn. A cool breeze followed him before the door closed. He had seen it as a victory and it was enough for me to see red. I pulled myself to my feet before I felt three pairs of eyes watching me.

"What?" I spat.

A shadow of a smile played on Atticus's lips, and Cato bore a lopsided grin.

"Intriguing," Cato crooned.

Marcus murmured a warning, but I paid no heed and stepped outside. I caught sight of Remus's large body dipping into the shadow underneath the grove of trees. Thick roots gnarled the forest ground as moonlight bled through the jade green leaves.

Remus stopped at the top of a grassy slope. I halted a few feet beside him. The heat of his body made silent shivers run over my skin even from where I stood.

Torchlights dotted the city. Beyond it, the vast ocean. The moon's reflection, a strip of silver light, shimmered softly over the dark water.

I watched him from the corner of my eye as he continued to gaze at the city. How his midnight hair touched his shoulders, stray locks caressed his jawline. How the corners of his jaw tightened. His tall figure was silhouetted by the bright moonlight as the trees bent over him, covering him in half darkness. The deep red tunic capped at his shoulders clung to the hard frames of his body. A bronze belt was cinched at his waist, leaving the remainder of the garment to fall to his knees, above his leather boots. The straps of his sandals crisscrossed along his calves.

"Enjoying gossiping about me?" His voice was molten darkness, breaking the quiet.

"Oh yes," I drawled. "Conspiracies and theories, what made the brooding Lone Wolf the male he is today."

He snorted softly, but silence thickened once more.

A thought came to mind. "Does Drusus actually know why you left?"

There was a slight roll to his shoulders. "He knows enough."

I tipped my head back and laughed mirthlessly. My hair tumbled against my back, brushing at the waist. Remus looked at me with a hardened expression.

"To think I was willing to reconsider trusting you." I laughed even louder. "I thought that Drusus would have *your* complete trust. If anything, this makes me more hesitant. Who are you really, Lone Wolf?"

His heavy gaze darkened. "Funny you ask, lotus. How about you? With that dark power of yours, who are *you?*"

My teeth clicked at his retort. "Stop calling me that, and these are not my shadows. The Ram did something to me."

Remus looked amused, taking a long stride toward me. "Keep telling yourself that."

He prowled closer, and I felt the darkness grow sharper.

Remus's eyes ran over my body, as if he could sense the power brimming inside me. He smiled wickedly. In a blink, his hand was around my wrist. I tried yanking back, but it was futile—his grip was ironclad.

My lips peeled back over my teeth. "Keep putting your hands on me, and I will have to remove them from your body."

A smirk poured over his lips. "Ah, but my hands could be put to good use."

"Inappropriate."

I pulled against his grip again. He snarled, tugging me forward until we were breaths apart. I could smell his scent of ocean and cedar. Flickers of silver ran over his arms.

Heat radiated from his touch, and the shadows felt drawn to his power. To him.

Aether wrenched from me, freeing me from his grasp. Remus grunted. "Not your she-wolf power, lotus. Your darkness. Show it to me."

I spat a curse at him, and he only laughed wickedly. Remus raised a palm, and a silvery torrent of flames exploded from it. Beautiful. Like fiery white gems that tousled and rolled together. I crossed my arms as a wall of aether halted the flames. The fire made impact, and the aether's unseen tendrils shimmered and stretched like a spiderweb.

Remus's energy was different. Different, like the aether of the Ram. Almost otherworldly.

My teeth clenched as a groan seeped through. Black tendrils broke from me, smashing through my shield and colliding with the moonlight fire. The energy building was so foreign I stumbled. The powers broke, and I found Remus gazing at me victoriously.

I panted. My gaze never left his as I slowly backed myself against a tree. My eyes drifted closed for a moment, and when I opened them again, I found Remus had moved even closer.

"I knew there was more to you." Cold. Indifferent. "How about we make a deal?"

I snorted. "Fuck off."

The corner of his lip twitched. His eyes glinted with something else. "Teach me how to control this aether, and I will keep your dirty little secret."

"You're barbaric."

"I prefer 'clever.'"

I bit my lip as I rested my head against the tree, eyes gazing at the treetops. Remus's fate was now bound to the Pack. Could I really avoid him? I could very well try. Or perhaps I could entertain this idea of his until I could find a way to distance myself from the Lone Wolf. "Fine. I will help you."

We stood in silence.

I refused to meet his eyes. Refused to meet the intensity.

When he spoke again, his voice felt like a caress down my cheek. "You're right about one thing. You shouldn't trust me. You don't know the things I've done to see my justice through."

Light flared, and the enormous black wolf stood before me. Midnight fur, blue under the soft light, fangs the size of a grown man's hand peeked between thick lips, and large claws punctured the leaves. Only last night those very claws had torn through flesh.

I watched as the Lone Wolf left me, almost breathless, against the tree. My fingers slipped against the rough bark.

A thought raided my mind as the black wolf disappeared within the dark woods. The stains of his ledger must run a deep red.

TWELVE

Remus

Dawn was at its peak. Its orange glow bathed the green leaves and grass.

Sage hills had rolled gently into thick woodland. The ocean was now far enough from view. The harbor city was almost a week's travel behind us. We'd made camp throughout the wilderness and stayed in inns when a settlement was within reach.

I still slept in my wolf form. It was easier when we made camp in the woods, the others doing the same. Diane would sleep curled up among the heap of furs. If we stayed at an inn, however, I would find solace on a rooftop or amongst the trees. I never slept indoors. Habits were hard to break.

With the newfound aether running in my veins, it was as if I could sense the presence of the various energies around me. The very ground was teeming with it. Pulsing. Communicating. It was like the aether had a mind of its own and purred against the thrums of others who possessed it. Especially Diane. It seemed to draw me to hers and I suspected it was because she carried the essence of two different forms of aether. She-wolf and shadows. It made me even more interested in her. A mystery to unfold. Her eyes seemed to darken with each passing day. The heavy energy residing in her impatient and growing.

A fire was burning at the center of our makeshift camp, which was nothing more than the leaves on the ground and the canopy of branches above. My stomach was settling, with strips of dried meat and nuts. We rested out of our wolf forms, stretching our human legs. Traveling as wolves was much quicker for obvious reasons. Diane always stuck to Marcus, straddled atop the brown wolf's back, her hands buried in the furs of his neck. I was unsure why, but my eyes had narrowed the first time I'd noticed. It had slightly irritated me, to say the least.

Atticus's voice rumbled, slicing through the quiet like a blade. "I remember the times when bandit raids were high. You led many of the attacks against them."

He didn't have to confirm he was speaking to me. I felt the curious stares. My eyes measured the red flames before meeting the male's gaze. Sunset and firelight embraced the inked patterns and images that covered his body.

"Women and children thrown in cages, settlements' riches and resources stolen from them. How could I forget?"

Atticus hummed in agreement. "I was captured by bandits once. Held me in a cage for two weeks with hardly any food or water. Even then, I remember hearing those cowards talk of the one called Remus. The black wolf. How he raided the raiders. An executioner. Your forces saved me, and I was never given an opportunity to thank you. So, thank you, Wolf."

Pulses of tension amid the silence. How it all threatened to choke me. No one had ever thanked me before.

Marcus was staring at his brother, Atticus. Warmth rested in those icy pools. That blue gaze moved to me. His jaw ticked as if he was fighting among his thoughts.

He flicked a random piece of wood to the flames. "It's interesting."

My expression smoothed into one of indifference. I arched an eyebrow. "Oh? Still trying to probe into the depths of my conscience?"

Marcus only grinned. Brilliant damn teeth. "I simply find it odd that the Lone Wolf decided to up and leave everything he'd worked for. You were son of an Alpha. Aspiring for greatness. Fought and saved countless."

His smile disappeared as he lowered his gaze. I braced myself for his next words. "I understand you lost your family. That is a pain unlike any other, but you don't strike me as someone who would simply give up. You have vendettas. Your arrangement with Drusus was enough to reveal that much." He looked up sharply, the blue of his eyes flaring. "So, why would a wolf of your stature just leave everything to the dust? It doesn't add up."

I allowed the silence to return. To swallow and eat at his words. Marcus wasn't fazed. He waited, refusing to drop the subject.

Wood from the fire cracked and popped.

"There is nothing more about me you need to know," I responded.

Marcus ran a hand over the light stubble across his jaw. "See, that is not true. I need to know what kind of wolf I'm bringing back to our people."

There was a terrifying tremble to my lips. I withheld the roar that wanted to rip from my chest. "I am no enemy to your people, Marcus. If I were to do anything that may bring them harm, I will give you the blade myself."

Marcus observed me another moment. Distrust showed plainly on his face as he stood and looked to the others. "I need a damn walk."

Cato fumbled after him with a mumbled, "I will check on him."

Another beat. Another pause, until I opened my mouth.

"I am no hero, Atticus. Your words are accepted in kind, but my determination to eradicate the raiders did not come from a place of nobility." I met the male's curious gaze. "Bandits killed my mater. Marcus was right. That was just another vendetta."

Atticus eyed me before a corner of his lip tipped upward. "I see through the façade, Lone Wolf. Say what you want, but we know the truth. You are not as bad as you want to seem."

Later that night, when the camp was deep in sleep and I had shifted back into my wolf, Helena's death emerged behind closed eyes. Blood-stained palms. A heartache that pounded the blood in my veins.

It wasn't until I could no longer bear the weight of the shame and guilt of my past that my body let me tumble into oblivion.

Thirteen

Diane

Roads teemed with bright colors and a myriad of smells. Lemon, thyme, rosemary, and basil fell over my tongue. The scents sifted throughout the stalls of fabric, pottery, and random trinkets that lined the forum. This was just one of the many thriving cities near the city of Rome. The people, dressed in their fine tunics and dresses, were lively this late afternoon, meandering their cobble-stoned streets without a care for the dangers lurking at their borders.

I leaned against a wooden post, under the soft shadow of an erected stall with a peach in hand. Atticus, who stood to my left, handed me a new dagger. Remus loomed at my other side, leaning against a wooden post, arms folded across his solid chest. The dagger danced between my knuckles, the movement slowly drawing Remus's attention as I slit the fruit open. Juice spilled down my wrist as I wrenched out a slice and popped it in my mouth. His gaze felt heavy as my tongue lapped across the blade before running down my arm.

Marcus and Cato were shopping for more supplies. After Cato's constant bickering, Marcus relented at his request to stop here for the remainder of the day. Cato had refused to sleep another night under the trees. And gods' honest truth, I was glad. Their backs were toward me, bronze light winking off their armor as they leaned over the seller's stall.

Wandering eyes, both female and male, gravitated toward my

brothers, and Remus—with that dark, dominating presence he was hard to ignore. Lust was vibrant in many of their stares. If they knew who Remus was, it didn't seem to faze many of them. However, there were a handful of citizens who steered clear of his path.

Out of the many lewd gazes, I felt some interest flicker to me as well, but I hardly paid any heed. Though I had to admit it was flattering. I dug my blade in for another slice.

"Can you stop eating that?" Remus glowered before looking away. "It's . . . distracting."

Somehow, even under the light of day, darkness still folded around his features. Power etched along the breadth of his shoulders and tall frame.

Shadows trickled under my skin but remained unseen to others. She-wolf aether hummed in response. It was too much. Two sources of power coursing through me. It was a new sensation, and it would take time to adjust.

I raised a finger, my eyes returning to the fruit. "One moment. Let me see if I can find a fuck to give you."

Remus's answering growl brought a smile to my lips. Atticus only chuckled softly. I tossed my warrior brother a wink when something caught the attention of my senses. It was like an energy that carried through the air, drifting among the tumultuous forum. A whisper of a voice that called to me, silently begging for me to notice. My feet began to move.

Atticus's voice sounded distant. "Diane, are you well?"

Shoving my unfinished melon in Atticus's hands, I sheathed my new dagger. "I'm going to check something out," I mumbled.

I walked, winding between the stalls and through the forum. The whispering became a buzzing, the row of stalls starting to blur. A persistent beckoning made the hairs on my skin rise. The gods-given aether rustled as if disturbed. Within the cyclone of sounds, I heard the words.

Your power speaks to me.
I will show you what I intend.
My vision will be your remaking.

Passersby brushed against my shoulders. Some shot me annoyed looks. Others sidestepped me, careful not to disturb a she-wolf. My feet kept going. I swerved corners, diving deeper into the market where walkways were thinner and crowds thicker. The whisperings continued, and I became frantic searching for the source.

Someone clutched my arm, and I peered down at a woman's large eyes. A cold detached expression in them. It was the same look I'd seen from those in the Order. I felt like I was being watched by someone other than the woman. *The Ram*, I thought. My fingers touched the hilt of my dagger. A man appeared behind her, his hand on her shoulder. To anyone, they looked like an ordinary couple, but I knew better.

The strangest thing was that I did not sense any malicious intent from the couple. They weren't here for a fight. I gazed at the woman warily.

She gave me an empty smile. "The king wants you and the black wolf. He wants you."

I pulled back from her grasp and glared at the woman—at the Ram, "Leave me be, swine."

The woman giggled then, fingers covering her lips. "The she-wolf is angry. He wanted to show you that he can always find you, can always see you."

Fear like a knife dipped in ice ran a sharp line through my chest. My hand clutched my dagger without removing it from its sheath. "Get the fuck away from here or I will remove you."

The woman clucked her tongue. The man behind her did nothing but wrap an arm around her waist. Now it truly looked like I was merely speaking with a romantic couple.

"Careful, she-wolf," the woman added. "You have no proof that I am part of anything. I merely came as a messenger. But I look forward to seeing you at our king's will."

I snarled, finally unleashing my dagger, and took a step forward. The couple stepped back. Both of their eyes were trained on me with faint, wicked smiles on their faces. The crowd thickened momentarily and they disappeared between the passing rows of citizens.

I could've sworn I heard faint whispers of laughter. I stood waiting, trying to listen out for anything else that may be amiss until a heavy presence pressed against my back. It was enough to burn through my fighting leathers.

"Everything all right?" Remus asked.

Inhaling, I debated whether or not to share what had just happened. My thoughts were still jarring. "It seems like it."

I turned to look at Remus. My half-eaten fruit in his hand. I raised my brows, hands on my hips. "What are you doing?"

The Lone Wolf was still, his eyes darting over my head. He ignored my question. "Are you sure? You seemed distressed."

"I have it handled."

Those green eyes fell on me. Bright, with a spark I couldn't put a name to. "I know you can handle whatever comes your way," he rumbled.

Slowly, as I focused on Remus, the effect the encounter with the Order had had on me lessened. His words then registered, the sincerity undeniable. It was knitted within the deep roughness of his voice, of his words. It soothed the fear and doubt within me.

Remus brought the peach to his mouth, the center of the fruit lined against his parted lips. Those eyes never leaving mine. I felt as if I couldn't move. This level of intensity was new to me. My lungs were starting to burn. Such a simple act, eating fruit, but it felt . . . dirty.

"I wanted a closer view of the show, but it seems like I missed it." His mouth closed on the fruit, juice trickling down his chin. His throat worked as he ate. My lips parted involuntarily, a shiver skimming over my skin.

Sweet gods and goddesses.

—◆—

I stepped out of the sodden clothes that pooled at my feet. Thank the gods we'd found this inn. My brothers and Remus had their own rooms and luckily mine held a private bath chamber. Small and quaint. Its window opened to the fresh batch of stars that dotted the ink sky. Vines crawled along the rims of the window space. The smell of the blossoms and leaves permeated the bath chamber, along with the rose and vanilla oils I had poured into the water. I quite adored the ambiance. The water was scalding hot, and I sighed as my muscles came undone.

"Praise Mars," I breathed.

I scrubbed the dirt and flakes of dried blood from my hair and the stubborn spots between my fingers and toes.

The Ram had been haunting my thoughts. I couldn't help it. I had been the huntress. The warrior in armor and glinting silver. Now, I was what—prey? The stories surrounding the Ram had broken into various versions, but the core of its story remained the same. The daemon king hated the gods and sought to destroy what they had created. Us. Mortal kind.

And if the encounter with the strange couple in the marketplace meant anything, it just further confirmed my growing fears.

I dipped my head under the water, allowing the thoughts to be drowned along the way. A new image appeared in their place. A dark, brooding presence. Tall. Black hair. Green eyes. The way Remus ran a thumb over his bottom lip. The deep sound of his voice. The way he was cold and indifferent to the world around him only seemed to draw me in.

How his lips pressed into the godsdamn peach.

I suddenly lifted my head out of the water. Rivulets sluiced down my naked breasts. Heat began to coil between my legs. My fingers drifted lower to where I was beginning to ache. I groaned. Was I really thinking about the Lone Wolf? *Well, it has been a while, and since there is no one else to think about . . .* My legs spread, heels hitting the ends of the tub. Perhaps it had simply been too long since I had found release, and I was craving this reprieve.

Fingers pressed to my clit. My head rested against the bath's rim as I rubbed myself in slow circles, replaying the images of Remus in my thoughts. Over and over. Around and around. A moan slipped from my lips. My other hand ran across my heavy breasts, the tightening nipples.

I imagined it was him. His rough hands. Those calluses scraping along my skin with flickers of flame. His liquid dark voice, whispering dirty things. What he would do to me. Praising me. How he would make me scream. I continued to rub myself, growling in frustration at the slowed stimulation from being under water. I lurched upward and grabbed a towel, drying myself enough to crawl into bed. Gods, I needed this.

As soon as I lay back, my hand dove back between my legs. I closed my eyes.

Good girl. Let me watch you as you fuck yourself.

I whispered a curse as my fingers slipped inside me. After several minutes of my breathless moans, my fingers returned to my throbbing clit. I imagined Remus's mouth over my core, his tongue running up and down my center.

You taste so good, lotus. Imagine how my cock would feel inside you? Stretching and filling you.

A moan battled behind my tightened lips. My hips lifted on their own accord, slowly grinding.

Keep going, beautiful. Keep going.

I kept moving my fingers in tight circles, faster and faster until I felt myself tip over the brink of bliss.

I cried out, a jolt to my hips. The release was quick, but I felt as though it had done nothing to stop the lingering heat.

Fates be damned.

The sound of rattling chains echoed. It was neither night nor day but smoke and fire. A valley of death. Burning pain rubbed at my wrists, the cold bite of iron. An emptiness swallowed whatever warmth my soul contained. Shadows poured from my lips and fingers. Remus emerged at my side, roaring in fire and light. Moon-white flames licked the ground, rolling forward in waves and engulfing anything that breathed. We stalked the battleground. No, not battleground.

The massacre we had created. The Ram, crowned by demise and darkness, stood behind us as if we were its leashed creatures. Its executioners.

No. I didn't want to do this.

My fingers curled into fists, pulling against the chains. They wouldn't come off. A sob threatened to choke me. Why wouldn't they come off? My hands shook, the rattling grew louder and louder. More shadows spilled from me as I tried to break free.

A warm hand wrapped around my own, somehow calming the burn under the chains. Remus looked as empty as I felt. His lips parted and the voice sounded close.

Too close.

"Diane."

I snapped awake. Instinct took over and I drove a fist against the intruder's chest. There was a grunt, and I lunged further. I pinned them with my legs on either side of their torso, the dagger I normally placed underneath my pillow finding its way into my palm. I pressed the blade to their neck. Underneath the deep moonlight, Remus looked at me with wide eyes.

"Shit," he breathed.

I sucked in a breath. "Gods, why, of all people, are you here?" I hissed.

His eyes assessed me. "I should've known not to sneak up on a she-wolf. I came to check on you."

My eyes narrowed. "You could've sent someone else."

Remus shrugged. "I could've, but everyone was asleep. But I don't mind how my fate has turned tonight."

I paused, noticing I was still straddling him. Then I remembered what I had done while thinking of him just hours ago. Clearing my throat, I slowly removed myself from him.

Remus sat up. There was a softness to his gaze. It was such a rare sight, and it broke through the usual stone indifference he carried. It humanized him. "You haven't been sleeping much, have you?"

I only nodded, not able to find the words. My teeth grazed my lip. The Lone Wolf was in my room—my bed.

"The Ram had us," I whispered, watching as his eyes widened slightly. "It had us chained and under its command. We had destroyed everything, Remus. The Pack . . . Rome. We lost."

He stilled, dark locks curled at his jaw and neck. Green eyes roamed my face, and I felt myself burn under his gaze.

I found myself continuing. "Something did happen earlier in the forum. A woman spoke to me . . . on behalf of the Ram. Said it wants us. Told me how it would remake this world and show me the level of destruction our aether could cause. And it did, Remus. That dream. It showed me what it intends for us."

"We won't let that happen," he spoke softly but the force of his words could've shuddered mountains.

It was only the sound of our breathing, nothing but grim words and misplaced hope hanging above us. Before I could register what happened next, Remus was moving. He laid me onto my back, pulling the sheets over me. I watched as he grabbed my dagger and returned it underneath the pillow. His eyes met mine briefly.

"We can't do anything at the moment, but we will." His voice startled me from the deafening silence. "I'm glad everyone else was asleep since it let me be the one to help you tonight."

Before his words had even registered, the door was closing behind Remus. Something in my chest skipped a beat.

Footsteps faded down the steps of the inn. He was not going to sleep inside. I noticed he always returned outdoors, to the trees and the moonlight. The Lone Wolf always slept in his wolf form.

I laid there watching the stars through the window, afraid that the Ram's vision would return if I closed my eyes.

FOURTEEN

Remus

Rome's gates had never looked so unappealing.

The Tiber River rushed in its pale blueness underneath the wooden bridge. As we passed the entrance, my eyes rose to meet the city in its fullness.

Gods, it had been too long.

Rome rested upon hills and hills, pillars and deep red-brown tiled roofs erected as far as the eye could see. Citizens were like ants, wrecking chaos at every corner. Satyrs, humans, and the occasional minotaur strutted through the busy roads. Businesses and temples strung along the crushed brick and gravel roads. There were far too many people for my taste. Smells of sweat mixed with spices wrinkled my nose.

People bowed their heads to the wolf warriors and Diane, casting blessings and wishes for good fortune. The wolves took the awe with grace and humility, bowing their heads and clasping their hands with those who asked for it. Wandering eyes brushed over me, while others gave me a critical look. My jaw clenched at some of their whisperings. The Lone Wolf's return. I recalled the drama that ensued when I left the Pack; rumors had seeped throughout the cities like a wildfire. It was why I found solace among the outskirts of the Roman region. Not many knew who I was there.

Diane was watching me. I could tell a question was brimming behind her lips. I slid my gaze to her. "Like what you see?" I taunted.

She rolled her eyes and looked away. I grinned. "Don't look away now, perhaps I like you staring. What do you want to ask me?"

Diane flipped her hair over her shoulders, hands skimming through the thick strands. My eyes tracked the movement a little too heavily. "I was recalling some rumors, but I'd rather not make assumptions." Her eyes went to the sky before giving me a sidelong glance. "Were you and Caius close?"

My stomach churned, but I didn't allow the unease to show. I held the question in the air debating whether to squash it or not. "Yes. We were like brothers once."

"What happened?"

I arched a brow. Diane mirrored my expression. I sighed. "He wanted answers I couldn't give."

When I had sensed her distress the night of her nightmare my heart had started racing. My chest had felt constricted, like a pillar of stone tightly wrapped with vines, and I had barreled through her doors to find her whimpering and clawing at the sheets.

The Ram's vision, her dream, was repulsive. The daemon king had made its intentions clear. It wanted both of us, the power that resided inside us.

She was about to ask another question when I interrupted her. "Don't forget our little arrangement," I murmured.

Diane glared. "Prick."

"Devious, you mean." Intrigue loosened my tongue. "But I have a question. I did not know you while I was in the Pack. I'm assuming you were in the Academy?"

We strolled down a more crowded road. Diane sidestepped a pair of bustling women. "Yes," she responded. "But I heard of you. The infamous Remus. The black wolf. Son of the great Alpha." As she spoke, her hand motions grew more exaggerated, teasing me.

I nudged her arm, scoffing. "That's enough. I didn't come up with those titles."

Diane chuckled, the dark smudges under her eyes seeming to soften. As if remembering she wasn't supposed to enjoy my company, her expression smoothed out.

"What was the Academy like for you?" I pressed.

Her golden eyes gave me a considering look, her hand brushing against the laurel wreath tattoo on her arm. "Terrible, but entertaining all at once. My power seemed to excel past the average she-wolf, so the elders trained me harder than most." A smile grew on her face. "I remember the nights we snuck out of our rooms to meet with the boys and go to whatever dinner party was being hosted in the villas district."

I didn't realize the corners of my lips had slightly tilted. "Sounds like it was a wonderful time. I'm glad you were able to experience that."

Diane shot me a curious look but I looked away, keeping my eyes on the road. Listening to the contentment in her voice made me wonder what the typical life of a youth would have been like.

A blacksmith's shop emerged round a corner, sharp rhythmic clangs of hammer meeting glowing steel. The minotaur manning the small forge paused his work as he met Marcus's gaze, and dipped his curved horns. Marcus saluted in return.

Known for their blacksmith skills, many of the minotaurs had ventured away from their mountain kingdom to establish their armories throughout the Roman region. Those with the experienced skillset oversaw the Pack's armory. The minotaur answered to a king who went by the name Cain, and while many resided here among the Roman region, their primary homeland was within the mountain ranges. In all my years of travel, I had yet to see their central city.

Eventually, where the main city of Rome thinned, we came upon the blossom groves. Pink and white petals filled the space between us and the Pack haven. My heart pinched with a mixed sense of familiarity and unease as I stepped underneath the archway. *I really shouldn't have come back.*

The others seemed just as on edge. Cato and Atticus hung close to my sides, and I wondered if Marcus had advised them to keep an eye on me. If that were the case, I would be thoroughly unamused. Diane took position beside Marcus. Light danced through the leaves, gliding along the pommels of their weapons, caressing Diane's shiny hair and Marcus's breastplate. The two made an immaculate image. Regality founded in bronze and steel.

The orchard parted, and two marble statues greeted us. The twin demigods, Fathers of the Wolves, stood guard at the Pack's entrance. No one knew what the twins had really looked like but much of the inspiration stemmed from the features of the god of war which consisted of curled, tousled hair and carved bodies. Romulus bore a spear while Remus had a hand on the sword at his waist, glowering at whoever dared enter his home. I frowned at the statues.

The aether in my veins stirred awake as if it were taking its first breath. *Home.* I tried to shrug the sensation off, but the rapid beating in my chest didn't falter. *No,* I wanted to snap. *This is not home.*

Villas began as the orchard ended. Soft columns of daylight cascaded over the red tiles and through the fields that stretched on either side of the Pack's center. Wheat, olives, and wine grapes were cultivated in those fields. Farmlands also made up the spaces between the houses. Cattle lifted their heads from the tall grass.

The Pack's forum, smaller than Rome's, was stacked with shops and taverns. Citizens strolled about: she-wolves, harpies, satyrs, and some humans. Many of the wolves were in their human forms, save for the few who meandered the roads with their paws and fangs.

Conversation dimmed as most eyes gravitated to us. Curious. Concerned. Angry. Some of the wolves prowled closer. Their hairs bristled at the sight of me. They circled the group of haven locals who seemed to have temporarily forgotten about me as their attention beamed upon the wolves I had traveled with. Welcoming them home.

A child hobbled closer with her pater at her heels. In her small hand was a flower, plain and white. She stopped abruptly to peer up at Marcus. The male smiled, warmth melting the frigid planes of his face, as he bent on one knee before the girl. She offered the flower to him, tucking the stem behind his ear. Marcus bowed his head to the little girl before returning to his feet and acknowledging her pater. Atticus was on his knees too as multiple children decorated his head and the neckline of his tunic with blossoms and leaves. His smile was soft yet bright. The wolf had hardly shown any emotion, so I was stunned at the sight.

Diane was crouching down, balancing on her heels as other

children crowned her with a makeshift wreath of flowers. Her eyes shone a liquid gold. The desert lotus looked more like a nymph with her crown of petals. As if she could summon waters and trees and not the shadows and darkness that followed her.

Marcus growled when he noticed how long I had been staring. I didn't care. She was breathtaking.

Cato nudged me, holding a small bouquet of his own. "It's tradition for the children to welcome the warriors home with flowers and small gifts. It started not long after you left."

One child ambled their way toward me, flowers in hand. My traitorous heart skipped a beat until the child's pater batted them away from me and toward the others.

Cato scowled, but I responded, ignoring the drop in my chest. "It's a good tradition."

We made our way to the Pack's meetinghouse. It stood off the center of the haven forum, surrounded by trees and perched upon a small slope. Stone steps led up to pale columns. Upon entering, I recognized the shelves of books and scrolls lining the walls of the main floor. Dark marble lined with crimson red covered the ceiling.

A giant griffin stood in its center and I recognized him immediately. Valens had spearheaded the academia among the Pack and provided private lessons to Helena and me. Griffins had always been a true rarity, even when I was a child. Old creatures who lived hundreds of years beyond the extensive lifespan of a wolf. As far as common knowledge was concerned, only one—Valens—lived in the actual Roman region, while the rest thrived in their kingdom above the clouds.

Golden wings unfurled, and talons clicked against the floors as Valens approached us. My jaw clenched when those eagle eyes, like freshly forged bronze armor, fell upon me.

The griffin chuckled deeply, causing the stray parchment on the wooden tables to tremble. *The Lone Wolf has returned.* He watched me as I passed. *Good luck, little pup. You will need it.*

Irritation crept up, along with a twitch of my lips. We approached the back doors that led to the war room, a room I was all too familiar with. I was partly afraid that I would hear my pater's voice booming along the walls. That he would appear, storming the halls with war at his heels, to send me to battle.

The doors opened to high ceilings and walls made of stone. Torches lit up the darker corners as sunlight penetrated through the open windows.

Advisors consisting of humans, satyrs, harpies, and she-wolves were gathered around the room. Three individuals stood in the center, their heads bowed as they debated and observed the parchment that was spread out on the main table.

But it was the fourth individual who caught my attention. His broad shoulders set confidently, dark eyes brimming with life as he huddled with the others. No wound to be seen.

Drusus.

He seemed fine. Considering he had broken the rules in regard to associating with the Lone Wolf, I would have imagined him in a more dire situation. His head jerked up as I huffed a sigh of relief.

He broke into a bright grin. "Finally, you made it."

Drusus skirted the table, crushing me against him as his arms wrapped around my shoulders. I chuckled warmly. "You're well."

I took a step back to examine him, and he lightly pushed me away. "Such a busybody, brother. I am fine; the Pack has the best healers, you know."

"Of that I have no doubt." I smiled.

Diane rushed past me and flung her arms around Drusus. He caught her with one arm, swinging her around before setting her on her feet.

"Never do that again. You scared us." Diane pointed a finger at him, scowling. She was still wearing her wreath of flowers. In fact, they all were.

Cato and Drusus practically crashed to the ground in their embrace while Marcus and Atticus laughed, watching the two roll on the ground as if they were pups. Diane slipped past them, running into the arms of one of the males who stood by the center table.

He was a brawny man with a short-clipped beard and dark hair. It dawned on me that I already knew him. Aurelius, the Beta wolf of the Pack. He was a veteran of the battlefield, well known for claiming back resources and people from the bandits. Diane was daughter to the Beta. It made me all the more interested to know more of who this she-wolf was.

There was another she-wolf at the main table, her dark skin akin to the dark tone of Laelia's. Her silky black hair was plaited into a crown around her head. She had sharp blue eyes dusted with gray and muscles that coated her lean body. She was stunning. She wore a sleeveless dress that hugged the outline of her breasts and hips and revealed the sharp edges of her shoulders and biceps. Her eyes weren't on me, they had gravitated somewhere else. To Drusus.

Intriguing.

That smoky blue gaze met mine. The sharpness in her eyes caused me to bow my head. Only then did her lips curve up. "I am Sabina, Commanding She-Wolf."

My lips lifted. "It's an honor." I looked to Drusus. "Are you well? I feared the Pack would retaliate against you."

Drusus looked sheepish. "Well, as it turns out—"

"He has another role to serve."

That voice.

My eyes collided with the last person at the table.

And the world went silent.

A sickening sensation coiled in my stomach, a bitter taste at the back of my throat.

The male was tall, with a sharp jawline dusted with a faint stubble. His eyes were a deep brown. Sinewed strength rolled underneath his beautiful dark skin, a lighter tone than that of Laelia's and Sabina's.

The closest person I'd had to a friend a lifetime ago.

Caius had changed his hair since I last saw him. Short dreadlocks were pulled back by a leather band, and the lower half of his head was shorn. Ink decorated the shaved part, trailing down and along the length of his shoulders. A lone dark band was tattooed around the ring finger of his left hand.

The power of the Alpha emanated from him. Demanded that I fall to my knees.

I didn't.

Alpha and Beta. Caius and Aurelius.

I drew a deep breath. Caius blinked as if he hadn't recognized me at first, then his nostrils flared. No one dared speak. This was my godsdamn reckoning. Caius rounded the grand table. I lifted my chin as each heavy step drew closer.

The Alpha stopped before me, standing slightly above me. Just slightly.

"Time has been unkind to you." His voice struck me like a bolt of Jupiter's lightning. It had been years since I'd heard his voice . . .

I inhaled. "Likewise."

Time hadn't been kind. The harsh edges of exhaustion and battle had carved the tautness of his cheekbones and showed in his eyes. He hadn't asked for the position of Alpha. When I left, my pater claimed it for him. By custom, it would've been Aurelius's right to take on the role when my pater died. Word was that Aurelius had declined, stating the Pack needed someone younger, with new ideas and beliefs. That his time of leading was long gone.

Caius was still irritatingly handsome. I recalled the days we would lounge amongst the older warriors, and the females that were visiting the barracks would always giggle at the sight of him.

My thoughts returned to the present as I caught the corners of his lips twisting in disgust. "There is nothing more you want to say to me?" he asked.

The bile returned. I wanted to hurl. I had handled mutilated bodies and daemon gore, but it was facing him that tore at me. I knew what he wanted, but the words stuck in my throat.

My voice came out in a low whisper. "I cannot give you what you seek, Caius."

He closed his eyes as if he had already known what I would say. Before I could blink, pain beamed at my jaw.

Caius pulled back his fist, eyes bright like steel. "Unbelievable. Even now, after all this time."

Drusus came to my side and placed a hand on my shoulder. The gesture was small, but it meant a lot. I couldn't look him in the eye, though. My attention was trained on the current Alpha. There were things I wanted to say but couldn't. Why couldn't I? It almost physically hurt to try uttering the words.

Caius clasped his hands behind his back. "Drusus had the pleasure of relaying everything that occurred in the harbor city. His role is to ensure you use this aether bestowed onto you for the Pack's benefit."

I ground my teeth, but I remained silent. I wasn't going to say anything if it would risk Drusus.

Caius continued.

"Rumors of a battle brewing between Rome and Egypt have been spreading like a disease. The late Caesar's nephew, Augustus, has been leading the taskforce. He wants the wolves involved with the war efforts."

It was common knowledge that Augustus was the adopted son of the late Gaius Julius Caesar. Augustus was young, but it was said he held a wisdom beyond his years. The makings of an emperor.

There was a hum of disapproval in the room. Caius raised his hands. "I know. We aren't part of their armies. The wolves have extended their services and are spent fighting the daemons and hunting the Order. Now with this Ram creature, it is only a matter of time before the Order rains their horrors upon us and all of Rome."

Aurelius spoke. His eyes met mine with a glimmer of recognition. "We will discuss more of this tomorrow. The more pressing question is what role the Lone Wolf will play in all this."

Caius watched me with an unreadable expression. "The Lone Wolf will live here temporarily. You will train in the ways of the aether until further plans are made. Sabina can show you."

I thought of something better. "If I may, Commanding She-Wolf . . ." I bowed my head to the gray-eyed warrior, casting her a smile. I didn't miss Caius rolling his eyes. "I would ask that Diane be my teacher."

Sabina raised her brows, sliding her gaze from me to Diane. Diane looked like a cornered rabbit, eyes running wildly between us. She shook her head, ready to dismiss the proposal. I arched a brow with a silent question, a challenge. Diane squared her shoulders, the sardonic smile she gave me telling me exactly where I could shove my deal. The female was stubborn. "I don't think that's a good idea."

Sabina's lips twisted in amusement as she observed our exchange. "Actually, that's a very intriguing idea."

Diane whipped around to look at her. "Absolutely not. Sabina, you are more skilled than I am. Surely, you are the better option," Diane protested.

I wanted to laugh. Conniving she-wolf. She wasn't going to get rid of me that easily. I looked to the Commanding She-Wolf instead. "I imagine someone in your position would be too busy to have to constantly observe me."

My gaze trailed back to Diane. She stood with her hand at her hip, the hilt of her sword at her side, the fighting leathers failing to hide the power of her body. My eyes flitted to hers. That golden gaze drew my attention, grasped it. I leld it in a chokehold. My chest lifted as I allowed myself to drown in her formidable stare, in the frustration and mistrust brimming there.

Diane's gaze shifted; I saw it—felt it. There was the slightest change where the anger turned into intense curiosity. My lips dared a smile, and Diane broke away, disrupting our silent war. I slowly slid my gaze to Sabina, who I realized had been watching the entire time, her lips twitching in amusement.

Sabina eyed me for another breath. "Diane, you will train the Lone Wolf. My word is final." Diane began to protest once more but Sabina waved her hand, laughing. Odd.

Caius prowled closer. His presence alone cast rivulets of power and authority around him. "Remember one thing, Remus. You are a visitor at the haven, and you will abide by my orders."

Perhaps it was some form of defense mechanism, but something about the notion of following orders from the Pack, how it felt being *back*, triggered me. "I understand. But let me be clear. I am not part of the Pack, and you are no Alpha of mine."

Voices spurred in shock. I paid them no mind, engrossed in the tremors of anger that began flickering to life.

OF FANGS AND SHADOWS | 113

A low rumble sounded in Caius's chest. His eyes flared a deep orange, the pupils dilating. Wolf eyes. "So it seems."

Aether exploded, and heavy paws pinned me to the ground. A wolf the color of snow-capped peaks with glossy pearl fangs hovered above me.

"You may disrespect me, but you will respect the Pack. They were yours once. However, they would rather toss you to the dungeons now. A traitor to his Pack, to his pater, even to his own twin sister," Caius snarled, pressing into my chest. There was a groan and the stone beneath me cracked.

At the mention of my sister, my blood boiled. I roared, ripping into my wolf skin, shoving Caius off me. I landed on all fours, snarling, as one paw clawed the ground.

Aurelius bellowed. "Stop this at once!"

Caius and I lunged at each other, a booming clap as our claws and heads met. As we thrashed against each other, we edged further into the war room. Shouts and screams echoed. Those closest to us sprinted out of the way as we crashed through the back wall, the sun now witness to our brawl.

Shouts and barks erupted all around; wolves jumped to cage us with their bodies, isolating us from bystanders. Caius snapped his jaw, snarling. I kicked him off, and we began to circle each other.

"Pathetic," Caius snarled. *"You are a coward."*

I knew it would come back to that. How could I blame him? How could I explain what had happened that night?

"Caius, I can't."

Caius swiped at me, ebony nails grazing my chest. I lunged back at him, and my fangs pierced his shoulder. We grappled and rolled, blood spraying the grass. Heavy paws met my chest, slamming me to the ground again. Stars raced across my vision.

"Try, Remus! Try! You didn't give an explanation. Helena was dead and you just left!" Caius's fangs dripped saliva and blood. *"We were close once. You and I. Then you left. Not me, you."*

I squirmed, panting. Gods, I could feel a dizzy rush spiral through my head. The words got stuck once more, threatening to make me hurl the contents of my stomach. *"I can't."*

Caius's strength wavered at the words. His yellow eyes revealed a flash of complete agony amidst the anger. *"Can't or won't?"*

I maneuvered out of his grip. Caius stumbled back, dirt swirling at his paws. *"You bastard,"* he cried. *"I was in love with her!"*

The hissing and roars silenced.

I knew this. Shit, I had introduced them. During our training, Caius and I had become close. When my pater brought me along to his battles, Caius was with me. He had been my brother.

I remember the moment he first laid eyes on my sister, something had dawned in his eyes. *Who is that?* he had asked in a daze, only for me to grab him by the back of his neck and threaten his life if he made an attempt on her. But Helena had seen something in Caius, too. She started coming to our training grounds more often, and I could see the warmth between them when they stared at each other. They would disappear into the night together, travel together, fight together. They fell in love, and I was truly happy for them. For her.

My chest panged. I saw her dead in my arms again, dead by *my* hands. A sob readied to choke me. I had carried my sister's lifeless body back to the villas that night. Caius was running to us—to her. He had stopped when he saw her in my arms.

Helena?

What the fuck happened, Remus?

No, no, no.

Caius had fallen to his knees as I placed her body in his open arms. He had held her tightly as if, somehow, he could force her soul back. We had mourned together.

"I'm sorry." My voice managed to steel itself, obscuring the agony that coursed through me.

Caius howled. In rage or pain or both. We collided once more, pushing against the other's shoulders. He threw his head back, exposing his neck. Fangs poised, I was suddenly blinded by the exploding white flames that erupted from my jaws. The power shocked both of us, so much so that Caius jumped back. I snapped my mouth shut, the fire now gone. Gasps rippled through the people, and the wolves braced themselves with their fangs bared for my throat.

His white muzzle dotted with red, chest heaving up and down, Caius's eyes ran over me curiously. I could barely manage to get up until I felt a heavy weight press against me. In his wolf form, Cato helped me up with his snout.

Marcus appeared between us. *"Enough!"* He swerved his head to Caius. *"I understand that you are angry with him, but fighting him is not going to bring her back."*

Caius hissed, snapping at the air toward Marcus. The brown wolf hardly flinched. *"Don't overstep, Marcus. There is unfinished business between me and the Lone Wolf. But to the Pack—"* he cast his gaze at the wolves and she-wolves surrounding us—*"I apologize. I don't intend to let my emotions deter me from being your Alpha. My priority is you and the safety of those who live in these lands."*

Sunlight made the white of his fur shine like beads of crystal. He gave me one final glance. *"As Fates would have it, it looks like we are going to be stuck with each other for some time."*

Cato nipped at my neck to get me moving. My leg gave out, and I stumbled. Drusus's wolf appeared at my other side, holding me up like Cato. Atticus and Diane emerged from the crowd. Atticus trailed behind us. Diane didn't look my way as she strode toward Marcus and Caius.

Fangs lined the pathway that led deeper into the haven. Snarls reverberated from the ground into my very bones. I could sense the hate and distrust the wolves shed as I limped past them.

This was not the story of the long-lost wolf returning home to be redeemed. No, it was of a shameful warrior who had returned only to be put in the very chains he had created.

FIFTEEN

Remus

"So, that went well."

Cato snickered as Drusus punched him in the arm. "Shut up."

I hissed as the ointment was spread over the graze on my chest. The she-wolf continued to dab at my wound despite my protests. I had learned that her name was Camilla and she was Atticus's beloved. Her hair was a dark blonde, tied in a loose knot with strands straying over her temple. Her body was soft, unlike the more hardened physiques of Diane and Sabina. Her skin held a lighter olive tone, though she had a condition called vitiligo, with various lighter pigmentations along her arms and neck. Atticus watched her intensely as he leaned against the wall.

I'd been taken to Drusus's villa. It was smaller compared to the other giant homes that crested the Pack's hillsides. The entrance led to a small courtyard that was used as a training ground, or so I had gathered from its racks of weaponry. Vines crawled up the pale walls, tall plants lining the corners of the courtyard. White columns stretched out at the back of the villa. It held a breezeway leading to the bedrooms that sat on opposite ends of the halls. The view consisted of the fields and other villas below. Simple in its elegance.

Camilla rested her fingers above the pale green spread. My skin tingled as I felt the aether stretch from her dainty fingers, seeping through the ointment and dragging the medicine into the wound.

There were healing properties within the aether as well, and certain she-wolves held a knack for calling upon its power.

I leaned against the cool limestone, a sigh pulling from my chest. "How long have you and Atticus been together?"

A gentle smile touched her lips as she worked. "Ten years now. Atticus had been called to intercept a rebel raid, and I was one of the healers for that assignment." A soft blush bloomed over her cheeks. "He was captured and became my patient after he was freed, and one thing led to another . . . A typical love story."

My lips curved softly, eyes darting to Atticus. He held my gaze, the look he gave reminding me of the night we spoke beside the campfire. The story of his capture by the raiders. How my forces freed him. It led him to her.

"I like love stories," I admitted.

Cato cackled. "I didn't pin you as the lovesick sort. Does a certain male or female have your heart, Remus?"

"No." My teeth clenched as the aether rushed back into Camilla's hold.

"There you go," she said. "It should heal fine on its own from here."

I bobbed my head against the wall. "Thank you. Your healing capabilities are seamless."

Gratitude shimmered in her eyes as she shrugged. "I've learned much since my time at the Academy, but there's always room for improvement."

"You're being modest," Atticus replied, his hazel eyes glimmering with heat.

Camilla smirked, running her hands over her dress before making her way to him. He wrapped an arm around her waist and pulled her close.

He crushed his lips to hers, then murmured, "My Camilla."

Drusus cleared his throat, giving them a lopsided grin. "You know, Atticus, Camilla took *very* good care of me while I was on the brink of death."

A growl rumbled in Atticus's throat, bright eyes darting to him. "Don't push me."

Cato was sitting on the granite railing that opened to a veranda, cream-colored drapes billowing on either side of him. He swayed his long legs. A conniving grin similar to Drusus's stretched on his face. "Do it, Drusus. You can practically smell the sexual angst from the poor fool."

Drusus sighed, placing a hand over his heart. "The softest of hands—"

Atticus snapped his human teeth, an animal hiss escaping his lips. Camilla rolled her eyes before pulling Atticus away by his sleeve.

"Sorry, Camilla," Drusus called out.

She tossed a wink at him, and I assumed she was very familiar with the wolves' banter. "I'll take care of this while you boys tend to your business." Camilla waved to me. "It was lovely to meet you, Remus."

The couple disappeared from the room, their steps fading past the courtyard. Faint giggles echoed, followed by low chuckles.

Drusus raised his eyebrows, warmth in his expression. "Well, they'll be busy for a while. They're perfect for each other."

"Lucky bastard," Cato commented as he flicked random debris from his shoulder. "I'll take my leave as well. I will see you both at dinner."

He lugged his large body from the rail and sauntered out of the room, leaving only Drusus and me. The room was wide, holding a large bed with white sheets, a desk along one of the walls, and a plated mirror above it. A long rug that was the lightest shade of brown stretched from underneath the bed to the center of the room. The scent of pine and wood. And a faint taste of lemon.

"Your home is beautiful," I observed.

Drusus moved from the desk he had been leaning against and strolled to the veranda. He placed his palms on the railing as he looked at the view.

"All thanks to my duties in serving the wolves," he said. "This room will now be yours."

I tilted my head, narrowing my eyes. "Why haven't you moved on? You have this beautiful villa, a great standing with the wolf army, surrounded by people who love you. Has there not been anyone who's caught your eye?"

Drusus twisted to face me with a look stuck between a smirk and disgust. "Move on? How can I when I've been serving Rome and fighting its enemies most of my warrior life. Why would I attach myself to someone, potentially raise a family, only to risk losing them? Or them losing me? I could easily die on duty, as you well know."

The thought of that made me flinch. "You're afraid to open yourself up to the possibility. I saw how the Commanding She-Wolf looked at you. Is there a history?"

A dazed look overcame him, as if he was peering into a treasured memory. "There is history, but I've complicated it."

"You slept with her."

He shot me a look. "She wasn't simply a fuck," he snapped.

I winced as the ointment cooled the gash. A ragged breath escaped me. "I meant no offense, brother. You're protective of her. I only regret that you didn't feel comfortable enough to share these parts of your life with me."

A sudden sadness pinched his brow, and Drusus began making his way closer to me. "I felt guilty," he admitted. "Guilty that I had a life here in the home that was once yours."

I pulled myself to my feet, gritting my teeth against the sting. My fingers wrapped around the back of Drusus's neck, and I tugged him forward to press our brows together.

"Never." My voice was firm. "Never feel guilty for having something beautiful and enriching. I am your brother by bond, and there is no greater joy than hearing stories of your life. I'm sorry I never asked to know more. I've been too selfish, drowning in my bloodlust."

A low chuckle left him as Drusus clasped a hand around the back of my neck. "I was beginning to wonder when your softer side would make an appearance."

I broke the hold, lightly brushing him off. "Be honored, as this may be the last time you see it."

Drusus chuckled and made his way to the breezeway. "So

dramatic. Come, I'd say it's due time that you see what has become of your old home."

Realization struck me cold. The grounds were familiar. The walls, the homes, the fields—all held a semblance of who I was so long ago and a reminder of what I'd lost. I'd always considered Drusus family, my home, but even now, with him beside me, I felt disconnected. No sense of belonging.

I wasn't sure if I remembered what home felt like. I don't think I ever knew.

SIXTEEN

Remus

All I could do was stare at the fields. The trees. Inhale the citrus smells. Awe and a touch of envy twisted in my chest as I listened to Drusus rattle on about the Pack's growth.

The wolves had taken over part of the crop and winery businesses. While the services of the wolf warriors were in high demand, Caius began expanding the Pack's efforts. Even the Academy was being progressed. Initially, it had been solely made for the she-wolves, to teach them the ways of medicine, battle, and even negotiation. Now, it was beginning to open its doors to other Olympians such as harpies, satyrs, and human females. The population seemed to have grown as well. Caius had accomplished much in his short time as Alpha.

Stone roads soon turned into soft dirt paths, peeling in various directions to the villas and townhomes that rested among the hills and trees. We were in the outskirts of the Pack haven. I was grateful for the escape, hardly caring about the stares and whispers. Years as the Lone Wolf had hardened many parts of my heart.

We came near a lonely townhome with a small barn. A satyr was tilling the ground, and a donkey watched its owner with utter boredom. The satyr lifted a hand to shield his face from the blinding light as Drusus hollered and raised a hand in greeting.

We stepped underneath the shade of the trees, the dirt road expanding before us. The cry of birds sharpened the peaceful silence, small bodies darting from the branches above us.

Drusus placed a hand on my shoulder. "Would you like to see her?"

I stilled. The path. Up the hill, around a bend, where all the wolves were laid to rest.

Helena.

My throat bobbed. Emotion that had been chained deep down all these years tugged at me. "You were going to take me to her?"

I sensed Drusus's faint smile. "Only if you want to."

It had been years. Gods, I missed her.

I quickened my pace. "Take me to her."

The Pack had dedicated a lone hill to their dead. Its lush green grounds were dotted with tombstones and mausoleums. Soft jade leaves floated across the resting place. Burned incense lingered, from all the regular visits to this place. The songbirds were all I could hear.

Stories said that the Mother Wolf—the very wolf who suckled Romulus and Remus—welcomed fallen wolves to the afterlife. The large white wolf would guide the fallen wolf through the celestial golden plains. These were stories, and yet I hoped the Mother Wolf had welcomed my sister.

I stood before Helena now, in front of a mausoleum dedicated to our family name, surrounded by blossom trees. The gates had been left open; apparently many from the Pack still visited to pay their respects.

Stray blush-colored petals rested over the face of her erected tomb. It was made of the finest stone, a dusty gray that had paled over the years. Drusus lingered outside the building, giving me a moment.

"Helena, I've been so lost without you." My fingers trailed over the carving of a pegasus, its wings stretched over the face of the sarcophagus.

Helena had been a Daughter of Mars. An elite warrior who found her bonded pegasus during the completion of the Rite which provided she-wolves with the title.

It was said her pegasus had died of a broken heart. His body, white and silver like a diamond, was found slumped against her tomb, wings draped over the stone. It had been named Nike, like the Greek goddess of victory. Helena had thought the name to be fitting for the winged stallion. He had been cremated, and his urn now rested on an altar alongside her tomb.

The world exhaled slowly, its breeze brushing the hair from my face and causing the petals to skitter over the stone. Remnants of Helena's death pressed against the constrictions in my chest.

My throat tightened. "I put you here, sister."

I closed my eyes and lowered my head until I felt the cool kiss of her sarcophagus on my forehead. Helena was no longer here among these mortal planes. I fought to find the words, to reveal the remaining truth of that night, but everything was lodged in my throat. Stuck in the heavy shame and guilt. My knuckles ran over the stone, welcoming the rough edges that scratched my skin. I pressed my lips to my sister's tomb.

I straightened as Drusus's steps grew louder. His shadow dipped into the mausoleum entrance, an ever warm and welcoming presence. "Are you ready?" he asked.

My hand slowly slid from the tomb's surface, an emptiness coiling around my palm. My fingers furled to a fist. The emptiness latched onto my chest, ready to swallow me whole. I began walking toward the exit.

"Did you want to see your pater?" Drusus asked.

I stilled. My gaze settled on the glow of the setting sun. Trees rustled their leaves, whispering words I could never hear.

His sarcophagus rested at the center end of the mausoleum. Close, yet so far . . .

My jaw tightened. "No."

I left the wolves' resting place. And not once did I look back. With every step, my heart beat louder. I hadn't even thought of visiting my pater's tomb before Drusus mentioned it. I wasn't sure what that meant, but the only thing I understood was the lack of guilt at the realization.

My visit had only been for Helena.

SEVENTEEN

Diane

Being summoned by the Alpha was not a common occurrence. At least, not for me. If had been Sabina requesting my presence I would think nothing of it but knowing that Caius wanted to meet made me curious. And maybe slightly nervous.

I walked up the steps to his villa. His place was not as grandiose as others where long fountains would make up the courtyard. Caius's home was surrounded by lemon trees and small gardens. The villa was partly hidden by the wine-grape fields, far away from the loudness of the Pack forum. I could see why Caius preferred this location. It was like a hidden paradise.

Passing through the courtyard, I opened the doors to the main space. Before I could take a step further, I stopped at the scene before me. The living quarters had large arches that overlooked the fields and trees and underneath them Caius and Marcus lounged on settees.

They were eating breakfast. There were plates of cheese, fruit, honey, and milk. The Alpha popped a grape into his mouth as he murmured something to Marcus.

Marcus glanced over his shoulder, the curls on his head fell over his brow as he squinted at me. "Are you just going to stand there or are you going to join us?"

"Sorry," I spluttered, making my way toward an empty settee between them. "I didn't realize our meeting was also going to be a little feast."

Caius hummed a sound as his large body leaned over to grab another piece of fruit. "Well, to make devious plans we must have full stomachs."

I eyed the plates on the center table and snatched some of the cheese and honey. I groaned as I ate. "That is the most sound logic I've ever heard."

Marcus snorted as he leaned back in his seat, unnecessarily spreading his legs out. Males. "So," his sky-blue eyes landed on Caius. "Would you like to ask her or should I?"

I raised a brow, my gaze going back and forth between them. I wasn't sure why but my initial feeling of intrigue was now muddled with suspicion.

The Alpha sighed and stood from his seat. "I'm going to need a drink before we dive into that." He passed us, pointing a finger in our direction. "Honeyed wine?"

Marcus scrunched his nose and we shared a look. "Wine with honey?"

Caius scoffed from wherever he had headed to retrieve the wine. "Don't tell me you've never tried it. One drink for both of you and that is an order."

I chuckled as Marcus rolled his eyes. Caius returned with a bottle and began pouring honey and wine into a few glasses. Seeing the Alpha act so . . . domestic was almost endearing. I'd hardly ever had the experience of seeing him conduct such mundane tasks when he was always acting the role of Alpha. I briefly imagined what he would've been like with Helena. I wondered how the sculpted planes of his face would have looked without the harsh lines that now surrounded his tense mouth and the heartache behind those dark eyes.

The morning breeze brushed against the collar of his tunic, revealing all the ink that decorated his neck and upper body. He offered us each a cup of the honeyed wine. I sipped on the sweet drink, pleasantly surprised, as I eyed Marcus. He hesitantly took a sip, eyes widening for a moment before guzzling down the entire cup.

Caius's expression seemed to lighten. "Never doubt your Alpha again."

After a breath, his eyes snapped to me and I felt myself stiffen. "Diane, I have a task for you, if you will take it."

I shifted in my seat. Wine forgotten. Stomach now uneasy. "What do you want me to do?"

The Alpha held my gaze. "Sabina tasked you to train the Lone Wolf. And *I* need you to keep an eye on him. In other words, I need you to get him to trust you."

I watched him, my heartbeat quickening nervously. "Why?"

Caius's eyes flashed like flint against stone, igniting an angry fire. "Remus left the Pack just before the daemons appeared. Alpha Anthony had just died, the Pack was in disarray, and the Order were spawning like rats. That enough is cause for suspicion."

I recalled Marcus saying something similar, when he'd questioned the Lone Wolf and his intentions as we sat around the fire. Remus had become guarded and hadn't encouraged Marcus's questioning. Atticus and Cato hadn't seemed bothered by it, or sensed any hostility from him. However, I suppose it was always wise to practice precaution. Who was the Lone Wolf really? It had been warring in my mind since I'd met him.

I thought of Remus and the cold expression he usually wore. But I also remembered witnessing flashes of something different. A tortured look. Heartbroken eyes. Much like the Alpha's. I recalled how the Lone Wolf had saved me from my nightmare and helped me into bed. The rare sight of him being kind and soft made me hesitate.

Marcus pulled me from my thoughts. "I would do it myself, Diane, but we all know how well he and I get along."

"As for Drusus," Caius interjected. "There's a clear conflict of interest. It's painfully obvious he has an undying loyalty to the Lone Wolf."

Marcus began to smirk. "Besides, he seems to have taken a liking to you. You are able to get through to him in a way none of us can."

"Hardly," I muttered. "Half the time we just bicker."

Caius watched me, surveyed me. "He knows something, Diane. He knows more about this war than he is letting on. Something happened the night Helena died. Remus—" The Alpha's voice broke. His teeth clenched. "Helena didn't tell me what she was planning on doing that night. They both suddenly disappeared but only one returned home. Remus is the *only* person alive who was there. He knows what happened. After that night, daemon sightings rose and those odd cloaked humans started practicing aether. It can't be a coincidence."

Silence fell over us as Caius's words lingered in the air. I could understand where the Alpha was coming from and he had a right to feel suspicious. Gods, why was I still doubting this? I hardly knew Remus.

I took a deep breath. "Alpha, if you have such hesitations about him, why am I training him at all? Why not lock him up until we locate the Order?"

Marcus looked to Caius. "She has a point. Why make someone who is potentially an enemy of the Pack stronger?"

The Alpha stared at the wine grape fields. Another breeze caused the leaves on the trees to rustle.

"An enemy of my enemy is my friend," Caius said. "One thing is certain, the Lone Wolf hates the Order. And with him being able to will aether, I'd rather have him on our side than against us."

The Alpha sighed and took another long drink of wine. He looked to me then and I saw the plea in his eyes. "He may be working with us, but that doesn't mean he has our best interests at heart. Of course, I want to know how the love of my life died, but I have this sense screaming at me that there is more to the story."

I mulled over the Caius's words. My stomach twisted at the thought that he may be right. Marcus leaned in, elbows on his knees, as he waited for my response. As they both waited.

I finally responded. "The Lone Wolf cannot be trusted. I will befriend him and obtain the truth from him." I met the Alpha's steely gaze. A cold resolve swept over me like a winter's wind.

"I will do it."

The sound of beating wings caused me to look up and I saw Laelia gliding down towards me. The mid-morning light transformed her shimmering wings into crystalline beads as she landed.

"Even from above, I noticed your gloomy expression," Laelia said as way of greeting. "I thought I would come to your rescue."

I cringed. "Gods, is it that obvious?"

Laelia cocked her head, offering me a smile. "You wear your emotions on your face, Diane. What's on your mind?"

The Pack's fields and hills were dipped in sunlight. It was calm and quiet, only a few people meandered through the fields. The haven would soon liven up and fill with crowds, business as usual. A war council was being held later today and we were to attend.

I had only managed to make it halfway to my pater's villa when Laelia found me. Lost in thought from the conversation with Caius and Marcus. They wanted me to keep my task a secret.

I rubbed at my temple. "Sabina is forcing me to train the Lone Wolf. I hoped she would train him. But alas, I am being forced to do it."

Laelia laughed, just as my Commanding She-Wolf had done when I'd pulled her aside. "Sabina sees what you are too stubborn to acknowledge."

"Funny. She said something similar." I grumbled.

Laelia smirked. "I wonder if it has anything to do with how the Lone Wolf is always staring at you." I stilled, my eyes sliding to hers. Laelia's wings flared as she threw her head back on a laugh at my expression. "Oh good, you've noticed. I was afraid we were going to need a conversation on how blind you have become to a male's obvious attraction to you."

I rolled my eyes and waved a hand in dismissal. Trying to bat the small sting of guilt at the reminder that I would have to get close to said male and pull information out of him. *No, I don't even know him. I will not be deterred.*

"Honestly, that's the least of my worries right now," I said.

Laelia continued to walk with me as we moved onto other topics, her and Meredith, the Pack, and life within the haven. We neared the villa just as shadows darted from above. I looked up and my heart went erratic. It was a sight I always welcomed. The pegasus. Their powerful bodies soared through the sky, their bonded she-wolves atop of them. The Daughters of Mars were the only ones who could ride a pegasus, thanks to their connection to them, laced with aether, established during the Rite.

The Rite. If the she-wolves chose the path of the blade, it was tradition for them to participate in the Rite and be named a Daughter of Mars, an elite warrior serving in the name of the god of war. The Rite consisted of a week-long trek. With only a satchel of food and a weapon of choice, the she-wolf would travel among the hills and mountain sides in search of the pegasus. Once the bond was realized, the she-wolf and pegasus were to go to the lone temple of Mars, accessed only by flight among the mountain peaks between the clouds. And finally, be proclaimed a Daughter of Mars.

It seemed they were training this morning. Upon their mounts, they conducted a series of makeshift battle routines in the sky. It was glorious and terrifying to watch.

"Will it be soon?" Laelia's voice made me jump.

Knowing she was referring to the Rite, I shrugged. "I am not sure. It doesn't seem appropriate given the current circumstances."

"That's a lie," Laelia quipped.

I looked at her, baffled, and she scoffed. "For as long as I've known you, the Rite is all you've wanted to do."

She was right. The Rite had been something I'd been looking forward to for so long. I had told myself I would complete it when I returned home, but with everything that had happened, and the power underneath my skin, that dark, ravenous mystery inside me . . .

"Laelia, I've been feeling this . . . power. It does not feel like that of my she-wolf-born abilities. I felt it more dominantly when I faced the Ram, but I've realized it's something I have felt throughout my life."

Laelia gave me an odd look. I knew she wanted to push me further on the topic of the Rite, but eventually she sighed and moved past it. "You've always been strong. Your aether, even stronger. Emotion plays a significant role. The aether must have been responding to how you were feeling at the time."

My teeth pinned my bottom lip, unconvinced. "That's what I wanted to believe too."

Laelia's brows bunched. "Is there something going on, Diane?"

The shadows. I wanted to shout the words. *There is a darkness inside me and I don't know what it means.* My lips thinned, fighting a sense of dread. *There is something wrong with me.*

But I didn't say anything. My fear of this unknown thing had taken advantage of me. I shook my head. "It's nothing, everything is fine."

Though, with the nightmares and shadows haunting me, my heart was screaming otherwise.

The war room was full of Olympians. The gaping hole that Caius and Remus had broken through had been sealed shut, as if the brawl had never happened. I followed my pater into the room, acknowledging the bows and murmurs of respect toward the Beta and his daughter. I shifted on my feet.

"You seem fidgety," a deep voice drawled.

His voice. Ice and fire. It spiked a thrill down my spine as the aether in me stirred with excitement. I took a step away from Remus, trying to avoid the heat his large body emitted. A dark colored tunic hugged his body today. Quite beautifully, much to my distaste. Or taste? No, distaste. The dark locks of his hair curled slightly at the ends, brushing his shoulders. The Lone Wolf looked amused. I realized I'd been staring.

"You can mind your own business," I retorted.

He leaned down toward me. His low voice tickled my ear. "Is it the power crawling up your skin? Deep, ravenous darkness. It must have been a while since you've found release."

"I sincerely hope you mean the release of my aether."

Remus looked smug. "Maybe."

Groaning, I strutted away from him. His long legs met my strides easily. "Is everything a sexual innuendo with you?"

He chuckled. "I really didn't mean it like that, but I'm glad to know where your thoughts are."

I gritted my teeth. "To think the Lone Wolf is known as something to be feared when to me you're simply annoying."

"You mean charming. Also, you look lovely today."

I hated how my heart jumped at the compliment. I was only wearing an ivory tunic, my hair now washed and running freely over my back. The Egyptian-made ear cuffs decorated my left ear.

"I'm not wearing anything extravagant." I was never this flustered. Or fucking shy.

When I met Remus's gaze, it could've set me on fire. The brimming . . . heat that sparked from those jade eyes. The longer I held his stare, the more I felt my power shift. His throat bobbed. His eyes flitted downward along my curves and to my eyes once more. Then he smirked and walked away. The heat was flushed away and replaced with coldness. And irritation.

Gods, this was the male I had to get close to?

We joined Marcus and the others. Atticus kept his arm around Camilla's waist. I went to wrap my arms around her, shooting her a flirtatious wink, much to Atticus's amusement, before I settled between Drusus and Remus.

The harpies entered the war room. Their brilliant wings swept the marble floor, colors cascading like gems across it. Laelia strode in with another harpy at her arm, Meredith, who had porcelain skin and deep gray wings. Her wine-colored hair was pinned neatly on her head and freckles dotted her cheeks and small nose. She wore a gown that hugged at her neck and seeped down to her feet, the color of pale rose. Unlike Laelia's competitive nature, Meredith held a softer, more refined demeanor.

Caius stood at the head of the war room, dressed in a fine tunic with armlets and leather bands around his large arms. Dominance was etched into his battle-worn body and his baritone voice. He ran over the details of the food and supplies that were to be delivered to the outskirt towns, especially those that had been impacted by the daemons.

Caius then spoke of the Ram. The responses were tainted with disbelief.

"Children's stories!"

"The Ram is a myth."

Caius's eyes coasted across the room, and silence fell. "It is a children's story made real. The Ram *is* here and will destroy us if we do not prepare."

From the crowd, an older male spoke. "Alpha, are we to ignore the fact that the Lone Wolf walks among us, among the very Pack he abandoned, and now sits with the war council? What do you have to say of this?"

Caius held his composure. Didn't pause for a breath. "What I have to say is that I am Alpha and you're to trust that I wouldn't allow the Lone Wolf within our presence unless deemed absolutely necessary."

The steel bite in his words made the elder flinch. Remus shifted uncomfortably at my side, and even Drusus tensed.

The elder's lips thinned to a line. "I do not mean to disrespect, Alpha, but there are rules—"

"Have you considered why the Lone Wolf is here? What purpose he might serve in this war?"

There was a stunned silence that brought a sly grin to my lips. Caius pressed his fists to the grand table. The muscles in his forearm went taut as he leaned forward.

"Since we are on the topic, I do require something from our *beloved* Lone Wolf."

Some chuckled, others trained suspicious looks on Remus. My father and Sabina stood by Caius. Their expressions were not that of surprise, so they must've discussed this beforehand.

The Alpha finally turned his head toward Remus. The hatred in his eyes was bright and apparent. "With your . . . powers, whispers are bound to carry. A demigod reborn."

Remus frowned, flickers of his silver aether darting across that darkened gaze. "That's ridiculous."

"Is it?" Caius pressed. "For too long the daemons have tormented the people's livelihoods. They need hope to cling to."

"What does that have to do with me?"

Caius grinned wickedly. "I plan to secure the alliance of all Olympians against one foe. For this to work, you must be their symbol. I want word of the Wolf Born of White Flames to spread to the edges of the sea. I want them to know the Pack fights for them, and therefore secure the support of the other Olympians."

There was a deep rumble beside me, but the Alpha took a step forward and bared his teeth. "You don't have a choice."

Remus didn't respond. A haunted look rose within him. I wondered again what hid behind those mental walls. Constant, brewing war, no doubt.

Marcus mercifully interrupted the growing tension. "Caius, we already have the support of the harpies, satyrs, and humans. Who else is there?"

"We will need to secure the support of the minotaurs and the griffins."

Cato chuckled. "And the sirens too? This is ambitious, Alpha."

Atticus swatted Cato's arm. "That's nothing to mock. You know the sirens only serve their Leviathan."

Caius looked between the males. "The minotaurs and the griffins are our main focus as of now. I have asked Valens to send my request for an audience with their griffin king."

It was said that the griffins lived in a fortress high in the mountain peaks. Valens had described it as a castle that floated above the clouds. No mortal or other Olympian race could manage the trek to the fortress.

One of the elders spoke from the crowd. "Would Valens be able to advocate our request to the king of the griffins?"

The griffin's voice reverberated throughout the main room of the meetinghouse. "*This matter is between you and the King of the Sky. I will not insult her by being your spokesperson. They would be offended if the wolves of Rome did not ask for support directly. I will only conduct the courtesy of delivering the request to my king since you wolves do not have wings.*"

Caius folded his arms. "While Valens conveys our message, the next step would be to go to the minotaurs. The Lone Wolf and I will meet with King Cain. I am Alpha and I will meet with the minotaur in person. I would not ask a leader to risk the lives of their own otherwise." He pointed a finger to Marcus, flashing a smirk. "I expect you and your team, including the Lone Wolf, to join me. I will need Remus's power to convince others to support our cause."

Another male waddled from the group to speak. "Caius, no one has ever managed to rally the Olympian races to unite as one. What makes you think the griffins would even dare fly down from their floating fortress?"

Caius turned his body toward the crowd. He tilted his head slightly as his eyes roamed over their heads. "The entire Roman region, even the mortal realm itself, is at risk. We need to unify. All people of all cultures will stand together to fight the evil that plagues our lands. This is our home, and we fight for it."

Hope. This is what it amounted to. Those who shared this land, this continent, this realm, could fight under one cause. Though peace seemed to always skitter away from our grasp. A continuous fight to keep trying. Relentlessly.

Aurelius and Sabina took the mantle, concluding the meeting with the following courses of action: the harpy scouts were to leave immediately, track the daemons' movements, and see where the Ram may have gone. It also meant Meredith would leave. Laelia's lips tightened at the announcement, and I noticed the subtle squeeze in their clasped hands.

We were bound to leave for the minotaurs' land in a month's time. Caius sent a meaningful look my way at that. My lips thinned, though my heart was beating wildly. One month to train the Lone Wolf. One month of having to deal with his irritating charm. Time was not a luxury, for who knew when the Order would strike. The fact that there was a male wolf who could will aether could never have been anticipated. I couldn't help but feel a flicker of excitement at such a phenomenon. At the slight notion of a challenge.

I needed help.

Teams of wolves were to be dispatched to rally the other wolves scattered throughout the Roman regions. Legions of wolves. The Alpha was calling them home.

Deep bundles of dark aether pushed against the mental bands I had willed. I shifted in place. I didn't want the Lone Wolf to know how right he was, how the shadowed aether was pestering me the more I withheld it.

In an attempt to distract myself from the unease, I looked at Remus with a mischievous grin. "Get ready, Lone Wolf. Training starts bright and early tomorrow."

Dark locks fell forward as Remus angled his head. Ocean and cedar brushed my mouth, curling around my chin and tipping my face upward.

A gleam sparked in those green eyes. "I'm looking forward to it."

I had failed to remember one thing. Remus may have been the Lone Wolf, but he was a warrior through and through. He'd led armies, won countless battles. He was the son of an Alpha, and that truly meant something to the wolves. Training would come as second nature to him. And I didn't doubt that the addition of controlling aether would only make the name *Remus* even more formidable than it already was.

EIGHTEEN

Remus

Drip. Drip. Drip.

It was the only sound in the cell. I blinked through the haze. The light of a candle was nothing but a blur as I fought to keep my eyes open. My arms were bound in metal. The slightest movement caused my body to scream.

Drip. Drip. Drip.

My hair had grown longer. The once mere dusting at my jaw was now overgrown and untrimmed. I hadn't seen my reflection for gods knew how long, but I was sure I looked wild. I continued to blink, the candle becoming clearer and clearer. I blinked once more, and someone was there, right in front of me. No, it was them. My captors.

Fangs. Dark, glittering eyes. I felt the curve of a unique blade brush strands of hair from my face. "When we return, we will hear the son of the Alpha sing."

I was alone once more.

Drip. Drip. Drip.

What was that sound?

Oh. Droplets of my blood. From my brow, down my chest and arms, to the growing pool on the cell floor.

My eyes snapped open to the dawning light. Claws unsheathed, hackles raised, on the cusp of a vicious snarl. My tail brushed against the damp grass as I looked at my surroundings wildly. Trees. Sky. Grass. Villas. There was no danger here. I was here and not . . . *there*.

Odd. I hadn't had a vivid dream about my time in Egypt in a long time. My usual nights consisted of Helena's death, which had not failed to torment me last night, but I wondered why I had begun to remember the time of my capture, too. It must've been all the recent changes stirring up old, tortured memories.

My nostrils exhaled a puff of air as I began to stretch my legs, claws dragging against the dirt. I had slept underneath a group of olive trees, a mere few feet behind my assigned room. I never slept in a bed like a normal mortal. Couldn't. For whatever logic, I felt it was more manageable to face the traumas of my past in the body of my wolf.

The taste of lemon was ripe in the crisp morning air. The haven was silent. It took me a moment before I managed to haul myself to my feet, shaking the dawn's residue from my fur. I shifted into my human body and slipped through the room's veranda before Drusus could sense me. He would question me, feel remorse, and try to find a way to help me. I didn't want that from him. My brother had done so much already.

I eyed the bed, its ivory sheets untouched. Hesitantly, I sat on it and leaned against the wall. I watched as the light brightened and crawled further into the room. I was truly back at the Pack haven. But things were different. I was different. Changed somehow with the ability to will aether. Not to mention the Ram had managed to enter our realm. It all felt overwhelming. I ran a hand over my face, trying to deter the path of my thoughts. I could only work on what I could control, I had to remember that. Even if it was a fucking painful truth to acknowledge.

When the time came, I stripped off my tunic. I donned trousers and washed my face and teeth. Still shirtless, I met with Drusus in the courtyard. His chest was equally bare. He stretched his arms.

"Good morning, princess." He grinned.

I took the waterskin hitched at his side and took a long sip. "Maybe we should hurry before the she-wolf finds me."

Drusus barked a laugh. "No way will I be your accomplice in this. You wouldn't get far, I can tell you that."

I arched a brow and wiped stray water droplets from my mouth.

"So you're fine with being an accomplice in rebelling against Pack tradition, but you'd avoid pissing the she-wolf off."

Drusus rolled his eyes. "To be fair, she can be quite scary. But you were the one who insisted on her training you." He paused, eyes glittering. "Why is that?"

I remained silent. Drusus took a step closer and narrowed his gaze. "She interests you." He snatched the waterskin from my hand. "That's what it is, isn't it?"

A growl rumbled in my chest. "Not in the way you think. Haven't you noticed how powerful she is? Her aether feels far superior than the average she-wolf; you can practically taste its strength. That is what interests me."

Drusus made a sound of disbelief. "I've always known her to be strong. She is daughter to Aurelius. His legacy is infamous, akin to that of your pater's. The Beta's power was bound to be passed on, and to his only child no less."

I refrained from touching further on the subject. Diane wanted the other half of her power—those shadows—to be a secret. I may have been branded as a traitor to the wolves, but I always kept my word.

To change the subject, I added, "I remember Aurelius. He served alongside my pater. A kind and hard-working male. At the time, if I hadn't been so busy, I would've wanted to get to know him better."

Drusus patted my shoulder. "Well, you are here now. No point in dwelling on what could've been. Now we just have to figure out what in the realms is going on with you and those flames of yours. Have you managed to summon them since?"

I shook my head. "Just once during the attack at the harbor. I haven't tried since, which is why I need the she-wolf's expertise."

Drusus looked to the courtyard's entrance just as I felt her presence. Diane leaned against the threshold, her body wrapped in leather and tight strands of fabric. Leather topped with plates of bronze covered her shoulders and thighs. A sliver of her stomach bare to the morning sun. Her hands wrapped in cloth. She wore skin-tight trousers as well, which wasn't traditional for human Romans. Faint beads of sweat already dotted her light brown skin.

I realized I was staring and forced my gaze upward. Diane was looking at me. Eyeing my body just as much as I had been hers. It was as if there had been a silent acknowledgment of the mutual appreciation we had for each other—physically, at least. Most times, the she-wolf preferred to test my patience. It had been both amusing and intriguing.

Then Diane leaned her head against the entrance to the courtyard, wicked glee overtaking her face. "Are you boys ready?"

I sighed as Drusus cackled. We started into a run along the outskirts of the Pack haven. Drusus matched my stride, his dark hair bouncing across his brow. We bounded between the trees, passing more villas, and skirted along the fields toward the Pack's main training ground.

Trees surrounded the large courtyard. Shading the spectator stands and brushing against the pillars of limestone that held a pavilion. A grand villa stood tall beside the training ground.

Wolves were already there. Some in similar attire to Diane, fighting wraps and leather, others in loose tunics. Many were exercising in their fighting forms. Stretching their legs and arms as they pulled their weapons through various movements. Some of the warriors were actually in their animal form. Large wolves either lounging in the courtyard or tussling in the dirt.

But as expected, all eyes gravitated to us as we entered.

Diane led Drusus and me toward the farther end of the courtyard. Many of the males leered my way while others watched with curiosity.

One male spat at my feet. "Fucking traitor. Anthony would be ashamed to call you his son."

My jaw clenched but it was Drusus who bristled at my side. "Enough," he warned.

The male scoffed and strutted away toward the growing group of wolves I assumed were his comrades. Drusus watched the males and growled, an animalistic sound between his human teeth. The wolves' hearing was sharp enough to catch it, and many of them turned their attention elsewhere. It seemed Drusus held that much power and respect among the Pack. The knowledge gave me a sense of pride in my brother.

Diane waited by a weaponry rack, watching the entire scene with wariness. We walked to the outskirt of the courtyard to keep enough distance between us and the other wolves.

"How about we start with some exercises, then move onto the aether?" Diane suggested to Drusus.

Drusus shrugged. "Fine by me. I'm sure Marcus and the others will come to watch once you and Remus start practicing with the aether."

Drusus lifted a blade and began to move. He had healed remarkably well and while the stains of the Ram's blade still marked the skin of his abdomen, they did not slow Drusus down. His legs swept the dirt as he stretched into position, sword above his head.

I fell into the movements, almost like in a trance, shadowing Drusus with a sword I had chosen from the rack, the chaos of my thoughts dimming to nothing as I found comfort in the swings of my blade. The tightness of my shoulders loosened. My breathing calmed the longer we practiced, even though blood pumped excitedly through my veins.

At one point Drusus turned on Diane and they began a mock hand to hand combat. She ducked his hits, slid to the side and docked him in the ribs. Drusus grunted obscenities, which only made her laugh wickedly. It was easy to see how comfortable they were with each other. They were comrades, had been in battle together, just as Drusus had been with me.

All of the wolves, including Atticus, Cato and, dare I say, Marcus, treated each other like they were a pack within the Pack. The way Drusus and Cato would muss Diane's hair as siblings would, how they all laughed and teased one another. Something began to gnaw at my chest, pulling from deep within.

Was it longing? For gods' sakes. This godsdamn place was already affecting me in ways I would have never imagined.

They stopped sparring and Drusus glanced my way. "Remember the old days, brother?"

I smirked and made my way to Diane's place, shoving my practice blade in her hands as I passed her.

My hair was already slick with sweat and clinging to my neck. I ran a hand through it, eyes on Drusus. "All the times I kicked your ass? How could I forget?"

Drusus chuckled and raised his fists. He leapt off the ground and threw a right hook. I blocked the attack and jabbed at him with my fist. Drusus pivoted a step back and followed with a quick lunge, releasing two more punches. This continued for another half-hour, and I felt every muscle in my body come alive. Blood thrummed with energy. Light burned brighter. Even the godsdamn trees seemed to dance. I sensed Drusus's intention even before he prepared to charge at me.

My feet skidded against the dirt as Drusus lunged at me. We rolled until I pinned him to the ground, my knee on his back.

Drusus squirmed underneath me. I chuckled, tilting my head. "Just like old times."

"Fuck you, Remus," Drusus growled, a smile in his voice.

I patted his head. "Not today."

Diane stood to the side, watching us with an odd expression, eyes bright and lips parted. Our gazes clashed, and she arched a brow.

"Seems like that aether has had an effect on you," she observed. "Let's see how well you can actually use it."

An hour later, I was hunched over with my hands on my knees. My body shook, and I could see spots skittering across my vision. The she-wolf was going to kill me.

Her face was flushed, sweat dampening her attire. But she also seemed to be beaming. The shadows under her eyes had almost completely disappeared, but I imagined her body was exhausted from all the withheld aether. None of that seemed to matter; the mock battle ground seemed to exhilarate her just as much as it did me.

She had started the session by having me simply summon the moon-colored flames. My current task was to will my power to compete against hers. To call on the aether was not difficult. It was the next step that caused me to falter. I wasn't sure how I had willed the fires back in the harbor city. I had been lost to adrenaline and blood-lust, and everything had come so oddly naturally to me.

Diane's hair slowly lifted in the air as her power caressed her. "Again."

I heard cackling from the sidelines. Marcus, Atticus, and Cato had finally joined us and were watching alongside Drusus. Their chests and arms were naked to the sun, as they had also trained.

Cato and Atticus gave me wolfish grins while Marcus just stared, arms crossed. Some of the more curious wolves had actually begun to circle around us.

"Don't die," Cato called out.

I rolled my eyes. Diane's eyes lit with a challenge. The she-wolf was actually enjoying this.

"Take the time to breathe." Diane's voice was a lace of smoke and iron. "You will the aether from your mind. See it, call to it. And it will answer."

The air vibrated around her as her aether prepared to launch. I inhaled and called upon the flames. White fire sparked to life along my skin until my entire upper body was doused in it. I imagined how I wanted the power to react, and the flames circled me like rings of bright, jeweled light.

Diane didn't hesitate. Her power careened through the air and slammed into me before I could even think.

I crossed my arms over my face, the silver fire following the move-ment into a shield as I fought against the pressure of Diane's aether. I cursed, falling to my hands and knees, as the weight of it all over-whelmed me.

I heard Atticus's voice, followed by Cato's chuckle. "That must've hurt."

Diane was cackling. "You look a little pale, Lone Wolf."

My chest rose up and down as I fought for breath. Still on my knees, arms dangling loosely at my sides, I flipped my damp hair away from my eyes and met Diane's heavy gaze. I did feel a little faint, but I wasn't going to admit it. "You are definitely enjoying this, aren't you?"

She hummed and began to inspect her nails. "I will neither confirm nor deny."

Marcus's voice interjected. "Remember, we need to ensure Remus can control the aether, and fast, especially so he can showcase it to the minotaur king. It won't be long before we venture there."

I gave the curly-haired male a sidelong glance without bothering to move, but it was Diane who responded. She waved a finger, a smile growing on her face. "Trust me, Marcus. *I* was the one charged with helping Remus, and I know what I'm doing."

Marcus closed his mouth, dipping his head in a bow. His normally ice-cold eyes were warm with respect. "My apologies, she-wolf. I know you do."

The wolf was still wary of me. I couldn't blame him, even though at times it could be irritating. It didn't change the fact that Marcus exuded respect and trust from his fellow wolves. I had to admit, he reminded me of Caius, in a way. Marcus was determined to help his Pack, and he had taken it upon himself to oversee our progress.

The training continued, day after day. Marcus and the others always joined us, to train or merely to observe. They had me practice in their mock combats, during which I had the opportunity to face Marcus. Blood was smeared along his battered lips, my knuckles still sensitive from the punch I had landed. Yes, 'mock' combats hardly meant anything to the wolves. My victory was short-lived when Marcus threw a fist across my jaw. *Godsdamn it.*

"What do you know, Remus," Cato breathed heavily, wiping the sweat from his brow. We had finished our group combat session, and he was beaming at me. "We finally had an even number to pair off. Usually, poor Drusus has to wait on the sidelines while we take turns to train. You completed us."

Atticus made a disgusted sound. "You did not just say that."

I chuckled and wiped the saliva from my mouth before slapping a hand on Marcus's shoulder. "Next time, I will have the last hit."

Marcus scoffed, a hint of a smile on his lips as he brushed me off. He ran a hand through his curls. "I'd like to see you try, Lone Wolf."

After the group session, I went against Diane. She was relentless.

A brilliant instructor, if a bit brutal. Much to my liking. After another beating from her, my body collapsed with exhaustion. Again, on my knees before her. The wolves laughed, some mocking while others whistled in awe.

Diane flashed me an innocent smile. My heart flipped. The corner of my lip curled upward, and I could've sworn Diane's cheeks flushed.

I, the Lone Wolf, known for my tenacity and brutality, had finally found my match.

The she-wolf was becoming part of my every morning and evening routine, of my day and night. She dictated most of my daily schedules, but I was finding myself more willing to follow whatever left her lips. Drusus was there to supervise, his presence a saving grace whenever Diane and I bickered.

I hadn't seen Caius in those weeks, but I felt his presence all the same. There had been additional meetings among the wolves, she-wolves, and harpies, none of which I had been allowed to attend, though Drusus never failed to inform me of the ongoing plans to prepare against the Ram. Caius avoided me like I carried a plague. The unfortunate events that had brought our paths to cross . . . it was too much for us. Overwhelming emotions and unmet closure. My own internal suffering prevented me from being able to speak about it. To help him. To help me.

One thing was certain. Aether was beginning to call to me like a mother's song. Natural and warm. Moonlight flames danced over my arms, rising higher and higher like wings. My palms opened upward at my sides, and a sigh slipped through my lips.

The sun was bright, its heat spreading like an embrace. Lemon and thyme, perhaps a hint of vanilla, could be tasted in the air, the chattering of the Pack forum was a distant sound. And the crowd of wolves who had been watching Diane and I train only grew. She-wolves and harpies had joined the spectators, and even some curious children.

I inhaled, the power strumming the chords of my dark

heartstrings. It rippled, cracked, and rushed through my veins. Pale smoke seeped from my lips. The flames burned brighter, growled.

I opened my eyes and looked at Diane, who waited several yards ahead of me. Her eyes widened upon meeting my gaze. Her expression turned calculated, arms loose at her sides. Then she reacted. Invisible threads rolled forward in waves, splitting the ground with a terrifying snap.

My lips curled into a feral grin. I willed the aether, and a wall of white fire materialized before me. Diane's power made contact, and the two entwined, sparking and flaring until nothing but silver embers drifted toward the trees.

The crowd fell silent. Marcus arched a brow, looking mildly impressed. Eventually the throngs of spectators began to disperse. Drusus and the others hung back, creeping closer to join Diane and me.

Diane began a slow clap, a smirk playing at her lips.

I flashed her a smile. "It's been two weeks. No, almost three? I'd say I'm a fast learner."

Drusus clapped a hand on my shoulder. "When you breathed smoke, Remus, I swear your eyes began to glow."

I ran a hand over my jaw. "It's odd. It feels like this is something I've always known. Like my muscles are simply remembering the aether."

Diane drew closer, tightening the wraps around her knuckles. "Male wolves are made of aether themselves. It makes sense that you feel it so naturally. It's similar for us she-wolves. Power that calls upon power of a similar essence."

I looked at my hands. The flames were gone, but I could still feel the warmth of their touch. "Let's hope this aether is worth something."

"It has to be." Marcus frowned. He met my gaze, and I saw a shift in the male's usual cold stare. "We are all counting on you."

"No pressure," Cato chuckled. He placed a hand on his abdomen. "I'm starving. Can we go eat?"

Atticus sighed, folding his inked arms. "Dinner will be ready soon."

They turned and headed out of the training ground. Cato's voice grew distant. "But can we have a snack?"

Marcus looked between Diane and me, before turning on his heels without another word. Once the male was out of earshot, I scoffed softly. "He has a stick up his ass, doesn't he?"

Drusus fought back a smile. "Marcus tends to care a little too much about everything. He means well, but . . . yes, essentially he has a stick up his ass."

Diane snickered as she walked to the weaponry racks. My eyes followed her. That confident gait, the way her long hair bounced along her back as she moved.

I heard someone clear their throat. My eyes snapped up to see Drusus's mischievous look. I glared. "What?"

Drusus shrugged and lightly brushed my shoulder as he walked past. "Nothing, my darling Remus."

I made to shove him, but Drusus pranced out of reach, laughing. He disappeared into the villa and left Diane and me alone in the courtyard. I walked to her side and Diane silently handed me a weapon and a damp rag. I immediately began to clean the pommel before re-stacking it. We had fallen into a habit of tending to the training courtyard after everyone had left. Even with Drusus around, it had become somewhat of an intimate experience.

Diane's brow was pinched, and I wondered what sort of thoughts were riling in that beautiful head. Her callused hands moved the rag down the thin sheet of a blade.

"It's a good thing you are already an experienced warrior." Her smoky voice broke the silence. "Like you said, it is almost as if you are remembering a past skill."

I glanced at the she-wolf. "I have a question."

She snorted. "This should be good."

My lips twitched in amusement at her retort. *Always so feisty.* "It seems like you don't have a bonded pegasus. I'm assuming you have yet to complete your Rite."

A shadow darted under her skin. She looked up sharply, checking to see if Drusus was around to witness it. I felt the energy emanating from her. It was restless. Diane still hadn't released her aether since the night of the daemon attack. It must have been *eating* at her.

Diane ran her trembling hands through her hair, eyes dancing along the plants and vines that encompassed the courtyard. "I was supposed to, but right now I think I need some time." She looked at her palms. The black ink stretched along her veins for another moment before disappearing.

Diane was afraid this newfound power was a curse the Ram had wrought upon her. I didn't believe it had come from the daemon king. My aether reacted to hers, recognized it. And it was not because of the Ram.

Aether stemmed from the gods and goddesses. So, where had her power come from?

Or from whom?

Drusus reappeared, yawning, interrupting our conversation. It wasn't long before Diane took her leave, her golden eyes meeting mine before she left.

Back in Drusus's villa, I gazed at my reflection in my bath chamber. My hair had grown, now a few inches past my shoulders. I ran a hand along my jawline; the dusting of fine hairs had thickened. I wasn't unkempt, but there was a ruggedness to me, something that hadn't existed before I became the Lone Wolf.

I hadn't bothered to really look at myself since. The basics in hygiene and self-care, yes but I had not taken the time to truly look at myself. My eyes seemed brighter and my skin tone had deepened from the sun. I looked more . . . alive. There was a light that I hadn't noticed before.

I reached for the razor and scissors.

———◆———

The dinner lodge was lined with long tables. Wolves and harpies hunched over their meals, chattering comfortably. A fire burned at the end of the room. Pillars of limestone lined the walls in addition to the torches.

Drusus nudged me forward and we made our way to the end of the dining hall where Diane and the others were already seated.

Cato whistled. "I like the new look, Remus. You look dashing."

I felt warmth bloom on my cheeks, and I absentmindedly ran a hand over the smooth skin of my jaw. Drusus had actually helped me trim my hair so that it reached just above my shoulders, though it was now pulled back into a loose knot with a leather band. Drusus had nodded appreciatively, as if he were an artist admiring his finished piece.

Atticus was seated at the farthest end of the table, Camilla at his side. He was grinning. "Handsome, indeed."

Drusus slung an arm around my shoulders while a small smile twitched on my lips. I felt Diane's stare and briefly wondered what she thought. I flicked my gaze to hers, allowing my smile to curl into a knowing smirk. Her golden eyes were fixated on me as she slowly leaned back in her seat. She met my silent challenge, allowed me to see that she was indeed looking.

Before Drusus and I could take a seat, a burly figure stood from the table adjacent to ours. He had an exasperated expression. "Drusus, we have done more than enough in giving the Lone Wolf food and a roof over his head. Why must you continue to associate yourself with him?"

While it was obvious that my brother was deeply respected among the Pack, it was becoming obvious that many were appalled by his friendship with me. It made me wonder if that was the reason for Caius's lenient punishment for Drusus. The inevitable judgment and doubt would be consequence enough for him.

Drusus took a deep breath. "For gods' sakes, Brutus. It's been almost a month. Regardless of Caius's orders, Remus is my *friend*."

The wolf called Brutus snarled as if Drusus's words had personally offended him. His eyes sharpened to a bright yellow. Other wolves growled and bristled in response. "Disgraceful. You'd choose a traitor over your Pack," Brutus spat.

I snapped. My hand wrapped around the collar of the wolf's shirt and jerked him across the table. Cups and plates crashed to the floor, drinks spilling onto the stone.

"One more word and I will have your tongue," I snarled.

Another male lunged over the table, meeting Drusus square in the chest. Drusus easily grabbed him, slammed his head onto the wooden surface, and held him there.

Brutus writhed against my hold. I almost thought he was going to shift into his wolf until Marcus appeared, ripping the male from my grasp. He threw him down the walkway between the dining tables. Drusus did the same with the other wolf. Some of the onlookers only stared while others growled—on behalf of Marcus or Brutus, I could not tell. But I had an inkling that it wasn't for the latter.

Marcus's blue eyes were eerily bright as his gaze roamed the room. "I expected better from my fellow wolves. The she-wolves and harpies have accepted the Lone Wolf with the nobility you wolves lack." The entire dining lodge fell deathly silent. All eyes fixed on Marcus, as if no one could look away from the composure and authority the wolf held. "Rumors and gossip go only so far. We are in the middle of a godsdamn war—keep the petty behaviors to a minimum."

Stray murmurs began to rise, but the overall tension of the room seemed to defuse, and Marcus turned back to his seat. He briefly met my gaze and gave me a stiff nod, which I returned. Drusus's jaw dropped—even he was shocked.

Marcus had gone out of his way on my behalf.

It didn't take long for the crowd to forget the debacle. The sound of chatter and clinking silverware returned. My back faced the crowd as I sat across from Marcus and Diane and began to eat. We had nearly finished our dinner of stewed meat and bread when I felt a body slide into the seat beside me. A she-wolf with fire red hair leaned over my arm, enough to reveal the deep plunge of her bodice.

"You've been stirring quite a commotion, haven't you?" she asked.

I was acutely aware of the others watching. I cleared my throat and turned to the female, raising a brow. "Clearly Pack life has been dull if I'm the most exciting thing here."

The she-wolf laughed. It was *not* the sound of summer rain. "Point taken. Do you have any plans this evening?"

Bold. Something I could appreciate from anyone. "You're not afraid of mingling with the dishonored Lone Wolf?" I asked.

She waved a hand only to lightly trail her fingertips along my arm. "The thought of it sounds fun, don't you think? An enticing scandal. It doesn't have to be anything serious. If you ever feel the need, come find me."

With a sultry wink, she strutted away. After a breath, I looked across the table. Diane was fiddling with her food, not looking up. She gripped her cup, knuckles bone-white. Drusus was watching me, clearly humored. I had nothing against the she-wolf and for her showing her advances, but for some reason, I was not particularly fond of the encounter happening in front of Diane.

I lifted a cup to my lips and wondered why I cared at all.

NINETEEN

Remus

I had nearly fallen asleep when I felt a massive presence enter the room. A snarl ripped through my throat as I felt my teeth sharpen to fangs. I lunged toward the figure, teeth ready to plunge into its neck. A large hand smacked my lower jaw. I grunted and noticed the familiar set of broad shoulders and dark hair.

"Fucking Drusus," I growled, rubbing the sting from his hit. "Did you just slap me?"

Drusus gaped. "Are you joking? You were about to rip my throat out."

I only glared.

Drusus leapt out of the bed. He was dressed in a casual tunic, a brown leather belt cinching his waist. No weapon in sight. Excitement gleamed in his dark eyes. "There is a tradition we usually follow before we leave the city for Pack business. You may have heard of the underground fighting rings."

Genuine interest sparked within me. I *had* heard of them. The unorthodox version of gladiator fights. Bloodier, if that was possible.

Drusus grinned. "I knew you'd be excited."

I pulled myself up and froze. I was . . . *in bed*. A disgusting weight landed in my chest. "Drusus, did I fall asleep on the bed?"

He gave me an odd look. "Don't you normally? You collapsed after dinner."

I couldn't recall the last time I had slept in my human body. It had been years. I used my wolf form as protection. It also served as a reminder of who I was and what I had done, punishment for the acts of my past.

Within a month of being with the Pack, everything had been fucked with. Routines. Training. It was becoming too much. Guilt began to gnaw at me with another realization.

These past nights, I hadn't dreamt of Helena.

Her death hadn't visited me as much as it used to. Logic told me that it was a good thing, but I didn't like it. I could toss theories as to what was bringing me back to a sliver of normalcy, but I knew. Within the scarred crevices of my heart, I knew who had caused this shift in the wheels of my thoughts.

Diane stepped out from the darkened breezeway that connected to my room, a form-fitting gown the color of wine and temptation melded to her skin. The wink of light at her thigh told me she had a weapon strapped underneath. Her lips lifted into a soft smile when she saw me.

I faltered. Something was happening to me every time my eyes landed on her. A skip in my heartbeat, a flutter in my chest, a growing need. Diane kept pulling me in. I needed to stop this before it developed further. I pushed myself off the bed, catching the slip of her smile. The sight tightened the muscles on my back, and I turned away to change. I hated myself a little bit more for causing it.

The statues of Romulus and Remus peered down upon the wolves waiting in the orchard. Marcus, Cato, and Atticus were dressed casually, with simple tunics and no sign of steel—apart from Diane's weapon. She drifted toward Laelia, Camilla, and Sabina, who had emerged from the forum.

The streets of the city were quiet. Wood creaked as wandering breezes knocked against the doors of apartments and shops. More and more groups of citizens appeared and fell into step with us.

I stopped to look upon the bathhouse we were approaching. "You have to be joking."

Cato snickered. "You'll see."

Marcus led the group into the building, joining the thin crowd. Voices echoed along with the sounds of sandaled steps. The waters of the bathhouse were untouched, utterly still under the pooling starlight. My hand slid across the stone as we closed in on a male harpy who was leaning against a pillar at the opposite end of the space.

One look from Marcus and the harpy nodded. The wolf glanced over his shoulder before disappearing behind the pillar. The females followed and then the remainder of the males.

I approached the entrance, and a mirthless chuckle touched my chest. Behind the pillar was a makeshift door that had been slid open and led to a descending stone staircase. Underground fighting rings were quite literal.

"This seems rather cultish," I murmured. Cato's laugh boomed along the walls.

Once my feet met the last step, the air seemed to lift. The space opened to a dome, tall and wide. The fighting ring stood in the center, a crowd gathered around it. Tables and seating were on a raised platform at the base of the back wall. The same wall held arches with railings for more spectators to view the fights from above. A bar was at the other side of the dome, servers bustling in and out from it.

A band of musicians gathered at the edge of the ring, far enough to avoid the wads of spit and blood. Lively string music reached the highest point of the dome. Sweat permeated the air, and roars riled the crowds.

There was already a fight in the ring, a minotaur against a harpy. The minotaur was on one knee, its onyx horns spun with jewelry and blood. Red inked the harpy's torso and legs.

Drusus's voice intruded on my astonishment. "This used to be a catacomb of some sort. The structure was here long before the fights started. Many believe it was used for sacrifices and other religious practices. Now," he snatched a cup from a bypassing server, "it is for the battle-hungry."

"Do they fight to the death?" I shouted over the crowd.

Marcus scoffed, his eyes fixed on the ring. "No, that obscene practice is held solely by humans. These underground fights are only till one is rendered unconscious or yields."

We ambled closer to the ring and sat at a table alongside the base of the archways and railings. My eyes gravitated to the fight as I took my chair. The minotaur bellowed and charged, but the harpy's wings fluttered upward before the minotaur's horns could make contact. She wrapped her legs around the minotaur's neck and tightened her grip around its horns, forcing the minotaur into the wall.

As soon as the harpy was announced the winner, the females jumped up and started cheering loudly. I cocked my head, admiring how Diane's face lit up as she hollered and raised a triumphant fist. A smile danced on my lips.

A cup of wine was shoved into my face, nearly bumping my nose. Marcus smirked at my scowl. "Don't give me that look. I may be wary of you, but I am not your enemy, Remus."

I eyed Marcus and took the drink from his hand. His smirk deepened, and he tipped his own cup to me before taking a sip.

"What better way for us to bond than over alcohol," I mumbled. The sweet burn was a welcome feeling between my lips.

"It's best if I don't remember my attempt at calling a truce, Lone Wolf."

I barked a laugh at that. More fights ensued in the ring. Drink after drink after drink began to drown out the blare of the crowd's cheers. The world slowly slipped into a warm haze, the constant, wild thoughts sparing me for a while.

My legs were perched on our table, muscles relaxed as I slouched in my seat. Eyes drawn to her. It was hard to look elsewhere. I hadn't spoken to Diane the entire night, practically tried to avoid her or at least establish some semblance of distance between us. The flash of hurt I'd seen on her face in Drusus's villa didn't seem to have affected her evening. Good. I was glad she was enjoying herself.

Her hips swayed as she danced alongside the other females. Camilla laughed at something Laelia said. Sabina had an arm around Diane's neck as they moved closer to each other. Diane flashed her a smile as they grinded in slow, erotic circles. Drusus sat beside me, his eyes heavy with wine and lust as he watched the Commanding She-Wolf.

I kicked his chair. "Dance with her, you fool."

Drusus hesitated. The mere possibility that this she-wolf had him by the throat was intriguing if not highly entertaining.

Then he gave me a lazy smile. "Hold my drink."

Drusus swooped in between the she-wolves and began to grind his large body against Sabina's. Cato jumped in as well and started rocking his hips against Drusus, throwing Diane, Sabina, and Laelia into fits of laughter. It didn't take long for Atticus to encase Camilla with his body, their arms entwined with each other. I remained in my seat, watching these ferocious warriors who could render a town red dance and frolic.

I almost didn't catch Drusus pulling Sabina away from the group. His burly figure disappeared among the crowd, Sabina laughing and leaning into him. Wicked wolves, up to no good. My eyes naturally went back to *her*. And my body went still as a raging burn unfurled in my chest.

Diane was dancing with someone. Another male, human or wolf—I did not give a damn—was holding her body too close. Something simmered in my blood, heated, and a mist drifted in front of my eyes. It was ridiculous that I was feeling this way. I shouldn't care.

And I also could do nothing. She could dance with whomever she wanted, and yet . . . I wished that it was me. Why? Why did I wish it was me? Seeing her walk into my room had twisted my heart both in a painful and delighted way. I had been happy—more than happy—to see her, but I also felt terrible that Helena's death didn't torment me anymore before sleep. The mere notion that I had forgotten my sister, even for a moment, had catapulted me into a vice-like grip of guilt. I couldn't get comfortable here. There was a purpose to being with the Pack. A retribution to be claimed. I owed it to Helena.

So, I could only watch from a distance. Diane looked happy. She twisted and dipped, the male's hands lingering too long on her hips. I was unable to look away, the mist of red only thickening. My jaw clenched, and my gaze snapped up to hers. She was looking my way. Her black hair fell wildly over her chest, damp strands stuck to her neck. There was a wicked light in her eyes as she continued to watch me. I spotted the slight curve of her lips, as if in challenge.

Two can play this game, lotus.

I stood and made my way into the crowd, not too far from Diane. My eyes landed on a woman and I immediately recognized her as the she-wolf who had approached me at dinner. She was among her own friends and I drew up from behind, sliding a hand around her waist. The she-wolf glanced over her shoulder, fire-red hair falling over my arm, and a sultry smile fell over her lips. She pressed her ass against me and we began to sway together.

My gaze shot up to meet Diane. Her eyes were on the she-wolf, specifically where her curvy body was grinding against mine. Diane glared, and twisted around to press her back along the male's chest, mimicking the other she-wolf's movements.

I couldn't look away. My eyes were pinned on Diane as she rolled her hips against the male. I wanted to rip him away from her. I growled, allowing my hands to slip across the red-haired she-wolf's waist, dipping my head to the crook between her shoulder and neck. My eyes never left Diane's. Stars seemed to glimmer in her darkened gaze and I was eager to feed that light, to see it spark and brighten.

Gods, I was about to break. Diane slid her hands up her stomach, over the swell of her breasts, reaching for the male who lowered his face to her neck. Her fingers slipped into his hair and he pressed himself tighter against her.

I was going to kill him.

The mist was nothing but a thick wall of red now. I was completely blinded by it. I cleared my throat, preparing to excuse myself and leave.

The red-haired she-wolf grasped my arm and tugged me closer. "Why don't we head somewhere more quiet?"

I shook my head. "No, but thank you for the dance."

I turned away from the crowd, unable to bring myself to see what Diane and that male would do next.

Dim light greeted me as I entered the archways. The hall was crowded as spectators gathered along the railing, peering at the ring below, sounds of fists meeting skin echoed by cheers.

I sensed her before I saw her. Her mere presence was like the setting sun, radiant and consuming. Diane followed as I entered an alcove. As she stepped in, I twisted around, pinning her to the wall without actually touching her. I slowly raised an arm and rested it on the wall above her head as she threw daggers my way. I couldn't help it. There was something about her presence that drew me in.

"What's wrong?" Her breath had a hint of wine and honey, the sultry sound of her voice dripping with sarcasm.

My teeth grinded with frustration. "Enjoying your evening, lotus?"

Her chest rose as she tried to catch her breath. "Absolutely. As you were, it seemed."

Twin flames ignited in her golden eyes and they burned beautifully. I stared at her, words failing me. The ability to comprehend and verbalize my emotions failed me as well.

Diane's voice pulled me out of my trance. "What's going on with you? You looked like you were on the verge of committing murder back there."

A deep rumble coursed through my throat. "So did you."

Frustration flickered across her face, and she began to step away from me.

I snatched her wrist and dragged her back against the wall. "Fine," I growled.

Her eyes brightened at the sound, and her throat bobbed. I leaned closer, pinning her hand once more to the wall beside her head.

"I wanted to rip his hands off you," I admitted. "To see you dance with another male was . . . aggravating."

She sucked in a breath, teeth tugging on her bottom lip. My eyes strayed to her mouth. What I wanted was to let my fingers trace over the skin of her throat, let the pads of my fingers run mindlessly down to the curve of her neck and across her shoulder. What I wanted was to break my walls and let her in, to bare my wounds to her and receive the same in return. But I didn't do any of that. My grip on her wrist loosened, and I released her from my touch.

Diane rested her head against the wall with the usual, calculated stare. "You could've danced with me, instead of *her*."

"Sounds like you're jealous too." My voice rumbled with a lick of dark humor.

Her eyes coasted from my face down to my chest, tracing the pattern of the tattoos that could be seen through my tunic. "Perhaps," she mused.

"It probably wouldn't have been a good idea to dance with you, anyway," I murmured

Diane slowly folded her arms. "Why?"

I wrapped a strand of her hair around my finger as my gaze bore into hers. "I would have been no better than that idiot. With my hands on you," I dipped my head lower, "and my body pressed against you, I may have wanted to do a lot *more*."

Diane tipped her chin higher, her breaths becoming irregular. Her tongue ran over her lips, and I almost growled at the sight. Earlier this evening I was telling myself not to let this go further. No good would come from it. But what if I had a taste? Just one. From the look in Diane's eyes, the feeling was mutual, and I so badly wanted to lean in, and run my tongue over those lips.

There was an eruption of applause, and the spell between us broke.

She blinked and exhaled heavily. "But you've been ignoring me this evening. Why?"

I didn't know what I was doing. I was frustrated and confused by the changes that had happened since I arrived at the Pack haven. The more infuriating truth was that no matter the change, unadulterated guilt still racked through me.

I stepped back. "I was . . . upset."

Diane's brow pinched, her nude-colored lips twisting. "Have I done something wrong?"

I shook my head. Something fluttered across my chest with my next words. "No, you're perfect."

She didn't seem convinced. "You're not being completely honest.

At some point, you may have to say what you really feel. It may do you some good."

My lips curled. "What's to say I feel anything at all?" Lies. Lies. Lies.

She scoffed. "Right, I forgot who I was speaking to. The mighty Lone Wolf. Perhaps you are only filled with ice and violence."

I turned away from the alcove, heading to the view over the fighting ring. My eyes focused on the crowd below as I felt Diane appear at my side. I grasped the railing, the structure surprisingly weak, as my grip tightened.

Without looking her way, I said. "Maybe ice and violence are all I am capable of."

I felt her gaze on me for a beat. "No, that's not entirely true. You forgot that you can also be broody, crude, and hate all living things."

My lips twitched at that. "How foolish of me to forget."

My senses reacted, and I glanced at Diane in time to witness a flicker of shadow run under her skin. She flinched and tore her gaze away. My gaze darkened, and I tipped her chin up with two fingers.

"You still haven't released your shadowed aether?"

She suddenly paled. "I don't want anyone to see, and I myself do not want to see it either." Then her eyes darted away with a rekindled anger. "You have this over me, you know. You could easily throw me to the wolves and say the Ram tainted my aether."

"What an ironic twist of words," I crooned. My fingers wrapped around her jaw, and I forced her to look back at me. "Do not let this thing win over you, Diane. You are not one to cower before an obstacle. Face this fear, and you will begin to understand yourself more. Overcome it, and you will be stronger."

Diane hesitated, then jerked away from my touch. "The Lone Wolf giving me advice? I must truly be desperate."

I began to smirk. "I'm the only one who can bear your secret, my lotus."

The dome exploded into cheers. Those in the halls banged their cups against the railings. Something about the energy caused me to look below to the cheerful chaos of the crowd, their smiles and hollers as they parted. Marcus sauntered toward the ring.

Before I could ask my question, Diane answered. "We come here often, and Marcus seems to have created a fanbase. Out of all of us, he's fought the most in the ring."

I was genuinely shocked. "I didn't think he'd be the type."

Diane shrugged, still annoyed and frustrated. "We all have our demons, Remus. This is how Marcus deals with his."

Marcus leapt from the ground, ripping into his wolfskin. The crowd went ballistic as Marcus held his head high, tail sweeping the dust up into clouds. The brown wolf's lips lifted into a snarl as a minotaur entered the ring. Once the bell rang, both charged. Loud booms hurled against the stone walls as the two beasts collided. We watched his fight for a moment, and I felt Diane's eyes on me.

"I'm sorry," I said. "Truly, I am. After all my years of solitude, with all the sudden changes, I feel like I am losing a sense of control. And you've done nothing but help me."

Diane cocked her head. "I was raised to understand that there is more to a person's story than what we see and that no one is obligated to share more than what they want to," she said. "I simply wish to know you."

I shook my head. "I was an ass."

"You were."

I chuckled. "Appease a part of your curiosity. Ask me a question."

I could see her mind churning, debating what question to ask. Diane wouldn't ask what she really wanted to know. She knew I wouldn't go near that topic, but I waited for something else. Some attempt to carve deeper into the damaged parts of me.

"What's your favorite color?"

A beat, the question lingering in the air, before I burst into laughter. Deep and rough. Gods, when was the last time I laughed? Her eyes glittered and her lips twitched at the sound.

I cleared my throat. "Black. Yours?"

Diane snorted. "How obvious. You're so gloomy all the time, it makes sense. I like deep red."

"Like blood? Seems a bit obvious for you too."

She laughed in return. "I'm not *that* bloodthirsty."

"You say I'm violent, but you are the most terrifying creature I have come across."

There was more than a kernel of truth to that, and she knew it. Another thought came to mind and I couldn't hold back my curiosity.

"As you're part Egyptian, what are your thoughts on this entire war? The tension between the two Empires must be complicated for you."

She sighed, her fingers trailing up the laurel tattoo around her bicep. "It has placed my pater and me in a difficult position. I have never been to Egypt, but my mater was born and raised there. My pater respects her homeland and we have always had a special connection to the Empire. From the beginning, he had made it clear he had no desire to fight against Egypt and remained on Roman soil when the Pack had to stop the rebel battles that took place on my mater's homeland. I believe you were there for that."

I felt a sour pit in my stomach. Yes, I definitely recalled all the lives I had taken during my time there. As well as the torment I endured. Though I admired her wish to explore the other part of her heritage, despite the difficult position it must put her in.

"Your dedication to honor your mater's memory is admirable," I said.

She shrugged. "Our fight is solely against the daemons."

I nodded. "The Ram made sure of that."

Diane pursed her lips. "What if the Ram follows through with its word? What if it has sent mercenaries or daemons to hunt us down?"

Silver skittered over my skin. It was quick but I felt it mirror the flare of emotion inside. "I swear to you, by every godsdamn star in the sky, that I will *never* let anything happen to you."

Diane blinked. "I would do the same for you." The conviction in her voice was unquestionable, but it almost seemed as if she were surprised she'd uttered the words. "It makes me wonder."

"Wonder what?"

She folded her arms and leaned to the side, causing the deep red dress to sway with the motion of her legs. There was a slit to her gown, and it parted to reveal a peek of skin. Gods above.

Diane snapped her fingers, light dancing in her eyes. "Eyes up here, Lone Wolf. I was about to say that Atticus has a point."

Hearing the wolf's name drowned whatever lustful thoughts were about to creep in. I arched a brow in question.

She smiled. "That you're not as bad as you want to appear. It makes me wonder what happened to cause you to hide underneath the cold mask." A bell rang as the crowd chanted Marcus's victory. I stole a glance toward the ring to see the brown wolf standing proudly, fur spotted in blood and dirt. I returned to Diane's softened gaze. She was an indomitable fire, yet she was also gentle.

My expression smoothed out, and I tapped her nose with my finger. "You don't get to have all of my secrets, lotus."

TWENTY

Diane

The clangs of the chains binding my wrists echoed through my bones. The bloodshed forced my eyes to stay open. The horror and pain plunged into my heart like a blade. My knees weakened as I continued to watch the shadows, flames as black as night, tear into the city. Smoke billowed through closed doors and cracked walls. Screams followed, sharp as glass. White tongues of fire crawled along the buildings, lighting them into bright sconces. Remus stood beside me, watching as his power brought an entire city to its knees.

The daemons followed. Their gnashing teeth gutted flesh. Silent tears ran down my face. Soundless sobs raged at my chest. I felt myself slowly slide to the ground. Strong hands swept under my arms, pulling me up. Up and up as I fell into myself. I wanted the darkness to take me. Drown me.

My eyes opened to bright and crazed eyes. Large, rough hands were gently cupping my face. A hard body caged me to the bed, suffocating me with his heat.

Remus released a breath. "Gods, I didn't think you'd ever wake up."

I was fighting for air, clinging to reality. It was only a nightmare. "What are you doing here?" I hissed.

His brows pinched as his thumb brushed something wet from the corner of my eye. His voice came out in a rough whisper, deep and almost raspy. "I came here with a proposition for you, but then I heard you whimpering in your sleep. You were *crying*."

My heart skidded. Images of death and darkness still poised to attack me. I shook my head and moved strands of hair from my face. "What kind of proposition requires you sneaking into my room in the dead of night?"

We had returned from the underground fighting ring only a few hours ago. After our conversation under the archways, we had rejoined the others. My warrior brothers and sisters had managed to get drunk, which left Remus, Atticus, and me to ensure they got home. Dawn was sure to be near by now.

Remus watched me, and the look in my tired gaze told him I didn't want to speak of what had plagued my sleep. He seemed to relent, and his lips curved before he winked. "Not the kind of proposition you've been craving, lotus. I know your shadows have been itching at you." When I only gave him a questioning look, he beckoned toward the door. "Come with me."

Remus's hands drifted to my own as he pulled me upright on the bed. His long legs were draped over the edge of my bed. The moon was bright enough to beam through my room, over the cream-colored drapes, tall bookshelves, and long rug.

I realized Remus was wearing a cloak. He pulled the hood over his head until I could see only the hard lines of his shaven jaw. "Scared, she-wolf?"

I scoffed, then slid from the bed and rummaged through one of the chests in search of my own cloak. I could feel Remus's hot gaze on me. And I liked it. I liked when his attention was on me, and I'd certainly allowed my eyes to feast on him. And when he had walked in the dining hall earlier, I'd liked the sharpness of his new look, his hair tied and knotted upon his head, the clean-shaven look making him appear younger.

I shouldn't have been entertaining this thought.

I cleared my throat, tossing Remus a raised eyebrow. "You've never seen a woman in her sleepwear?"

Remus blinked before a charming smile appeared. I saw through it. A wicked creature rested underneath, ready to bite and draw blood. "I've seen plenty, Diane."

Plenty. My teeth pinned my bottom lip as I raised my cloak over my shoulders. Of course, the bastard had slept with plenty of women. With all that running around slaughtering the Order, surely the poor Lone Wolf had needed to find ways to relax. Remembering how one of the she-wolves had propositioned herself to him suddenly tightened something in my lungs.

I brushed past him. "I'm sure Luciana would be happy to oblige if you ever felt any urges."

"Luciana?"

I rolled my eyes. "The she-wolf you danced with."

He hummed, face obscured from the darkness of his hood. "I'd rather not."

I was not sure why, but I felt a coolness spread through me, loosening the ugly knot from within my chest. I followed the Lone Wolf, both cloaked in shadow and moonlight, and we strode into the woods.

***

We stood in a clearing, surrounded by thick branches that stretched and webbed together. I would like to say that I would not normally follow a male into the woods just based on his word. But the aether was indeed aching to be released, scratching under my skin like a caged animal. It craved destruction. And regardless of his cockiness and secrets, I knew I could trust Remus.

The clearing was far enough from prying eyes. Remus sauntered around me in a wide circle, the starlight clinging to him like a pair of wings. The hood of the cloak was still drawn over his face, but his long fingers were splayed over his lips while he was deep in thought.

"Do you trust me?" he asked.

My throat suddenly felt dry. This was unnerving me. Why? I had never felt this level of fear. When facing the Ram, it had been as if the aether inside me had snapped awake, like a beast waking from its slumber. Had the daemon king willed it? Had he poisoned me with this darkness? I wanted—no, needed—answers.

Remus stood over me and placed his hands on my shoulders. I was suddenly very aware of how tall he was. How I had to tip my head up to meet his eyes. The strength of his rough hands. Only the fabric of the cloak between our skin.

What was wrong with me?

Remus's voice was like a river of night sky. Deep, soft, and powerful. "It's not going to do you any good if you keep fighting the aether. You're scared, Diane, I can understand that. Gods, I can understand feeling afraid. Tame this fear, this beast inside you, because it is you and only you who should be in control." He placed a finger on my chest. On my heart. "Give yourself the opportunity to trust in yourself. You may be surprised by the things you are capable of."

My lips twisted, struggling with how I felt. This male, the Lone Wolf of all people, was telling me to face my fears. To regain control of my power and ultimately myself. There was some irony there.

Remus curled his fingers around my chin, forcing me still. "No one can see you. It's only me, and I'll be here in case anything goes amiss."

A shaky breath escaped my lips. "It's precious, seeing this soft side of you," I teased.

He shot me a playful smile. "I am precious, thank you."

Cocky bastard. Cocky, adorable bastard. "Stand back," I whispered. "But don't go too far."

Remus bowed his head and tugged the hood of my own cloak further over my face before retreating a few steps. My limbs trembled, and nausea churned. I hated this. I hated how weak and scared I felt.

It was like this deep power was encased in a tiny jar. A tiny, painstakingly small jar pushing at its weak walls. Ready to burst. I released the aether in a steady stream, nervous that if I simply let the power loose, it would come out in torrents. Black tendrils lifted from my hands and began to spiral up to the stars. It was small, but it already felt as if the air were lighter. *More,* it seemed to beg. My mouth opened in a silent cry, and shadows billowed from my entire body. Like a thread of yarn being spooled from a tight ball.

As the power continued to unfurl, my mind seemed to fall. Or rise. I was looking at the sky, at the jeweled lights that decorated the darkness above. And I felt like I was rushing upward, racing toward them. Faster and faster, my consciousness suspended, like I was floating. And there, the night took shape. The figure was speckled with the stars, with tall pointed ears. My blood thrummed as if in response to a song, and my heart beat faster and faster—

I sighed as the last of whatever I had bottled inside left me, propelling me back to reality. My head dropped, shoulders sagging. No sense in trying to understand what had just occurred, so I stared aimlessly at the ground until boots stepped into view.

His hand came around my neck, thumb pressing underneath my chin to tilt my head, and I met his luminous gaze. I felt the brush of his thumb down the column of my throat.

"So powerful," Remus murmured. "Beautiful."

"Thank you," I said softly. "For pushing me to do this. You were right. I . . . I needed it. I feel like I can breathe again."

His voice was gentle. "I've been thinking about your power, and Diane, I don't think it came from the Ram."

I stared at him, speechless. I wasn't so sure, but after what I had seen in the deep roots of my thoughts, perhaps Remus was right. Or maybe that was what the Ram wanted me to think. It had the ability to plant its nightmarish visions on me—what's to say it hadn't done this as well? Still, I wanted to hope.

"Then where did it come from?" I asked.

Remus dropped his hand, and my skin immediately felt cold. "I don't know, but if it is coming from you then I do not fear it."

My heart fluttered. Under the moon, under the curious eyes of the Fates, the Lone Wolf had helped me. I had been stubborn and afraid, but he hadn't judged me for it. He had been attentive to my needs and been there to support me. And I found myself wanting to do the same for him. I'd noticed the weight looming over his shoulders. The way he would always sleep in his wolf form. The occasional haunted look in those jade, feline-like eyes. I wanted to support him too.

A tendril of guilt rose at the thought of my 'task'. I had a duty to my Pack. Whatever naive notion I was feeling toward the Lone Wolf, I needed to squash it.

We began walking back toward my villa. Leaves crunched under our boots.

After a beat of silence, Remus nudged my shoulder. "Remember the deal I made with you? Well, let's toss that one and make a new one. You've been helping me, and I wish to help you too. When you feel the need to release the aether, come to me."

I smiled. "Your deal was shit to begin with. You tried to hold my secret over my head when you were going to be stuck with me anyway."

We stepped into a column of moonlight, and I caught his glittering eyes. "Or perhaps the deal and the Pack's arrangement had the same goal."

My cheeks threatened to redden, and I looked away. "Someone may think you're going soft, Lone Wolf."

He chuckled deeply. "The audacity."

We walked the rest of the way in silence. Awareness hummed to life between us. It skimmed over the skin, begging for touch and words. It almost felt like a dream, and it would be gone by tomorrow. We would leave for the minotaurs' lands, and whatever this was would most likely dissipate. I wasn't sure I wanted this to end. I had never met anyone like Remus.

He left me at my room's door. He bowed before taking off, his footsteps soundless like a spirit. My heart thundered for a moment as I leaned against my door. *Powerful and beautiful.* The words stuck with me much longer than I would have liked. My hand rose to my neck, remembering the touch of his thumb. It had been so subtle, but it felt like my skin was on the verge of catching fire. I went and fetched a basin of water, hoping I could stop this flame before it burned me whole.

TWENTY-ONE

Remus

S hades of amber flickered behind my closed eyes. The dark was so thick, it almost swallowed whatever torchlight existed here. The taste of copper filled my mouth, and a line of spit fell from my battered lips. The slightest movement had my body screaming. No chains held me. They had removed them, and I lay limp on the soiled strands of hay that had been scattered across the floor. One of them unlocked the cell. Their teeth skimmed over my neck.

"It's time to wake up and play."

"Remus?" I looked up and met Drusus's wolf eyes. "Where did you go just now?"

My time in that cell, the wounds inflicted there. It had all stayed with me. Evidenced by the marks on my skin.

"Egypt," I said.

Drusus nodded. He didn't have to ask further. I remembered the fury he had unleashed upon seeing my beaten body. My captors had managed to escape, but Drusus still saved me. Covered my eyes with a rag against the bright sun from all that time in the dark.

"Does it happen often?" he asked.

"Sometimes. It's been a while since it last did."

Drusus gestured toward my paws. "I remember when you tattooed your knuckles. The symbols you had etched—"

"—to remember," I finished.

Drusus said nothing. He knew there were no words and that I

wasn't looking for comfort. An amicable silence soon followed. We had been traveling among forests and plain hills for almost a week, only stopping to rest and eat. Toward the lands of the minotaur. The harpy was currently flying ahead to scout for any signs of life and possible threats. Camilla and Sabina had stayed behind with the Pack, the Commanding She-Wolf to tend to the she-wolves, whereas Camilla's duty was among the healers in preparation for battle.

"*What happened between you and Sabina?*" I asked Drusus.

Drusus's gray wolf seemed to smile, ears flickering. "*This has been something we've been skirting for years. She's had lovers as well as I, but something always draws us back together. I have been fighting it because it feels too real. I don't want to lose this, but that night at the fighting ring I was overwhelmed with how much I wanted her. Everything about her.*"

I watched him for a moment. "*What about her? How does she feel?*"

"*She made her feelings known once, long ago, and I denied her. It was everything I wanted, and I made a stupid decision. The lust is still there. We have succumbed to our carnal desires more than once, but there's a lingering question whether or not this could be something more.*"

I hummed in thought. "*Sounds like you need to speak with her. I've seen the way she looks at you. There is more there, brother. Of that, I am sure.*"

Drusus released a sound between a laugh and a sigh. "*I always imagined what it would be like to talk to you about these things. I know you have taken lovers, but you've never shown an interest in having anything more either.*"

My thoughts turned to a female. Dark hair and golden eyes. I clamped the thought down before it went further. "*I told you I liked love stories, even though it is not a possibility for me.*"

Drusus's eyes gravitated to where Diane sat. Her legs straddled upon Marcus's back. Her attention was on the deep conversation she was having with Marcus, Atticus, and Cato.

"*Well, perhaps not a she-wolf,*" Drusus surmised. "*That doesn't mean you can't find love with someone else, but if you were to pursue a she-wolf, I wouldn't completely shut down the idea.*"

I hated how this intrigued me. "*Why do you say that?*"

Humor twinkled in the amber hues of Drusus's eyes. *"Let's just say that I have never seen two particular warriors challenge each other and become so aggravated it almost seems that they are very enamored with one another. It's all very enthralling."*

Something skipped a beat inside my chest. A warmth dared to spread. I didn't want to hope. I was the Lone Wolf and the topic of love, no matter how beautiful and meaningful, wasn't an option. I would never place that shame upon her, anyway.

———

Thwack. Thwack. Thwack.

Blood coated the ripped skin of my knuckles. The wooden post I had been assaulting with my fists had dented and smoothed. Helena drew up to my side. Her brows furrowed.

"You've been at it for over an hour," she commented. I grunted and thrust another fist at the wood.

Thwack.

My twin flinched at the sound and caught my hand to inspect the wounds. "Pater has returned. He's with the conqueror in the war tent."

We'd been waiting for this. I nodded and began to wrap a bandage over my knuckles and palms.

"Let's go."

Helena and I parted the flaps of the war tent. My pater, basically an older version of myself with his dark hair and green eyes, looked up from a map. At his side was a male with blond hair, thin lips, a hooked nose, and cold, calculating eyes.

"Alpha Anthony. Gaius Julius Caesar." My pater didn't like it when I called him anything else in front of others.

My pater's eyes flared at the intrusion. "What is this?"

Helena emerged from behind me, and a pang of envy hit my chest when my pater's eyes softened at the sight of her.

"You're planning on using the wolves," she said. "We heard you."

I did not recognize my pater, with the thunder that rolled in his eyes. The Roman conqueror seemed amused by the exchange and stood back.

I gritted my teeth. "The wolves are not to be used as a means to conquer land. We are not Rome's weapons."

Pater threw us out. The cost of us standing up to him would be the wounds on my skin. Wounds that would scar. That was his form of punishment. The constant demand to train overtime was often an excuse. He never laid a hand on me. Pater craved perfection.

My knuckles broke as the wooden post finally snapped.

Trees appeared. The moon shone. Helena stood at its center, staring at the sky. A blink and the daemon stood in her place. It lunged at me, and I drove my dagger up its ribs.

The snapping of bone and gutting of flesh.

My ebony claws dug into the earth. I snapped awake to a dark sky glittering with a sea of stars, a canopy of trees above me. Starlight showered through those tall trees in soft beams. When I remembered I was still in my black wolf's form, I sighed with relief.

I silently fought for breath, wondering why more memories were slipping through my thoughts. First, the time I spent in Egypt. Now, it was the time Helena and I had spent trying to defend the wolves. Relentless advocation that the Pack will never know about.

Helena's death had returned to me, albeit not as harshly and not as often. But she still came, and I remembered the weight I had to carry, the revenge I vowed to uphold. How the Pack was a means to an end. This attempt to befriend and cultivate relationships with those of the Pack was becoming a distraction.

I welcomed the lashing of my thoughts. A bloody, guilt-laden reminder.

TWENTY-TWO

Remus

"It smells like death."

Atticus was sniffing the air. His glacial wolf eyes flashed Sunlight seemed to have dimmed in these parts, replaced by a grayness that thickened the very air. The birds chirped less, and the trees seemed to darken. The gnarled branches angrily condemned the gods.

"Peachy," Cato replied, narrowing his gaze on the tree trunks. *"There are claw marks. Jagged and crazed, which make me think it was daemons."*

Caius cursed under his breath. His white wolf pelt gleamed like fresh snow even under the gray sheen of light. *"I hope we aren't too late,"* he murmured.

The stench of rot and burnt wood thickened. My hackles rose as Drusus tensed beside me. The wood's edge peeled open to desolation.

It did smell of death. Reeked of it. Stretching ahead of us was a town. Or what remained of it. Oh gods. Dark red streaked the low, rock-made wall. Stone houses were destroyed, gaping holes in the brick and stone. The buzzing of flies was a constant hum.

Caius growled at the sight. *"The daemons have gotten to the mino-taurs already. There is no life here. If we keep going, we can reach their main city by nightfall."*

As I looked inside the doors of the minotaur homes, the buzzing grew louder. My nostrils twitched. Daemon carcasses heaped in piles, maggots chewing on the thick meat.

Drusus ducked under my head to peek in. "*Shit, that's disgusting.*"

"*There aren't any minotaur bodies,*" I observed.

My body tensed with Caius's voice. "*No, the minotaurs would've buried or burned their dead.*"

I met his piercing yellow eyes. It was the first time we had spoken to one another since our initial brawl. The Alpha didn't say anything else, his gaze sliding past me in dismissal. We reached the end of the town where more woodland greeted us. The day was waning, ribbons of deep gold and purple enveloping the sky.

Pointed ears flickered, listening to the sounds from the woods. Leaves rattled, and the sharp sound of hisses erupted from deep within. Someone cursed, and we watched as crescent-shaped red eyes glowed from amongst the trees. Rows of them. There must have been about twenty daemons charging our way. And something else. Another sound followed the daemons. Deep thundering like hooves.

Diane waved her hands. "Wait! Look! What's in front of the daemons?"

A dark figure popped out from the shadowed mounds, stumbling and grunting until I could see its curved horns. The daemons were chasing a young minotaur.

The youngling stole a glance over his shoulder. "Come for me, you hungry bastards!"

A javelin hissed over the low stone wall. It missed the daemons and was aiming for Caius's neck. There was no thought. Pure instinct drove me forward.

"Caius!" My teeth clamped over the javelin before it reached his neck, snapping the wood in half.

Snarls erupted, and the wolves readied themselves as the minotaur led the daemons toward us. Caius paused, then slowly gestured to me with a nod of his head.

An ear-grinding screech and a daemon lurched forward, managing to tackle the young minotaur. Diane sprinted to the minotaur's aid and rammed her shoulder against the daemon, tumbling to the ground with it and throwing punches under its jaw. She unhooked a dagger and jabbed it up its neck. Black blood poured onto her chest.

She groaned, kicking the daemon off her. "Gross."

Another javelin whistled from the trees. This one made purchase as it pierced another daemon. More red-crescent-eyed creatures began to pour out of the shrubbery, the clang of metal and the thunder of hooves at their heels. There was a loud bang, and a daemon went flying from between the trees, landing with its neck in a crooked angle. A minotaur emerged, black gore smeared over his war hammer.

An entire herd of minotaurs appeared with fighting leathers and wicked weaponry. The minotaurs hacked at the daemons with axes, war hammers, and curved swords. The wolves leapt over the low border wall. My fangs punctured the leg of another daemon before it could reach Diane and the young minotaur. I dragged it away and slammed it against the stone wall. The sharp snaps of bone sang to me. I drove my fangs into another, its wailing cut short as my teeth dug deeper into the flesh of its neck. Gutting and wrenching. I spotted Laelia land, graciously swinging her twin blades in the air as the daemons came for her.

All of the daemons were soon disposed of, and Laelia began to wipe her blades clean with a cloth. Diane scrambled toward the youngling she had saved.

"Are you hurt?" Her brow creased with worry.

His jaw dropped at the sight of Diane. The movement caused the silver ring of stars that was pierced through his nostrils to jingle. "You saved me."

Diane huffed a sigh of relief. "Think nothing of it. Here, let me help you up."

He wasn't as big as the average minotaur, which must have meant he was still in early adulthood. On his head sat a crown that looked to be thick iron melded to resemble entwining branches.

The herd of minotaurs sheathed their bloodied weapons. Axes and war hammers hung at their hips as javelins and wicked swords were hooked over their backs. Leather, fur and jewelry adorned their burly bodies. Some had ringlets of silver and bronze around their horns, while others wore armlets and wristbands.

The massive minotaur who held the war hammer rushed to the young minotaur's side.

"Your Highness." His baritone voice could shake bones. "I told you, you shouldn't be the one to lure the daemons away."

Your Highness? By the gods, that explained the damn crown. This was the prince. Son of King Cain. The prince rolled his eyes. "I wanted to help, Octavius."

Diane was scrubbing the black gore off her chest plate, her eyes flashing in interest. "Your Highness?"

The prince minotaur's eyes beamed at the sight of Diane before he dipped his head. Curved horns and all. "Prince Theon at your service. I have never met a she-wolf before. May I ask the name of my hero?"

Sweet Fates.

She smiled widely. "Diane."

Diane gestured to Caius, who padded among the warriors, his muzzle tinted with daemon blood. "This is Caius, our Alpha."

Caius bowed his head. *"Prince Theon, it is a pleasure and an honor. We were actually on our way to meet with your father."*

Theon nodded, suddenly solemn as he looked at Octavius. "I'm sure you are, Alpha."

Octavius's fists clenched. "With all due respect, Alpha, if you come seeking aid from our people then you should turn back now. As you can see, we have problems of our own."

"I do see." Caius observed, his paw pushing a lifeless daemon on its back. *"I see we have the* same *problem. Now, I have a whole pretty speech prepared, and I would rather present it to you and your king under the appropriate circumstances."*

The corner of Theon's lip tilted up as he folded his thick, gray arms. "My father is not home. He is away tending to some of our outer cities. Out of respect for Diane, my minotaur and I can escort you to our home. From there you may attempt to speak with my father once he arrives, but your efforts may be futile, as he has been away for some time, and there is no anticipated date for his return."

Octavius stepped forward. "My prince, is this necessary?"

Theon whirled on the minotaur. "Do you wish to rob me the opportunity to repay a life debt? She saved your prince. This is the least we can do."

Octavius clamped his mouth shut, frowning. The minotaur then began to shout orders to the others, who opened a pathway for their prince. Theon offered an arm to Diane. She grinned and looped her arm in his. I watched as he led her to the front, the other minotaurs marching in a protective formation around them.

Drusus crept up beside me. *"It looks like you have competition."* He snickered.

"Excuse me?"

Drusus shot me a dry look, but Caius was already snapping for us to move. We flanked the minotaurs as Caius and Marcus walked alongside the prince. Laelia stayed behind with the rest of us, soaring above.

Caius's deep voice droned from ahead. *"What were you doing with the daemons, Your Highness? It looked as though you were letting them chase you."*

"Yes. The point was to lure the daemon herds away from our kind and kill them in the process." Theon's gaze was solemn, and he gestured to the lifeless city that was now at our backs. "What can we possibly offer you now, when we can't even save ourselves?"

TWENTY-THREE

Remus

Beads of torchlight weaved throughout the night-kissed land, signifying that we'd reached the minotaurs' homeland. Rocky hills surrounded the city. Towards the left, etched into the sides of the hill and deep in the mouth of a massive cave, more of the city's lights and buildings could be seen. The cave was said to have been the home of an ancient Norse god who gave their land to the minotaurs before taking their place in the realms where the gods and goddesses resided.

We followed the prince past stone homes and a thousand armories. As the night drew in, the city teemed even more with life. Children ran around and adults—both male and female—worked. Metal clanged, fires hissed, and steam rolled in the air as the minotaur blacksmiths worked their weaponry.

I recognized the look in their eyes, the sheer ferocity lined with anger and purpose. The emotion echoed in every stroke of their hammers. It was the call of a battle rising, the promise of bloodshed that would arrive on an incoming horizon.

Upon the prince's appearance, the minotaurs bowed. Sharp and curious eyes followed us. I noted the onslaught of construction. Homes were being built, crammed together.

Octavius noticed where my gaze had wandered. "We have to make room for those who lost their homes."

"I understand. Where I'm from, the situation is nearly the same."

He grunted and said no more. Before long, we were at the mouth of the cave. Torchlights rimmed the cave walls and the streets within. Businesses, shops, and market stalls.

"*Shift into your human forms,*" Caius ordered.

Aether hummed as we shifted, the massive bones of the wolves warping into nimble human bodies. My feet found the ground, and I groaned as I stretched my arms and legs. The minotaurs watched us with intrigue.

My gaze collided with Diane. The last proper conversation with her had been the night I urged her to release the shadow aether. *Strong. Beautiful.* The words had escaped me before I even realized I'd uttered them. I was beginning to lose my edge. We hadn't spoken much since. I'd kept my distance, and it seemed Diane preferred the same. She broke our gaze.

"It's like another city." Drusus's awe served as a perfect distraction.

Cato brushed against his shoulder. "It's been a long day. I feel like getting drunk again."

I snorted as we followed the minotaurs into a massive brick and stone building near the entrance to the cave. The colors inside were of deep blue and bronze, and the floor a dark marble. The main room looked . . . like a home, albeit a grandiose home, but at least it wasn't a throne room or a war room. A dining table stood in the center, a fireplace at its end. Decorated shelves and paintings were on either side, where hallways split off into other rooms. A chandelier of melded iron that looked like entwined branches, similar to that of Prince Theon's crown, hung above the dining table.

Theon beckoned us into the space. "Welcome to my home. This is where you will be staying. I imagine my father will be here within a few days and you will be able to speak with him then, Alpha. Though I can't promise much will come of it."

Caius ran his eyes across the room, his dreadlocks still pulled back with a leather band. "I fear we don't have a few days, Prince Theon. Time is truly our enemy these days."

Theon simply shrugged, Octavius remaining close behind him.

"You came here. You are more than welcome to turn back around and return where you came from."

There was a low grumbling from Cato. "Oh gods, please no."

Caius's jaw ticked. His war-born eyes measured Theon. "A king in the making, aren't you?"

Theon seemed to puff out his chest, and after a jerk of his horns other minotaurs filed in and led us to our rooms. When I entered my designated room, my eyes gravitated to the open windows that revealed the city's nightlife and the wide bed underneath them. The weight of my boots seemed to echo upon the marble floor.

I drew a bath and shrugged out of my armor and clothes. When I eventually walked out with a towel wrapped around my waist, a new set of clothes had been folded and placed on the bed. I changed and stood, staring at the silk sheets. Wondering. I guessed I could walk out of the king's house and find some trees to settle under. Perhaps no one would notice—

The door opened, and the smell of soap and blossoms hugged my back.

"Don't leave." That voice.

Fuck. I turned to see Diane slipping into the room, closing the door with her back. Her long hair was still damp, and a nightgown that stopped mid-thigh clung to her body. Dear gods and goddesses above. It was like the Fates had asked Venus herself to sculpt the she-wolf.

I hesitated. "What are you doing here?"

Warmth hinted at her cheeks. "You think no one has noticed but I have. You never sleep indoors." I kept silent as she drew closer. Determination brightened her eyes. "There is no need for an explanation, not unless you wish to share. But I ask you this: don't sleep outside tonight. Stay here."

I should've known the she-wolf would notice. Her keen observation missed nothing. It was not like I had tried to keep it a secret. The others might've simply chosen not to say anything about it.

Throat bobbing, my voice deepened, an odd feeling coming over me. "I don't think I know how."

A pained expression passed her eyes. To see someone feel for me something like that was touching. "You punish yourself too much, Remus," she said softly. "And you are in pain. I see it in your eyes and the way it weighs on your shoulders. You've helped me, now let me help you. To at least have you sleep in the comfort of a bed. You deserve that much."

An image of Helena flickered through my thoughts. "I am not sure I do, lotus. The things I've done . . ."

Diane raised a palm, stopping me from speaking further. "You don't have to elaborate." She gingerly took my hand and squeezed. "Whatever it is that you are going through, remember that you are a fighter, a warrior who has been carrying a burden for so long and deserves to sleep in peace. Besides, it might help ease all your constant brooding."

I gave her a dry look. "How charitable you are."

She smirked and pulled me toward the bed. She actually intended to help me. Dumbfounded, I could say nothing as I followed, slipping under the sheets with her. Every muscle and all my senses were hyper-aware of her body next to mine.

Diane was on her stomach and propped her chin on her folded arms. She was quiet, allowing me a moment to adjust and feel comfortable. I shifted onto my side to face her and considered her words, running a thumb over my bottom lip. Parts of the truth slipped out.

"My sister's death finds me at night," I began. Diane waited patiently for me to continue. "It's been years, and still her passing is a nightly reminder of why I do what I do. It is why I always sleep outside in my wolf form. It makes me feel stronger and safer."

My eyes shifted up to the window. Shame burned through me. Diane's presence was soft, a radiant enchantment that caused me to close my eyes.

I shuddered. Diane scooted closer until her body was slightly above mine, and she began to run her fingers through my hair.

I opened my eyes, meeting her soft gaze. "You don't have to stay."

"But I want to. Now sleep, Remus."

Her fingers continued their tender touch through my hair. Eventually, with the warmth of her body and the softness of her hand, the heaviness began to settle, and my eyes drifted closed. The memory tried to claw its way to me. Blood. My sister's body in my arms. Footsteps in the distance. My pater—oh gods, my pater—

A soft voice, smoked with steel and fire, drifted from the far corners of my mind. "Sleep. You are safe."

Diane.

Something in my chest shifted. Filling the emptiness. Slowly.

The darkness drifted over me again, but this time it was not one of horror or nightmares. It was a gentle blanket of night where only dreams could thrive.

Twenty-Four

Diane

I awoke to a large arm wrapped around my waist, hot skin pressed against my thin nightgown, and soft breaths at the back of my neck. The silk sheets felt slippery under my touch, and I noticed one of my legs was trapped between two thick male thighs. The smell of the ocean, cedar, and pure man was drugging.

I wouldn't mind waking up to this more often.

I stiffened. Last night hurtled back at me, and I remembered the impulsive decision I'd made.

Remus. I was in bed with Remus.

The morning was still young. A pale blue with the last of the stars still peeling away from the rising sun. I slowly shifted, my curiosity urging me to catch a glimpse of the sleeping Lone Wolf. His lips were parted slightly, eyes closed, rimmed by thick lashes. The pale scar that slashed through his right brow. My gaze wandered to his arm, now able to observe his tattoos up close.

Blossoms and vines twisted and turned along his left arm. Intricate, delicate patterns completely covered his skin. The tattoo continued up to his clavicle, and my fingers were suddenly tempted to trace the design.

My eyes snagged on his bare chest, and a breath caught between my lips. Angry scars marked his skin, continuing lower, beyond what the bedsheet covered. *What happened to him?* My heart pinched at the thought, and my mind began conjuring many questions and theories.

His pain. The sadness that followed him. His coldness. The mask of indifference. All shields to hide the scars beneath. I meant what I'd said last night. Despite his secrets, the Lone Wolf had been living a tortured existence, and I believed he deserved a break from that reality. It had taken him a while to fall into a deep sleep. He had been restless. Pinched brow and quivering lips at whatever haunted him. I wasn't sure I even wanted to know what awaited him behind closed eyes.

I shifted once more, slipping my leg from his hold. The movement stirred him, and his eyes flickered open. Bright green and angry. With supernatural agility and strength, he flipped me onto my back, and pinned my arms above my head. His knees parted my legs. Teeth elongating into a snarl.

"Remus," I breathed.

I kept my voice low. Remus couldn't *see* me. I noticed the blank look in his gaze, the way his eyes were glazed and unfocused. I waited and hoped that whatever had a hold of him would wash away. This wasn't exactly the right time for it, but I couldn't help but notice his beauty, lethal.

"It's me. Diane," I soothed.

Remus stiffened at the sound of my voice. My skin tingled, and heat trickled to the lower parts of me. Gods, help me. My aether shifted along my skin. Remus jerked back, blinking, and the blank gaze cleared.

"Fuck," he rumbled. "This is awkward."

I released a nervous laugh. "You don't say."

Remus's eyes flashed as if suddenly realizing how I lay vulnerably beneath him. He cleared his throat and rolled onto his back beside me. The heat of his body left me prey to the cool draft in the room, but warmth still weighed between my legs.

"I'm sorry." Remus's voice was rough from sleep. "Clearly, I'm not used to waking up next to someone."

The thought that I had been the only one in a long time to wake at his side made my stomach clench. I needed to do something, absolutely anything, to distract my lustful thoughts.

I began to lift the bedsheet off me when Remus's voice stopped me. "How are your shadows?"

The shadows flickered over my skin as if in response "Better. I feel I have a stronger hold on them. They don't bite back as much."

Remus watched me carefully. "Have you considered using this aether in battle?"

"No," I responded quickly. It wasn't a difficult decision to make. "I will never let this power see the battlefield."

I glanced up to see Remus with a thoughtful look. "And you want to keep this part of yourself a secret from everyone?"

Well. That was a bit more complicated. "I have considered telling my brothers about it," I admitted. "I want to be sure I can handle it before I consider telling the others. They will need to know eventually."

"How come?"

I gave Remus a dry look. "The Ram's intention is to have control over both of us. My brothers and Caius are going to need to know. And I'll need to control it so as not to scare them."

A dark look crossed his eyes, as if the mere name of the daemon sent him tumbling through a void of darkness and horror. I wasn't entirely convinced he'd shared the full extent of his knowledge of the Ram. My intuition hinted that there were missing fragments to the story.

Remus's eyes slid to mine. The morning light brushed over his piercing gaze. "Release it. I want to see."

Here I lay in the Lone Wolf's bed. I'd only wanted to repay him for the support he'd shown me in the short time we'd known each other. But I had not meant for our interaction to go in this direction. Especially when it came to sharing more about myself, to becoming more vulnerable.

"Why are you so intrigued by these shadows?"

Remus looked amused. "It's a part of you. I'm finding myself wanting to know more and more about you."

I could feel my cheeks warm under his intensity, and I turned away. I opened my hand, watching as a narrow stream of black smoke slithered out from the center of my palm. A hum resounded in my blood. *Powerful.* My eyes squinted as I noticed flecks of light entwined with the laces of dark aether. Dusts of light that looked like stars. I wasn't sure why I hadn't noticed this before. This didn't look like the aether the Order had conjured. *Beautiful.*

An involuntary gasp pulled from me as I released more plumes of shadows. They expanded, now drifting out from the skin of my upper body. Remus's hand slid along my arm. The rough pads of his fingers awoke blissful stings of awareness. White flames danced along his skin as his hand slid further down.

"Is this okay?" His question pressed against the back of my neck.

My head lolled back in answer, landing against the crook of his shoulder. His hard body melded against mine under the silk sheets.

More shadows pulled from me, and I gritted my teeth. The power danced through me. Heavy. I could feel the potential of its strength as if I were pressing a hand against its glass wall.

Remus held me as I continued to release my aether. Flickers of his moonlight flames joined my dark twilight in the air. My back arched, a foot running along the hairs of his legs.

He chuckled. The deep rasp of his voice shot a hot line down my back. "Keep moving like that and I will have to toss you off the bed."

I fought a smile. "What if I wanted you to toss me *on* the bed?"

Remus shifted in place. "You are trouble, lotus."

I felt something thick and hard rub against my ass. The sheer size of him made my mouth water, and I bit my lip. Needing to break away from this consuming moment, I flipped the sheets off me. Remus remained on the bed as my feet met the cold floor.

"How did you sleep?" I asked. One final desperate attempt to shift the climate of the room.

I glanced over my shoulder, and it was impossible not to notice the raised sheets below his waist. I briefly—very briefly—wondered what it would feel like to taste him. To wrap my lips around his . . .

I snapped my attention to Remus, his eyes already on me. There was a softness in his gaze. "The best I've slept in a long time. Thanks to you."

The lust slowly dissipated, only to be replaced by a kernel of warmth. I gave him a small smile. "Good. You deserve it. If you have trouble sleeping again, you know where to find me."

"Lotus, are you wanting to share a bed with me again? Just so you know, I have no objections to that."

I rolled my eyes, throwing a vulgar gesture over my shoulder as I left his room. The timbre of his chuckle tingled over my skin on the way out.

I was starting to genuinely care for the Lone Wolf. This should not have been happening and yet, I was finding myself more than willing to step deeper into the unknown with him.

We were dancing on a thin blade. A bloodied, cursed blade. Something deeper, more powerful below it. Not just carnal desire but . . . intimacy. I couldn't help but feel a sense of rightness at the possibility.

TWENTY-FIVE

Remus

The weight in my chest shifted. An unwinding of chains. It was slight, but it was enough for me to feel as if I was breathing for the first time. Diane may have left my room, but her presence stayed like a damn brand. I felt the rush of heat thicken my cock even more. *Think of something else, Remus. Swords, armor, bloodshed. Oh, gods. That doesn't help.*

My hand wrapped around my hard length, and I thought of her lips upon mine. My mouth and teeth marking her skin. The sounds she'd make as I feasted on her. My tongue lapping at her delicious core, getting drunk on her taste. Her fingers would rake through my hair, pulling hard as she grinded against my mouth. The heels of her feet would run down my back while begging me to let her come. I hissed between clenched teeth at the thought, still stroking myself. The image shifted to Diane on her knees before me. Her sensual lips wrapped around me, taking me to the back of her throat, bright eyes flitting upward as she continued to suck. My length in and out of her mouth. The sound of wet skin. I groaned as I came, the hot ropes of my release landing on my bare stomach.

Once I cleaned and changed into a dark tunic and fighting leathers, I glanced at the rumpled bed sheets. If someone had told me a month ago that I would be touching myself while fantasizing about a member of the Pack, I would've given a cruel laugh. *How absurd,* I would have thought. For so long, I'd been hiding behind my hate, directing it toward the Pack. But now, the tide of my tormented mind was changing. I didn't understand what it meant. I was still angry. I was still guilty. My desire for vengeance was still alive. And I had pushed away the Pack for a reason. A reason no one knew.

And yet, I was beginning to want more for myself.

My fingers brushed against the silk sheets. To be able to sleep in a bed again alone. I rubbed mindless circles on my chest, my feet steering me to the door. No. To be able to sleep in a bed again *with her*.

I would like that.

Later, it was made apparent to me that Caius had made plans with Theon for us to help the minotaurs with their construction projects. Those who'd lost their homes to the daemons were moving back to the central city. It was the prince who'd made the call to expand since the attacks had started. And as the minotaur king was still away, we would make ourselves useful.

Hours dragged as we lugged slabs of stone and brick alongside the minotaurs. Even the prince began plastering the mortar and stacking bricks to make a wall. The steady rhythm of the work was a welcome distraction. I hadn't seen much of Diane and the others as we all tended to our own duties. In the late afternoon, I found myself chopping wood under a small grove of trees. My muscles clenched with every swing of the axe.

Cato emerged from the trees. His dark, wild hair clung to his slick brow. The tattoos on his body peeked out from underneath his tunic. He was hauling a cart of unchipped wood. "You look like you're angry at it."

I frowned and gestured to the cart. "More for me?"

Cato dropped the handles of the cart and took the axe from me. "No. Sit back for a moment, Remus. I can handle this batch."

I leaned against a tree, drinking in the sight of the wood snapping under the axe's blade. The steel lacked its shine, but the force of Cato's swing was enough. I found the motion oddly satisfying.

"So, how come you and the Alpha avoid each other like the plague?" Cato went to retrieve another piece of wood, setting it on the raised platform.

I folded my arms, eyes on the log. "Why do you need to know?"

Cato rolled his shoulders before raising the axe. "I don't, but Caius intends to have you showcase your power. If we want to obtain support, we need to be a united front."

The next log was splintered in half.

"Obviously," I mused. "My decision to leave the Pack led to a terrible fallout between us. Caius and me."

Cato glanced at me. I saw understanding there. "Do what you will, but it may help both of you if there were a conversation, and some closure."

I offered a grim smile. "It's not that simple."

"It never truly is, but it may be worth it to try."

With that lingering thought, and after Cato finished his stack, we returned the wood to the construction sites. Cato's hand landed on my shoulder.

When I glanced back with a glare, he only gave me a wild smile. "The best of friends, Remus. You and I. Drusus will need to find a replacement."

I laughed at that. Cato patted my back as he went to help the other minotaurs. Somehow, when the sun descended to where the oceans lay, I found myself lingering against an empty cart close to Caius and the minotaur prince. Some of the families in the area had offered wooden bowls of cooked meat and potatoes. Thick wafts of rosemary made my mouth water, but even the delicious meal was not enough to distract me from the awkward silence. It was only me, the prince, his seemingly disgruntled guard, and Caius. The others were still at their designated sites, presumably eating or resting like we were.

Caius's voice almost caused me to jump. "What city did you say the king was visiting, your highness?"

Theon kept his eyes on his meal, pushing the potatoes around with his utensil. "I didn't. I said my father was visiting the other towns and cities in the outskirts in general."

The Alpha nodded his head and placed his empty plate down. He stretched his arms and returned to leaning against the cart opposite me. "Right," he continued. "And what of your mines? I'm assuming you've been amassing more weaponry, with everything that's been happening."

Theon slowly put his plate away. He leaned forward in his seat, placing his elbows on his knees. Those oxen eyes leveled with Caius. "Of course," he responded simply. The prince might not be betraying anything in his calm demeanor, but I caught how Octavius shifted on his feet, a guarded look on his face. I narrowed my eyes. Caius seemed to have also caught the shift.

Caius folded his arms, cocking his head. "Are we able to tour the mines? The minotaurs are famous for their ore and their skills as blacksmiths. I'd love to see them for myself."

Theon seemed to deliver a colder smile than intended, "No visitors are allowed in the mines for now." Octavius shot a nervous look toward him, but the prince remained unmoved. "We have blacksmiths in the central city. We can certainly have you shadow one, if they're willing."

Caius's eyes went to the hills in the distance. There was calculation behind that look. I was all too familiar with it. "I'd really love to see the mines."

Octavius cleared his throat. "Your Majesty, we must return. There are still some public matters to address."

Theon clapped his hands on his legs as he stood. "I'm sorry, Caius. Perhaps we can tour the mines at another time." He took a few steps on the dirt road before he stopped and looked over his shoulder. "I recommend staying away from the hills, for safety's sake." There was an odd glint in the prince's eyes that made me think he almost *wanted* us to defy him. Was the bastard taunting us?

Caius bowed his head as the prince and his guard left us alone. I had finished my meal and wiped my hands clean with a spare rag. My eyes wandered from the foundational structure we had finished, the rest to be done in the coming days. I caught Caius glancing my way before he turned his attention back to the hills.

"They're hiding something." His voice caused me to still.

Cato's previous words echoed in my thoughts, sinking into my bones. Godsdamn Fates. I rolled my shoulders. "The prince seemed a bit cold. A bit off script to his usual boyish, carefree demeanor. Did you notice the way the guard looked at the prince when you mentioned the mines?"

Caius startled at the sound of my voice. He looked at me like he was surprised I'd even responded, as if he'd thought he was alone. "It was an innocent question at first, but when I sensed how guarded they became, it had me curious to probe even further."

My brow pinched in thought as I ran a thumb over my lip. I remembered how prickly the prince was during our first encounter. How he'd gestured to the obliterated city. *What can we possibly offer you now, when we can't even save ourselves?*

"It makes me wonder," I started. Caius gave me a sidelong glance, waiting. "Where is the minotaur king, really?"

The descending sunlight caught on the ink along his neck and his partly shorn head. He arched a brow. "You think the prince lied to us?"

I shrugged. "It's a working theory."

His large arms were still folded, but his fingers began to tap at his arm. "So, what do you make of it?"

I tried not to consider how my chest tightened at Caius wanting more of my insight. "I think it's worth looking into," I responded.

Another thought came to mind, and whether it was Cato's words or some desperate action to repair the damage between the Alpha and me, I stood and began to walk toward the hills.

Caius's voice reached for me. "Where are you going?"

I turned, my hands outstretched as I continued walking backward. Dust speckled his cheekbones and fighting leathers. I flashed my teeth in a sly grin. "To the mines. How else are we going to find out what they're hiding?"

Caius's eyes widened slightly, but I saw the glimmer of excitement. He looked back toward the central city, but his feet were already moving to follow me.

A harsh laugh escaped me. "I knew you were still bad, Alpha."

Caius snorted. We stayed among the trees, away from prying eyes. As I walked with him, I felt a strong sense of nostalgia. Long ago, we were always at each other's side. Ravaging battlefields, plowing through bandit strongholds. Strategizing and hunting.

Caius and I followed the harsh smells of smoke and fire and the dark trails of wheels along the hills. When we arrived at the mines, there were some minotaurs pulling carts in and out, but there didn't seem to be much movement other than that.

Caius pointed toward the farthest entrance. "That one. I haven't seen anyone going in or out of it."

Firelight flickered within the depths of the entrance. My nose wrinkled at the fumes. I could hear distant sounds of wheels, rocks clattering and voices echoing out of the tunnels. Caius and I shared a look before I stepped in ahead of the Alpha.

The tunnel was deserted and dim from the torches that lined its cavernous walls. My fingers suddenly itched to reach for my sword. It was probably nothing, but the sensation nudged at my senses. The minotaurs had been prey to the Order's misgivings just as much as everyone else.

Wisps of cold air stroked my hair. A heavy weight drifted over me. It ran along the width of my shoulders like soulless fingers. It promised a life without pain, void of emotion. What would such a life be like?

A hand grabbed my shoulder, breaking the connection. My eyes snapped to Caius, who lifted a finger to his lips. The Order's aether. The Ram's power lurked here. There was a break in the tunnel ahead, and voices echoed from within the cave.

Caius prowled ahead of me. His hand hovered above the pommel of his sword as he edged toward the tunnel's end.

A deep voice made the loose rocks on the walls tremble. "I told you, there is no other ore of value within this region."

Another voice. Feminine and raspy. "Why do I sense a lie? Don't play me for a fool."

Caius stiffened at whatever he saw, so I peeked around him. I gritted my teeth. Our intuition had been right. The godsdamn minotaur king stood with a member of the Order, who wore the signature cloak and mask. The mask only hid the top portion of the woman's face, her red-painted lips exposed. Shadows danced and twirled around her body. The sight made me think of Diane, but I knew she was *not* like that. There was an evil way in which this female carried herself, even under all that attire. A promise of cruelty.

King Cain stood in the center of the space, more tunnels branching out behind him. The minotaur king was larger than most, his thick, gray skin corded with muscle. A pair of silver rings hung at the base of his horns, and a jeweled net hung over his long snout. Atop his head was a gnarled crown of obsidian, much like Theon's. The king looked quite comfortable working alongside the Order.

Rage quaked through my bones. Hadn't the minotaurs allied themselves with the wolves? I remembered the days when my pater had ventured to visit Cain, when he'd formalized the partnership between the two Olympian races.

"Traitors," I hissed quietly.

I felt Caius straighten beside me. He ran a hand down his tunic, and adjusted his leather bracers. "Well, it's only a matter of time before they sense us. There's no point in hiding."

I unsheathed my sword. "After you?"

Caius's dark eyes glimmered as he removed his blade from where it hung over his back. "I think assholes can go first, today."

I rolled my eyes and strolled into the clearing. "Rumor has it," I said aloud. The minotaur king and the woman of the Order jerked their heads to me. I pointed my blade to Cain. "That you were touring the outlying cities. Tending to them. But I had a feeling that was false. Am I right, Your Highness?"

Cain's eyes widened as he looked from the blade to me. Recognition flared. "You're the spitting image of him. What is Anthony's son doing in my mines?"

The female sneered, red lips spreading into a wicked glee. "Oh, you've been caught, your highness."

"Shut up," Cain growled.

I noticed Caius hadn't followed. Bastard, what was he plotting? I decided to trust in the trajectory of this encounter and follow my instinct.

"Why?" I snarled. "Why betray your people?"

The female laughed, the sound void of real emotion. "Poor Cain. What a conundrum you are in."

The minotaur king suddenly looked tired. A pained look flashed across his face. "I *am* helping them."

I snorted in disbelief and disgust.

The woman must not have seen me properly from underneath the mask, because she suddenly gasped excitedly. "Oh, I recognize you. I was there when you brought my king back from his prison realm. He's been waiting for you."

Waiting, not looking. The change of words sent a chill down my spine. The Ram was biding its time, and now I was beginning to understand why. He must truly be gathering his forces.

Her red lips split into a vicious smile. "Did you come alone?"

I didn't indulge her as I raised my sword. Shadows materialized before her, charging forward like sentient beings. I pivoted away from the strike, flipping a knife out of my belt toward the Order member's head. She laughed as the knife was slapped away by a hand of black smoke. The woman's attention was on me as Caius's figure appeared behind her. He slashed his blade across her back. She merely hissed even though blood began to fall from her torn robes like rain. Perhaps the Ram's aether really did protect his followers from pain.

The female shrieked, twisting around to face both of us as shadows shot against Caius's chest, throwing him onto his back.

My blood went cold. "Caius!" I was ready to rush to him when he raised a hand and pushed himself up.

The woman tilted her head, the mask following the movement, making her look more monster than mortal. "Caius? So, this is the Alpha?" She ran a pale hand through the air and wicked blades appeared. "I didn't know the Alpha wolf was so handsome. Maybe I'll have my way with you before slitting that pretty neck."

The minotaur king was roaring. "You fools! Leave!"

The woman angled her head toward Cain. "Oh, that almost sounded like you care what happens to the wolves. Will they care in return? It's unfortunate this was all for naught, as you've lost your value to us. We can't have you blabbing to anyone, can we?" she crooned.

She threw the daggers, not at us but at the king. Shit. If anything happened to him, it would be detrimental to what we were trying to accomplish. The Order already held the upper hand in the grand scheme of things.

And that is why Caius started to run. He sprinted toward Cain to save the traitorous horned bastard and was now within the blades' trajectory.

No. Not Caius.

Blinding light erupted from me as every fiber of my being was torn open by white flames. Wild energy intercepted the aether-made daggers, making the Order member's shadows disappear.

Her jaw dropped as she stared at the white flames that licked at my skin. I could taste her wariness as I stalked toward her.

My lips curled into a sneer. "This is your end."

The woman began to laugh, a morbid resolve seeming to hold her in place. As if she was accepting her fate. "I can see why the daemon king wants you. With you at his will, he can rule this realm. Clean it of its iniquity."

She jerked as my nails elongated into claws and sunk deep into her chest. An agonized wail rose from her mouth as my flames spread to her skin. White fire ate at her flesh, and I held her as she burned, until her screams were no more and her body slipped from my grasp.

I gazed at her lifeless body with the same empty void I had felt when I killed those of the Order. A chasm had opened in my heart. "Ironic. For someone who was promised a life without pain, that seemed to hurt."

The white flames caressed my skin. I exhaled. Unfathomable energy, so potent that it vibrated against my bones, rippled through my blood. I was falling deeper and deeper into its lethal embrace.

Until I heard the deep, guttural voice of the minotaur king. "Dear gods."

Cain was on his knees, gaping at me. Caius approached me warily. "Remus?" he asked, as if unsure it was still me.

I blinked and willed the flames to quiet. Caius watched me and jumped to catch my arm when I stumbled back. There was a tremble in the king's shoulders as he shook his head.

"No," he moaned. "No, no, no. What have you done?"

I growled. "We just fucking saved you."

"Remus," Caius snapped.

Cain groaned, his face falling into his hands. "You don't understand. I didn't want to work with the Order. They threatened to continue killing my people if I didn't comply. They took control of the mines, taking ore for themselves."

Caius hissed between his teeth. "The Order has been taking your ore?"

The king growled. "The Order has been amassing an army. They have a fucking battalion behind these hills. And they said that if anything were to happen, they would unleash it upon my kingdom! You fools doomed them!"

Caius cursed, placing a hand over his mouth. He snapped his fingers. "No, Cain. The Order is not going to do shit. We are going to fight."

The king laughed in disbelief. "How do you expect us to win? There isn't enough time to prepare."

Determination flashed in Caius's darkened gaze. "Yes, there is. I know you were doing what you thought best, but your kingdom wasn't truly free, nor were they safe. This is the only way."

The minotaur king gritted his teeth in a pained expression. My chest tightened. Caius and I looked at each other. The chances were slim. But the daemons would be heading our way, toward the city of the minotaurs. This was a pivotal moment for the Olympians to unite their forces and kingdoms, and I recalled Caius's vision. It was coming to fruition.

Twenty-Six

Remus

The city fell into shock on seeing their king walk amongst their dirt roads and wooden stalls. Cain revealed that he had been held hostage for weeks. The sacrifice their king made had been made known among the minotaurs. I could understand the dire situation, the desperate call for survival. Though a part of me wanted to scream at the knowledge that the Order had managed to take enough ore to support an army. The Ram was becoming stronger.

The king walked into his home, the minotaur guards blinking as if they couldn't believe their king actually stood before them. Prince Theon was seated at the dining table, reviewing some pieces of parchment, when his attention snapped up. His eyes flashed with emotion. The chair toppled to the ground as Theon jumped up, breaking into a run to Cain.

"Father."

Cain caught his son. The massive minotaur shook as he slid to the ground, rocking Theon in his burly arms. "My boy." The king tightened his embrace. "My boy."

The wolves and Laelia were at the table, their gazes focused on the scene as Caius relayed our findings.

Theon broke away from his father's embrace, his young oxen face unashamedly bearing the overwhelming emotion of reuniting with his father. "I have to admit that I had hoped you and Remus would go to the mines. I knew you were suspicious, yet I was afraid of telling you the truth of the situation. The Order had threatened us, and many of our soldiers have fallen to their blades and daemons. I knew we couldn't get out of this on our own."

Cain leaned back, observing his son with a rekindled brightness. "Son, you practically orchestrated this. Didn't you?"

Anger flashed over the prince's eyes, reflecting the fire that burned at the hearth. "I knew that something needed to be done. I thank the Fates for bringing the wolves to our doorstep. Now, with them at our side, we stand a chance."

The king stood. The shadow of his height crawled along the floor. "You may be a better ruler than I ever was."

Caius flinched with a hiss. I jerked my head to him and saw him clutching his side. He fumbled with the straps of his fighting leathers, and Diane stepped in to help. Once the attire was removed, Caius lifted his tunic to reveal deep purple bruising all over his torso and side.

"I didn't feel it till now," he muttered.

Diane headed in the direction of her room. "I'll get some ointment."

Marcus was already moving and paused at Caius's side, his blue eyes bright like ice. "The evening is darkening. I can help evaluate the city and see what we can use to our advantage before the daemons arrive."

Theon took a step forward. "Octavius and I will go with you. We know these lands and can help find a suitable place to station our army."

Caius gripped Marcus's forearm. "I trust your judgment, Marcus. Do what you think is right."

Marcus beckoned to Atticus and Cato. "Let's go. Drusus, you and Remus help organize the minotaurs within the city borders."

Once Marcus and the others had left, Caius looked to Laelia. Tiredness stretched along the width of his mouth and the creases at his eyes. He still looked young, but he was exhausted. Utterly exhausted. "I hate to ask."

The harpy held up a hand, her wings ruffling. "Do not worry, I will send for aid. You wolves always slow me down, anyway."

A grateful smile took the Alpha's lips. "Thank you, Laelia. Fly hard and safe. Come back to us."

Diane emerged from the hall just as Laelia prepared to leave. The she-wolf and harpy strode toward each other, pressing their brows together as I'd seen them do before.

Once the door closed behind Laelia's powerful wings, Diane rushed to Caius's side. Her fingers dabbed the ointment onto his wound. Caius grunted, but eventually leaned into her touch. The massive, corded muscle of his arm brushed against her.

The Alpha lifted his eyes to Diane and offered her a genuine smile. Diane winked. The interaction was clearly platonic, but the image of them sitting there gave me pause. An Alpha and a powerful she-wolf. A male who was self-sacrificing and noble, a female with a heart of iron and gold. It made me think of how imperfect I was. How unworthy I was to even wish for an alternative future. To desire for more.

I ran a hand over my face and followed Drusus out of the room. I would bury these impossible but growing hopes, shove them deep within me where every other dark truth was hiding. And I would lose myself in the inevitable battle, dive into the bloodbath, unleash every emotion in the fight, and allow the red to stain my skin as it had already stained my soul.

Almost another week passed and the time dragged like waves clawing at the sand. The world fell silent to the aether that was growing hungry in my veins. Tents had been pitched in the land between the hills and the minotaur city. Smoke curled from their fires. Atticus and other scouts had gone in search of the forces that King Cain had informed us of. That had been three days ago.

There was nothing to do but wait. Sunset stretched its golden wings, bathing the hills in its embrace. I stood at the camp's edge. The Alpha was at my side, his arms folded and tattooed skin taut with tension.

"A wonder," Caius said. "The way our paths have been drawn and twisted."

My jaw worked as my thoughts mulled over his words. "The Fates must be having a laugh seeing our courses change with every minute decision we make."

I felt Caius's gaze on me, a weight to it. It bared over my shoulders, and I closed my eyes as he spoke.

"I need to know what happened to her." His voice lowered, turning into a plea. The sound dug a dagger in my chest. "*Please*, Remus."

My stomach twisted. Words got stuck in my throat. Caius, the wolf warrior who was thrown into the role of Alpha months after losing the love of his life. I wanted to scream at myself, at the part of me that was chained by grief and guilt.

"Did our friendship mean so little?" Caius asked.

My eyes opened as the deadly mask of indifference fell over me. Hiding the anguish underneath. I steered my gaze to Caius, and I almost wished I hadn't. *No*, I told myself. *Look at the male you're torturing with your cowardice.*

Caius watched my face. His eyes pooled with sorrow, but there was also a sharpness there. As if he could see right through the mask.

"You deserve to know," I replied.

My voice was immovable, coated with steel and ice. *Please*, I begged myself. *Tell him.* My lungs constricted, and I fought the urge to hurl. Instinct told me to shield the way I was crumbling. The truth of Helena's death. The reasons behind my becoming the Lone Wolf. A storm raged inside me. I took too long.

Caius released an angry breath. The anger of a broken man. "I still love her. And you. I need to know what happened to my *wife*."

Numbness dulled the storm. My lips parted. "You got married."

Caius nodded slowly. "Helena and I were going to tell you and then hold a formal ceremony, but she wanted it to be secret at the beginning. Something just for us. Helena also knew your pater would be difficult. She said you would understand that."

That I did. But an onslaught of emotions roared at me. Caius was my brother-in-law. Helena had been married and happy. I needed to say something. *Anything.*

"I'm sorry," I breathed.

Pain flashed across Caius. He gritted his teeth, but whatever he saw in my gaze had him taking a step back. He turned away. Something wild and panicked stirred inside me.

"I love you too," I said. Caius stopped and I continued. "You deserve better. From me, especially. You both did."

Caius didn't move for a few breaths. The soft movement of his back revealed that he was fighting a war similar to my own. He cast a glance over his shoulder. A tortured look. He hadn't got what he'd been looking for, but he accepted it for the moment.

"I'm trying," I managed to say.

I wasn't sure if he was able to hear the plea underneath the cold-ness. The damn mask I couldn't seem to withdraw. The Alpha's jaw ticked, and he walked away from me.

I don't know how much time passed before I felt her presence. Diane stepped to my side. Her black hair was pulled back by a band, kohl rimming her eyes. Fighting leathers and a breastplate gilded her body. The tattoo of a laurel wreath wrapped around her arm.

We didn't speak, finding comfort in the silence. I felt the soft strums of her aether caress my skin. Like she could sense my distress. I welcomed it, was grateful for it.

Light turned to dark. Distant thunder echoed in the earth from beyond the hills. A deep horn bellowed. Atticus bounded into view, the beige wolf sprinting down the hillside with the minotaur scouts not far behind him.

The daemons were here.

TWENTY-SEVEN

Diane

The hills looked like dark mounds of ash. Soon the air would taste like death. I exhaled.

Atticus had arrived and shifted into his human form. The news was grave, but we would give everything. Fight for more time until Laelia arrived with reinforcements.

My brothers surrounded me, their bodies clasped in armor and steel. The moon was bright, silver ribbons of light that touched tattooed, sun-kissed skin. When it was dark and the angle was right, their eyes would reflect like the common animal. Like a band of ungodly beings, we stalked closer to the base of the hill, the minotaurs and their king at our heel. Our Alpha at the helm.

Marcus began to speak strategy. "We will lead the second line of defense in our wolf forms. Caius will be at the front line with the king. Diane will be ahead of both lines."

I grinned. Excitement stirred the aether in my veins. I willed the shadows into silence. I began to inspect my fingernails, feigning boredom, and whirled my dagger with my other hand. "Of course, the males should stand back and let the female take charge."

A streak of amusement lit Marcus's eyes. "You will also have Remus."

My heart skittered, both with bitterness and intrigue. I shouldn't have been surprised, though. Remus's power was the catalyst, the blade that Caius would use for all to see. A symbol that we stood a chance.

Marcus barked a laugh at my pout. "No one is going to steal your thunder, Diane."

I sheathed my dagger and crossed my arms. "No one would be able to anyway."

The comment earned a chuckle from Atticus. He ran a hand over his jaw. "Is it a good idea to have Remus, whom the Ram is very keen on having for itself, on the front lines?"

Marcus ran a tongue over his teeth. "We need to show our strength to the minotaurs. Caius was very clear on that. Once the second lines move forward, we reconvene and cover him."

The first line of defense began the march. Caius and Cain bled within the forefront as they led the minotaur army. I felt my arms reach for my brothers. Their grasps tightened around my shoulders. Marcus bumped his brow against my own.

"Give them pain," Drusus grinned.

"But leave some for me." Cato winked.

Remus waited. Wrath and vengeance incarnate underneath the starlight. The breeze whistled softly and brushed some dark strands out from the knot he'd tied. His broad shoulders were draped in fighting leathers, an ivory tunic underneath.

The minotaurs parted for us like rippling water. I felt Caius and Cain's heavy gazes at our backs as we wandered farther ahead of the first line.

Remus's dark voice rolled over my shoulders. "Funny how everyone believes *I* am the one with unbelievable power when you stand amongst them. With an aether that knows no bounds."

I could hear the smile in his voice, but I didn't look his way. "I don't need to release the aether in my veins in order to feel validation."

"No, you don't," he agreed. "But you should be honest with yourself. Embrace everything that makes you *you*."

I suddenly felt flustered. "Enough. I'd rather stand here in silence before the daemons arrive."

Remus didn't respond. He stood at my side. It brought a sense of familiarity, like I'd experienced this before. Remus and I standing before a battlefield. The Ram's vision. There was a sour feeling in the pit of my stomach at the thought.

It didn't take long before a score of screeches carried through the light winds. The hills came alive. Like rippling blackwater, the daemons' languid forms appeared over the hills' edge. Thunder rolled through the ground. My boot slid over the dirt.

"There's perhaps a few hundred," Remus calculated.

Three figures emerged from the hilltops. Riding on horses, their black cloaks billowed in the air like ribbons. I could see the faraway glint of their masks. The Order had arrived.

"The Ram isn't with them," I observed. "We would've sensed a greater energy."

Remus cursed under his breath.

I slowly cocked my head, staring at the rider in the middle and the wolf mask he wore. He was the one who was always alongside the Ram, almost like a second-in-command.

I jerked a chin toward the wolf-masked member of the Order. "Look, I think it's your friend."

Remus snarled. "That's the bastard who took my blood in order to summon the Ram."

I stared at the darkened expression that loomed over the Lone Wolf. My fists clenched. My previous agitation shifted, directing all its strength toward the Order that had violated both of us. The daemons were fast approaching. King Cain shouted a command, and the first line fell into position several yards behind us.

The aether in my blood stirred. A laugh escaped my lips at the sensation.

I flashed a wicked grin to Remus. "Watch this."

The Lone Wolf stared as I took a few steps forward. I planted my legs firmly, tension bracketing my muscles. Power purred loudly against my skin. The daemons had now reached the base of our hill. Not yet. Ten more seconds . . . five seconds . . . Arms hanging at my sides, my palms opened toward the army of demons.

Now.

The vibrating hum paused, followed by a sharp blast. An unseen

206 | JESSICA J. AYALA

wall of aether stretched out before me, extending along the length of our forces. Faint, pale blue lines rippled through the seams. A she-wolf's aether unleashed.

With my teeth clenched and a roaring in my ears, I willed the wall to move. It charged forward, ripping the grass of the hillside in its wake as the daemon army continued to run down.

Five, four, three, two, and—

The world flashed in electric blue and black blood. Screeches ripped through the night. The first line of daemons that met the wall exploded in heaps of bone and gore. Others began to claw at it, masses piling on each other, pressuring the aether to crack.

I closed my hands. The wall was on the urge of breaking. It was enough for now. I glanced at Remus and cackled at his baffled look.

"Can you do any better?" I crooned.

Remus flashed his teeth, eyes brightening with wicked glee. "Step aside, she-wolf."

Another crack of blue light, as if the god Jupiter had torn through the skies with his thunderbolts. Daemons ripped through the wall. My power disintegrated into wisps, and the daemons continued their charge.

Remus ran a thumb over his lip as he prowled to my side. Tendrils of silvery white danced over his skin as his power began to rise. Curls of white smoke seeped out of the corners of his eyes and mouth. He lifted from the ground. Threads of jeweled fire materialized around him.

My lips parted at the terrifying sight.

With a roar and a focused sweep of his arm, an enormous arc of blinding flames appeared overhead. It fell upon the creatures, crashing in vicious waves, engulfing the daemons with its burning touch.

Remus's body was still aflame as he slowly returned to the ground. His gaze settled on the obliteration before him. It wasn't the lifeless look I'd seen in my nightmares. I could've laughed with joy. Twisted, malicious joy. *Come for us, daemon king.*

Green eyes moved to me. His voice was a humming, a song that my inner aether harmonized to. "Like what you see?"

Gods, yes. I smirked and unsheathed my sword. "I thought the floating was a little dramatic."

He began to look sheepish. "That was an accident."

I choked on a laugh and started to run toward the hill. "I wonder who can kill more daemons?"

Remus laughed as he shifted. The black wolf ripped through the grass. His snout crushed against my abdomen, flinging me onto his back.

I swiped my blade downward on the daemons that attacked his sides. A deep howl penetrated the starry sky, and I grinned. It was a show of power and hope. The minotaurs and wolves roared and bellowed, weapons banging against shields. Caius and Cain hollered the command, and the first line was unleashed.

Army met army. The gutting of flesh and cries of the fallen suffocated the air. Though Remus and I managed to obliterate the first half of the Order's forces, daemons seemed to be sprouting like wildflowers. The Order riders remained at the top of the hillside in front of us, merely watching the bloodshed at their feet.

Minotaurs swung their axes and war hammers, the sound of bones being crushed following. I spotted daemons attacking in groups. The multitude of fangs and claws were enough to overpower the minotaurs.

The command for the second line blared. A tumult of snarls and howls followed as my brothers in their wolfskin careened down the hill. Fang met flesh. Claw punctured skin. We gained ground, the daemons seeming to diminish as we fought our way through.

My eyes went to the Order riders. The one who wore the wolf mask raised his hand. The stars themselves seemed to shy away from the gesture, clouds covering the sky, and the other two riders spurred their horses to a canter. The horses were halfway down when the *sky* came alive.

I couldn't see what it was at first. Dotted figures blended in with the night. Then the crescent glow of hungry eyes. How the dark sky *rained.*

I felt the blood drain from my face. "Winged daemons."

Moonlight reflected on the veined velvet of their batlike wings.

Their cries were the sound of a thousand voices. I shouted as one swooped me up from Remus's back. The black wolf roared and leaped in the air, snapping his teeth. I felt the graze of them at my leg before I was taken to the sky. The battlefield below grew smaller, and I cried out as the winged daemon's claws dug into my arm.

I bucked and kicked. The daemon banked, turning to where the wolf-masked rider stood waiting. No, no, no. Remus followed us. Had he noticed how the daemon was practically leading him to the Order rider? I had a feeling he had but simply didn't care. Remus ripped through the swarm of daemons. Yes, they were luring him in and capturing me in the process.

"Remus, stop!" I shouted, but my screams were drowned out in the wind from the terrifying height.

My limbs stopped moving as the aether called to me through my veins. I willed the energy, and my power broke through the daemon's grasp on me. The creature shrieked, and I fell. The stars could do nothing but watch as I plummeted to the ground.

The daemon above me unfurled its wings and dove for me. I gripped my blade. Power exploded, pushing at the daemon until it was forced to fly below me. I grunted as I speared the daemon's back with my blade in an attempt to steer it as we continued to fall. It couldn't fly anymore, and I noticed that my aether had ripped through the velvet of its wings with invisible claws. Shit.

The ground grew nearer and nearer. I released a flood of aether toward the ground in an attempt to slow us down. Bone and blood splattered over my face as the daemon crashed, and I flew away from the force. I rolled, pain surging up my body. I laid in the grass until a pair of fangs hovered above me.

"*Fuck, Diane,*" Remus snarled. "*That was risky.*"

He helped me to my feet with his snout. I groaned. "I survived, didn't I?"

Screams chilled my skin. The two Order riders that had come down the hillside somehow didn't look from this world. They honed in on the minotaurs with jagged blades made of stolen ore, cutting through the minotaurs like weeds. Daemons created a pathway for the riders, who prowled closer to Cain and Caius.

Remus snarled, pushing me with his muzzle. *"On me, Diane!"*

Pain screamed through my muscles as I straddled the black wolf. The moment my fingers curled in his thick fur, he plunged back into the battlefield. We could do nothing but watch, no matter how fast Remus ran.

A rider lifted their sword and aimed for the minotaur king's neck, both Cain and the Alpha deeply distracted by the battle. Theon slipped through the gap between the Alpha and the king, his arm raised, his blade violently colliding with that of the Order member. The rider swung once more, and the blade sliced through Theon's abdomen.

No.

The cries of the minotaur king—of a pater—pierced the realms of the gods. The king held his son's body close, blood pouring through Theon's hands as he pressed them against the wound. I couldn't see what happened next as Octavius roared, stepping in front of his king and prince. His war hammer rang against the rider's blade again and again until it finally crashed against the head of the rider.

The daemons responded with angry shrills. Caius ran ahead, his white paws gouging the second rider's neck. My brothers were also in the fray. Daemons plunged their teeth and claws into the wolves. Our forces were strained.

Shadows pressed against my skin. *Do not cower. Conquer the fear. Battle is my mantle. Death poised in every breath. I am a wolf.*

Dark twilight smoke simmered from my skin. Remus halted. His hairs bristled at the power. At me.

"You are strength," he said.

It was all he needed to say. My head snapped back, eyes meeting the night sky. And the shadows roared. A wave of darkness blanketed the starry sky like a black mist, swallowing the battlefield whole. Many daemons suffocated, their insides burned. I felt everything, every death, through the seams of my star-speckled aether. I could feel my brothers' shocked gazes on me, but I didn't look their way.

Remus pawed the ground, white flames licking between his fangs.

He roared and opened his jaws to unleash a plume of fire, burning a row of daemons to ash. The smoke willed away, and the battle paused. The last Order rider, wolf mask gleaming, stood among the ashes.

His voice was a brewing storm. "The daemon king seeks his claim. By the power of those two wolves will his reign return once more. If you come voluntarily, fewer of your allies will fall."

He began to saunter through the burned pathway. Shadows of his own making unfurled, spearing the minotaurs that tried to close in. Remus paused. He was considering this.

My hands tightened into fists, gripping his fur. "You will not give up yet," I seethed.

Remus said nothing. I couldn't blame him, though. Surrendering myself to spare the others had passed through my thoughts, but I knew better. Violence would persist even if we surrendered.

A deep roar erupted in the distance, startling those around us. Powerful. Majestic. And another. The sound of howling.

Wolves spilled out of the woodlands. The treetops rustled as wings appeared. Shimmering colors that beamed even in the night. Laelia led her warrior sisters into battle, their war cries rattling the moon.

They'd made it. The minotaurs cheered as they raised their weapons to continue the onslaught, with the wolves and harpies joining the forces. The wolf-masked rider didn't stop walking. Winged daemons gravitated to his sides as he neared.

Caius snapped his teeth to grab Remus's attention—his and every one of my brothers'. "*You and Diane need to leave. All of you.*"

"What?" Marcus snapped.

The Alpha bristled. "*The Ram is gaining the upper hand. We cannot, by any means, allow it to obtain more power. We have reinforcements now, we can handle this, but all of you need to be far from here. Guard Remus and Diane. Run. Run till blood breaks through your paws.*"

When we didn't move, the Alpha snarled. "Go!"

Remus hesitated. A look passed between the two wolves. Something like sadness and regret. Marcus barked an order, breaking the hold, and we ran for the trees.

Rose-gold wings banked for us. Laelia unsheathed her dual blades. "What is going on?"

"*We have to get Remus, and apparently Diane too, out of there,*" Marcus barked, eyes sliding to me. "*And you better explain yourself.*"

Remus growled at Marcus's tone. My fingers gripped his fur tighter as we plummeted through the trees. That was a conversation for later.

We fled deeper into the woods. The sounds of hooves and high-pitched screeches tailed us.

TWENTY-EIGHT

Remus

"**B**e ready," Marcus warned.

Daemons that could *fly*. They looked similar to the daemons we had been dealing with, with faces that resembled the skull of a snake and red crescent eyes. Their bodies, though, looked more humanoid, with batlike wings. This was the Ram's doing. It had probably managed to use enough energy to bring creatures back from the same prison realm he had escaped from.

The Ram was an ancient being, had once wandered the realms with the gods and goddesses. As such, its aether was different from ours. The aether in the mortal realm was more limited in nature whereas the Ram's was much more akin to that of a god. Well, until me. And Diane. Whatever the Ram sensed in Diane's aether intrigued it enough to want her. The mere thought sent my blood boiling.

My lungs pumped harder, legs ran faster. Till my paws bled. My thoughts went to Caius with a painful jump in my chest. He would be fine. He had to be.

Trees parted, and I saw the stars greeting us. I cursed. *"Wait, there's a cliff—"*

Diane's shout echoed through my bones. She must've sensed the attack before it happened. The ground exploded beneath us, and I felt the impact of someone's aether against me as my body flew.

Drusus roared as the winged daemons emerged from the dark, their claws nearly grazing Cato and Atticus. Atticus leapt in the air, his jaws wrapping around the neck of a daemon before slamming it to the ground. Laelia flew between the trees, spun her blades, and cut down the other flying creatures.

Diane stirred beside me. I crouched around her body as she came to. Daemons continued to spill out of the tree lines. They avoided me and Diane, herding the other wolves farther away. Shit.

Marcus also seemed to catch their intention. *"Regroup! To Remus and Diane!"*

The rider stepped into the starlight. The copper snout of the wolf mask glinted wickedly, and his black cloak unfurled behind him like a graceful shadow. The daemons continued to push the others away, allowing the male to approach us.

"Why must this be more difficult than it has to be?" he asked with a sigh.

My brow furrowed at the sound of his voice. A whip of dark aether appeared in the rider's hand. He swung it toward Diane. I whirled around, curving my body over her as a sharp burn lashed at my back. Diane flinched, her eyes wide with horror.

The male's voice returned. He almost sounded angry. "I thought the Lone Wolf would be stronger."

My legs slid as I felt another sting of the rider's whip. The crack of flesh almost caused me to collapse. But I would take this so she wouldn't have to. Angry lashes burned my back as the Order rider continued to whip me. I heard Drusus scream my name, but he and the others were held back, fighting the daemons.

Skin broke, but I refused to cry out. This follower of the Order would not hear the voice of my pain. When the next lash of the whip came for me, tongues of silver flames formed between my fangs as I snatched the whip midair.

Smoke curled around the Order rider. "There's that power. Your king wants it."

My claws dug into the ground as I yanked the whip from his grasp. "That daemon is no king of mine."

The rider chuckled as he willed dark aether from his hands. My power clashed with his, and it shook the cliff's edge. Shit. Cracks crawled underneath us, and a portion of the cliff began to fall. Some of the daemons that were within range fell as well. I shouted for Diane to run—she was too close to the edge, but it was too late. In a desperate attempt to survive, one daemon clawed at the air before sinking its teeth in Diane's thigh. Her wild scream pierced my heart. A fucking terrible sound that I never wanted to hear again. The daemon held onto her as it toppled, and she lost her footing.

Diane's eyes met mine, and the world seemed to suck in a breath. The ground crumbled underneath her, taking her and the daemon over the cliff.

My heart stopped.

Maeruu's roar ripped through the air, echoing the words trapped in my lungs. "NO!"

I didn't care about anything. Not about the Ram, the Order, the daemons, the Pack, nor the godsdamn war. Only one purpose drove me in that moment.

I jumped.

The wind howled, whipping angrily at my eyes as I fell. The cliff rushed past me as the vast darkness taunted me from below. Diane was fighting the daemon, punching and kicking until the creature fell into the dark, empty oblivion.

Diane cried out when she saw me. Her hand reached for me. I felt the light brush of her fingertips, and I swerved my body around to encase her. Logical reasoning didn't exist anymore, and I did everything in my power to give *her* a chance.

Silver rimmed her eyes. *Please,* she seemed to breathe.

I closed my eyes and waited for death.

TWENTY-NINE

Remus

Death didn't come. Not yet. Sharp bites of icy water greeted us as we plunged into a river, the current dragging us away like lost souls to the Underworld. Air was kicked out of my lungs. Pain was temporarily numbed by adrenaline and shock.

Hands tugged at the nape of my neck, and my eyes snapped open. Still in my wolf form, I could fight the current. Diane's grip tightened, and I clawed my way to the surface. The moment my paws reached the riverbank, I shifted and felt Diane slip from me. I groaned at the pull of skin from my back.

The world spun for a moment before landing on piercing golden eyes. My name echoed from her mouth. Water ran in rivulets down her blanched skin. She was in shock. It was clear from the tremble in her fingers. When she winced and I saw the lines of blood down her thigh, I snapped into focus.

I lurched upward and clenched my teeth in pain. Diane's hands swooped underneath my arms. "Stay with me, Remus. We need to move. We're easy targets out in the open."

"You're hurt," I rumbled, reaching for her.

Diane batted me off. "No, *you* are hurt. I can manage."

She slapped my hands again at my next attempt to help her. With a frustrated growl, I let the she-wolf guide me into the woodlands.

My thoughts were a blurred mess as they went to Drusus and

the others. What had happened after we fell from the cliffside? Had they survived?

The fact that we'd had to flee from a battle soured my stomach. Reinforcements had arrived, and I knew we could've won the battle. I was confident Caius then would have secured the minotaurs' support to join the war. Though if something had happened to the minotaur prince, I was unsure how the king would react.

I lifted my feet to step over a low-hanging branch, and a hiss escaped my teeth. Diane's grip squeezed on my arms. We managed to slip into a tight group of trees. Leaves and branches hugged the space, creating the semblance of a nook.

Diane and I settled in between the gnarled roots that crawled all over the forest ground. We were silent as we began to remove our armor and fighting leathers. Diane winced again, and without a word I reached for the leather of her sheathed sword, lifting it from the belt.

My fingers found the straps of her breast plate. I untied it and raised the armor from her arms. Diane didn't hesitate to help me loosen my armor pieces. We continued to help one another strip, avoiding the wounds and bruised muscles until we were both in our tunics.

Diane's ivory tunic was drenched and plastered to her flushed skin. The nasty wound on her thigh was bright and angry. Growling to myself, I ripped the seams at the end of my tunic to make a few strips of cloth. I wrapped the gash, red already seeping through the fabric. My fingers ran over her arms as I inspected her for any other wounds. Diane relaxed against the trunk of a tree, her eyes catching my movements.

She snatched my hand. "You don't have to dote on me."

I shook my head, ignoring how my back hollered in pain. "I don't have to—I *want* to help you."

Diane scoffed, her brow bunched. "That bastard *whipped* you. What he did was so vile, and I want to wring that mask from his face and bash him with it."

My lips twitched, threatening a smirk. "So violent," I murmured.

I brushed the damp strands from her face. She flinched and when

I paused, her face seemed to flush. "Sorry," she mumbled. "I'm not used to others taking care of me like this."

This fierce and independent woman. I was overcome with the need to show her what it could feel like to be taken care of.

Diane refrained from looking at me. Perhaps she was feeling embarrassed. "Change the subject, please."

I hummed a deep sound, obliging her. "If I didn't know any better, I'd say you're protective of me."

Even under the dark of the night I could see her rolling her eyes. "You wish."

There were no other wounds worth being concerned over. Once I was satisfied, I pushed myself to my feet. "I'm going to scout the area. I'd rather not have daemon teeth in my neck before morning."

Diane narrowed her eyes. "Can you sit back for a moment? You are injured, Remus. At least let me take a look."

Now I did smirk as I started to retreat into the trees. "Don't worry, my lotus, you'll be able to have your hands all over me in a moment."

She groaned. "Never mind. I hope you trip."

I chuckled as I returned to the quiet of the forest. It seemed absent of daemons and murderous mortals. I stood at the forest's edge with my eyes on the river. The Fates must be applauding us. We should've died tonight, but the realms had other plans.

It was *too* silent. I strained to hear a wolf's howl, anything, but I couldn't. It would most likely take us a day or two to find a way back up the cliff. With our injuries, maybe longer. It would be easier and more worth our energy to simply return to the Pack haven. Caius and the others would head there eventually, and it was where our armies would gather anyway. But I didn't want to risk luring the Order back to the haven.

I rubbed my eyes with the heel of my palm. Perhaps my decision to jump off the cliff had changed the Fates' course. Perhaps us fleeing the battle had doomed our futures. And perhaps all of this had been for naught, and the Fates were paving our paths, laughing.

Thirty

Diane

Underneath the canopy of branches there was very little protection from stray droplets that sprinkled over my hair and face. I welcomed the chill. Anything to distract me from the pain and the ache.

Everything had turned to shit. There had been some success, but the casualties, the loss . . . I wished I was there to help instead of being in hiding. We were no longer the hunters but the hunted. It wasn't the first time I'd been separated from my brothers during a job. We always had contingency plans, and I was scolding us in my mind for not being more prepared. But it was either return to the Pack or continue fleeing in the hopes of the Order straying farther and farther away from the haven and Roman cities.

I was not so foolish to think we would be able to avoid going back home forever. The Pack was preparing for war. We would have to return eventually.

Remus had thrown himself in front of the whippings to protect me. Every lash had resounded in my chest. I feared that if it hadn't been for the cliff falling apart, we would now be in the Order's grasp.

My skin tingled, remembering Remus's softness when he removed my armor. How uncharacteristic of him. That was something else that had unsettled me. The kindness and affection. It had whispered to me with every brush of his fingers and dip of his brow as he examined my injuries.

My cheeks warmed, and a heat coiled in my lower abdomen. I fought the urge to rub my legs together. It had been a painful month with this unsatisfied thirst. The Lone Wolf was slowly slipping the world from under me.

At the sound of a branch snapping, I heeded my sense of alarm and flung my dagger in the direction of the noise. Remus caught the blade with ease, ducking his head to the side with a measured smoothness. His deep olive skin was splattered with dirt and bruises, contrasting with the lines of coarse muscle running down his forearm and broad hands. The skin on his knuckles tightened, flexing the vein on his hand as he held the dagger.

Remus's eyes narrowed, looking more catlike in the dark. "That's twice you've tried to kill me."

"And twice you've snuck up on me." I grimaced as I sat against the tree trunk.

The creases on Remus's brow deepened as he sat next to me. A lock of black hair fell over his brow. "Has the bleeding stopped?"

I laid my head back, briefly squeezing my eyes shut. "I think so."

Remus's finger lightly grazed my leg, just above the wound. "May I?" he asked, voice suddenly drawn into a whisper.

I nodded, staying silent as he unwrapped the bandage, his large hands surprisingly gentle. Remus took a sharp breath at the sight of the gashes, deep crevices of skin filled with dried blood.

"See," I said, fighting to maintain a steady breath, "not bleeding."

He didn't move, green eyes locked on the wound. "I will fucking kill them all."

The deep tremors of his voice trailed a line down to my core, lighting it to a blaze. Remus rewrapped the wound and was about to pull away when I latched onto his hand. I was beginning to realize it was becoming hard *not to* touch him.

"He whipped you," I repeated. "And *I* will fucking kill him. Now let me look at your wounds."

Remus's gaze lit up, flashing bright with a hunger that caused my throat to dry. He shifted to sit directly in front of me, and I wondered how his large frame could even fit within this small space between the trees.

His tunic had dried but it was almost completely ruined. Remus lightly pushed my hands away as he lifted his arms and pulled the linen over his shoulders. My eyes widened at the broad expanse of his back. And the lashes. Streaks of beaded red bubbled along the wounds. My fingers hovered above them. *He took these for me.*

Pale jagged lines snagged my attention, and a gasp caught in my throat. It was not uncommon for wolf warriors to carry scars from battle, both literally and figuratively. But this. It covered his entire back, defining his history. My heart cried out at the sight.

Remus must've felt my lingering gaze. I'd been silent for so long, trying to read the stories behind every cursed, tortured wound. The words left me before I could take them back: "You're beautiful."

He chuckled, deep and mirthless. I shook my head, my hand sliding across his bare shoulder blade. "You are beautiful, Remus. Every jagged scar."

The muscles underneath my hand tightened, and a rumble shuddered through him. "You don't know what you do to me," Remus breathed.

Warmth and safety. That's what I felt. What I had been feeling with him all along. "I was supposed to take these whippings. Instead, you did. I fell from the cliff. And you went after me."

His head snapped to the side. "And I'd do it again."

Each word landed with ironclad conviction. His voice rolled over my skin.

I ran my tongue over my lips nervously. "We are going to need to find a town and get some medicine. Our aether will have already started the healing process, but we will need proper medical attention."

Remus grunted and pulled his tunic back on. He slid beside me, lying on his side so as not to aggravate the wounds. He faced me, expression pale and tired.

"Hopefully, we can stay ahead of the Order. We may need to come up with a contingency plan if anything were to happen." I was rambling, falling prey to my rising worries.

Silence. I stole a glance at him to see that the Lone Wolf had fallen asleep. The creases in his brow had smoothed out, and his lips were parted. The pain in his cold gaze was gone.

Suddenly I began to feel a dull ache in the back of my head and curled beside him. Sometime later, I woke up trembling from the chilly night air, my teeth chattering, and big arms looped around me, tucking me against a hard chest.

"What are you doing?" I whispered, relishing the heat that moved from his skin to mine.

Remus nuzzled my neck. It was subtle but I could feel the touch throughout my body like bites of ember. My toes curled at the simple action. *Diane, what are you doing?*

"What does it look like?" he teased. "I'm making myself comfortable."

"I think you just can't sleep without me."

A deep chuckle. "Don't flatter yourself."

Despite my previous attempt to restrain myself, I snuggled closer to him, and Remus tightened his hold. "Sleep, Diane."

———

Death pooled out from my hands. Distant cries of agony. Marcus, Drusus, Cato, and Atticus. They were at my mercy, tormented by my power. Marcus was on his hands and knees before me, his face twisted in disgust.

"Monster."

No, this wasn't me. I begged him—all of them—to listen to me. I wasn't trying to harm them. I could never. My brothers disappeared within the shadows, and I chased after them. Only for me to stand before Remus and the daemon king. The Ram bore its crown while ordering us to continue the bloodshed.

Towns lit in silver aether. Remus raised his hands. Not a flicker of emotion in that gaze. I cried for him. For myself.

It was only until I felt something brush under my eyes that I snapped awake.

"Diane," Remus soothed with another sweep of his thumb. "You're safe."

My hands fisted the collar of his tunic, frantically seeking the feel of his skin. Remus said nothing as he leaned closer, letting me know that he was real and here with me. A sob escaped me. My hand ran down his forearm, and Remus turned his wrist to wrap his palm around my hand.

He exhaled a steady breath, holding my gaze. "I am here."

My lips trembled, but I couldn't speak. Remus tugged me closer to him, murmuring sweet promises and comforts, but I couldn't hold on to them. I was slipping beneath the cracks and crevices, the ground ready to swallow me whole.

THIRTY-ONE

Diane

Sunlight kissed my brow and gently prompted me awake. My limbs ached, but the faint pulse in my head had stopped. I admired the morning glow that shone through the forest, watching specks float in the soft beams of light. Somewhere in the distance, birds sang.

The warmth beside me was absent, so I knew Remus was gone. I rolled to my feet and limped over to a tree to relieve myself. My skin strained against the wound, and I bit back a groan. I shrugged back into my armor and fighting leathers, abhorring the feel of the dirty attire. Twigs snapping announced Remus's arrival. He, too, wore his armor and leathers, sword already strapped to his back.

His bright eyes landed on me, the slightest tilt to his lips. My breath caught as we watched each other. I could've sworn Remus's gaze turned heated as it roamed from my face and down my legs. That heat soon morphed into anger as his eyes latched onto my wound. Ridiculous, his concern when he was enduring so much more pain than I.

"How are you feeling?" He asked.

A sarcastic smile plastered on my face. "Like a king. You?"

"Like a queen." Remus breathed a chuckle, taking a step forward. "The woods seem to be clear."

"You worry too much." I stretched my arms out, groaning at the release of tension.

The sun grazed the sword pommel strapped to Remus's back. He flicked my nose. "No, I just survived this long because I'm *that* skilled."

"Oh, mighty Lone Wolf, I praise the gods that you are here."

The soft beam of light rimmed his massive shoulders. A halo gilded him, and a smirk was sprawled over his lips. "Enough," he chided, bumping against my arm. "Although, there is something I find a bit funny."

"Oh?"

There was a devilish glint in his expression. "That a good girl such as yourself wants a taste of the life of a Lone Wolf."

He was making it too easy. "I don't ever remember saying that I was."

Something ravenous flickered over Remus. His pupils flared with silver before it disappeared. "That you were what?"

The way his voice deepened was a distraction, and I found myself becoming flustered. Before I could muster the words, Remus leaned forward, that unabated hunger growing stronger. "That you were what?" he repeated. "A good girl?"

My mouth opened, but no words found me. I felt a rush of red run up my cheeks, while the other unashamed part of me felt heat curl between my thighs.

The sound of Remus laughing at my embarrassment had me punching his arm. "Bastard," I grumbled.

Remus had planned to shift into his wolf to make travel quicker, but I'd immediately shot down his suggestion. He was still healing, and I had no intention for his back wounds to worsen. Sleeping in the woods again was out of the question too. We planned to find shelter in one of the towns outside of Roman jurisdiction.

After a while of us walking, Remus broke the silence. "You revealed your power to the others."

There was a tightening in my stomach, and I suddenly felt lightheaded. "I had to," I muttered. "We would've lost otherwise."

Remus scoffed. "You almost wiped out half of the army."

Leaves crunched under our boots, and my stomach began to growl. "I don't think the others fully processed what they saw," I mused. "Perhaps they will cast me out too, and I will be the first Lone She-Wolf in history."

I didn't mean it as an offense, but I regretted how it sounded. "Don't doubt their love for you," Remus said after a long pause.

Mountain peaks soared in the distance. My thoughts went to the griffins. It was said that their kingdom sat above the mountains, surrounded by clouds. I wondered if the Pack had received word yet on the request from the griffin king. Securing the minotaurs' support had been successful given the circumstances, and word of Remus's power was sure to continue spreading.

Now that my power had been revealed as well, I was unsure how that would affect this war. The heavy threads of aether rolled endlessly within me, and I yearned to know more. This was so unknown to me but at the same time felt natural, a part of me.

Needing to disrupt my train of thought, I glanced at Remus. "Tell me something about your childhood."

The Lone Wolf snorted. "What is there to tell? I didn't have a pleasant childhood."

I frowned, the response sparking my curiosity even more. "Really? Your pater was *the* Alpha. The pater others wanted. Surely there were good memories with someone like that."

Remus looked away as if irritated. His hands clenched, and I noticed the ink dotting his knuckles.

I found myself reaching for him, but he jerked away. I paused. "Sorry, I was curious about the tattoos you have."

I was about to pull away when he snatched my wrist.

"Don't." His voice roughened. He watched me with the usual intensity, something like a plea echoing in those jade eyes.

My throat bobbed as I went back to examining the tattoos. And his large hand covered in calluses . . .

"These are Egyptian." My voice turned to wonder as I ran my fingers down the hieroglyphics printed along the length of his fingers. Images of feathers, falcons, cups, and reeds.

"My story is of scars," he translated. I eyed him with curious astonishment, and his lips parted slightly as he stared back.

I brushed the pad of a finger along the ink, my brow furrowed.

"There are scars underneath your tattoos." I looked back at him. "Like you've punched walls every day."

His eyes widened at my observation. His lips thinned almost with bitterness. "Might as well have. My pater craved perfection."

"What do you mean?"

He jerked his hand away and continued walking. I tried to catch up but winced, the wound on my thigh flaring up. Remus heard my struggle and slowed enough for me to reach his side before he turned his back on me.

"Remus."

His voice was hard. "No."

I wanted to keep pushing, to understand more of what he meant I should've caught on to how he acted whenever I spoke highly of his pater. Even in the Pack haven, the legacy of Alpha Anthony was honored. The wolves adored him, but Remus always seemed reserved. Had something happened between him and his pater? I assumed there must have been tension when Remus decided to leave the Pack, but those scars on his knuckles were saying something else that I couldn't understand.

Fine. I was not going to drop this topic, but I would wait until he was ready. I also couldn't help but feel slightly hurt that he didn't want to confide in me. Perhaps, however, it wasn't a matter of not wanting to speak to me but of not being able to face the deepest parts of himself. Time. I would give him time.

I asked another question. "When did you get those tattoos?"

"I had them done after my time in Egypt." He kept walking but glanced my way for a breath. "You can't read hieroglyphics, can you?"

I knew I should've been able to as I was part Egyptian, but there hadn't been much focus on that part of my heritage. I felt a bit of embarrassment, maybe even shame

"How come you know how to read hieroglyphics?" I asked.

Remus didn't look back. "I told you. My pater expected perfection from me. In both the blade and academics. I can teach you, if you want."

I smiled, grateful that he couldn't see how much his offer meant to me. "What of your mater? You mention her."

Remus tilted his head to the side, a soft smile on his lips. Warmth overtook his face as he peered into a memory.

"Yes. Before my sister and I were of the age to begin training, we lived in a villa by the sea. My mater often took us to the beach; she would lounge in the boat while my sister and I swam along the shore."

I tried to imagine a younger Remus and adored the image my mind fabricated. A boy with dark hair and bright green eyes. He probably laughed and smiled often once, but while some parts of that boy lingered, other parts of his innocence had been killed off. What had happened to him?

Remus stirred out of his memory and noticed how my expression had fallen. "And your mater?"

I gave in to his attempt to change the subject. "She died of an illness that not even our healers could help with. She was from Egypt, had been abducted and taken to the Roman lands by common thieves and raiders. My pater saved her. They fell in love along the way."

"Beautiful," Remus murmured. His eyes brightened the longer he stared at me. "It sounds like your mater was very resilient and strong."

This time I felt a soft smile bloom on my lips. "That she was."

When night drew in, we made camp alongside a thin creek. Remus disappeared to hunt for game. It wasn't long before his large black wolf sauntered back into our makeshift camp. Moonlight caressed him, the dark flanking him. A wolf of night and ruin.

He held a pair of rabbits in his teeth. I took my dagger from its sheath, the blade dancing between my fingers as I grabbed our dinner from the wolf's mouth.

I sighed. "I'll do the skinning, but you do the cooking."

The wolf snorted and nudged my hip with his snout, the force of it almost knocking me off my feet. I whirled around, ready to chastise him, but he shifted, and Remus towered over me. His grin froze me in place, and I didn't notice his arm sliding around me and taking the game from my hand.

"Sit that pretty ass down while I make dinner."

Gods.

———

I curled my exhausted body against a tree and drifted to sleep with the gentle sounds from the creek. It wasn't long before I heard a deep voice muttering near me.

My hand flew to my sheathed dagger, and I staggered to my feet before realizing it was Remus, his large body at arm's length. Remus lay on his stomach, shirtless, the lashes on his back cleaner and less angry than the night before due to the aether coursing through him. Even in sleep, he was restless. His body shook, a slight sheen to his skin. Flickers of silver flames skittered over him.

His teeth were clenched. Hands curled into fists as he kept mumbling the same word over and over. *Ielena.* His twin sister's death must have been hurting him more than he let on. The sight wrecked me.

Remus's voice was a pained groan. "I'm sorry."

I lay on the ground next to him. He was too big, so I curled my arms around his shoulders and brought his head to my chest. Remus twitched, the flames running along his skin in anxiety. The fire didn't burn me. It felt warm, a feather-light touch. I held him, brushing the damp locks of hair from his face until his body finally went slack in my arms.

This continued throughout the week. Nightmares always haunted me, but something deeper, more wicked, loomed over Remus. Throughout the nights we pulled each other from our personal demons. At times we both lay awake and watched the stars. Other nights, we talked or relaxed into a comfortable silence. Slowly, like the budding of a blossom, the nightmares started dissipating. And every morning, without fail, I found myself in his arms.

———

Deerskin and leather strapped with weapons of steel, tooth, and bone. The baying of cattle and the squeals of pigs. Small corrals and log structures. The town was a welcome sight after the constant backdrop of trees. People strolled through their small settlement. Remus and I remained hidden among the bushes.

Remus rested an arm over a propped knee. "We don't know if they're friendly to Romans, though I doubt they are. Hardly anyone likes the Romans. I wouldn't blame them for not forgiving Caesar's conquest of their lands, but they may like the wolves."

I stole a glance at him. "Have you encountered many independent communities?"

A shadow crossed his eyes, and he ran a thumb over his lip. "Yes and no. I helped many of the rescue and defense efforts. My pater and Caesar focused on their conquering. They both had a desire to rule over these peoples' lands and wanted to use the wolves to do it."

I sucked in a breath. "What? I don't remember ever hearing that. I don't think anyone in the Pack has ever spoken of such a history."

He shrugged, avoiding my gaze. "We stopped the invasion before it could happen."

My stomach twisted. I didn't like where the conversation was headed. I wasn't sure I wanted to know more, but I had to ask. "We?"

Remus lifted his chin. A vacant look concealed whatever he felt inside. "Helena and I."

They had stopped the wolves from becoming conquerors. It was the only conclusion I could muster. Although Rome had had its bloody history, something I wished I could scrub away and rewrite, the wolves had never taken part in that hunt for power. It wasn't who we were as a species, and many other Olympians weren't interested in the conquest either.

If he and Helena had stopped the attacks, what's to say they hadn't stopped other ruthless efforts on behalf of the Pack? Yet, he had still become the Lone Wolf. Deemed a traitor and mocked for abandoning his people. But there was more to Remus. If this was all true, then Remus had been so much more than a warrior for his people.

Remus pushed a branch out of the way to peek at the town. "We need cloaks. Something to obscure our faces. We don't know if they will take to strangers, especially Roman ones."

I forced my attention on the town. "What do you suggest?"

"Stealing cloaks," he rumbled.

"You have to be joking," I hissed. "It won't work to simply hide our identities. They will know who we are."

Remus ran a hand through his hair. "We have to leave our Roman armor."

I lugged off the fighting leather pieces, remaining in my dirty, tattered tunic. Remus did the same, and I hid the armor pieces under a thick root while he drifted off to find cloaks.

At a sound I flicked the dagger in my hand. Remus appeared, and he cocked his head. In his hands were two cloaks.

"You're going to stab me one day," he said, handing me one.

I rolled my eyes. "Unlikely."

He grinned, pulling up the hood of the cloak until only his jawline could be seen. "You almost did when we met."

"It was barely a graze," I retorted.

I pulled the hood over my head, and we began making our way into the town. Luckily, the sky was darkening. Less chance of being recognized.

Families were tending to their gardens and animals, but they all stopped to stare at us as we passed. I instinctively reached for Remus's arm and moved closer to him.

"What are you doing?" He lowered his voice, keeping his gaze straight ahead.

"I am your wife. We lost our horse and belongings to daemons."

When Remus tugged me closer I knew he agreed to go along with the scenario. A man strolled toward us. His head was shorn, save for a strip of plaited blond hair down the middle. Deep blue eyes ran over us as he gripped the axe in his hand.

"What's your business here?" The man spoke in the Roman tongue, though that was not so surprising as it was the common language in the region.

Remus raised a hand. "My wife and I lost our horse to daemons, and she is wounded."

I peeked under the hood. The man was handsome. Corded

strength and power carved the width of his chest and torso. I pulled the cloak and tunic back to reveal the bandaged wound on my leg.

The man grunted and turned toward a longhouse. "Come with me."

We shared a glance before following the male. His scent was human, and I sensed nothing to be wary of. Yet.

The longhouse was warm from the fireplace and candlelight. Bear furs and other animal skins were draped over wooden chairs. A bow hung on one wall, a quiver full of arrows perched just below it.

A woman sat at the main table. A long, simple gown hugged the curves of her thighs, brown hair braided back from her soft face. She was pregnant.

Her eyes widened, and she dipped her head. "Welcome."

I recognized the accent to her voice. I almost gasped and pulled forward. Remus still held me to him. "You are Roman?"

She looked to the man behind us before returning to us with a warm smile. "Aye. Aidan, my love, who are our guests?"

Aidan strolled into the main room and planted a kiss on the woman's lips. "Travelers in an unfortunate situation."

His eyes had melted at the sight of her. The love could be seen in the gentle caress on his fingers against her neck and how his body angled around her and her belly.

Aidan looked at us, the fire flickering within his blue eyes. "It's quite easy to tell that you are not from around here. You may eat with us and sleep in our spare room. Sit. I will bring you some medicine."

Remus gently guided me to our seats and pulled out a chair for me. When he sat beside me, his hand grabbed my seat and dragged it closer to him. Quietly, I ate the meat stew the woman offered us. Remus's large frame almost suffocated the space beside me.

"Thank you for the food," I said. "I am Diane, and this is Remus. I know the name of your husband. May I have yours?"

The woman wiped her hands. "Junia. I am sorry to hear of your harsh journey."

"Thank you," Remus replied.

A lone trickle of stew ran down his chin. I lifted a finger to brush it off. He stilled and looked at me, eyes turning a brighter shade of green. His gaze fell to my mouth as if the shape of my lips entranced him.

Junia cleared her throat. Aidan chuckled and murmured, "Must be newly wedded."

Remus's lips kicked up. I pulled back, tucking a strand of hair behind my ear.

Junia got to her feet and made her way to me. "Let me tend to that wound of yours."

I insisted that I could do it myself, but she shrugged me off. She began to clean the wound, and I sat in silence as I listened to the conversation between Remus and Aidan.

"No, I am thankful for the wolves." Aidan leaned back, kicking a foot up on the table. "They have saved members of this town before. Back when raids were frequent and daemons less so."

The words brought a soft smile to Remus's lips. "The wolves try their best."

Junia had finished applying the salve and wrapped my thigh up with a clean cloth. I grasped her hand.

"Thank you," I said. "How far along are you?"

She smiled and began to rub a hand along the curve of her abdomen. "The babe is due within a month. It can't come soon enough. I need my body to myself again." I chuckled as she placed an extra canister of the salve in my hands. "Just in case the wound festers. Have that husband of yours take care of it for you."

My expression sobered. "He actually has a few injuries of his own."

She patted my hands. "Even more need for it."

It wasn't long before Aidan showed us to the room we were to stay in. A candle had already been lit, clean clothes folded on one single bed. Aidan closed the door behind us, a knowing glint in his eyes, and his footsteps soon faded away. Leaving me and Remus alone.

THIRTY-TWO

Remus

The cloak pooled at my feet. Every muscle kicked and pushed against the urge to turn to the warrior behind me. I yanked the top part of the tunic over my back. I waited as she dabbed the salve onto the lashes on my back. It was sensitive, but the aether was doing wonders to the wounds.

I turned to face her as her fingers skimmed across my skin to my chest. She dropped the canister, eyes watching me. Requesting answers.

"My pater caused the scars." I paused at the way she held her breath. I battled with the havoc inside me. The tainted memories that thrashed and confined me. To tell her everything about me, about my past. I wanted to—yearned to. The words were still lodged in my throat but I found myself giving her a few small truths.

"My pater wasn't always . . . the male the Pack saw him as. My mater was his strength and weakness. He was away on Pack business and returned home to find his wife had been killed, his two children terrified and hiding in the villa. That is when we moved to the Pack haven. My pater was never the same after that. He had always been a broody person, but my mater's death broke something inside of him. He began obsessing over perfection. He honed us, my sister and me, into killers of his own making. My pater was kinder to Helena, though, allowed her more freedom. He cherished her. As for me, he wanted me to be more like him. Cunning, clever, fierce in every way an Alpha was intended to be. My pater never laid a hand on me, but he required my training to be strenuous tenfold. To the point the skin on my knuckles broke every day." I gave Diane a grim smile. "That was my life. These scars here were from some of the battles I led. The majority on my back are from—"

"Egypt." Diane exhaled slowly. "You went to Egypt. I remember hearing of this. There were rebel groups conspiring against Rome, taking innocents, and the wolves were sent there. Marcus and the others were there as well."

I nodded and sat next to her on the bed. Diane shuffled behind my back and ran her fingers over my scars and tattoos. I felt a sense of safety with her presence, and it helped me speak, letting this dark memory unravel. Small truths.

"Drusus and I were already friends at this point. Caius was not in Egypt. He had stayed behind to manage the haven, as most of the wolves had been sent across seas. The bloodshed happened on the sands, in an old, crumbling temple, I think. Pyramids loomed over us like spectators to the mayhem. My pater was leading another battle miles from us, so it was just me and my battalion. We fought against the jackal-shapeshifters." I remembered the scene so vividly. Their warpaint and crowning chest plates lit the dunes in sparkling gold. Beautiful and terrifying. I paused, swallowing thick emotion. "Many of my wolves died. We retreated. I made the order and stayed behind to ensure every breathing wolf escaped. But I couldn't find Drusus, and I fucking *panicked*. I searched the dead for him, like a mad man, until I saw him being cornered by a group of jackals. So I surrendered myself in exchange for Drusus's life. As I was the son of the Alpha, the jackals were more than happy to oblige. The bastards." My hands clenched into fists as images rushed to me. "They tortured me. Held me in a cell, wanted to know Caesar's and the Pack's next moves. I didn't break, but I think they liked having me around as their plaything," I grimaced. "It was months before Drusus came barreling in to my rescue. He and my pater were leading another attack, and they managed to find where the jackals were holding me. I remember the light of the sun being so harsh, Drusus had to wrap my eyes until I became accustomed to it."

Diane was leaning into me. I felt her gaze on me, and I was shocked that I had revealed so much in one evening. Speaking to her so freely was becoming natural.

She grabbed my hand, her slender thumb running over the back of it. "The stories of your pater," she began. "Are not what is told among the Pack. Anthony was revered. Everyone saw him as just and brave. What he did to you, Remus . . . it angers me to the core. Wolves are warriors by nature. Training comes with that, and we are all familiar with cuts and bruises. However, what your pater did to you was in-humane and vile. You were just a boy. Yet he accomplished what he wanted. He made his son into an invincible weapon."

A mirthless chuckle escaped me. "My pater would probably say otherwise."

"And your sister? How did he treat her?"

"Better than me. I think it was because she reminded him of our mater. I'm not sure, but he always had a soft spot for her."

Her grip tightened. "You deserved so much better."

I didn't believe that. Diane sighed and untangled our hands. She gave me a thoughtful look. "You were imprisoned. Survived months of torture. You say I am powerful. What about you? You have endured pain unlike anything I have known. God-like aether now runs in your veins. Kingdoms could bow to you with all that you have experienced. I admire *your* strength."

Diane. My friend and supporter.

The corner of my lips kicked up. "Thank you. I don't believe I am deserving of it, but I am grateful nonetheless."

She smiled, minutes passing until awareness rose between us. The candlelight flickered patiently on the bedstand. I'd shared a tortured part of me. Slowly, like a melting ice cap, I felt the sickening sensa-tion lighten as I spoke to her. She didn't realize how deeply she'd been affecting me. I wondered if there would ever be a day when I would think of my past and not feel the urge to hurl.

Small truths.

Thirty-Three

Diane

I was enthralled by him. Remus had shared a part of himself with me. And I wanted more. To hear his voice, to take his hand as he led me through the dark corners of his being. Yes, I wanted more. It was becoming a thirst I feared would be unquenchable.

Guilt began to seep in. It gnawed at my heart, reminding me of the initial ulterior motive behind getting to know the Lone Wolf. Gods, I actually enjoyed speaking to him, being with him. Words couldn't accurately describe how natural and comfortable it felt to be around him and to simply talk.

A part of me wanted to serve my Pack. It was an instinctual re-action to follow orders and uphold my duty. Another part of me was . . . starting to see things differently. As I learned more about Remus, there was always something deeper, darker about him to be discov-ered. And I was finding myself caring about every piece of him.

Not everything is black and white.

I remembered Drusus's words from all that time ago, when I had just met Remus.

He and his sister interfering with Anthony and Caesar's conquer-ing plans was something I really wanted to inquire further about, but I held my tongue. Remus seemed worn out, and I could understand why. It could be emotionally draining to open yourself up to another.

Remus was a man and wolf who had been raised by fist and blade, becoming one of the most skilled warriors among the Roman lands. He had become the Lone Wolf, name cast in shame. He had been feared, hated, and loved. Now, touched by aether, he truly was one of the most powerful beings. Caius had said it himself: *Wolf of the White Flames.*

The wool and linen of the new clothes felt loose and soft between my fingers. We sat on the edge of the bed, seeming to drown in our thoughts, ignoring the obvious tension that had risen between us. The sensation thrummed along my skin and awakened every nerve of my body. Remus was the first to move as he stood from the bed, turning to face the corner of the room.

He didn't bother with a warning when he slipped off his clothes. My jaw fell. With his back to me, Remus stood gloriously naked. A body carved with strength and marked by battle. His long legs were thick, the lines of his muscles ran and curved over his back and across his broad shoulders. The dark ink that decorated his arm and part of his chest added to the delicious look. My mouth began to water.

Remus was still facing away from me as he began to dress into the new clothes Aidan had provided him.

I whistled. "Training has shaped your ass well."

Remus barked a laugh, the sound tickling my chest. A sudden surge of courage took hold of me as my feet found the floor, and I walked to the corner where he stood. He stiffened as I drew closer but didn't look my way as he pivoted around me to give me the space to change.

My fingers trembled as I began to remove the tunic over my head. There was a sound akin to a growl, a clearing of a throat. The thought of disarming Remus the way he was disarming me gave me a spurt of strength, and I let the tunic fall from my hand. I had never cared much for modesty, anyway.

I glanced over my shoulder to see Remus facing away. My idiotic heart fell at that. The words left me before I could think twice.

"Look at me."

Remus tensed. "I don't know if that's a good idea."

Air caught in my throat. The awareness singed my lungs, and the ache in my breasts was becoming too much. I wanted this. I wanted *him*. Badly.

I forced the words out, my voice thick. "Why?"

Remus kept his eyes averted. His chest rose sharply. "You're making it incredibly difficult not to want to kiss you."

My teeth grazed my bottom lip. He hadn't been this forward before. The desire had been kindling on both sides. It was obvious from the way he had watched me in the past months. We were warriors, but we were on the precipice of a different kind of battle.

"Then kiss me."

The soft flicker of the candle stirred the thick tension in the room.

Remus was unnaturally still for a moment before slowly facing me. I was partially naked, my breasts bared before him. Silver light glowed around Remus's pupils; it pulsated before he blinked, and the jade-green returned. He prowled toward me, reminding me of a wildcat.

I took a few steps back, hitting the wall. He caged me in once more with little to no effort, his height forcing me to look up at him. A primal look of hunger and desire ignited in those green eyes.

"Do you really want me to?" he asked.

"Yes."

Remus didn't move at first, his eyes pinned on me as if he were giving me another chance to change my mind. And when I didn't, he slowly bent his head. His lips skimmed over my lips. I felt the rough touch of his hand as it trailed up my arm to cradle my cheek. Sparks lit up after his touch, setting my lower abdomen aflame. The scent of cedar and ocean was so close, and I yearned to taste it.

"I have to confess something." His voice was deep, raspy, and it curled my toes.

I waited, his thumb brushing over my cheek. Remus's breath kissed my lips, and I felt myself lean into him. His body responded, pressing me harder against the wall. The thick length of his erection beneath his clothes was difficult to ignore. I fought the urge to roll my hips.

"I want to do more than kiss you," he whispered. The sound

trailed down my skin, and I closed my eyes. "I want to taste you, feel every part of you. Watch you come undone."

I shivered as Remus's other hand rested on my hip. He squeezed, and a sound between a moan and a gasp got trapped in my throat. I wanted to surrender myself to him. My lips parted as I tried to reach for his mouth.

My breathing turned rampant. "Please."

I opened my eyes to see him simply staring at me. Warmth and hunger battled like beasts in his gaze. Strength and softness. Lust and something . . . more.

And then Remus kissed me.

The taste of cedar and man finally greeted me. Lips that were both gentle and hard. Remus moved his hand from my hip to cup my other cheek. He held my face as our tongues collided. He tasted like untamed power. We continued to kiss, the only sound in the room our heavy breathing, under the protection of the candle's shadow.

I dared bite his bottom lip, and a growl rumbled through his chest as he slid an arm around my waist, the sound rough and full of approval. It shot a thrill along my spine down to the tips of my toes.

My hands trailed down the length of his arms and his waist, exploring every dip and hard curve of his frame. Remus kissed a fiery line down my neck. I was ignited, utterly consumed by the feel of his skin against mine. He cupped one of my breasts, sweeping a thumb over my tightened nipple, the hot press of his tongue licking along the base of my collarbone. I ran my hands up the back of his neck and into his hair. Remus lifted me, I instinctively wrapped my legs around his waist, and he slammed me against the wall as he continued the assault on my lips. Teeth and tongue. Fire and ice.

"What are you doing to me, lotus?" He broke off and growled against my ear. "I find myself falling to my knees before you every passing day."

I whimpered at the sound of his voice, so rich and deep it sank into my bones, making every nerve shudder in my body. Remus twisted us around before gently placing me on the bed. My hands went to my waistband to remove the remainder of my tunic. Remus took over and slid the rest of my clothes down my legs, leaving me completely naked. He leaned back a moment, admiring me with twinkling eyes.

His fingers traced up my calf and leg. "Beautiful," he murmured. "I like seeing you like this. Laid bare before me, like my own personal feast."

My tongue ran over my lips as I slowly spread my legs. His eyes burned brighter as he leaned over to kiss me. His mouth then moved lower, and I gasped once his lips wrapped around a nipple. The soft scrape of teeth, and I yelped. He licked the sting away and continued to explore my body with his tongue and lips, drawing sighs and moans from me. My hips rolled against his hardness, and Remus trembled.

"Fuck," he rasped.

Remus slid lower, his calluses scratching my skin. Gods, it was the sensation I had been craving all this time. My hips continued to roll, desperate for friction. His hands held my parted thighs, green eyes igniting. His desire was so tangible I could taste it.

His gaze flicked to mine. "I will be savoring this, lotus."

I bit my lip in anticipation. Remus kept his eyes on mine as he dipped lower and ran his tongue up my center. My hips bucked, fingers bunching on the sheets underneath me. Remus continued to slowly lick me from entrance to clit. He feasted with reverence, and the occasional deep rumble of satisfaction. Hot pleasure rushed through my veins. I trembled, unable to stop myself from fisting his thick hair.

"Remus," I moaned.

He growled, and my back bowed at the thick sensation of his finger entering me. He stroked me slowly at first then began to thrust into me with a steady rhythm.

"Remus," I groaned again.

"I know," he purred. A second finger entered me. "So wet for me."

Moans fell from my lips. Over and over. He continued to thrust into me with his fingers, plunging in and out as he lapped at my clit. I felt drunk on these sensations. On him. I was at Remus's mercy, my panting filled the room. His touch brought me higher and higher, and I fell into wondrous oblivion.

My chest fought for air, and my legs went slack. Remus pulled back, his lips swollen and glistening. His eyes glimmered as he brought his hand to his mouth and sucked on the fingers that had just been inside me. I had never experienced such a strong fire with someone. This heat that kept spreading surpassed lust, turning into something I was nervous to acknowledge. But I wanted to hold onto that sensation, feel it again, and would have gladly succumbed to it.

"You've made a monster out of me, Diane. I will now always crave your taste."

My name rolled from his tongue like dark, sinful liquid. I grinned and began to sit up. Remus's hand came around the back of my neck to bring my lips to his. We kissed, sharing the taste of myself between our tongues. I pulled on his bottom lip gently.

"Sit back," I ordered.

Remus arched a brow and shook his head. "Tonight is for you, lotus."

I raised a finger to his mouth and pushed him back on the bed until he leaned against the wall. My lips brushed against his ear, and his hands came around my back.

"Tonight is for both of us," I said. "You pleasured me, and now I want to pleasure you."

Remus stilled as my lips began to explore his skin. I dragged my tongue down his neck. He groaned, dropping his head against the wall. I slid down his body and kneeled between his large legs. My hands pulled at his clothing until I freed his hardened length.

Oh my gods.

Remus was thick and long, full of veins and soft skin that caused my mouth to water even more. I ached to know how he would feel inside me. I wrapped my hand around the base of his cock and leaned down.

My eyes flitted upward as I dragged my tongue up his length. Remus hissed, and warmth raced through me at the sound. I ran a hand along his thigh and over the hard lines of his stomach.

My lips wrapped around the tip, and I ran my tongue along the slit. I took him to the back of my mouth, making myself gag. Remus cursed.

"Take it for me, I know you can." Remus's hand wrapped around the length of my hair once, twice, and held it as I bobbed my head along his thick length. "Fuck," he panted. "Just like that, lotus."

I moaned at his approval, nails digging into his thighs as I continued to lick and suck him. His deep voice, laden with sex, was becoming an addiction.

"You look so beautiful with my cock in your mouth."

His hand was still entwined in my hair, and he began to thrust. *Yes.* I peered up through my lashes, watching him tremble under my touch. He was nearing the edge of release. Remus paused, but I wrapped my hand around his cock once more.

I smiled softly as I licked the head. "Come in my mouth."

Remus's eyes brightened. He flung his head back as I took him again. With my hand pumping him at the same time, Remus found his release.

His deep guttural growls unleashed a fire in my core. "*Diane.*"

I moaned, swallowing every last drop of him.

He let go of my hair and pulled me toward him. Remus looked at me with drunken bliss, his thumb wiping the wetness from my lips. He tugged me closer for another lingering kiss. I pressed further into his touch. Let this not be the end; I never wanted it to stop.

Remus released me, a soft smile resting on his lips. "You have no idea what you do to me."

Warmth trickled through my chest and squeezed. "Nor do you."

Remus stilled. His lips twitched, but he smoothed his expression, shutting me out from how he was truly feeling. There was no need to probe further tonight, and I slept again in the arms of the Lone Wolf.

No nightmares came for either of us.

Thirty-Four

Remus

A sharp knock snapped me awake. The brisk morning breeze crawled through the room. My skin chilled, and I recalled I was still naked under the sheets. With Diane. I'd crossed a line last night, broken the rule I had set for myself. I bared parts of my jagged heart, and she'd been kind enough, patient enough, to gather the broken pieces in her hand. And the way she had looked at me—a tenderness that complemented her usual fierceness. A sunset in her eyes, power and beauty, it was so alluring that I'd had to reach for it. Taste it. Be embraced by it.

She had managed to roll out of my arms during the night. Her naked back was to me, and I noticed the crescent moon and array of stars that danced on a thin blade along her spine. I wanted to run a hand down the dark pattern, perhaps squeeze her ass. She was still asleep, and I could wake her with my face between her legs. My cock twitched at the thought. I would kiss her, bite her, mark her skin until she was begging—another knock.

"For gods' sake," I grumbled, slipping into my clothes.

I pulled the bedsheet over Diane until she was fully covered before opening the door to Aidan. A pale, fear-stricken Aidan.

"What happened?" I asked, alarmed.

Aidan swallowed and I then noticed the wide blade in his hand. "Daemons are heading our way. Townsmen spotted them earlier this morning. We are to fight them. Junia is in the cellar; Diane can hide with her."

I looked back to see Diane already awake, her eyes wide as she silently communicated with me. I returned my gaze to Aidan, my eyes shifting into the bright eyes of my wolf for a breath.

"No need. Diane and I can lead the daemons away from here."

Aidan didn't seem surprised by my declaration. He arched a brow, a knowing look in his fearful gaze. "I knew you weren't completely human. There seemed to be an . . . energy surrounding both of you. The moment you two walked into my room, Junia and I both felt it. True, unfiltered aether."

I offered Aidan a grim smile. "I'm sorry we lied to you. The daemons will have more interest in us than in your town, I can assure you."

Aidan nodded and beckoned us to follow once we were fully dressed. I left to retrieve our armor and weapons and returned to see Diane at the doorstep, hugging Junia farewell. In Diane's hand were bread and fruits.

The she-wolf met my gaze, and the softest hue of pink kissed her cheeks. She and I were getting too close. I felt a pull in my chest, but something like panic stamped it out.

You're tainted. Wrong. A monster.

Aidan raised a hand in farewell and watched us depart. The small settlement disappeared behind the wall of trees. The day now didn't seem as bright, and the leaves shuddered at our presence.

The cloak drifted behind my legs. My senses were on alert, eyes darting to every corner and every brush of wood. The daemons had been spotted coming in this direction. It wouldn't be long before we met them.

"You're staring," I noted. I looked down to see Diane's expression turn into a pout. My lips curled again, and I winked. "Remembering last night?"

Diane's eyes went to my lips before she flashed an innocent smile. "Maybe."

I leaned toward her. "Good. I want you to remember just how wet you were around my fingers and mouth."

Her eyes heated. "And you say I'm trouble." She cocked her head, and I could almost see the thought as it crept in. "Have you slept with many others?"

I threw my head back and laughed. "I like where your mind is headed. Yes, I've had my fair share of fucks, experimented a bit. But it had been a long time before you. And you?"

Diane hummed and kicked up a wad of dirt. "Of course. I've slept with multiple males, sometimes more than one at once." That caught my attention. "My first was actually Marcus."

As quickly as my intrigue started, it was smothered out. My nose scrunched up in disgust. "Gross."

Diane laughed, the sound of summer rain. "It was ages ago; we are completely platonic now."

"Marcus is so . . . ordinary. I can't even imagine how the sex would be."

She laughed even more at the implication. "Do you really want me to expand on that topic?"

I growled. The thought of someone else touching her sent tendrils of red through me. I pushed that out as well. I was the Lone Wolf. I couldn't truly have her in my life. The realization caused my stomach to drop.

"I know Atticus is with Camilla, and Drusus seems to be quite taken with Sabina. Has there not been anything with you and Cato?" I asked.

Diane shook her head. "No. Cato had quite a wild past, which I've always admired. He would jump from one partner to the next, both male and female. No one could tame him. Until very recently, it seems. We've spotted him quite a lot with another male wolf, Felix. He isn't a soldier, he actually assists the healers."

That was surprising. From the moment I'd met him, I didn't imagine Cato as someone who would settle. My thoughts soon returned to Marcus, or any other potential male touching her. I gave her a sidelong glance. "I still can't imagine you with *Marcus*. Just know that I would cater to every one of your wildest fantasies." I dipped my head low, allowing my voice to curl against her ear. "And if we were to fuck one day, I would make it so you wouldn't be able to stand straight for days."

Diane inhaled a breath, the desire evident by the hungry look on her face. Then it morphed into something like realization and conspiratorial glee.

Her hand clutched at my arm. "You mentioned Drusus and Sabina. What have you heard?"

I chuckled and leaned closer, almost dropping into a whisper. "That Drusus is head over heels for her even though he's too stubborn to admit it."

Diane threw her head back in delight and clapped her hands. "I knew it! The bastard has been avoiding how he feels for years. I know Sabina well, and she cares about him. Deeply. They would be beautiful together."

We chuckled and continued to talk about the Pack's idle dramas. It didn't take long before I felt a different presence thrum against my skin. It was heavy and dark.

I halted, hand raised. "Our party has arrived."

I began to shift, my lips curled, fangs beginning to unsheathe as a growl rolled through my chest. Black fur sprouted, ebony claws snapped, as my black wolf pawed the air.

The winged daemons exploded from the trees. Flames burned in their crescent-shaped eyes, echoing the anger of their king.

Diane was already on my back, and we ran, the horde nipping at our heels. Trees hissed at us as we passed. Diane kept them distracted, shooting pulses of aether at them. We managed to lure the daemons farther away from the settlement, and then I quickened my pace even more as we tried to lose them completely.

A daemon dove for us and managed to dig its claws in my leg. I roared in pain. Diane swung her hand toward the daemon, aether slicing its arm off. The creature wailed, wings flaring as Diane's power shoved it off me.

Light exploded, and the world spun. I was now on my human legs, running with Diane in my arms.

"Follow my lead," I commanded.

White flames enveloped me. Diane's feet slid to the ground as I landed and spun on my knees in front of her. Fire fell out in waves before me. Diane raised her hand to the sky. The sky darkened. Shadows billowed from her palm, exploding into a spider web of darkness.

Only the screams of the daemons could be heard. The silver flames burned some, and the black-webbed power pierced through the bodies of the others. The screaming suddenly stopped, and only the silvery light and darkness remained. Dark aether continued to roll from Diane's body, claiming the forest and sky with its ebony touch. Her lashes fluttered, eyes turning completely black, swallowing every inch of gold.

She was terrifying. Beautiful.

I walked toward her. "Diane."

My white flames penetrated the dark, kissed her skin. I slid my hands around her back and pulled her into my chest. My nose dug into her hair. Blossoms.

"Come back to me, Diane."

Her eyes snapped open. I had never been more relieved to see the gilded brown of her eyes. The light of the sky returned, and Diane slumped into my arms. My aether fell quiet as I continued to hold her, slowly guiding us to the ground. She shivered once and I tightened my hold.

Diane gave me a weak smile. "I am still getting used to this aether. Did I get them all?"

I searched her face, unable to resist the lift of my lips. "You managed to kill half of the daemons. I had the other half. . . . Well, I got more than half. But it's not a competition."

A weak laugh puffed from her chest. My lips grazed hers. It was light, but it spread alike wildfire at my lower back. I knew I shouldn't touch her again, especially so intimately. I couldn't resist. Her hands reached around my neck and into my hair. I leaned down as she pulled, our lips quivering in anticipation.

I jerked. A sensation that I couldn't put to words. Something was wrong. My lips parted as if in question. Our eyes drew down at the same time. A thin blade, its narrow point made of shade and shadows, protruded from my abdomen. Pain suddenly bled through me. Damn the Fates.

"Remus?" Diane's voice sounded small. Her face went bloodless.

She reached for me as I stumbled forward. My forehead pressed to her chest. I felt something tug at the blade that impaled me and I was yanked from Diane's grasp.

"Fuck, that hurts," I said through gritted teeth.

Behind us, an armored daemon emerged from the brush. Tall— taller than the average man. It had the same sickly, sweet scent of the common daemon, the snake-skull shaped face, antlers that protruded from the back of its head and crescent eyes. However this one had bat-like wings folded over its back. I realized it was one of the winged daemons from the battle with the minotaurs.

Its armor was black as night, and a long cloak draped over its shoulders. A long chain trailed down from its hands and led to the blade that pierced my abdomen.

Aether curled from Diane's hands. She angled herself in front of me and seethed at the daemon. "I'll kill you."

The creature slowly cocked its head. The movement was so measured yet animalistic, it was almost frightening. I had a sense that it knew what Diane had said.

More winged daemons appeared. Each held their own ungodly weapon. They stood before us in a semicircle, but they made no move to advance. The first daemon pulled on the chains once more, and I hissed at the flare of pain. Diane shook with rage, her aether flaring out enough that I could feel its angry touch against my skin.

"Now, now. No need to keep taunting him. I think the wolf knows when he's been caught." *That voice.* It sent a shiver through me.

The Order member with the wolf mask stepped into the clearing like a spirit and stopped beside the daemon that held me.

"Sentinels, keep your guard up. These wolves like to bite."

In unison, the sentinel daemons raised their blades. Deep, hungry power vibrated in the air, the ground, the trees. The Ram's aether. It was strong here. I tried to move closer to Diane, ignoring the pain. I had to protect her. I would do anything to ensure her safety.

I shuddered again at the voice. "Who are you?"

A dark laugh. "I'm a little offended. Don't you recognize me?"

The rider raised a hand to his mask and lifted it.

Long black hair fell down the sides of his face, revealing a gray speckled beard with a wide-set jaw. Deep green eyes.

I had gone still. Everything from *that* night rushed back to me. All the blood I had spilled since then. There had been a purpose to the bloodshed, to every Order member I'd killed, and now—*now*—I began to tremble, rattling the chain jammed to my back.

"*Pater?*"

THIRTY-FIVE

Diane

The late Alpha stood before us. A dark grin grew over Anthony's face as he commanded the sentinel to tighten its hold on the chains. Chains that were attached to his *son*. My legs felt numb, and my gaze slowly slid to Remus, who looked absolutely devastated. As if he were seeing a ghost. I was confident I looked just as shocked as him. Alpha Anthony was supposed to be dead.

"You lied." Remus gritted in pain, and shock. "I thought you—"

"Died?" Anthony snapped. "No. You didn't kill me, son. I thought I'd taught you better. Always confirm your kill."

What?

My blood went cold. I couldn't formulate a coherent thought. Then the sentinel yanked on the chains with so much force that Remus fell to his knees, his curses drowned out by the roaring in my ears, and I couldn't help my shout of protest.

Anthony watched his son, an emptiness in his gaze. "You knew so many of my secrets. If you hadn't served a greater purpose in the king's plan, I would've silenced you the night of your sister's death."

Remus shook, flames flickering over his arms and hands. Anthony waved a finger in admonishment. "Careful now, we wouldn't want anything to happen to your she-wolf."

There was a hiss. It was quick, bolting out from the dark clouds that had formed at the hands of another sentinel. Remus swerved round to protect me, wrapping his arms around me. He jerked forward, grunting as another chained blade pierced his back. I cried out for him, my hands trying to hold him up, but we stumbled to our knees. Silver flames flared from Remus's skin only to shudder and dim.

"My aether," Remus ground out. "It's almost like it's suppressed."

Anthony sighed. "These chains hold a specific element of aether that can suffocate the power of its user. Something only the sentinels can conjure. Save your energy for what the king has in store for you. For both of you."

Remus roared, the blades tugging at his back and stomach. His fingers lifted my chin, and I looked at him. Those green eyes were nothing like Anthony's. These were gentle and kind, tortured and sad, though right now they were utterly consumed by a fierceness that enraptured.

Remus's murmured voice was thick with emotion. "Diane, you need to run."

Something in my chest broke. I shook my head. "No, I can't. I won't."

His hand, large and warm, cupped my cheek. Tears began to blur the handsome face before me.

There was a subtle brush of his thumb. "We are at a disadvantage. They want us alive, but it is better they have one than both of us. You must run, Diane. If those sentinels manage to get their chains on you, then there is no hope left. The Pack needs you more than it needs me."

The nightmare returned to me, taunting, laughing at me. Remus in chains, enslaved to the Ram's vision for this mortal realm. His blank gaze as he became death incarnate.

No, no, no.

See, the Ram's voice seemed to croon. *You were never going to outrun what you fear most.*

"But I need you."

The realization settled in my chest, and no storm or daemon king could shake it. I'd rather die than see him taken from me. Remus must've seen the resignation in my face. He quickly shook his head, grabbing my face with both hands. Panic in his gaze.

"Don't you fucking dare," he growled. "For me, Diane. Run."

"I can't let you go," I whispered. Agony sliced through me, and my heart hammered against my chest at the mere thought of leaving him behind.

Remus smiled softly. Sadly. "You will never lose me, lotus. I will find my way back to you."

Fate refused to give us more time as the sentinels began to march toward us. My fingers squeezed around the rough wrists that clasped my face. Remus brushed his lips over mine. My eyes fluttered, and then his hands shoved at my chest. Screamed for me to run. The shock, adrenaline, the sound of his cracked voice pushed me to my feet. I choked on a sob, holding his gaze for another moment before the band of sentinels rushed toward me. Remus wouldn't let them pass so easily. Silver flames roared and blinded me. I ran, screams echoing behind me, but I didn't look back.

Remus had bought me time. I ran till my legs burned and my chest heaved. Forests thinned and thickened. Rivers tore through rolling hills. I managed to lose the daemons at some point, but I didn't stop moving. Blisters bit into my feet. Whether it was the maddening adrenaline or sheer willpower, I pushed myself till all I could feel was numbness.

Dusk cascaded in ripples of gold and purple. The smell of citrus and blossoms rose. A familiar grove of trees appeared.

I dragged myself over the crest of a hill, relief hitting me, when a pair of sentinels floated from behind me. They must have been following me the entire time.

Dual blades made of shadows and darkness formed in my hands. The sentinels lunged for me. I parried their attacks. The aether of my she-wolf blood surged through my legs, and I leapt into the air. A sentinel rose to meet me, our makeshift weapons colliding. The other daemon swung out its blade and collided with one of mine. The force of it caused my dark aether to falter, and the sword shattered in my hands. I cried out just as the first sentinel grabbed my head and slammed me against the ground. Pain burned along my spine. My limbs went weak;

I could no longer fight. At least not by hand. With one final, desperate attempt, I willed the shadowed aether, the foreign darkness that lurked in my soul. It was like I was diving headfirst into the depths of my power. Just hours ago, I'd done this and accidentally fallen into a trance. Remus had pulled me out of it. But he wasn't here, and I needed to survive. I continued to call upon every stream of energy, breaking through the mental barriers, and the world around us—the sentinels and I—exploded into darkness.

Death. I could taste it here.

Realms of gods and goddesses and endless stars spread before me. The twilight plane hummed an ancient song. It felt familiar, attuned to the rhythms of the aether in my veins. The night carved out a figure. Tall and lean, its body filled with the sea of stars. Pointed ears like a dog's.

The realms of the endless twilight and night fell, and I plummeted down with them.

The world returned to me, and I fought to stay conscious. My body could not move, the aether inside me completely depleted. Smoke curled beside me, and I saw the remains of what I assumed was a sentinel. Nothing but burnt flesh and ash. A flash of pain as something tugged at my arm, dragging me back down the hill. I turned my head, caught the sight of antlers. One sentinel had survived. Barely. Its armor was broken, pieces of gray skin exposed and mottled. Black blood ran down the crack of its snake-skull.

The ground rumbled and the sky flickered with large figures. I was drowning, suffocated by my dying thoughts, when I heard familiar snarls. Flashes of gleaming fangs. Wolves surrounded me, tearing the last sentinel away from me. A pair of yellow eyes hovered over me. A brown wolf.

"Marcus." Blood fell from my lips. "They have him."

A dark gray wolf drew up beside Marcus. Even in his wolf form, I could see Drusus's distraught expression reflected in the wolf's amber eyes. "No."

My hand touched grass, drawing on every torn muscle to pull

myself up. I cried out, and a snout dove under my arm. Dove-gray fur. Cato.

Every word was absolute pain. "Alpha . . . Anthony . . . is alive. Remus. Captured."

Whatever strands of strength I'd been able to hold on to broke. Something swept under me, and I felt Cato's arms and chest. But it wasn't the body I yearned for. More pieces of me crumbled. The last thing I heard was Drusus's deep, mournful howl piercing the godly skies.

PART II

DAUGHTER OF MARS

THIRTY-SIX

Diane

My foot pressed against the writhing daemon below me. Sword in its chest, my shadows ran down the silver blade. The black aether sank with the sword, spreading through the daemon's body like liquid fire. Wails of agony rang in my ears.

Death by my hand. I watched it unfold, numb and bored. As I unsheathed the blade from the lifeless daemon, the shadows dissipated.

"Are you making sure I don't go berserk?" I asked without lifting my gaze as I cleaned the blade.

Marcus watched me from a distance. Daemons lay dead at his feet as well. We'd stumbled on a random herd and hadn't hesitated to attack it.

Despite the evening's dim light, I still saw his gaze. Uncertainty. Concern.

Marcus's jaw tightened. "You know I don't think that of you."

I scoffed, stalking toward him. "No, you've just been tasked to watch me. All because I can do *this*."

I stopped within inches of him. Darkness plumed from my shoulders and arms, spreading behind me like wings. Veins of black ink crawled along my forearms and up my neck.

Marcus flinched at the sight, but he shook his head and planted his feet before me. "No. Caius just wanted to make sure that you are still *you*. The Ram ... we've seen what it can do, Diane. Please, try to understand this from our perspective. So many have fallen victim to the Ram's obsession with conquest, even its own followers. Mortals who don't even seem to be alive anymore. We've seen the odd light in their eyes. Something unnatural happened to them, and we were worried something similar had happened to you."

We'd had this conversation multiple times. A month ago, when I awoke back in the Pack haven, I was questioned. Laelia had been the first person I saw when I woke up. My head had been pounding, my body aching. Heartbroken. She had no fear in her eyes when she tended to me. Neither did Camilla and Sabina. They were all in the room with me when Caius had entered, the thirst for war etched in his gaze. The Alpha had bent to one knee at my bedside, meeting me at eye level.

"How are you?" His voice had held no malice. No evidence of violence or anger.

I had stared at the Alpha almost blankly. "They have him."

It was all I could say. Pain was lodged so deeply in my chest I was worried that if I spoke any more the agony would consume me. The Alpha had nodded, and I'd seen it. Quick like lightning on a summer's night, but it was there. Pain. Worry. Fear. The Alpha cared for the Lone Wolf.

"I know," he had responded softly. "We will get him back."

When I hadn't responded, the Alpha had exhaled through his nostrils. "Diane, what you did back there with the minotaurs. Have you always been able to do that?"

Sabina hissed. "Caius, that is enough. Let her rest, and then she can answer whatever godsdamn question you want."

My throat had bobbed in worry. "I think I have always been able to. I've felt it for as long as I can remember, but it only awakened the night the Ram entered our realm."

Caius's gaze had remained unreadable. He had only nodded and shared a quick look with Sabina. "Rest, Diane. I'm sorry to have disturbed you this way."

The Alpha had left my room that day only for the door to open straight after. My brothers had filed in, their somber gazes locked on me. Oh gods, Drusus. His face was gray and pale, as if he hadn't slept.

The skin on his knuckles was bloodied. I recalled the distant scream-ing and sounds of fists pounding against the wall.

Cato had crawled into the bed with me as Atticus sat on the edge, his hand placed over my head in comfort. Marcus hung back at the wall. His brow pulled forward in concern. My family had stayed in the room with me until I'd managed to find the strength to return to my feet.

I was irritated with Marcus now for keeping an eye on me, but I knew, in the deepest parts of my heart, that he was simply worried about me. I hadn't been quite the same since that day.

One month.

It had been a month since Remus's capture. One goddamn month of him being in the Ram's grasp. I hadn't been able to sleep much since the day I lost him to the Order.

We'd been searching every day. Hunting throughout the Roman regions. Other wolf packs had been sent out to search as well, but there had been no word. No sightings of the Wolf with the White Flames.

Marcus placed a hand on my shoulder, gesturing for me to walk with him. "I'm sorry, Diane. For doubting you. It's just I have never seen a power like yours."

I sighed, rubbing my temple. "Remus never shied away from me and my power."

Marcus hung his head, the guilt plain on his face, but I couldn't focus on that. Remus had seen my power and had never doubted me. He'd supported me, pushed me to confront my fears. I was still hes-itant about using this power. But I was trying. At least that is what I'd been telling myself.

There were too many questions unanswered. Where had these shadows come from? What did all this make me? I sighed once more as we entered the camp.

Tents were pitched among the trees. Marcus and I strolled past the burning campfires, and I fought the urge to duck my head from the whispers. The questions and doubts. Most of the Pack were now wary of me, though none would say it to my face. They had all known

260 | JESSICA J. AYALA

me my whole life, and yet they were now almost afraid of me. Marcus nudged me in support, and I shared a grim smile with him.

We entered the main tent, the inside surprisingly warm.

Marcus shook his head. "No, we should be sorry. We've known you our entire lives. You have given so much of your own life to the Pack, and you are owed our trust."

Caius looked up from the parchment in his lap. His eyes landed on me and softened.

My brow furrowed, the frustration from our failed scouting attempt surging up again. I relayed what we'd found. "The town hasn't seen a damn thing. No trace of the Order, the Ram . . . or Remus."

"We killed the daemons in the area," Marcus cast a quick glance my way, "but yes, no one has seen anything amiss other than them."

Caius still watched me. His lips twisted, and he stood, placing the papers on the desk. "Another group of harpy scouts has been sent to search the mountain ranges. There is a lot of land, but I am confident they will find something. Where else could the Order be? It's clear so far that they aren't residing near any of the towns and cities."

I folded my arms. My patience had already been dwindling, and Caius's words severed whatever thread I was hanging onto. "And the griffins?" I snapped. "Have those stuck-up birds responded about us having an audience with them?"

Caius didn't react to my tone. His voice remained calm and strong, but that only irritated me more. Fates above, this male hardly ever cracked. "They haven't yet. I'm going to return to the haven and speak with Valens."

Aether rumbled through me. My eyes shut as wisps of darkness seeped between my fingers. "That's not good enough."

Caius said something, but everything was muffled, muted, as shadows exploded out of me.

"That's not good enough!" I cried out. "We wander north to south, east to west, kill and kill, with nothing to show for it. Nothing! Maybe, Alpha, you are okay with leaving Remus in their hands. I mean, I never truly followed through on my task, did I? You both wanted me to keep an eye on him, befriend him, have me get close to him so I

could find out his secrets. But he remains a mystery to you, untrust-
worthy, a liability, right?"

Marcus cringed as Caius looked ashamed, but they didn't flinch
away from me. They knew how much I was hurting and let me continue, but that only angered me more. I couldn't stop myself. I *wanted*
to lash out.

"By the way, I am absolutely *thrilled* to report that he did confide
in me on a few things. Would you like to know what I discovered?" I
sneered, glaring at Caius. "Remus has been suffering in silence. While
everyone spat on his name, it turned out that he had always been advocating for the Pack. Helping us when we didn't know it."

Shadows covered the tent in darkness. Someone shouted, but the
world was still muffled as sorrow claimed me. I felt large arms wrap
around me. My feet slipped against the ground as I curled against
their chest.

"No, Marcus. It's okay, I have her," Caius murmured. "Leave us."

I sobbed against the Alpha's chest. Eventually the darkness dissipated, the candlelight returning to the tent. Caius didn't let me go.
He held me, his head resting on mine. I looked up and saw devastation in his gaze.

When he spoke, his voice was a rasp. "I have been angry for a
long time, but I don't hate him. I'm sorry I asked you to do such a
thing to Remus, especially as something has developed between the
two of you. There are things that he and I need to resolve. I hope it
isn't too late for that."

Caius looked away briefly, his jaw clenching under the amber light.
"You're right, though. This isn't enough. I will return to the haven and
demand Valens take me to his king. I will climb the fucking mountains
if I must. We won't be able to win this war without them."

I slowly unwrapped myself from the Alpha's grasp. He held my
shoulders as I wiped the tears from my face.

"Diane," Caius said gently. "I'm also sorry for how the Pack is
treating you. Marcus is right. You've done so much for us and don't
deserve to feel this way."

I sucked in a shaky breath. The Alpha's words meant a lot to me. I didn't hold anything against the Pack—my focus had been on searching for Remus, and I hadn't had the energy to think of much else. But Caius's apology soothed an ache in my heart that I didn't realize was there.

I met his tortured look. "Helena's death has affected both of you deeply. You haven't seen him, Caius. Her death haunts him day and night. You and Remus need to confront this and move forward."

Caius didn't respond. He looked away with another clench of his jaw. He squeezed my shoulders. "We aren't giving up on him. I promise."

I returned to my own tent, unfeeling and hollow inside. I felt useless. Like I was wasting time. I was here, safe and surrounded by loved ones, while Remus was not. My heart twisted at the thought of what could be happening to him right now.

I peeled back the flaps to see Drusus sitting on the edge of my bed. His head was bowed, arms draped over his legs. He looked up, purple smudges still lingering underneath his eyes.

I propped my sheathed sword against the bed. "You look as shitty as I feel."

Drusus smirked, though it didn't meet his dark eyes. "I failed him."

I saw the agony and guilt in his expression. I crawled into the bed and curled at his side, wrapping an arm around his shoulders. "You did *not* fail him, brother." Drusus hardly spoke these days, I knew he wasn't doing well, but I didn't think he actually believed something like that. He leaned into my embrace. Seeing his heartbreak reopened the wounds in my heart. Not that it could fully heal to begin with.

Drusus's voice was hoarse with emotion. "He's gone through so much. I vowed to help him find his way and to be there for him. And I failed him."

We sat in silence. The firewood that flickered outside the tent snapped and popped. Chatters of wolves, she-wolves, and harpies surrounded us. Crickets chirped somewhere.

"We will find him," I said finally. "I will rip every tendril of aether from the ground until he's back with us."

THIRTY-SEVEN

Remus

No dreams existed here. It was a soulless void, a voice that iced bones and blood. Glimpses of sunlight and stars slipped through the slitted windows. I didn't hope for freedom. If it meant that she was far from wherever I was, I'd take it all.

I was familiar with this. Captivity. The binds and gnawing pain. Hunger and thirst. Cold air brushed at my feet, a damp wall at my back. My wounds had been healing, but it didn't matter. They would be reopened soon enough.

Days. Or had it been weeks? I couldn't tell. I had been drifting in and out of consciousness. I saw trees and canyons. Teeth and horns. The Order had covered my eyes when they'd brought me here, and I couldn't tell where I was. They had made sure I was barely conscious the entire time.

Since my capture, no one had entered my chamber except for the occasional sentinel who checked my bindings as well as the odd Order member who brought me droplets of water and what couldn't be considered proper meals. I'd started to think I had been left here to simply rot. But I knew better. The Ram was prolonging my torture, keeping me waiting, trying to anticipate its next move.

One thought remained clear: my pater was alive. He had stood before me, and I hadn't recognized him. We'd been estranged before his supposed death. Well, my attempt to kill him. He had committed wrongs—more than just wrongs—and Helena and I had fought to hold onto the Pack's dignity. But everything had been in vain. Helena had died, and the Ram still roamed this mortal plane.

I could hear someone walking on the other side of the cell's door. Two of them. I shut my eyes and kept my head low as the door slammed open. I sensed the two figures prowling closer.

The scent nudged on a memory. Lemongrass and rose, with a faint taste of sand and sun. It reminded me of Diane, but it was muskier. My thoughts exploded with images of pyramids and that tiny cell I'd spent months in. Shit.

I snapped my eyes open. The two figures standing before me were tall with slender muscles that coursed through their dark, thick skin. They had pointed ears and a long snout like a dog.

Jackal-shapeshifters.

The jackals of Egypt were here in Rome. Assuming I was still in Rome. What were they doing here? Their breastplates curved around their chests and shoulders, glimmering in gold and beads of turquoise. Armlets and ear cuffs, much like the ones Diane wore, shone on their attire. Ivory leather and fabric hung over their thighs. Gold paint streaked from their temples down to the point of their snouts so that they resembled the god of the dead, Anubis.

The two jackals snickered, thick lips curling back to reveal fangs. "It's been a while, Remus. Good to see you again," one jabbed. The other laughed as he twirled a javelin in his hand.

My voice cracked through my hoarse throat. "What is going on? Where are we?"

The jackal closest to me placed a hand on his chest, feigning an offended look. "After all the time we spent in that cell together, Remus, you've forgotten about us?"

Of course I recognized the bastards. They'd tortured me endlessly in that cell. I was blinded by a sudden rage, a hatred doused in red.

I tried to move and bit back a shout. My arms were drawn upward, stuck to chains hooked to the walls on either side of me. Pain screamed through my arms and shoulders. Gods and goddesses knew how long I'd been hanging like this.

"Where are we?" I repeated.

The first jackal revealed his khopesh blade. The dark steel glinted wickedly under the chamber's light. "Don't worry, Wolf. We are still within Roman territory. Come on, Remus. Do you truly not remember us? Did you forget our *play times?*" The words rippled into a growl.

It then dawned on me. Every piece that had led to this war. I cursed aloud. "This has been in the works all along, hasn't it? The entire tension between Rome and Egypt. It was all a means to an end."

The jackal snickered. "You're catching on. Now, you can't do much, Lone Wolf. Don't bother with your aether. The sentinels have their uses when it comes to those bindings." The jackal stepped back, pointing a finger to his chest. "Jabari. And this is Omari. Ah, see, I knew he recognized us. Omari, Did you miss us, Remus?"

I would never forget my captors. They were the same jackals who had cornered Drusus all those years ago. My blood burned at the sight of them, my inner wolf hungering for their deaths, and I looked forward to the day I'd see the life stamped out of their eyes. "Fuck you."

Jabari cackled, while Omari settled before me, bringing the tip of his javelin to my throat. "Oh, I've missed playing with this one," he crooned. "How about we play like old times, yes? Before precious Pater comes."

As if summoned, the doors slammed open, the walls groaned, and a man walked in. Green eyes shot to me, and my breathing hitched. *My pater.* Seeing him again catapulted me into a confusing combination of emotions.

I thought I'd killed you.

Pater, why did you never care about me?

I could see his features more clearly now. His hair had grown past his shoulders, and he looked thicker with age and muscle. He strolled into the chamber and drew closer. I shifted uneasily.

Pater watched me with something like intrigue. He seemed different, in the way he held himself. It was too confident, his demeanor smooth like he was unfazed by the world. Different even from when I'd seen him in the woods, hunting me and Diane.

I remembered the night when the Ram entered our realm. The male with the wolf mask—my pater—had cut my hand, forced me to help the daemon king break free from his imprisonment. It had been him all along.

My pater tilted his head before glaring at the jackals. "I want a moment with him."

Jabari bowed, taking a few steps back. Omari still held the weapon at my neck and dug the point into my skin until I flinched.

"Omari," my pater hissed.

The jackal's dark eyes glittered with pleasure as he watched my pain. "The king says we are to watch him. That is what I am doing."

Jabari grabbed Omari by the shoulder, reeling him back. Omari snapped his jaws, and I slumped forward when the blade left me.

Pater jerked a hand to the door. "Leave us. Disrespect me again and I will send you back to Egypt."

The jackals sneered as they left the chamber. But not before promising to return to me. *For play time.* Once the door had closed, Anthony returned his calculating gaze to me.

"An annoyance, but they serve their purpose in the king's plans." He crouched before me. His scent was familiar, riling up old memories that I wanted to burn. "I know you despise me, but I ask that you quiet that thirst for vengeance for a moment," Anthony said, shadows dancing around his fingers. "I'm here to give you an opportunity."

My heart beat wildly. I laughed mirthlessly. "I can't believe it. You come back from the dead, attack me, and expect me to *converse* with you?"

He grabbed my chin almost forcefully. Shadows crawled from between his knuckles to my skin. The calm, collected look was still present. "Please, spare me. You speak like you have not been killing Order members since becoming the Lone Wolf." When he saw my eyes widen, his lips peeled back in a sardonic smile. "Yes, I had a sense it was you when I received news that my fellow comrades were being found slaughtered across the region. Didn't you leave one of my men with his throat slit while his wife slept beside him?"

I snarled and jerked away from his grip.

My pater snorted, stepping back. "My thoughts exactly. Enough of your vendetta against me and my king. I need you to see the greater purpose as to why I am here. I need you to know that I am doing this for our family."

Another humorless laugh escaped me. "What family? You betrayed your people, your own fucking realm, by serving that monster you call king."

Shadows snapped at his fingers as he curled them into a fist. "That's right. We don't have a family, you killed what was left of it."

I flinched as if I'd been slapped. My pater's lips curved cruelly. "Then again, you and your sister were against me from the beginning. Conspired to betray me. Neither of you understood the work I was trying to do."

He couldn't be serious. "You truly believe that? Pater, you manipulated politics in your favor. Helena and I saw you in the underground tunnels—"

"Yes, I know what I did," he snapped. A hiss of shadow leaked from his shoulders. "You and your sister pried too deeply in the matter without coming to me first. I had a plan! Then what happened? You both fell victim to the daemon king, and your sister's life was the price paid. I was going to tell you both. I did this," he waved to the ghastly chamber, "all of this, for our family. He can bring people back from the dead. The king has fought the gods themselves. You've heard the stories, and they are true. We can bring your mater and sister back. Unite our family once more."

I suddenly wanted to retch. My pater had gone mad. The dead could not cross realms. They belonged to the golden fields and crystalline waters. Tears burned the back of my eyes as I looked at him. I should've known something was amiss with him. From his corrupted plans of conquest with Caesar to what Helena and I had stumbled upon in the underground tunnels. The pieces were slowly falling into place, but some were still missing. I needed to know more.

My pater's chest rumbled so loudly, I was sure the walls were going to crumble. His inner wolf. It has been so long since I'd seen him in that form.

His lips lifted into a bloodless grin. "Before the Ram can bring your mater and sister back, it needs to make *room* for its kind. All those in its way will be eliminated."

I blinked. "Its kind?"

"Yes. Mars, our god of war, banished my king's kind to another realm. All of the gods helped. Unfair, isn't it? To now punish an entire Olympian race. Doesn't that go against what the Pack stands for? The Ram wants its people to be freed. And as a reward for my servitude, it will bring back my loves." A shadow danced across his face. "That is where you come in. With whatever power you've stolen from the gods, you will be able to make the mortal realm anew."

I groaned. The muscles in my arms were screaming. "Pater, please," I begged. "What you are doing is annihilation. Mater wouldn't want you like this."

His eyes flared at the mention of her. "Careful with your words."

I relented. I didn't want to bring my mater into this either. "And the alliance with Egypt?" I asked instead. "You have jackal-shapeshifters in your midst, yet you have killed many of their own before. How did this come about?"

The former Alpha tilted his head back with a pensive look. "The Order's influence stretches beyond the seas. Rome and Egypt have been on the brink of battle for many years, and the tension provided us the opportunity for an alliance. Many of the jackals have joined my king's cause. They agreed to obey his highness, to surrender their emotions and weaknesses to serve a greater calling."

"Surrender their emotions?" I asked. He ignored my question as he leaned forward. His expression turned serious. "Remus, you need to submit. For your own good, pledge yourself to the king. He will come to you soon, and I can't promise that he will be as kind as me. I was able to ask for a moment with you to try and convince you. The alternative . . . will not be easy."

I scoffed, flinching at the stings and cuts on my body. "I will *never* submit to that creature. I will always fight."

He tilted his head back, the look of detachment returning. I huffed a breath, smacking my dry lips. "Pater, are you still in there?"

He blinked, eyes flashing a deep green, his pupils dilating. His wolf appeared as another growl ruptured the air between us. Fangs poked from under his lips before his face became human once more. His voice was emotionless. "I am here, boy, but I am no longer your pater."

The ground shook, and the chains whined. Smoke seeped from under the chamber's door. Somewhere, I could hear the jackals' snickering. Within the smoke, curled horns emerged.

I strained against the bindings in trepidation and fear. The steel dug into my skin, and blood started coating the edges. Red crescent eyes glowed from within the dark. Deep trills echoed.

Anthony watched me. I could've sworn I saw a flicker of remorse. "It's too late."

I hadn't seen the Ram since that first night in the caves. I didn't recall it being so tall, now that it stood before me. Its hide was rough and dark, like that of a minotaur. The aether that lingered around its essence was what I'd felt in the cave. Old and angry.

The daemon king's voice rumbled down my spine. "I've been waiting for you." Anthony stepped aside as the Ram loomed over me. I kept my chin up, challenging those crescent eyes. It ran a finger down my cheek, the armor on its knuckles clinking gently. Its gaze felt cold and endless, like a void. "Now I can take revenge on the gods and goddesses, see my justice through."

"No," I growled.

The Ram placed a finger at the center of my brow. I jerked away and shouted as my back slammed against the wall. Darkness crawled along the corners of my vision. Chains banged against the stone.

The Ram's voice was a lethal quiet. "Your mind will be weakened, but I will show you what you refuse to acknowledge."

The blood in my veins began to boil. I thrashed and screamed. My vision dimmed as the Ram dragged me into the depths of my mind. A face emerged. Golden eyes. Dark hair. Diane. I held onto the image, wishing I could hold her in my arms, talk to her. Tell her how I felt, how I'd been feeling the entire time since I'd started to know her. Her face was the last thing I saw before the darkness swallowed me.

Thirty-Eight

Diane

"I didn't think you would hire us again."

It had been a few months, yet the scene seemed so familiar. Deep red wine swirled as my fingers slid along the smoothness of the cup. My eyes roamed the simple bar. Weary travelers and common civilians. I exhaled a breath. Battle was my mantle. . . .

"I told you I would never forget you," I chided. I drank the wine, wishing it was stronger.

The woman watched me, a rueful look in those eyes.

I placed the cup down. "What?"

"You're hurting," she said simply.

I rolled my eyes and chucked the bag of coin on the table. "I am not paying you for your observations."

She shrugged, looking more amused now. "Technically, you are."

I leaned back in my chair, propping a boot against the table's corner. "Godsdamn, you're right."

The woman made no move to take the bag of coins. To her credit, I was overpaying her. I thought she would simply take the money and flee. I would have paid any price—not only coin—to have any information on Remus.

We needed more eyes on the ground, in the sky, even under the fucking water.

"Just tell me if your girls found anything," I relented.

The woman's eyes returned to that apologetic softness. Pity. "No, my dear. They didn't. It is like the Order disappeared. Daemons haven't attacked these parts since the last time I saw you."

I looked away, trying to smother the overwhelming sense of disappointment. And anger. Why had I hoped for anything at all? Too much time had passed.

"They're hiding." My voice lowered into a whisper. "They're hiding and they're planning. This isn't over. Those bastards have something of mine, and I won't rest till I see them turn to ash."

My eyes went to the door where Drusus and Cato were waiting. *We are wasting time.*

"They have something . . . *someone* you love."

I jerked and glared at the woman but didn't respond. Couldn't. The woman sighed and reached for the coins.

"Strength to you, girl. Love can be a terrible but most beautiful curse."

I picked up the cup for another swig of wine. It was empty. I sighed, placed it down, and got to my feet. The chair scraped against the stone.

Before I could take another step, the woman spoke again, stopping me. "You have fire and heart, child. A killer of men. And I mean that quite literally. How many have died by your hands?"

I slowly turned around. My palms slid along the table as I bared my teeth. "They were all guilty."

The woman's lips curved. "Remember that fire you have. I hope you destroy all those who have wronged you."

I scoffed. "This isn't just about who has wronged me. The man they've taken from me has access to a power unlike any other, and if these fanatics manage to control it, then I fear the worst for all our lives."

She observed me, squinting her eyes slightly. "Then you better get moving."

I walked away a few steps before I glanced at her once more. "I never asked your name."

The woman grinned. The jewels around her neck and wrists

winked against the afternoon light. "I don't know yours either. Let's keep it that way. I like the mystery."

I turned my back to her once more, maybe forever. Drusus and Cato were leaning against the wall of the bar's entrance. The tattoos on their skin glistened with sweat. Drusus gestured to the exit with his head, and we began to walk in the direction of the city's gates.

"It wasn't for nothing," Drusus commented. "We need as many eyes as possible."

I made a noise in my throat but didn't bother to answer. We were in the harbor city where I'd met Remus. To think he'd been on a personal hunt for the Order while I was tending to official Pack business. The different paths of this war against the daemons drew us together.

My eyes landed on the temple that had been destroyed. It had been rebuilt since, as many of the other buildings in the city had. One never could have guessed that a horde of daemons had decimated the place. Or that a wolf of white flames had torn through the city's roads, saving its people.

"So," Drusus began. "How long have you been in love with my brother?"

I stumbled. Drusus was smirking, a wicked glint in his eyes this time. A drastic change from the somber wolf he'd been since Remus's capture.

I tripped over my words. "What? Gods, did you have to eavesdrop on everything?"

Cato chuckled and slipped an arm around my shoulder, forcing me to meet his pace. "I've seen the way Remus stares at you. That male has it *bad*."

I couldn't help but feel a flutter in my stomach at that. Heat bloomed on my cheeks as the intensity of *that* gaze came rushing to my mind. Those jade-green eyes. How they pierced through me, captured me. The dark look he'd sent my way when I had pressed my blade against his neck, as if he'd *liked* that.

As soon as the thoughts came, my heart fell again. Here I was, reminiscing, when he was out there, in the hands of those who wished to hurt him.

We made our way into the outskirts of the harbor city. The camp was stationed within mere yards off the ocean. Caius had remained at the haven in pursuit of an audience with the griffin king while we continued our search for Remus.

The minotaurs had been preparing as well. We'd received word that they had been forging weapons and would be spreading the shipments themselves among the wolf warriors, including the she-wolves. Sabina was a little too excited at the news.

I had been relieved to hear that Theon had survived the attack at the mines. He would bear a nasty scar, but he would live to see another day. I'd thanked the gods and goddesses for that mercy.

We entered my tent. Four pair of eyes met mine.

"How does my tent even fit all of you?" I asked.

Laelia raised her cup. "I truly don't know how or why but it's the comfiest out of all of ours."

Doubtful. Camilla grinned and stood from Atticus's lap. The cocky bastard was in a much lighter mood now that Camilla had joined our ventures. She beckoned for me to sit on my bed, small vials in her hands.

"Don't say anything and let me see how those wounds have been faring," she ordered.

Laelia and Cato had already taken up space on my bed, and I shoved myself between them.

Laelia's wing shifted to accommodate me. "Camilla, Sabina, and I were the first ones here. Wherever Camilla goes, *that* one follows," she said pointing at Atticus, who gave her a smug grin. "And wherever one of your little Pack is, there is surely another close by."

I stifled a chuckle as Cato rolled his eyes. "You like our presence, Laelia. Gods know why Meredith isn't here to keep you company."

The tip of Laelia's wing smacked his head. "She will be returning soon with her scouts."

A pop sounded as Camilla opened the vial with her teeth. The smell of lavender and rose wafted through the room, and I sighed. Camilla's fingers worked the oils on my temples and down my arms. Her aether sang, caressing the ointment into my skin.

Her full lips spread into a smile. "You need this. You didn't really give yourself enough time to heal when you woke."

I mumbled an agreement, casting a glance at our Commanding She-Wolf. Sabina's dark skin looked more toned than when I'd last seen her. She had her hair down and not in the usual braided crown. She gave me a mischievous smile, and it reminded me too much of a wolf my heart missed. *No*, I scolded myself. I couldn't think of him now.

Sabina's eyes shot to Drusus, who stood by the tent's entrance. I snuck a look at him and saw he was watching her with a dark hunger. Sabina and I shared an amused look, and I bit back a chuckle. Camilla had told me that when Laelia had brought an injured Drusus back to the haven, Sabina hadn't left his side, snapping at anyone who tried to get near him.

Sabina's voice broke through my thoughts. "When are you going to complete the Rite?"

I snapped my head toward her and glared at my Commanding She-Wolf. "This again? I thought I'd said I was putting it off until after."

Sabina sighed, rolling her eyes at the ceiling of my tent. "Diane, there will always be something happening. There will never be a 'calm' moment in our lives. Wouldn't it be nice to have your pegasus during battle?"

I knew it would be an advantage. To take to the skies and bend the battleground to my will.

"You would also find some closure. When you find your bonded pegasus, you make an offering to the temple of Mars. Every experience is unique to the she-wolf, but it may help you find some reconciliation within yourself," she added.

My heart skipped a beat. "What if I don't like what I find? What if I have been fooling myself this entire time and the power I possess is not of this realm?"

Atticus snorted, his lips tipping upward. "You are so hard on yourself, Diane. A long-suffering perfectionist. It is not always so black and white. Aether is aether. It is pure in its own essence, and whoever wields it decides whether it may be for good or not. You do not need to have all the answers, just the confidence in yourself that you will figure this out."

I leaned my head against Laelia's shoulder. Sabina was right. Perhaps the Rite would be good for me. I found it ridiculous to conduct the tradition while warriors were preparing for battle, but it seemed there may be some time for it. The thought brought a trickling feeling of surety. A confidence that this might be a good decision. *Later*, I told myself. *I must find Remus first.*

Laelia began to inquire about Egypt's recent actions against Rome. The rumors of Mark Antony's flirtation with the queen of Egypt had been confirmed. The general had been acting with the intention of giving Egypt Roman lands without Rome's approval. Now he had fled and was deemed a traitor to Rome. War had been officially declared against Egypt. The brewing tension had been a tightening chord that had finally snapped, and the blade of war would bestow its lethal cut. It was due time. Caius suspected the Order had taken advantage of the opportunity. It was a battle amongst humans and amongst Olympians.

The adopted nephew of Gaius Julius Caesar, Octavian, had announced preparations for a naval battle. He was to take legions of the human army to intercept the Egyptian ships heading our way. Egypt seemed to have been moving its game pieces far more quickly than anticipated.

The leaders of the Pack—Caius, my father, and Sabina—had been in close communication with Octavian. Each side was fully aware of the other preparing armies and of the destination of each legion. Thankfully, it wasn't something I needed to worry about. My focus was here, with my brothers.

The revelation of Anthony's faked death and betrayal had left a horrific sting among the Pack. Anthony had been loved and admired. He had been seen as a role model of Alpha leadership. How quickly that idea had crumbled. Anthony had done a lot for the Pack, but there were conspiracies of how he'd sold his allegiance to the Order.

More questions had emerged, but the wolves had looked to Caius. He'd had the vision of an alliance between all the Olympians. Uniting cultures and aether. Caius had taken the broken mantle, mended the shards, and led the Pack with a healed light.

When Camilla finished, she closed the vials and wiped her hands with a rag. Her eyes warmed as she clasped her hands over mine. We shared a moment of comfort and affection.

Until Marcus barged through the tent, his curly hair swept over his brow as if he'd been running his hands through it. "We are going back to the Pack haven."

I jumped to my feet. "Why? We have yet to find Remus."

Marcus seemed pale and exhausted. "We've received reports of daemon sightings. Masses of them have been traveling from the southern regions, along the west coast. They are heading to the city of Rome."

Cato cursed under his breath. Drusus stalked out of the tent, shouting orders to the wolves. Atticus kissed Camilla's brow before following.

"No," I seethed. "Marcus, we can't go back yet."

The mere thought of postponing the search for Remus, of *abandoning* him, had desperation clawing at my chest.

Marcus looked exasperated. "I'm not saying we are giving up, but we have to make sure there are enough wolves to defend our home. Your pater is leading armies to face the daemons as we speak."

I hadn't seen my pater since I'd returned to the Pack. I had left the haven as soon as I'd recovered. I couldn't bring myself to face him since the reveal of my shadowed aether.

Something in my chest twisted. Sabina cupped my cheek. Her smoke-colored eyes softened at what she saw in mine. "Trust in Remus. He's strong. He wouldn't succumb so easily."

Sabina jerked her chin to Marcus. "Walk with me."

They left the tent, and I slowly sat back down. Laelia's wing wrapped around me as my thoughts returned to Sabina's words about the Rite. I had an inkling that I wouldn't be able to avoid it for much longer.

Thirty-Nine

Remus

I was at the precipice of death. It taunted me; it stayed so close but never claimed me. The Fates were truly cruel. I relished these moments, though, when there was nothing but the drip from the damp walls and the ragged sounds of my breathing. It was the only solace before the jackals continued their *play time.*

They visited me often, pricking and poking me until I was blinking in and out of consciousness. The jackals were keeping me weak enough to prevent me from using my power. And once the jackals had had their fun, the Ram would appear and throw me back into the void. At first, there would be nothing but darkness until I'd feel the unseen claws rake through my mind. Like he was sifting through my thoughts, penetrating the mental walls in order to seek out my weaknesses. It was constant pain.

But without fail, within the twisted depths of my mind, I always thought of her. Since that vicious, beautiful creature had pressed a blade to my throat, I'd found myself starting to fall for her. Diane. Diane. Diane.

Night bled through the trees, dipping into the catacomb's entrance. Pater had walked through this pass. We followed his scent until it stopped at the foot of a tunnel. He must've gone inside.

"Well, are you going to stand there or are we going to keep going?" Helena's fingers drummed the pommel at her waist impatiently.

I smirked. "You still act like a child."

She jammed an elbow in my chest as she walked by. "I'm more mature than you."

We pressed forward into the catacomb, delving deeper underground until we began to pick up our pater's scent along with a few others. Our feet were silent, our bodies shadowing one another. Helena and I were one. We communicated with the flick of a finger or bat of an eye bending around corners and diving deeper underground.

That is where we felt the dark hum. A symphony of wails. The hairs on my neck rose. Helena brought a hand to her mouth, her eyes going wide with shock from what she saw. I couldn't believe it either.

Our pater stood in the midst of a crowd. People in cloaks surrounded him. "Brothers and sisters, we gather in preparation for a new realm. Undefined by the gods, where all people will have access to aether and will be able to bend it to their will. We will welcome those who were banished unjustly. A realm where our beloved dead can return."

We watched in confusion as the people began to chant foreign words. The humming grew louder, and a voice stood out. It wasn't loud, nor did it echo within the cavernous walls. It was in our minds. Helena's eyes grew frantic, her hands covering her ears. My heart pounded against my chest in terror. I grabbed her arm, forcing her to get moving.

"We live today and fight tomorrow," I hissed. "Now, we run."

It wasn't long before we heard roars and snapping teeth. The voice still followed us, and I shouted at the darkness. Helena and I ran out of the tunnel, figures darting between the trees. Red crescent eyes leered as the creatures hunted us. I had never seen such animals before.

We were forced to fight, our backs pressed against each other as we cut them down. The voice was even louder now, and I fought the urge to clamp my hands over my ears. More creatures came, and we tore through the woods, separating from each other. The voice kept relaying its story. Of its banishment. Of the banishment of its kind. How it wanted to be released. The voice asked if I could help free it. I ran until I saw my sister again. Her eyes were blank as she gazed at the moon.

I blinked, and Helena wasn't Helena. A daemon stood in her place. I staggered forward, breathing heavily as I neared it.

"What have you done with her?" I shouted.

The daemon turned to me. It had the skull of a snake. It snarled, claws scraping the earth as it lunged toward me.

I drove the dagger up its ribcage. "What did you do?"

My vision flickered. I blinked as the air in my lungs was trapped. It had never been a daemon. Helena's body, bloodied and limp, was now in my arms. My hand was still on the dagger's pommel.

I fell to my knees, clutching her, rocking back and forth, as my screams tore through my heart. My soul.

In the depths of my mind, the voice was laughing.

I woke up with a jolt. Sweat trickled down the nape of my neck. Gods. It had been years, and all I could ever see in my nightmares was me killing Helena. I had somehow forgotten about the daemon, had stamped it out from memory because of the sheer horror of what I'd done.

My head slumped forward, my back against the wall. My arms were no longer strung up by chains. The binds were now strapped to my ankles, but I was able to sit. There was a cot just a few feet away from me, but they kept me shoved in the corner.

"You think of your sister often."

Gods, I forgot he was in here. Anthony had also visited me often. I ignored him. He sat on a chair, leg crossed over his knee and a book in hand. A godsdamn book, as if his son was not chained before him.

He placed it on the table and clasped his hands in his lap. I avoided his gaze and kept my eyes on the floor at my feet, the redness around my ankles. I swallowed, the taste making me gag. They'd kept me alive with bite-sized meals and limited water. They would always feed me after the Ram had tormented my mind.

I had been fighting the temptation to surrender to the Ram. I had never been afraid of the dark, but this was entirely different.

"Remus."

I closed my eyes. "What would happen if I were to give in?"

There was no immediate response. In that pause, I tried to recall a time when my pater had showed even a sliver of affection but came short.

My pater's voice finally broke the silence. "It is an agreement between you and the Ram. You surrender your emotions, your humanity, in exchange for loyalty. As part of it, the Ram gives you access to his power, the shadows you've seen the Order wield."

"It sounds like you are selling your soul."

"You won't feel pain," Anthony continued. "You will be conscious and aware of your actions, but any mortal feeling will no longer exist. At least none of the strong, debilitating ones. Everything will become easier."

The crack at the last words made me look up. I eyed the smoothness of his brow, the relaxed curve of his shoulders and jaw. I realized I had never seen him more at ease than he was now.

"You succumbed," I observed. "So you didn't have to feel any more pain."

He shrugged, the corner of his lip kicking up. "It's less . . . distracting."

I ground my teeth in frustration. For the love of gods . . . "You tossed away valuable memories of mater and Helena like they were nothing. Solely because you were a coward and couldn't face the sadness and whatever guilt came with their memory."

"I may not feel remorse, sadness, or pain, but I still have my sense of purpose. I intend to bring them back," Anthony explained as if talking to a child.

My body screamed as I rolled to my feet. I glared at him, flames of pale moon flickering dimly over my skin.

White smoke curled angrily at the corners of my eyes. "They cannot come back. The only thing you've done is heighten the more dangerous emotion in you while shutting out the other part. The part that balances your heart. You are simply avoiding the inevitable hurt."

Anthony jumped to his feet, the chair falling to the ground. His eyes roamed over the fires that danced along my skin.

"Just imagine the destruction you can bring," he said.

"I'm sure Mater would be proud."

He snarled, and pain flashed under my eye. I tumbled back as Anthony shook out his fist. I refused to touch my rapidly swelling cheek.

I straightened, fangs protruding from my lips. "You said I think of my sister often. I do. Her death haunts me every day, but I refuse to let go of her memory. She deserves to be remembered, and I will *never* do what you did."

Anthony stared at me, the green of his eyes darkening. The doors opened, and the jackals entered.

Jabari snarled with glee as he spun twin sets of blades in his hands. "Pater and son bonding time has come to a close."

Anthony didn't leave immediately. I thought I saw a tightening in his shoulders. An animalistic growl spewed from his lips before he slammed the door behind him.

Omari ran a slanted hand down the slick side of his dagger. "So broody."

Jabari snickered and slashed his arm upward. It was swift, and I grunted as I felt the sting across my chest. A line of red bubbled from the slim cut.

Jabari tossed the other blade into the air, and then pointed it toward me. "We are going to continue adding more scars to the collection."

The silver flames returned with my anger. How they took pleasure in hurting me. I may have been chained, easy prey, but the jackals would never have me. They would never break me.

I growled and lunged at them. Jabari leapt back out of my range, the chains holding me back. "Ah, careful Lone Wolf. We are the only ones who can do the biting."

"You are sick," I replied, kicking at the string of chains.

Omari chuckled, swiping with his dagger at my shoulder. He did it again and again until I cried out from the pain. Omari cocked his head to the side, admiring his work. His jackal eyes held a hysteric gleam.

"Sick with joy," he responded.

They continued handing out cuts and gashes, taking turns as they cackled and snarled. I managed to grab Jabari by the throat only for Omari to drive a thick blade up my side. I shouted, stumbling back.

Dark claws nicked my skin as Omari placed his foot on my chest. "Why don't you take a seat?"

He shoved me to the ground, my head banging against the stone. And the jackals continued, to the point where darkness began to cloud my vision.

Eventually, I saw the Ram's horns and crescent eyes appear before me. Armored fingers tipped my chin up, and I felt a sharp prick on my brow.

Give in, and the pain will stop.

My body jerked. My blood began to burn, and screams ripped at my throat. I relived Helena's death. A repeat of me running the dagger up her side over and over. Chaos sank its teeth into the exhausted fragments of my soul.

Black hair . . . eyes of honey . . . who was she?

Diane.

FORTY

Remus

My ankles were still chained but this time to a hook at the end of my cot. The corner I had been held in before was stained with my blood. Dark smudges of it ran along the stone wall. The cot was a lot better than the stone floor.

I couldn't move. Every fiber of muscle had been expended as the jackals twisted my body and the Ram twisted my mind. My eyes flickered open and closed as I watched the light that snuck into the chamber be snuffed out by the night. On and on it went. I knew the routine. Jackals, the Ram. I hadn't realized until now, but it had been days since I'd last seen Anthony.

The doors opened. I expected to hear the usual cackles and sneers. A presence darkened the entire chamber, like a dark wave. I turned my head and cracked an eye open to see Anthony and the Ram. Dark clouds misted around the Ram's feet, but it somehow looked more 'real.' Mortal. *It is not a god*, I reminded myself. *It may be as powerful as one, but it isn't immortal.*

He, not *it*. The Ram was of his own species and not some rabid animal. Anthony bowed his head and left the room. My lips twitched in loathing.

The Ram loomed above me. Unease trickled through me. This was different from how the days usually went. I not want to go back to whatever mental cages he threw me in. "I want to tell you a story of my people," the daemon king said.

I slowly managed to sit up in the cot and pressed my back against the wall. "I already know your story, Ram."

The creature chuckled. The sound was almost ghost-like as it reverberated from the chains attached to my feet through my very bones. "I have a name. The mortals' ignorance in this realm will be the death of you all."

My lips twisted into a sneer. "Can't blame us ignorant mortals. The gods banished the memory of your name. Besides, I prefer *Ram*, it's simpler."

The daemon king ignored my jab. "Before this realm's creation was completed, before a single drop of breath was bestowed on these lands, the gods banished my kind to another realm. They said we were unfit to live here. Since then, I have vowed to return. I have armies on the other sides of the veil just waiting for me to release them. You are the key to that, as is the golden-eyed she-wolf. You both hold enough power to rip the seams of the realms open."

My brow furrowed at the mention of the she-wolf. Golden-eyes. Light brown skin. Full, parted lips. And the scent of blossoms. I held onto that image.

Smoke billowed out of the Ram's nostrils, curling like horns. "I spoke to mortals for centuries from the other side. I influenced their deeds and actions, waiting to find the perfect one. Then I found your pater. Ridden with sorrow and loss, he was willing to give anything to have his fallen wife back. From then on, he conspired against and thwarted Rome's governing power from the inside. It was easy to do so when he partnered with that conqueror, Caesar. After crossing lands and sea, your pater found my followers and formed what I hear you mortals call the Order. Yet, I still needed aether to let me into this realm. And I found it. That one night, many years ago, I found enough aether when I sensed you and the other she-wolf. You were searching for your pater. I tried to influence you both, but my efforts were in vain. I had to withdraw . . . but not without punishing you for the defiance."

My blood burned, and I lurched forward as I caught his insinuation. "It was you," I snarled. "*You* killed her."

Helena. My heart screamed her name. I had never understood what had happened. Her death had haunted me for years, and even in my nightmares the memories of that night were distorted. Never clear nor complete.

It had been the Ram. He had killed her and had me convinced I had done it on my own accord. The realization was sickening.

The Ram grabbed me by the throat, pinning me to the wall. Air choked out of me as he dragged me higher, my feet sliding against the stone, the chain on the cot pulling at my leg. I fought against his grip, but the Ram dug his claws in just enough to break skin.

The daemon king curled his lips in a snarl. His breath rolled against my ear. "I couldn't influence you enough to give away your humanity, but I managed to distort your reality." He tapped an elongated claw at my temple. "With this, I distorted the reality of your mind. You killed that she-wolf by *my* hand."

Dark spots fluttered across my eyes. I dug my nails into the Ram's large forearm. Anything to release the iron grasp on my throat. "Fuck you," I wheezed. "You used me. You took someone important away. Now, you owe me."

Intrigue lit within the depths of the Ram's fire-red eyes. "Owe you? What do you desire?"

My feet slid against the wall once more before I stopped fighting and hung limp in the Ram's chokehold. I was tired. So tired.

"My sister," I said weakly.

The Ram touched my brow, and the corners of my mind began to slip. "If you join me, I will do so much more than return the dead to you."

The roaring ache in my chest echoed with every sweep of my blade. Slashes of silver winked with every bloody arc. The screaming in the cat-acombs was a distant hum. I couldn't feel the splatter of blood on my face as I ripped my blade from the robed figure's neck.

The last body fell at my feet. My boots stepped through more liquid and kicked at the head of a snake-skull. I stood among the bloodshed, but all I could see was Helena.

Lost in my grief, I didn't notice the figure at the entrance of the catacomb. The voice of a male I now hated.

"What did you do?" My pater's voice trembled with what sounded like rage and despair.

A tear rolled down my cheek. I could not find the words. Helena's lifeless body still flashed before my eyes. The clang of the sword rang throughout the cavern as it fell from my hand.

"You don't understand. The work I've been doing is beyond what you and I . . ."

His voice was drowned out by the blood that roared in my ears.

"You are no longer a member of the Pack of Rome. I brand you . . ."

I finally lifted my head to the male who was my pater no longer. I walked past him, but he gripped my arm. Fingernails dug through my clothes.

His voice deepened into a snarl. "Try anything and the Pack will never support you. Your name is sullied, and I will not have your ignorance and stupidity halt what needs to be done. One day you will understand."

I shoved him from me. "I want nothing to do with you. Ever again."

He said nothing of my sister. She had been his favorite, and that was when I knew something had broken inside him. Left him unfeeling. Without humanity. I left the catacombs, brushing the branches out of my path.

The bloodthirst hadn't waned; it only hummed for more. I retrieved Helena's body. Aether rumbled through the ground while unseen claws tore at my heart.

And so I became The Lone Wolf.

White flames exploded out of me, wild and desperate, forcing me back to reality before I could sink into the memory once more. There was a faint image. Familiar. Black hair . . . eyes of sunset . . . I couldn't remember her name. Every burning feeling toward her was dimming. . . .

FORTY-ONE

Diane

It felt like someone was screaming for me. I jolted awake on the bed, hand flying to my dagger. My heart pounded against my ribs. I was breathing heavily as my eyes searched my tent.

But I was alone.

After several beats of silence, I slowly returned under the sheets.

My gaze strayed to the pale starlight shining between the slits of the tent as I tried to make sense of what happened. It wasn't a sound that had woken me, but a feeling. Like someone was shouting my name through the aether of the realm.

I was unsure what to make of it, and I tried to close my eyes.

A sense of foreboding surrounded me like a pack of hounds.

FORTY-TWO

Remus

The sunlight was too bright, and the sounds—gods, everything was uncomfortable to my ears. Members of the Order floated about the courtyard, disappearing through doors and beyond the gates. I felt their curious glances. Some bowed their heads to me, and a part of me enjoyed the sight.

Anthony was at my heel. He was like my shadow, constantly around. His face was cold and impassive, much like the other members, but there was a tightness around his eyes. An occasional twitch of his lips. He'd been wanting me—my power—at his side for so long, the least the old man could do was look a bit more pleased with the outcome.

I had been freed from my cell. My wounds had healed except for the new set of scars that I had collected. I was finally being given proper meals and water. Although I was free from the binds, the sentinels never strayed too far. If they needed to apprehend me, they could do so. Not that it was really necessary now, as my aether had been snuffed out and was rekindling at a very slow pace.

We walked the length of the courtyard. High towers of dark limestone walls surrounded us. The air was heavy ocean salt and sun. I continued to walk past the fortress, sensing others of the Order flanking me.

The ocean expanded before us. Endless water and light stretched beyond. We were on an island. Boats bobbed along the docks, and we began to board. I stood at the helm as members of the Order pushed the boat into the sea. More boats undocked alongside us.

Anthony gazed out at the waves. "Keeping you here was temporary. We have another residence on the mainland. It isn't far. Daemons have ravaged those lands so much that no mortal lingers there for long."

"Where have the armies been amassing?"

Anthony glanced my way, his eyes running along the placid features of my face. "It doesn't matter," he responded eventually. "Our forces are already moving."

The hours dragged as water sloshed against the boats. The second settlement, deep within the hills of the mainland before the mountains began, was a fortress of watchtowers and tall structures. Daemons, in addition to the winged sentinels, patrolled the area. Other followers of the Order meandered about.

Anthony and I were ambling along just outside the gates when jackals emerged from the trees. I hadn't seen them in some time since I'd been released. They had been sent to prepare for our return to the mainland. I'd found their absence quite liberating.

Their snouts were coated in blood. Javelins were latched over their backs, the bladed tips glistening red. My curiosity was piqued. Jabari and Omari stopped when they noticed me.

Jabari tilted his head, prowling closer. "Are you still in there, Lone Wolf? Or did you give up your humanity?"

I didn't respond as I eyed the two jackals before me. The absurd elation in their dark, wicked eyes made them seem high off whatever bloodshed they had returned from.

Anthony gestured to the blood stains on their golden circlets and robes. "What happened?"

Jabari gestured back to the trees. "The king will want to see this. A group of harpy scouts have been found. We killed them all, save for one."

Omari's lips parted, revealing red-stained fangs. "Wouldn't it be a great opportunity for Remus to show his allegiance to the king?"

I arched a brow, leveling Omari's conniving grin with an impassive look. Darkness seeped from the ground as the Ram stepped out of his cloak of ancient aether. The jackals and Anthony went to one knee. As did I.

"Show me," my king rumbled.

———

The bodies were in ribbons, scattered carelessly like the aftermath of a feast. The jackals had certainly had their fun. A small creek cut through the clearing, and its waters ran red. Wings had been ripped from the harpies' backs. Their throats and limbs were torn.

The jackals stood on either side of me as I examined their work. My nostrils twitched at the smell of blood. My inner wolf growled in agitation. It had been too long since I'd been in my wolf form, and I was beginning to feel uncomfortable in my own skin. But I could not shift unless the king deemed it so.

A follower of the Order stood in the clearing with a badly wounded harpy at their feet. I motioned the individual away as I stepped closer to the harpy, keenly aware of the crowd behind me. I knew the Ram watched amidst the trees.

The harpy squinted at me. She had ivory skin and wine-colored hair. Her dark wings had been torn but looked well enough to take flight. Blood covered her body, most of it hers. I cocked my head at her.

Her eyes widened. "Remus? Remus, it's me. Meredith."

The harpy's face fell as I looked at her.

Her eyes watered in despair and hope. "Remember me. Remember us. Laelia, Caius, Drusus . . . Diane."

"Enough," the king growled. Billows of black smoke unfurled around his feet and hands. "Finish it."

The jackals snarled excitedly, pointing their spears at us. I felt Anthony nearing me with a steady, if slightly hesitant, pace.

"Son, think about what you are going to do," he said.

Son.

I began to laugh and lunged. Fangs extended, I clamped a hand around the harpy's neck, squeezing. She fought me, scratching at my hand and arm, but there was nothing she could do. Her lips were moving, but I heard nothing. I slammed the harpy to the ground. I glared at her as she whimpered in pain.

"Find the others," I snarled. "Show them what happened to an entire group of scouts. Only two against you all, everyone dead except for you. Fly hard and swift, little bird."

I released the harpy, and she staggered back. Her wings lifted. She looked at me once more, her eyes glistening, before she took to the sky.

I turned to look at the Ram. "That harpy will find the wolves and show them the extent of your power. I am yours to will as you like, my king."

Jabari jammed his javelin to the ground. "I think I like this new Lone Wolf."

Shame, Umari grumbled, sheathing the blade over his back. "I'm beginning to miss the old one."

The Ram's crescent eyes lingered on me. Tendrils of darkness caressed my face. "I think it is time we pay the people of the Roman lands a visit."

I bowed my head and walked with him as we left the clearing, Anthony's gaze burning into my back.

FORTY-THREE

Diane

Dust speckled the light pouring between the trunks, the grass looking like golden wheat. At the edge of the forest and down a slope was a group of villas where a grove of lemon trees had ripened. The zesty smell filled the air. The Pack haven was now near, and with every passing day the dullness in my chest thickened.

A sharp cry pierced the woods. Skirting between the trees and bobbing in the air was a harpy. One wing bent horrifically, but she still clung to the air.

My heart fell when I recognized her. Meredith was coated in blood. She fell at the edge of the camp, and a crowd swarmed around her.

I shoved through the wolves, Cato and Drusus flanking me. A wolf already held Meredith in his arms. He checked her pulse and nodded. A sliver of relief. I looked ahead through the trees. There were no other harpies. Meredith had left with an entire group of scouts. Was she the only one to return? The thought brought a bitter taste to my mouth.

Another sharp cry pierced the air and my heart. It was a sound I never wanted to hear again. Laelia landed with a harsh thud, wings seeming duller in color as they folded over her back. She fell to her knees, scooping Meredith from the wolf's arms.

"Fuck's sake, Meredith, open your eyes!" Laelia's lips trembled as a hand wiping away the hair plastered on Meredith's pink skin.

Meredith's eyes fluttered. Her hand twitched at her side as if she was trying to muster all the strength she had left to touch Laelia, but the words fell from weak lips. "Everyone is dead. Jackals killed them. Remus was there. . . . He seemed so cruel, emotionless. I don't think he's himself."

Blood roared in my ears. I staggered back and felt a hand grip my elbow. Drusus's deep voice murmured something in my ear, but I couldn't hear anything.

The jackal-shifters of Egypt were here. How could that be? A damning suspicion inched its way to my mind, and the look I shared with Marcus confirmed it. The naval battle against Egypt. It couldn't have been a coincidence. It meant that Egyptian forces were being recruited to join the Order's army.

And Remus. Oh, gods, if Remus was no longer himself. . . My breathing went rampant. No, no, no. Remus wouldn't have given up.

"No." I didn't realize my whisper was said aloud.

Laelia's back stiffened, wings going taut. Meredith tried to say something to her, but Laelia turned to me. Anger burned in my warrior sister's eyes.

"Your Remus did this," she snarled. "She almost died. When I see him again, I can't promise I won't kill him."

"That's enough." Cato pushed between us, ushering a harpy forward to help Laelia and Meredith.

Drusus grabbed my arm gently, but before he could urge me to step back, a light flashed, blinding the world. Murmurs fell over the camp, and we watched as a column of white flames rose from the ground. It clawed at the sky, baring its fiery teeth to the gods and goddesses who watched from above.

Remus.

I didn't think—couldn't think—as I ripped out of Drusus's grasp and tore through the woods. He cried out for me to wait. Shouts and commands were bellowed, and soon wolves began running alongside me. I caught the familiar brown wolf at my side. Marcus's snout nudged me, and I swung myself over his back.

Harpies cried out and rose above the trees. Laelia was not among them; she would stay behind with Meredith where Camilla could treat her. I looked to my right and saw Sabina atop Drusus, no pegasus in sight. Aether hummed from her dark skin as she flashed her teeth and unsheathed her sword.

Atticus and Cato stayed close, barking commands and leading other wolves. Caius had yet to return to the camp, but we couldn't wait. There was no time.

The woods soon opened to a slope, unveiling the valley below. My brothers shifted back to their human forms. The hills before us were lit in moonlight fire. Villas burned as civilians ran away like ants. Screams echoed among the hills.

Remus had done this.

Cato padded to Marcus's side. *"We will get him back, Diane,"* he said, pressing his snout to the top of my head. *"Keep fighting for him, and we will figure out the rest. Fight for him and yourself. Fight for the love you bear for one another."*

Tears burned my eyes, but I made myself nod.

Sabina pointed at the people. "Harpies and wolves, help the people to safety. Kill daemons and any you find."

"My brothers and I will find Remus," Marcus confirmed. He glanced over his shoulder, his gaze landing on me, flickering with a shade of remorse. *"Cato may be more of a romantic, but I cannot promise the same."*

Drusus growled in anger before sprinting down the hillside, Sabina still on his back. Cato shifted back, and we rounded the streets and corners, edging closer to the beacon of flames. The heat was so intense that sweat dabbed my brow and back. Seeing the fire so close, it was difficult to deny that this wasn't the making of something *more.* Godly, even.

My brothers and I kept close to each other as we ran down a street. A pack of daemons emerged around a corner and charged toward us. Cato lunged, ripping through the horde. The wolves cleared the road, and a civilian ran around a corner from the direction of the fires.

Cato stopped him. *"Did you see him?"*

He didn't need to specify whom. The man nodded, fear paling his face. "The Wolf of White Flames is here. He came in fire and light, but he didn't burn the villas. Not immediately. We noticed the brightness and fled."

Cato gave me a sidelong glance. We rounded the corner onto a main road. Tongues of moonlight followed a tall figure clad in dark armor.

Flames bowed to his every step, crawled over the roofs and walls of the villas he passed. The heavy reality of his presence caught the air in my throat.

Remus's back was to us. Beside him, the tips of their javelins winking wickedly against the burning night, were the jackal-shapeshifters, who wore Egyptian armor. My gaze caught on their golden armlets.

Marcus's voice barreled through the street. *"Remus!"*

Remus paused and slowly turned his head. I felt the pull to go to him, but my blood ran cold when I saw his gaze. His eyes were empty. Gone was that wicked gleam. Drusus took a step forward, but Sabina urged him to stay back. Remus's gaze ran over us with detachment. No emotion behind those beautiful eyes. *Please, no.*

Anthony appeared behind him and leaned in to whisper something as Remus's eyes tracked us. There wasn't a shred of warmth in them. His green gaze then slid to me, and my heart stopped, as if holding its breath.

Remus turned away and walked into the night, leaving us with the flames that burned the town.

Forty-Four

Diane

My nose wrinkled from the harsh smell of burnt wood. One male had done this. I'd seen the enormity of Remus's power before, but this was something else. It had all been for show. The Ram wanted to show just how deep its influence ran.

Remus couldn't have given up years of hunting the Order only to succumb to it. I refused to believe it.

There had been no deaths, thank the gods. Only minor injuries and burns. Healers were tending to those affected. The villas had burned to soot and ash. The wolves shifted to their human forms, joining the she-wolves in lowering the flames.

It was odd that there hadn't been any casualties. Surely the Ram would've desired bloodshed and death, so I couldn't understand. Seeing the jackals and the Alpha again had rattled us and shocked the other wolves. Many of them had been distraught, heartbroken.

Harpies tended to the people, leading them to the shelter of barns or sheds. There were only so many resources available within our reach. People began to build makeshift campsites. Children and women slept in wagons and carriages while others lay in the grass.

Finally, in the dead of night, the wolves and harpies returned to the camp. All the while, I concocted my own plan. The candlelight in my tent flickered against the gold of my armband. The near silent sigh of the dagger being sheathed into my thigh strap brought me a sense of comfort. I slipped another dagger at my hip and slid to my feet, drawing the hood of my cloak over my head.

Silent like a wraith, I walked toward the tent of the only other person I knew would understand my plan.

"Drusus," I whispered, opening the entrance to his tent. "Are you awake?"

He lay on his bedroll, an arm draped over his eyes, his thick hair completely disheveled. The sparse facial hair that was beginning to grow over his jawline gave him a more wild, unruly look. I was sure Sabina liked it.

Drusus looked up, his eyes bloodshot. He eyed the hood of my cloak and the pommel of my sword. A smirk grew over his lips, and a wicked gleam shone in that dark gaze.

"Going out for a stroll?" he asked.

I gave him a lopsided grin, propping a hip against the tent post. "I thought you'd enjoy some fresh air."

Drusus's expression sobered. He stood, sheathing his own sword and clasping a cloak of his own around his neck. He ran a large hand through his hair. "I haven't been able to sleep, anyway."

"Neither have I."

He paused, eyes scanning the sleeping camp. "Should we bring the others with us?"

My teeth grazed my lip as I mulled it over. "No, they have duties here. Marcus would want to come up with a more elaborate plan, but I cannot wait any longer."

We trod into the wood's embrace. When we were far enough from the Pack's ears, Drusus shifted into his wolf form. His long tongue lapped at his muzzle, and I stifled a snicker. I clambered onto his back and held onto the fur at the nape of his neck as he waded through the thicket.

Moonlight kissed the grass, giving it a bluish hue, dawn a mere handful of hours away. We walked in the direction Remus had gone, but the wilderness was vast. No trace of him.

We gazed at the landscape. I felt a heaviness weighing on me that felt a lot like helplessness. Needing a distraction, I began to scratch behind Drusus's ears.

He squirmed in place. *"That feels good."*

"As in inappropriate good or just good?"

The wolf barked a deep laugh. *"Gods, Diane, no. Just good."*

I shrugged. "Just wanted to be sure. Can you catch his scent?"

Drusus lifted his snout, his nostrils flaring as he sniffed. *"It's faint. We can only head in the general direction and hope for the best."*

I tried to search the air for that familiar ocean and pine scent, scrambling for anything but coming up short. The male wolves had a much keener sense of tracking.

The morning sun was beginning to crawl over the mountain rim, and I was becoming more unsettled. His snout was plastered to the grass as he grunted and snorted. A growl rumbled in his throat, and he suddenly kicked off the ground, running toward the hills.

"I only needed to hang on to the unusual scent of the jackals," Drusus growled. *"Their scent is much more prominent. It seems they sweep through these lands much more than Remus."*

A horrid thought twisted in my stomach. "Do you think he's still there?" And still clinging to his humanity?

Drusus's pace quickened, understanding my true, unspoken question. *"He has to be."*

Between the hills, a watchtower of wood and stone emerged. The watchtower guarded a fort higher up the hill. Torches dotted the stone and brick buildings. Figures strolled about, and I could tell it was the Order. That old and heavy sensation was thick here.

My stomach rested on the grass as I peered over the hill slope and observed the fort. Drusus shifted back into his human form, laying on the ground beside me. He wasn't wearing the hard slabs of armor, just his fighting leathers.

His eyes narrowed. "This place smells like death."

My nose wrinkled. Between the scent of ash and a sickly-sweet odor, it reeked of the Order.

Atop the watchtowers, I could see the winged daemons. Their

batlike wings stood out against the fading moonlight. Even from this distance, the red crescent eyes on their skull faces glowed.

Imagining Remus stuck in a place like this sent my blood boiling.

I tapped the pommel of the sword at my waist. "Infiltrate the fort and find Remus."

Drusus caught my arm before I could move forward. "Not so fast. See those towers along the edge of the fort? We start with those, and if Remus isn't there then we move outward. But Diane, for the love of gods, do not run off without me. We are outnumbered and need to proceed carefully."

I wrenched out of his hold, irritated that he thought me to be so reckless, but that's also exactly what I would've done. "Then don't fall behind."

We glided to the fort's walls. We edged closer, hidden by the tall dark grass, avoiding the winged daemons. The fort had long been abandoned. It was very old, and I assumed it had been one of the first forts manned by humans. The stone was cracked, the wood splintered along the wall. I ran a hand over the surface. We needed to be as silent as possible.

Aether pulsed from my palms, seeping into the cracks as I pulled on the loose stone. Drusus dove and caught one of the larger stones before it fell to the ground, but it didn't stop other rocks from spilling onto the grass. We froze. There were distant murmurings and low conversations but nothing else.

I exhaled slowly and had begun to step through the space in the wall when Drusus stopped me. He pressed a finger to his lips and pointed. On the other side of the wall was a daemon. We were still hidden, but the creature must've caught the sounds.

Claws extended from Drusus's hands. He grinned and thrust his hand out as the daemon stepped in front of the hole. Drusus slammed a hand over the creature's mouth while driving a blade through the base of its spine. The daemon spasmed, and Drusus twisted his hands, breaking its neck.

We stepped through the makeshift entrance and entered the Order's fort, keeping to the shadows of the buildings. We rounded the corner of the tower we wanted to enter. Two daemons ambled by the clearing in front of it.

Drusus and I stepped out of the dark in unison and grabbed the daemons from behind. They squirmed and fought against our hold. Muffled shuffling sounds were followed by faint gurgles as Drusus's blade slit the daemon's throat. I used my hands, clamping one over the creature's bony mouth while shadows spilled from my skin into him, suffocating him from the inside. My other arm wrapped across its chest as the darkness slid over his body, and he went limp. Drusus's eyes were wide as I quietly placed the daemon's body on the ground.

"Remind me not to piss you off," he muttered.

I smirked as I skirted around him to enter the tower. The door opened to darkness. I stepped in, the shadows twisting along the length of my arms. The wood underneath my boots creaked, and I paused. Drusus hadn't come in yet.

Large arms wrapped around me, slamming against a hard body. I froze. Lips brushed along my ear. Warm breaths caressed my skin.

And that deep voice . . . "I thought I told you to stay away."

My traitorous heart thumped wildly at being so close to him, and despite the kindling of fear, the feeling quickly melted into heat. A delicious heat curled inside me. I wasn't sure what that said about me.

"Remus," I breathed. "Please."

I was still rigid in his grasp. I was not foolish enough to think Remus was still *Remus*. I kicked at him, aiming for his groin.

He growled. "I advise not doing that."

He dragged me outside. Drusus was on his knees, arms raised behind his head. Hordes of daemons and the Order surrounded him. Remus spun me to face him.

Silver flickered behind the green of Remus's eyes as his lips curled. His voice was melted darkness and steel. "Your highness, we have guests."

FORTY-FIVE

Diane

I staggered toward Drusus, keeping my own hands raised. I tried to ignore the gentle way Remus pushed me away. He was dressed in fighting leathers, painted the color of midnight and plated with deep silver armor pieces. The sinewed strength of his legs flexed with every step, the deep glow of dawn at his back. A demigod of war.

"Remus, come home," Drusus begged.

Remus's eyes drifted to him. There was some recognition in them, but it didn't ignite the way one would normally look at a loved one.

There was a long pause before Remus spoke. "You shouldn't have come."

Sounds of laughter neared, and the jackals emerged from the crowd of snarling daemons. Their javelins kissed the night sky as they came to stand on either side of Remus.

One leaned forward, its fangs dripping with saliva. "Friends of yours, Lone Wolf?"

Remus remained unmoved. Bored. "No."

I had been holding on to the hope that Remus was still himself, and a small, stubborn part of me still did, but to hear him speak like that . . . Cold pain chipped away at my heart.

The other jackal sneered. "We will see about that."

I didn't see the creature move. One moment he stood next to Remus and the next he was nearly on Drusus. My brother was quick, unsheathing his blade with unnatural speed. I jumped back as their

302 | JESSICA J. AYALA

weapons clashed, the two of them grunting. My hand reached for my sword.

Stars scattered across my vision as my arm was yanked painfully behind my back. Claws pulled on my hair, and the cool sting of a blade was pressed against my throat.

The other jackal's breath brushed against my ear. "What a pretty little thing."

Remus's eyes flashed. Silver flames roared from his body. "Do not fucking touch her."

The jackal cackled. "Doesn't seem like you've completely given up your allegiance with them."

His blade tilted slightly, pulling a hiss from my lips. Drusus roared and struggled against the other jackal to get to me.

Remus's gaze glowed a complete silver. White smoke twisted from his eyes and lips. "Either you have them stand down or I will make them, *your highness*."

The daemon king appeared, materializing behind Remus. The Ram strode forward, quiet and lethal. Wicked-looking scythes were strapped over its back. I remembered that in some of the stories the Ram was as much a warrior as it was a conqueror.

"Leave them," the Ram bellowed. "Do not touch what is mine."

The cold steel left me, and the jackal shoved me to the ground before strutting back to the daemon horde. Drusus was soon behind me, helping me to my feet.

The Ram continued walking. Drusus tensed as I wedged myself between them. Two blood-red crescent eyes stared at me. The creature towered over me, but I refused to cower, digging my heels into the ground.

"You thought you'd snuck into my hold? I *allowed* you to enter my residence, she-wolf." The Ram raised a finger, caressing a knuckle down my cheek. "Your power sings to me."

Every muscle in my body screamed to flinch back, to run home and scrub the atrocity from my skin. Instead, I tipped my chin higher and narrowed my gaze.

"My power is mine alone," I said.

The Ram drifted back. Chilling, ghostlike laughter skittered through the air, pebbles shifting from the deep reverberations. My skin prickled at the sound. It disappeared in a cloud of smoke and reappeared behind Remus.

"You've seen my vision. I planted it in your mind, but your fear only nourished it," the daemon king taunted. "You will make room for my kind. Wouldn't this world be better without your current state of corruption? If you started anew and allowed your lands to flourish once more?"

A scoff threatened to escape me. "Sounds like you are trying to be a god."

The Ram snarled, for once revealing something other than a calm, emotionless demeanor. "The gods are the ones to blame for all this, the hypocrites."

Darkness pooled from its feet, spiraling around Remus, and I hitched a breath. I wondered if the Ram was going to take him away again, a sense of panic rising at the thought. If Remus disappeared again, we may never be able to find him. He still held the empty gaze, though his fists were clamped to his sides, shaking.

The Ram's voice boomed in the wind. "She is of use to us. Bring her to me. Let her beloved wolf force her into our ranks."

Remus's power howled to the world as his moon-white flames burned brighter and hotter. They lit up the world, and it seemed to shudder in return. My shadows responded, rising higher and stretching out like the wings of a griffin.

My heart tugged as I looked at him, another desperate attempt to see if he was still in there. "Remus."

Between the rippling shadows and burning silver, we were locked in each other's eyes. No one, not the Ram nor the gods, could have intervened in this moment in time between us. Remus blinked, and there was a shift in his eyes, a light that returned. His lips began to curve up.

I knew what I needed to do.

My mouth opened into a scream, the dark claws of my power rushing out just as Remus spun around, redirecting his flame toward the Ram. Remus's large body was lost in the silver light as my shadows surged past him, billowing out onto the daemons and Order that surrounded us.

The earth shook from the bone-splitting roars of the Ram. Remus's and my powers collided, hitting the Ram square in the chest. The daemon king fell to a knee before creating a shield of its own, trying to hold off the force of our aethers combined.

Remus walked through the flames and shadow. He tore through the shield with a slam of his fist and the cry of a god, and Remus met the Ram face to face.

Remus, with silver eyes and the voice of thunder and angry seas. "You could never tempt me with a life without my humanity. You tried to destroy me, forcing me to relive the worst parts of myself. But it never worked, because I had been already created by the dark. You will never have me, and you will never have *her*."

The Ram's eyes glowed with fury. It snatched Remus by the throat, lifting him several feet above the ground. A scream of pure terror bubbled in my throat just as Drusus cried out. The skies screamed as beating wings pounded the air.

The Ram suddenly dropped Remus and frantically searched the skies as if the source of the noise unnerved it. A shard of brown darted to the ground from above. The winged daemons went wild, leaping off their perches just as a godsdamn griffin hurled down into the watchtower.

The magnificent beast dug its talons into wood and stone and *pushed* the watchtower over. The edifice moaned and began to collapse. Torches fell to the ground, and it didn't take long for flames to ignite.

From within the smoke, three figures emerged: Marcus, Atticus, and Cato. They rained their might upon the daemons. Marcus met my eye through the madness, understanding flickering across his gaze as he pointed to the sky with a knowing smile.

Another griffin careened through the winds, sweeping a winged daemon aside in midair. I recognized Valens, Caius on his back. The Alpha raised his sword with a war cry. Caius had done it. He'd obtained the griffins' support. I felt my limbs slacken in relief.

Anthony emerged from the smoke. A strange expression flashed over his face as he looked at his son before hurrying toward the Ram. "We must go," he urged.

The Ram growled angrily and grabbed Anthony. They disappeared with the Ram's aether, taking other followers with them. As soon as they'd gone, the shadows and silver flames evaporated. The air, a moment before thick with the Ram's aether, lifted. Remus staggered back. His black locks fell forward as he fought for breath. My heart went rampant as he turned to me, those jade-green eyes shining again with life and recognition. I couldn't fathom how Remus had survived, how he'd managed to stay true to himself. How he'd seemed so cold and unfeeling just moments earlier, nothing like the male standing before me now. The moment Remus met my gaze, the tilt of his lips and the subtle nod of his head told me all I needed to know. He was still with me.

Remus stilled, his eyes on me. They were glittering as if they were made of stars. He took one step, then another. His voice was rough with barely repressed emotion. "Diane."

I ran toward him, relief and so many other feelings warring in me as Remus yanked me to his chest. I felt the warmth of his skin and the feel of the hard lines of his body even through his fighting leathers. I could even hear the wild beating of his heart. And gods, I'd missed his pine and ocean scent.

"Fuck." His voice was still hoarse. "Stay close to me."

Always. I wanted to say it, but the words didn't come. After a moment, I pulled away to look at him, noticing the softness in his eyes. I wanted to stay here and bathe in the safety of his arms forever, but we edged back to where Drusus stood. The smoke from the fire was thickening rapidly, and it was becoming difficult to breathe.

I wasn't sure how we had missed the jackals. They might've used the destruction led by the griffins as an opportunity to sneak away. I would've assumed they left with the Ram. But I saw their forms emerging from the fire-red smoke like wraiths.

One moment I was holding Remus's hand and the next Drusus was pulling me away. I shouted in alarm as the jackals charged forward, their spears pointed at Remus. Remus caught the wrist of one, stopping the tip of the blade before it penetrated his chest. But the other jackal was too quick. Unabated fear sank deep in my bones as I watched him dive under Remus's arm and prepare to drive the weapon into his abdomen.

Cato suddenly appeared, pushing Remus out of the way. The fires behind them seemed to flare brighter as the blade pierced Cato instead. Something shattered inside me. Grounded to dust. *This wasn't real.* It couldn't be.

I screamed, but I couldn't hear my voice. Drusus held onto me, and we both stumbled together. Drusus's body trembled, and I was sure he was screaming, too. I watched as the jackal's grin grew wider, as he drove the blade deeper and higher. Cato's body lurched with each bloodied thrust. Once the jackal had unsheathed the blade from Cato's abdomen, a griffin landed in the center of the fort, making the shifters run away.

Remus caught Cato, clutching at his bloodied wound as they slid to the ground. I wrenched myself out of Drusus's grasp, frantically clambering toward them. Blood. There was so much. My hands shook as I pressed my hands over Remus's, and we both held the wound.

"Fuck," Cato rasped. "Don't say I never do anything for you, Remus."

Remus smiled softly, but it didn't meet his eyes.

"Please, Cato," I cried.

There had to be a way. Aether could heal him, couldn't it? But I knew in my heart it wouldn't. The blade had damaged vital organs. The blood loss was too much. The odds were stacked against us.

Only hours ago, he was with us. Running alongside us. Eating and talking with us.

Blood bubbled from Cato's lips, and a sob pulled from my chest. His hand landed over mine as his eyes followed me.

"I would've done the same for any of you." His breathing was ragged. Broken. "Remember what I told you, sister."

Tears blinded me. I ran a hand through his hair, pressing a kiss to his brow. My brother. The selfless one. The one who always laughed and found joy in life.

Cato smiled at me as light dimmed from his eyes.

Emptiness. Silence. I could not hear nor comprehend anything else as I stared at Cato's lifeless body.

Remus's voice emerged from the haze. "Peace be with you . . . brother."

We stayed there for a few moments before an explosion caused another tower to topple over. Daemons and griffins screeched, but I didn't care. No, I couldn't care about anything. I wanted to stay here with Cato.

Marcus and Atticus rushed toward us and stopped, their gazes pinned on Cato. Marcus's ice-blue eyes flashed with pain, but his voice was steady. "Get Diane out of here. This place is going to burn."

No. My words were filled with disbelief, until I began to shake with outrage. They were trying to take me away from him. "No!"

Atticus bent down to pick Cato's body up from the ground. His voice was gentle, coaxing me. I reached for Cato, but Remus caught my hands. His face was full of remorse as he pulled me away. I kicked my legs out, shouting and screaming in pure agony.

Remus wrapped his arms around me. The rage was short-lived, but it scorched everything inside me, leaving me breathless as a griffin landed behind us. Their wings drifted over us as Remus placed me onto its back. The griffin pushed off the ground. I felt helpless as I watched my brothers below. They climbed on top of two other griffins, one of which gently took Cato's body in its talons. They took to the sky as well but veered off in the opposite direction—toward the haven.

I struggled against Remus's hold, my screams having turned into desperate sobs. "Where are you taking me! Let me go! Cato!"

I cried out his name, begging the Fates for this to be just some drawn-out nightmare, but I knew. My brother was gone, and it felt like a blade had run its jagged line through my chest. I drowned in my anguish until I faded into nothingness.

FORTY-SIX

Remus

Diane cried herself to sleep. The sounds of her screams and sobs had clawed through the coarsest parts of my soul. I never wanted to hear those sounds from her again. My arm tightened around her waist as the griffin flew. Her body was limp against mine. Tears left pale lines streaking through the dirt on her face. I pressed my brow against her temple.

"I'm so sorry, love," I whispered.

Cato had saved me. He had died so I could live. I vowed to remember that for the remainder of my days. As his blood had poured between my fingers, a war had begun to brew within me. I'd heard the message loud and clear from Cato's lips. *No more guilt, Remus.* Gods. Now, high above the clouds, those words echoed within my chest, and I bowed my head, still clutching onto the warrior female I was falling in love with.

Thank you, Cato.

It hadn't been difficult to pretend I'd given up my humanity. I'd concocted the plan amid the torture and Anthony's visits. The cold mask of indifference was something I had lived under for so long, it should've concerned me how natural it felt to turn on that facade. I had to wait, suffer the pain for an extensive amount of time to the point that even the Ram considered the possibility that I'd pledged my allegiance to him.

Before they unchained me, I had felt the Ram's aether explore my thoughts and mind. He was trying to utilize any weakness in order to completely shut my humanity off. There was a brief moment of fear that he would overpower me completely and succeed, but I used the anguish over my sister's death as a cover. I used the emotion the Ram would consider weak, pretending it was the reason I wanted to let go of my emotions. I wasn't convinced I would be able to trick him, but when the daemon king ran a gentle finger down my face, a triumphant gleam in his eyes, and left, I breathed a sigh of relief. I'd done it.

The more challenging part was keeping my thoughts in a state of disinterest. I was afraid the daemon king would be able to sense the true nature of my mind, how far from loyal I truly was, so I could never let my thoughts stray. I refrained from thinking of Diane and the others. I didn't even allow myself to bask in the relief of finally feeling the sunlight and ocean air on my face. And when those damn jackals had Meredith, it took every sliver of strength to repress my rage. But I had to stay my hand, follow the plan. I fell back into who I was when I first became the Lone Wolf. A cold monster who killed without a thought. I'd hoped that Meredith would be okay after the attack, that she would let the others know we were coming.

The entire endeavor had been mentally draining.

And now I was back. And I intended to repay the favor of what had been done to me, to the others, to Cato.

The strips of pale pink in the sky reminded me of the blossom groves that rimmed the mountains. I learned the griffin we rode on was named Ethel. His wings swept in powerful strokes, lifting us higher and higher. Caius was still with Valens, flying beside us. I hadn't looked his way, but I knew Caius had been stealing glances at me.

I sighed. "I'm not going to grow horns, you know."

Caius looked confused at first, but his expression turned concerned. "No, I just worry. You weren't in their grasps for long, but I was afraid they might've damaged you."

I shrugged. "The damage had already been done."

Caius sighed in return, nodding. "That's true."

I finally took a moment to look at him, at the exhaustion and sadness in his eyes and body. "Are you well?"

Valens steered closer. Caius looked worn out as he stared at the clouds. "No. This may sound naïve, but I didn't think someone so close would . . ." He ran a hand over his face.

I understood what he meant. Cato had been one of the first to accept me for me, regardless of the title I held. For that, I would always be grateful for him. "It's not naïve. He was a good male—more than good."

Caius's chest rose and fell sharply, tension bracketing his shoulders and jaw. "That he was."

It was several minutes before I spoke again. "I'm assuming we are heading to the griffin's kingdom?"

He nodded. "Our welcome is for a limited time. That is why we are heading straight there, and the others are to go to the haven. The king of griffins only wanted you two with me."

There was a break in the painted clouds as the world was laid bare before us. The land was as regal as a queen on a throne of hills, mountains, and canyons, with rivers running through them. It was even more beautiful with the dawn painting its light across it. Stunning and menacing. A queen who bore a ruthless beauty.

It wasn't until we soared back above the cloud line that I was rendered speechless. It was as if the kingdom was floating above a mountain peak, the earth of it blended with stone and other materials to support the base. Logistically, the slim mountain peak should not be able to hold the entire kingdom, but it did. Scientists and philosophers would be baffled. Aether was an entity of its own.

The floating land was massive. Pale lines ringed and stretched across the expanse. Streets, I presumed. Rivers also coursed through the realm like ethereal snakes. At the center of the kingdom, the most prominent feature was a castle made of off-white stone speckled with gold. It stretched upward, and from the reflective shine of the dawn light, I could see it bore many tall windows.

As we banked, the air thinned, and my throat constricted. A stem of panic rose. My hold on Diane tightened. After a few moments, the restriction released its hold. I sucked in a breath.

"It's our kind of aether," Valens explained. "It is ancient, like the

Ram's. It enacts a sort of protective mechanism. We simply shifted it to help you mortals breathe our air."

Valens turned his head to me, his eyes like pools of sand. "I'm sorry, boy. About your pater."

I felt Caius's gaze back on me. Empathy emanated from both males. My stomach churned with something acidic, a bitter taste on my tongue. Guilt. They thought I'd only just found out of my pater's betrayal. I should've revealed the truth of my pater before leaving the Pack. But I'd been blinded by my cowardice. I truly believed I had killed my sister and thought I deserved to be cast out. At that time, I was the Lone Wolf, and my pater had spun the story of how I'd abandoned the Pack. That I'd fled when my sister died. In the Pack's eyes, that was the truth.

But it wasn't the complete truth. My pater had banished me to save himself.

The cold mask slipped back in place. "I don't give a damn about him."

Valens said nothing, but I saw the pity in his look. The sickening sensation in my stomach lessened as we grew closer to the castle. Gentle waves of dawning light cascaded over the clouds.

Diane stirred awake, and I heard a low gasp. She must've seen the beauty of the land ahead. My arms tightened around her, squeezing her lightly against me. I just needed to do something to soften the pain. Of everything. I despised feeling so helpless. Diane stiffened a moment before melting into my embrace. Her fingers faintly trembled as she ran her hands across my arms.

"You're really here," she whispered.

I pressed my lips to the back of her head in reassurance.

We landed in the castle's courtyard. The grounds held iridescent shades of rose-gold opal stone. Griffins greeted us. One was a snowy gray and the other a rich brown.

"Can you believe it?" Caius whispered, his eyes roving along the castle and its grounds. "We are probably the first mortals in thousands of years to see the griffins' castle."

He looked to Diane, who slid off the griffin, her gaze mesmerized by the view. Caius took a step forward, sweeping her into his arms. My heart pulled at the pain I saw in their embrace.

Caius cupped her cheek, his face stricken with grief and guilt. "I'm so sorry, Diane. I hate to have to pull you away after what happened"

Diane's eyes glistened. "We don't have the luxury of time. I understand."

Her voice. It was monotone. It didn't hold its usual spark and flare of fierceness. She looked at me, and her face lit up. Just slightly.

My hand went to her back as we followed where the griffins led. We entered the sparkling beast and were greeted with high ceilings and large columns of taupe and gold. Ivory velvet lined the walls. Massive windows with etchings of spirals and whorls filled the corners, nothing but clouds and sunlight on the other side. It looked like parties were held here. I noticed Diane grazing her lips, something I'd learnt she does when anxious, and her eyes scanned every crook and cranny of the place.

Valens padded down the hallway to our right. *"Come, mortals. It is still early. Our king will see you once you get some rest."*

Vines crawled up the arches that made the hallway, which was large enough for a pair of griffins to walk alongside each other.

Valens neared a set of doors, and they opened on their own accord. *"Remus, this one is yours."*

Caius followed the second griffin further down the hall. Valens waited for Diane to follow him, but she strutted into my room without sparing him a second glance. "I will tend to Remus. Where can I find toiletries?"

Valens didn't seem surprised. *"You will find everything in the bath chamber. Would you like me to escort you to your room?"*

Diane gave him a smile. A smile not reflected in her eyes. "No, thank you." Valens left, but not before giving me a warning look that probably said that if I mistreated her, he would come for my jugular.

The bedchamber was massive, perhaps the size of Drusus's courtyard. Glass windows filled the back wall. Deep blue and silver furniture. A large four-poster bed of lavish wood faced the windows. Thin drapes hung over the four posts; the deep blue sheets lined with silver looked like rippling water.

Diane had disappeared into the connecting bath chamber. I followed her, her presence a constant lure. After a month of being separated, my deepest fear was the possibility of never seeing her again, and I was *desperate* for her. I was a man who had had a taste of the sun and would forever ache for its warmth.

She had her thorns, the fears and anxieties that loomed over her beautiful heart. I wanted to know everything about her, I would welcome every imperfection, so I could embrace every part of her. I hoped she'd accept mine. So I could be worthy of the blossom underneath the thorns.

My lotus.

Diane was facing the mirror. Her shoulders heaved up and down as she fumbled with the straps of her armor. She cursed under her breath, her voice wavering, on the edge of breaking. I gently turned her to face me, loosening the cinches of her armor.

Her eyes clashed with mine. I saw the fierce storm there, the pain and anger that lashed across them. In the midst of it all, there was a lick of heat. A flame that brightened with every passing second.

We stared at one another, our breaths hanging in the space between us. My fingers hovered over the leather of her armor, but I couldn't seem to move as the scent of blossoms rushed through me. It dove through me, scorching my lungs. I felt like I could burn simply from being this close to her.

A moment passed before our resolve snapped. My hands wrapped around her waist as she clung to my neck. Our lips crashed. Hunger and desperation. Teeth, tongue, and possession. A beautiful madness. I pushed us against the counter. Diane grunted, kissing me fiercely as her hands roamed over my chest and arms. My hand slid up her back and into her hair, fingers twisting into a grip, and I tugged her head back. Her shuddering breaths stilled me, and I tried to see through the lustful haze.

"Diane," I began.

"No." She squirmed. "Please don't stop. Please, I need this—I need you."

I pulled back just enough to see the emotion in her golden eyes. "You're in pain," I said. "It wouldn't be right of me to let this go further."

Diane scoffed, anger unfurling over her beautiful face. "Now you want to be a gentleman. The rude, raunchy, broody male has found his manners."

"Lotus," I started, but Diane's hands curled into fists against my chest.

"I thought you would be as eager to touch me as I am with you," she said through gritted teeth. "I was terrified. So godsdamn scared of what was happening to you. I just want to feel you, to be with you, to fucking know that you're here. *Safe.*"

"Lotus," I said again, gently. "I am here. I am with you." I pressed my brow to hers. "You would be angrier if this continued. Besides, I'm not letting you go again."

Diane bit her lip. I could see through her at the battle she was facing. My hands went up to cradle her face. Her eyes lifted, silver lining them. My heart raced at the sight. She was so devastatingly beautiful.

I brushed my thumbs along her cheeks. "When and where you are, then and there I will be."

Tears ran down her face. Diane closed her eyes at the words, the promise.

I planted a kiss under her ear. "I thought of you when I was in that cell," I whispered against her neck.

"I thought of your voice." A kiss at the corner of her jaw.

"Your laugh." Another kiss on her nose.

"Your terrible sense of humor."

She released a breathy laugh as she silently cried. I beckoned her toward the bath tub. "Come, let me take care of you."

Diane continued to undress as I prepared the bath for her. The waters were warm enough that I felt a pinch of pain from the heat. She allowed me to lead her into the tub. Diane hissed as she dipped her feet in the water, but as she slid in deeper, her lips parted into a groan.

I tried ignoring the sound as I pulled off the remainder of my clothing. Diane's eyelashes were heavy with her tears. Her eyes widened when she saw me undressing.

"What are you doing?" she asked.

"I'm going to take a bath," I responded as if it was obvious. "Not sure if you noticed, but I am filthy."

Diane's cheeks reddened, but she turned her attention to her hands. Tears pooled once more in her eyes as she made mindless circles in the water. She stiffened as I slid into the tub behind her.

Fuck. I might've heated the water too much.

Diane held still as I began to scrub her shoulders with soap and a rag. Foam slipped over her skin. I was lost in the motion, giving her peace and quiet and a moment not to have to think of anything else. Diane's shoulders shook, and her muffled sobs echoed in the bath chamber.

I dropped the soap, wrapped my arms around her, and dipped my face in the space between her neck and shoulder. Diane cried, finally allowing herself to be lost to the heartache. To do nothing but *feel*.

<hr>

It was still early. The sun crawled higher in the sky. Only a few griffins could be seen flying outside. Diane rested her head against my chest. The water had begun to cool, and my fingers were running through the long strands of her hair.

She had stopped crying and had fallen into a quiet somberness. I knew Diane was mentally picking up the pieces of her heart, readying to forge through what was to come in the upcoming days.

I scooped her up from the bath, dried her, and carried her to bed. Under the sheets, we faced each other as the sunlight tried to pierce through the curtains I had drawn.

Diane's eyes roamed my face. Her nose was pinched red, eyes puffy. Her attention snagged on my shoulders and chest. She sucked in a breath, her eyes tracing the new map of scars and wounds.

"Those were the same jackals from your time in Egypt, weren't they?" she asked.

My silence was response in itself. A flash of anger as Diane grinded her teeth. "Godsdamn them. How could your pater allow that to happen?"

I thought of Anthony. In the last few days before my rescue, Anthony had watched me with a renewed interest. A gleam in his eyes anytime he looked at me. I didn't recognize the male at all.

"Anthony's been long gone. I think I've only ever known the man void of humanity, after he turned himself to the Ram," I explained. "And before then, he had been so busy being Alpha when I was younger that I didn't really get to know him. It was only when my sister and I were of age to train—just after my mater died—that I began to get to know him. I've realized he was already colluding with the Ram by then. I never got to know my pater without the Ram's influence."

Diane watched me carefully, offering a sad smile. "Thank you for taking care of me. . . . I missed you. I was going mad at the thought of what they were doing to you."

I frowned as a thought crossed my mind. "You have to know that I didn't want to hurt Meredith. They killed all the harpies and were going to kill her too. I tried being careful in how I damaged her wing. It had to look believable, without hurting her much and so that she could still fly. I thought if I could send her back as a sign and warning of what the Ram's forces were capable of, it would give her a chance to survive. I hated every part of it."

Diane's expression darkened, lips tightening. "I believe you, though you may need to convince Laelia of that."

"I understand."

She sniffed away more tears, running the back of her hand across her nose. "What happened when you went to the town?"

My eyes strayed upward to the thin drapes over the bedposts. "I thought making a bright show of it all would give the people enough time to realize what was happening. I burned random stalls and sheds, leaving the villas last. Anything. I tried to give them time to escape in hopes that the Pack would arrive in time."

Diane didn't respond and the silence quickly turned into

something comfortable. She rolled closer to me. Her eyes were fluttering sleepily.

I tugged on a hair strand. The words slipped from my lips in a hoarse whisper. "When I sensed you walking into the Order's fort, and when the Ram stood before you . . . when that monstrosity *touched* you . . . I was afraid."

Her liquid gold eyes found mine, and I felt exposed, like she could see between the cracks in the walls I'd tried so hard to keep up. Diane grabbed the hand that I had twisted in her hair and planted a kiss on my inked knuckles. "Careful, Lone Wolf. It sounds like you might be catching feelings."

I snorted, bringing her closer to me. She closed her eyes, her breathing slowing, and I lay there with her in my arms. I was way past catching feelings, I realized. Diane had been ready to sacrifice herself for me just as much as I would for her. We had been dancing around the flame burning between us.

"Cato told me no more guilt," I said, my voice still hoarse. "But I don't know what that means. I don't know if I can live without guilt. If I even deserve to."

Diane stilled. Her fingers splayed over my chest as her jaw tightened. "Yes, you do. More than you think."

There was nothing I could say. Some dark truths had the power to stain hearts and twist lives. I didn't believe in a future that could be ours. She deserved better than me. But I would always fight so that she may live. So she could be happy.

A loud knock snapped me awake.

I growled, "No."

Caius's voice was muffled on the other side. "Yes."

He knocked again, and I growled more loudly. Diane shot up. She was still naked, her eyes wide.

She mouthed the words to me: "He doesn't know I'm here."

My lips curled at a delicious thought. Something along the lines of *I can make it so that he can hear you screaming my name.*

Diane shot me a look. She must've read my thoughts and the mischief in my gaze. Her eyes went heavy with heat as she left to retrieve a thin nightgown from one of the drawers. Diane flipped her hair over her shoulders as she held her belongings, trying to cover what the thin garment was doing a poor job of.

She shrugged. "Best take this with some dignity."

Diane threw the door open and walked past Caius. The fierce she-wolf strutted away as if she had no care in the world. Caius stood frozen, his eyes on the spot where Diane had stood.

A brow arched in amusement as his eyes slid to me. "I had a feeling she was in here. It's time to meet with the griffin king."

The dynamic between us had certainly softened. I didn't realize it at first, but we had been reaching an almost amicable state.

I flipped the sheets off me. "Why did we even need to come here? Why couldn't the griffins just agree to join our cause."

Caius made a noise of agreement. "You know how this works. It's a formality, there'll be negotiation to ensure their forces can join us. Not to mention the king wanted to see you both in person. It won't be a long visit."

I nodded and began to make my way to the bath chamber when Caius's question halted me. "How?" he asked.

I paused, my hands tightening to fists at my sides, sensing what he was trying to ask. "*How* what?"

"How did you not succumb to joining the Order?"

Anthony was alive, and the only surviving member of my family. I could understand why Caius would think I'd be tempted. It could not be further from the truth.

I slowly faced him. "The way the Ram entices others to join his forces is by shutting down their emotions. He reveals to them their grief, anger, or fear and offers to take it all away. It is a means of escape. In return, they are given the ability to control aether, but it is borrowed power. Only by the will of the Ram can they hold that ability. The Ram tried with me but failed. He thought he could use the horrors of my past against me, but he didn't understand that I have been *made by* them."

Caius's brow pinched in confusion, so many questions passing over his eyes. But if he was curious about what those horrors were, he didn't ask. I wanted him to. Whether because I was standing before him in a moment where there was no anger between us or whether it was because I had grown so damn tired of holding this burden, I didn't know.

Caius's expression flickered from his initial confusion to a sense of awe. He looked proud. A sudden wash of guilt invaded me. "Your determination in staying true to yourself is admirable. Go change. I'll be back shortly, and we can head down together."

He turned to leave, and I found myself calling out for him. "Caius?"

Caius paused, turning back to me with a questioning look. I was at war with myself. *Again.* The words were strangled, and my abdomen rolled over itself. I fought against the sensation. He needed the truth.

I opened my mouth. "Nothing."

When Caius left, I rushed to the bath chamber, where I hurled all the contents of my stomach.

FORTY-SEVEN

Diane

Deep orange danced through the glass, casting its soft light onto the royal rug. Columns led us down the grand hall, Valens at the head.

My hands ran over the tunic that clung to my shoulders and legs. It was the color of dandelions. I felt the heated gaze on me. If I was feeling any better, I would've added a little sway to my hips. Remus would've grumbled with longing, making my heart skip a beat.

But there was a hollowness in my chest. Cato was dead. *Cato*. My charismatic, patient, and endearing brother. I squeezed my eyes shut, fighting the thick emotion that threatened to suffocate me.

My hair ran freely, curling slightly at the ends. I'd managed to pin jeweled beads along the length of it. I was curious as to why the griffins had human clothing and accessories at their disposal. Remus wore a tunic that melded against his toned body, along those long legs that strode down the hall with purpose. My eyes lingered on him, and I caught the wicked look in his eyes. Being with him again had felt like home.

Large doors opened onto a grand hall, a pair of mortals standing at the entrance. No, not mortals. The way they carried themselves and the air around them held a supernatural element. Aether hummed around their presence. A glittering shimmer coated their cheekbones, and they both wore laurel wreath crowns. They were dryads, tree spirits blessed by the goddess of the hunt. I had never seen any in person, and it was surreal to know that they lived among the griffins. One dryad had skin like Remus's, a deep olive tone, and the other dryad had a darker skin tone, much resembling Caius's.

The dryads nodded in greeting before they glided toward where I thought we would find a throne. Except there was no throne—just a massive griffin sitting on plush cushions, a tall crystal window at its back. The griffin was a gray-blue speckled with black and wore no crown. The beast lounged on the cushions, claws atop one another, as large deep brown eyes tracked our movements. We bowed as we approached the king.

Valens's voice bounded off the crystalline window. *"I introduce to you, King Aquila."*

"King Aquila," Caius stated.

The griffin king's wings shifted slightly. Curious. Judging. A strong feminine voice came out of the king's beak. *"So, these are the wolves the daemon king is so obsessed with."*

Caius lifted his head and glanced at us. "Indeed, they are. Which is why it was of utter importance to meet with you."

I perked up. "You're female and call yourself king?"

The griffin king heaved herself onto her feet. Claws clinked along the lavish marble, wings sweeping out gently. With the clouds and sunset radiating behind the window, the griffin seemed to be emerging from Olympus itself. *"Hatchling, I am leader of my kind so I can call myself whatever the fuck I like."*

I stared at the griffin king in awe. "As you should, your highness."

Aquila tilted her head in thought. *"Intriguing. I sense powerful aether from you."* Her eyes snapped to Remus. *"From you both. Care to give me a demonstration?"*

I hesitated as Remus made his way toward me. He gave me a subtle nod, his expression smooth and stone cold. His mask was in place. My lips twitched, and shadows whirled from my feet, twisting and dancing around me until they spread above my head like branches from a tree. I could taste the gravity of my power by the way the air hummed in the room.

Following quickly behind my shadows, light flared, and heat licked along Remus's skin. He was less artful with his power as the flames grew from him in waves. Steam rolled from his lips as he sighed, his eyes glowing a pale silver. Remus didn't look human at all. He was a vengeful god of fire and war. Together, we lowered our aether until the golden light of the day returned to the throne room.

"*Astonishing. Your power resembles that of the gods.*" Aquila was staring at Remus. "*Your eyes glowed like the moon and stars. How did you come across such power? Male wolves are not born with aether, aside from being able to shift into your wolf form.*"

Remus ran a thumb over his lip, the last of the flames flickering from his hands. "I am not sure, your highness. The Ram attacked me, and when I thought I was truly lost, the power ripped out."

The king stayed silent for a moment, as if processing what she was hearing. "*And you?*" She turned to me.

I felt my lips tighten in anger. "The Ram did this to me."

Aquila looked almost amused, wings lifting to reveal the muscles tensing under her blue feathers and gray fur. "*You don't truly believe that, hatchling. Try again.*"

I felt stunned but lifted my chin in defiance. "I do not know where this power came from, and that is the truth."

"*That's much more like it,*" Aquila replied. She peered at Caius. "*Tell me, Alpha. Why should I offer my griffins' help with your cause?*"

Caius inclined his head. Luckily, Remus had relayed everything he'd heard during his time with the Order as we made our way to the throne room. "King Aquila, I know you've heard what's been happening on the mortal lands. The Order has been fraternizing with the Ram. It claims to have armies waiting on the other side of this realm. They have also been colluding with governments, gathering support from the people of other continents. The Ram has no intention of leaving any survivors. It wants full domination."

"*He*, not *it*."

All eyes went to Remus. His level gaze met the griffin king's. "Your highness, I was the Ram's prisoner, and I was freed thanks to the wolves and your griffins. From my time with the daemon king, I can confirm he is angry at the gods and goddesses. The stories we've heard hold fragments of truth. His kind were banished from this realm, and this is his way of retribution."

The griffin king seemed enthralled. Her large head lowered, nostrils flaring puffs of warm air as her brown eyes lingered on Remus. The deep color rippled like scales of a reptile and refracted crystals.

"*I can sense you are free of any daemonic influence,*" she observed. "*The stories of the mad daemon king have been told over the centuries. Remember, griffins live hundreds of years, far longer than you do, hatchling, and one of my forefathers was amongst the first Olympians who lived in the mortal realm. It's been told that the gods and goddesses wanted to give another realm to his kind, but the daemon king was angry and led a rebellion against them. He was imprisoned, his name forgotten in history, and it was then that the daemon king promised he would return with a vengeance that would shake Olympus.*"

Remus's gaze darkened. "I've seen what he is capable of. He tried to destroy my sense of humanity, my connection to emotion. I am fighting to ensure that fate does not fall on everyone else. You griffins have remained a legend, safe in your fancy towers. While I applaud your efforts to keep your own kind safe and prosperous, there won't be a realm left to live in if we don't unite."

Aquila's eye moved to Caius. "*And you, Alpha? Anything else to add?*"

Caius folded his arms, a grim smile forming on his face. "The Lone Wolf stole the speech I'd prepared. But I would like to open the discussion of possible trade opportunities that may better serve your people moving forward."

The griffin king chuckled, the sound elegant and soft. It hummed off the crystal window. "*Ever the opportunist. I have to say you are much more than the praise I've heard.*"

Caius arched a brow. His smile turned cocky. "You have heard how great I am all the way up here?"

The leaders dove into deep conversation. Planning, plotting, securing agreements. The griffins would open their doors to trade among the wolves and minotaurs—something Caius was sure King Cain would appreciate. An invitation was also extended to the Daughters of Mars to visit the griffin lands. As they had their pegasus, and the kingdom was only accessible by flight, it was a fitting opportunity. Aquila still wanted to maintain a level of privacy for her kingdom, which Caius respected. The griffins opening their doors to the she-wolves would allow them another venue of academic training. My heart fell a little at that. I had been struggling to come to terms with the Rite—struggling with my worthiness in pursuing such an honor. Now, with Cato's death, I wasn't sure I wanted to complete the Rite. It didn't feel right.

I felt a hand touch my arm. Remus's expression was gentle, though his eyes glittered like a wildcat. The light scattered over his cheekbones as I knew it did over mine.

"You are worthy. And not *despite* your flaws, but *because* of your flaws. If anything, they make you even more worthy. Someone who holds their imperfections with pride and perseveres against all the shit of this world emerges a stronger, better version of themselves. That is what determines a person's worth. And you, lotus, are beyond worthy."

I was at a loss for words. I stared at this incredible male, but words continued to fail me. Remus kept his gaze on me but then seemed to drift off in his own thoughts. A growing darkness swept over him, a sheen of silver flickered over his eyes and he turned away from the throne room.

I suddenly wanted to chase after him and tell him that everything he'd said was also true for him. Tell him just how worthy he was.

FORTY-EIGHT

Remus

The place was too damn big. I walked along grand hallways that were so lavish that not even the rulers of Rome could have managed such a feat. They would shit their pants if they saw this place, and I was glad the opportunity would never arise. Humans could be greedy little creatures.

The walk was calming. I'd needed an escape. When Caius and the griffin king had started discussing the Daughters of Mars, I'd noticed Diane's expression. Her eyes went downcast. She wanted to pursue that calling but had been doubting herself.

I meant every word that I'd said to her. Diane held a worth that not even these fanciful, ancient halls could compare to. Though as I'd reminded her of her potential, I'd remembered the lack of mine. *The Lone Wolf.* I was not worthy of anything more than that blasted title.

A woman emerged from between the columns, books in her hands. I recognized her as one of the dryads who had opened the doors to the throne room. She smiled and beckoned for me to follow her. Curiosity took hold, and I went after her.

"Where are you taking me?" I asked.

We came upon the end of a hallway where tall doors made of dark wood stood. I held them open as she carried the books inside, and my jaw fell when I stepped inside. Ceiling high bookshelves lined the massive library. Elegant tables and chairs were placed among the main

326 | JESSICA J. AYALA

floors, cushions at the base of the tall windows, creating little reading nooks. Soft fingers of light trailed over the rugs and wooden shelves.

The dryad looked over her shoulder. "You seemed haunted by your thoughts. I thought a visitor such as yourself might enjoy one of our finer features."

My eyes roamed over the room. "It's incredible."

She looked proud. "I'm glad the griffins are supporting your war efforts." I jerked my attention back to her, and she shrugged. "There are other dryads and water spirits in your lands too."

I nodded in understanding. She wandered down an aisle and began to place the books back. Not a speckle of dust could be found among the shelves. The care for this place was unmatched.

The dryad kept her eyes on the books, absorbed in her work. "You know of the sirens?"

"Only that they are hardly ever spotted, and serve their Leviathan."

Her fingers ran over the old leather spines. She hummed happily and pulled another book from the shelf. "Do you know how to summon a siren?"

I gave her a dry look, but the dryad only smiled. "The griffins have gathered so much knowledge over the years that you can't even imagine." She shoved the book in my hand. "There are many ways to summon a siren but the most recent documentation is in here. The sirens are our cousins and should be made aware of what is happening on their shores."

The book was old. The pad of my thumb ran over the wrinkled pages. I looked up to see the dryad already making her way out of the library. She opened the doors, and Diane was on the other side.

Diane jumped, eyes bouncing between me and the dryad. The woman gave her a curt nod and brushed past the she-wolf. Diane cleared her throat but gasped when she turned back to the library.

"Oh shit," she said in awe.

I chuckled. "Beautiful, isn't it?"

"Incredible," she whispered. Her hands trailed over the shelves with the same reverence the dryad had shown. Her hand froze, fingers curling into fists as if remembering why she was here. "Why did you follow her here?"

I waved the book in my hand. "Apparently, she thought this would serve our efforts against the Order." I stopped and a wicked grin took over. "Why?"

Diane scowled and stumbled back against the shelves as I neared her. Her chest rose, and she sucked in a breath when our chests touched. My lips hovered over hers in a feather light touch.

"Are you jealous?" I asked.

Her knuckles whitened on the shelf behind her. "Like you've never been jealous before."

I caged her in, my arms above her head on the bookshelf. A rumble coursed through my chest. I knew she was referring to that night in the underground fighting ring when the damn male had had his hands on her. "Don't remind me."

Her eyes turned a golden blaze. I lowered my eyes to her mouth. Her lips parted, and I imagined pulling on her bottom lip with my teeth. Hear her sighs. Feel her body writhe against mine.

The Lone Wolf.

I pulled back. I was *not* worthy of her. "You deserve better than me, Diane. There are things about me that I haven't told you, that I struggle to say out loud, but you deserve to know everything. And you may not like me after all."

There was a flash of hurt. Diane's brow pinched. "I know you haven't been completely honest with me. I noticed your expression while we were in the throne room. I want to support you. And I don't want to push you if you aren't ready, but there is a part of me that is growing more frustrated that the closer we become, there is still so much I don't know about you."

My hands tightened to painful fists. She had every right to feel this way. Our relationship had been growing, past that of simple friendship.

"They are heavy and dark truths," I said.

Diane tipped her chin up. Defiance in all its breathtaking beauty. "Are you worried of scaring me off? Let me decide that for myself."

My face softened, and the beating in my chest roared with a warmth that could not be consumed. The chains in my heart tugged, wondering when the day would come to set the truth free.

"I truly don't deserve you," I whispered. "But there's someone else who needs to hear my truths before you, lotus."

Diane looked confused but I pushed off the shelf, shutting down the conversation. She lingered back, and I felt her watching me as I took the book that the dryad had given me and flopped onto the cushions. Eventually, Diane sat across from me with a book of her own. She didn't push the conversation, but her presence provided the comfort I needed in that moment.

Battles of guilt and fear rammed against my thoughts. Fear of how Diane would look at me. The inevitable hate that Caius would rage against me. Facing such truths was never going to be easy, and I was no longer ashamed of the emotions I felt. I had been running away from my demons long enough.

We read in comfortable silence. My eyes ate the pages of the book, enthralled with the findings on the sirens. I focused on a passage, and I almost couldn't believe what I was reading. That clever dryad.

FORTY-NINE

Remus

Even in the ashen light, the castle seemed to glimmer. The ground rippled in the sun. Over the courtyard, other balconies and launch pads extended out from the buildings. Many of the griffins in the kingdom were already taking flight.

This visit to the griffins had been short, but necessary. Caius had managed to secure an alliance with the griffins, and their forces would join the wolves within a month's time. Now there were more pressing matters and places we needed to be than in a fancy castle above the skies.

If the luxury of time had been available, I would've explored the vast land that floated above the clouds. The paved roads and ancient architecture. Lounge in the grand library and see what other works had been created in the far corners of the world. Perhaps when all of this was over, I would be able to. My standing as the Lone Wolf still prevented me from living a life amongst the Pack, and I was not naïve enough to hope anything had changed. I could request to live the remainder of my days here with the griffins, potentially travel to other parts of this world.

Aquila's claws tapped on the platform, her large eagle eyes focused on me. *"Did you learn anything new in the library?"* she asked.

I shrugged. It came as no surprise that she knew the dryad had given me the book about sirens. Perhaps the king of the griffins had planned for that to happen all along. "Maybe."

The king chuckled. *"I look forward to seeing how you manage this, Wolf of the White Flames. Though it saddens me that you might not be able to see this through."* I shot her a dark look, but the griffin's expression was of genuine sympathy. *"Think of it, hatchling. You hold a power that is not meant for the wolves. The gods could see it as you stealing shards of their power."*

"I didn't. I don't even know how it happened, I willed for something to help me and then the flames appeared."

Aquila's wings folded comfortably over her back. *"Will has a power of its own. It is not the aether or sword that drives the hand but the will of the individual."* She paused, gaze settling on the morning-kissed clouds. *"It will take everything you have to defeat the daemon king. Are you prepared for that?"*

My eyes landed on Diane, as if unseeing fingers had tugged my chin in her direction. She was speaking to one of the griffins. Her black hair trailed over the brown fighting leathers. Muscles flexed and lined her arms and legs. A warrior goddess born of Rome and Egypt.

"Yes," I murmured.

Aquila followed my gaze. *"Gods save you, wolf."*

The flight was just as solemn as when we'd arrived. Caius's face was stuck in a grim expression. Every effort up till now had been amounting to unavoidable bloodshed. It was all happening too quickly. My body was on the verge of collapsing. Soon, I would tell him soon. Once we arrived at the haven.

Clouds unfurled to reveal heavy smoke. The dark colors signaled that it was recent. Warning tingled at my senses, and all of us strained to look at the scene unfolding below.

"No." Caius leaned forward. His face paled. "No!"

Valens roared and folded his wings over his back, shielding Caius as he spiraled downward. Ethel followed suit, winds screamed and teared at our hair as we lowered toward the tree lines. Diane gasped in horror, and I squeezed her tightly.

The pack haven was destroyed.

Villas had been torn through, red tiles overturned, the limestone walls broken. Blood and gore drenched the dirt roads. The once golden wheat fields were now ripped from the earth, splattered with red. Roman soldiers were already at the haven, rolling wagons and collecting bodies.

This place had always been untouched by the outside world. It was a *haven*. I seethed. Damn the Fates. The daemons. It was the only explanation. The realization that the Order had been running through these grounds riled a sense of anxiety in me.

Diane jumped off of Ethel's back before the griffin could even land, disappearing among the mass of fading smoke. I didn't follow her. I knew she could handle whatever she needed to do. The griffins held back as Caius and I prowled through the damage. We rounded the heaps of debris. Red and black smeared the walls of the ravaged villas, and the foul smell of burnt flesh rotted the air.

Caius was asking the people what had happened. And the people reached for their Alpha. Caius took their hands in his own, listening to their words.

Daemons appeared while everyone was asleep.

Riders burned the villas.

Anthony was here.

Judging stares went my way at the mention of the former Alpha. I fought to remain detached. It would be futile to defend myself; my name would forever be associated with his. And it wasn't like I was the golden hero. Not with the bloodstains on my soul.

Perhaps I truly was Anthony's son.

Caius looked my way with something resembling sympathy. *I had to tell him the truth.* The Alpha returned his attention to the people, uttering soothing words and condolences, uncaring of all the dirt and blood being smudged on his tunic. I let my attention stray to avoid eavesdropping. It felt invasive.

Leaves now rustled gently in a somber song as the dead were being collected. Funerals would take place within a week. After the bodies were cleaned and donned in finery, their loved ones would hold them in their homes as tradition called it.

A sensation buzzed at the nape of my neck, beckoning for my attention. In response, the aether in my veins stirred. I honed in on the feeling.

My fingers wrapped around the pommel of Anthony's sword. "Caius," I warned, unsheathing the blade.

Caius didn't question me; he unsheathed his own blade and followed.

The strange sensation led me toward the trees, where the villas ended and the wheat fields began. Away from prying eyes. We approached a tree with a wide berth of leaves that sheltered us. The golden fields paled underneath the graying sky.

Amongst the blades of blood-stained wheat, standing like a phantom of death, was Anthony. The hood of his cloak was drawn, the sharp angles of his bearded jawline the only thing visible. No jackals. No daemonic army. Only him.

A growl rumbled in my chest, anger and hatred running through me. "Why are you here?"

Anthony was silent for a breath, angling his head. "Son-in-law, I've been waiting to see you."

Caius tensed. His grip tightened over the handle of his sword. "How did you know?"

Anthony chuckled, the sound dark and dry. "Did you truly think I wouldn't know of my daughter running off to be married? I'm offended it was done in secret, as I've always liked you Caius. That's why I named you my successor, instead of my own son."

Caius returned the mirthless laugh. "Fuck you, old man. Remus is better off without you."

The former Alpha cocked his head, seemingly amused, and clasped his hands together. "Interesting. You don't know much about your former childhood friend. Has he told you how Helena died?"

Blood drained from my face. My heart began hammering in my chest. A coldness spread over me and stole the air from my lungs.

This wasn't how it was supposed to go. I had planned on telling Caius everything. This couldn't happen like this. *You fool, you waited too long.*

Anthony raised a finger. "Just listen to Remus's wild heartbeat.

The truth has been within your grasp this entire time, Caius. Remus is not one to be trusted. Ask him of the secrets he's held since the night of Helena's death. Ask him what he beheld in those catacombs. Ask him who drove a dagger through his own sister."

Caius stilled. His face was a mixture of confusion and anguish.

"That's enough," I snapped. My heart rate betrayed the sternness of my voice. "You attacked your people just for us to meet with you? Weak, even for you, *Pater*."

Anthony turned toward the fields. "I came because the king tasked me to ensure the downfall of the Pack. Tip the scales in our favor. He also wanted me to relay a message. He no longer wants you and that she-wolf, but he will drain your powers dry and see your heads on a pike. So, I advise this: Be ready to fight, and bring everything you can if you wish to live." He paused, meeting my eyes. Gods, I wanted to believe I saw something shift within those green shades, some kind of emotion. My father's lips thinned. "I do hope you live, son."

He disappeared in clouds of smoke. Anthony must really have been favored by the daemon king to have such aether. I hadn't seen any of the Order with that much power. Anthony had tossed me into the fire. Left my sins and scars exposed in an attempt to further drive the wedge between me and Caius.

Caius was silent. His stare became a heavy brand on my skin. "Remus, what did he mean?"

My insides twisted at the sound of his voice. There was a shout and a cloud of birds took flight. Marcus, Diane and the others stalked toward us. Gods, of course they would be here now.

Marcus looked between Caius and me. "What's going on?"

Blood matted his brown curls. None of the wolves had any armor. The attack must've caught them unprepared.

Caius hadn't looked their way. His gaze burned into me. "What *the fuck* did he mean, Remus?"

I shuddered. I godsdamn shuddered. I knew, though, within the darkest, most hated parts of me, I knew I was ready for this. This was for me. And for Caius.

The words fell from my lips. Unwavering. "Caius, I've been wanting to tell you. For years I wanted to tell you, but I couldn't. The truth sickened me to the point I couldn't breathe."

The trees seemed to fall silent as well. Diane's eyes were on me, but I couldn't face her. Though a part of me was glad she was also witnessing this. She would now see me in my entirety. I locked eyes with the Alpha. Warrior to warrior. Brother to brother. And I bared my truth.

"Ever since my mater passed, my pater was not the same. He became more detached and cold. He suddenly had a drive for conquest and power. For years my pater attempted to use the Pack to overtake kingdoms and lands, especially when Caesar was in power. Helena and I discovered many of their plans for conquest and stopped them. We always managed to infiltrate his efforts and change the course of the Pack's future. One night, Helena and I followed Anthony into the woods. We suspected it was another attempt to abuse the Pack's power until we stumbled upon an entrance to one of Rome's underground tunnels." My jaw clenched as I remembered the sight of the people wearing cloaks and masks surrounding Anthony. How he preached to them.

"I didn't know this back then, but Anthony created the Order. That night, I saw him surrounded by cloaked figures. He spoke of a new future, a new realm, where aether would be given to all and the dead would return. There was a power, a darkness that Helena and I had never felt before. We heard a voice—it sang promises of a painless future, of power at your fingertips. And it wanted freedom. We didn't know what any of it meant. The first daemons emerged that night, and Helena and I ran. We ran from the voice and the daemons, or at least we tried to. We fought them, and at some point, Helena and I separated."

Caius's breathing was quickening. Ragged and cracked. The agony the young Alpha had felt all these years was beginning to resurface. My own chest tightened to the point of pain.

Fragments of that awful night kept hurtling toward me as I continued to speak. "Eventually, I found Helena but—" Something crumbled inside me, tears welling in my eyes. "A daemon appeared in her place. My vision was clouded. I didn't understand what was happening, and I was afraid the daemon had taken her. It attacked me. And I—" I shuddered. "I fought it, and when I came to, Helena was in my arms."

My voice cracked, and I forced myself to meet Caius's eyes. His fists slowly clenched as he braced himself for my next words, the truth I knew he sensed coming.

"I killed her," I choked out. "I killed my own sister. I thought it was a daemon but . . . it was her."

Silence thickened the air. My heart roared with untamed emotion and guilt. I'd said what I'd needed to say to Caius for years. I didn't know how I felt now that I had. My heart hadn't stopped racing, but I was numb inside. Perhaps I was on the verge of going into shock again, after unveiling the dark truths I'd withheld for years, and reliving those terrible moments.

The world seemed to shudder. The dirt beneath my boots vibrated. A ripple of energy rolled through the leaves and between the strands of red-stained wheat. Caius's body trembled as blood seeped between his clenched knuckles.

Rage roared in his eyes. It was the fire of a burned man, a betrayed brother, a bereaved lover. "It was you. This entire time it was *you*. You took Helena away from me."

Something punctured my chest. The stubborn tears finally began to roll down my cheeks. "I'm so sorry I didn't tell you sooner. I wanted to—I tried."

Caius clamped his lips shut and briefly looked away before turning back to me. What I saw in his eyes revealed all the unresolved pain, the long-suffering agony. "I've wondered. For years, I wondered what had happened to the woman I loved. *My wife.*" His lips curled into a low, feral snarl. "You killed my wife."

I didn't move as he took a step closer and raised his fist. I welcomed what was coming.

"You killed her," he repeated. His fist struck me across the face. I stumbled back, and he advanced on me again.

"You killed her!" Caius roared. "Your own sister!"

The relentless tears almost blinded me, but I didn't care. I'd killed her. I killed my sister. Helena. Helena. Helena. I did this. I was guilty,

I deserved to be punished. Yes, I'd been ready to spill my truth, but it still felt like lashes against my soul.

I hated myself.

Caius punched me again, his knuckles sliding across my jaw. Saliva dripped from my rapidly swelling lips. I didn't fight back, didn't want to. Caius pinned me to the ground. He was an animal unleashed, snapping my face to the side with each blow of his fists. Stars exploded behind my eyes, the skin on my face breaking.

Then something snapped inside me. My agony began to twist, corrupting itself until it turned into anger. Everything was boiling inside me. Every vein of pain and fury rushed through me and my mind couldn't keep pace with it. My breathing grew erratic. I was *so* godsdamn tired of all of this.

"Caius, stop!" The voice speared through the storm in my heart. Diane.

She was going to intervene. I would expect nothing less from my she-wolf, but I needed this to happen between Caius and me. I willed silver flames, and a blazing circle erupted around us, blocking Diane and the others from getting any closer. Diane's she-wolf aether tried to push through, only for the wall of white fire to rebuild again.

"Remus!" Diane shouted from the other side. "Let us through!"

I could hear Drusus's roar. "It doesn't have to be like this!"

My vision blurred as I focused on keeping the aether up. Caius paused, heaving violently. Blood streaked his knuckles and some was splattered across his face. I yelled, and bashed my head against his, pushing him off me. We both struggled to our feet. Our rage was equally matched now.

"Fight me!" Caius roared. His hands rolled into fists once more. "Hit me, Remus!"

I charged him. We collided, refraining from shifting into our wolf forms as we allowed our human skin to feel every emotion warring inside us. My fists met his face, his body, and soon we were both bloodied messes. We circled one another, Caius wiped the blood from his mouth with the back of his hand. One moment I was standing in front of him and the next I was grabbing the collar of his tunic.

My lips curled into a snarl. "I have grown *tired* of being called a traitor. I did everything I thought was right!"

Caius shouted, a sound filled with heartache than anything else, as he shoved me away. I loosened my hold on the wall of fire, and Diane's power blasted through it. Black veins etched on her skin as the shadows billowed out of her like wings.

Her eyes, those golden eyes of sands and suns, were full of sadness and hurt. I hated that I'd caused that look.

But they all needed to hear this.

Blood bubbled at the corners of my lips. Every word out of my mouth unleashed needles of pain through my throat. "I killed them all."

Caius froze, his body trembling as if he were holding on to my last bit of strength to not attack me. The others listened and waited, I could sense their hesitation and worry. So, I pressed on. Every. Broken. Word. "I went back to the catacombs, to where Helena and I had found Anthony, and I killed them all. Every living thing—mortal and daemon. That is when Anthony found me."

I coughed up more blood. Red liquid was beginning to run down my brow, making me shut my eyes.

Drusus took a step toward me but paused. I peered at him, saw the devastation on his face. "Remus, your pater wasn't good to you. Was he?"

I exhaled a heavy breath, my lungs rattling. I shook my head. "I never chose to leave the Pack. Anthony disowned me and dragged my name through the godsdamn mud. At the time I guessed it was just easier to leave than to let everyone know the truth about me or their beloved Alpha. I hated my pater, but I loved the Pack more. I was broken, and I made the promise to myself to hunt the Order down. As penance."

Something pulled at my ribs, and I groaned from the pain. "I killed him too. My pater. Or I thought I had. Everyone believed he died from the flames of a battle, and that's partly true. I was the one who pushed him. I destroyed what was left of my family. But I never intended to kill my sister, I didn't know it was her."

I lifted my head to gaze at the canopy of trees. The leaves were a pure green. Untainted. "I needed to be sure that voice never returned. So I hunted my pater, disguised myself as a soldier and entered the battlefield. We fought, and I pushed him into the flames. I thought it was finished, that the terrifying voice that had visited my thoughts would never return. Only to find that Anthony still lives, the Order still exists, and the Ram was behind everything, all along."

There was nothing left for me to give. The coppery tang of blood filled my mouth, and more saliva pooled behind my lips.

Caius shuddered, breathing heavily through his nostrils. "You knew about the Order's existence, the betrayal of our former Alpha."

"You must know that I wouldn't have left if I thought the Ram still had a connection to this realm."

Caius snarled. "You were fighting a war none of us knew about. I suspected something else had happened that night. It was why I had Diane get close to you to—"

Caius stopped speaking, as if catching himself. Every strand of aether that coursed through my veins, every tendril that created my heart and soul crumbled into nothing.

Wind strummed through the leaves and stalks of wheat, brushing at my hair. But at Caius's words, everything seemed to still. I stared at him, feeling a sickening sensation sink into my chest.

The Alpha continued to breathe heavily. "Remus. I'm sorry, I didn't mean for it to come out that way."

I slowly looked to Diane. Her shadows had dissipated, but her eyes flashed with something that looked like agony, like *guilt*. My heart fell.

"Is that true?" I asked. "Were you ordered to get close to me? To, what, find out what the terrible Lone Wolf had done? To see if I could be trusted?"

Diane flinched. Her reaction and inability to look me in the eye only confirmed what I hoped wasn't true. "Remus, please let me explain."

"I can't believe it," I said, anger rising inside me.

"It was how it started *at first*, but everything began to change the more I knew you." I thought I could hear desperation in her voice, but my mind couldn't focus on anything else other than what Caius had said.

"I thought you were different," I said. "You didn't trust me at first, yes, but you never hated me like the others, you still gave me a chance to just be *me*. But it seems it was all a means to an end. A soldier blindly following orders."

Her expression darkened. Even the gray light above seemed to shrink back as shadows flickered across her features.

"Really?" She said, stalking toward me like a tigress. "I am only a blind soldier? Perhaps. But what of you? Let's be honest, you didn't align yourself with the Pack out of the goodness of your heart. We were all a means to an end for you as well. All for the sake of vengeance. You believed in your purpose and so did I." She scoffed, "I suppose that makes us both blind to our purpose."

"I confided in you," I growled. "I trusted you with the worst parts of me and it meant *nothing* to you."

Diane stood before me, a mere arm's length away. How easily I could reach for her, embrace her. Her darkness rose in gentle waves around her like snakes waiting to strike. Subtle yet lethal.

Her lips twitched with anger, those golden eyes seemed to glow more and more with every passing second. "Listen carefully, Remus. Don't you dare say that your trust meant nothing to me. I *wanted* to know more about you, and it had nothing to do with duty, but you kept shutting me out. After everything we had been through, you still didn't fully trust me."

Tears began to line her eyes. I could see the battle of emotions that clashed viciously within them. Anger, pain, and sadness. My own chest rose and fell in rapid breaths. We were both at quarrel between our own hearts and minds. I wanted to hold her, take the tears away, but the doubt and hurt spiraling inside me, from the argument with Caius, the agony of my sister's death, and now this new betrayal, and maybe even from some form of self-preservation, stopped me.

She gritted her teeth as her fingers slowly curled into fists. "I know you've been hurt. I cannot even begin to imagine what you've been through in these years, but do not forget that I also have my own demons to reconcile with. And I still trusted you with my own darkness."

There was a small ember in my heart that was screaming at me to come to my senses. I knew—within the deepest parts of my soul—I knew everything that had happened with Diane had been real, but my heart was being consumed by its own poison of fears and insecurities.

The words still flew out of my lips, the taste of ash and dust on my tongue. My voice came out in a rasp, not caring that the others could still hear me. "I know I'm not perfect, but I didn't think you would be one to hurt me. Maybe everything was just a lie."

Something shuddered over her expression, even the shadows surrounding her seemed to wilt. "If you truly believe that, then there's not much else to say. You also hurt me, Remus, and I think you should go. I don't want to see you right now, and I think some distance would do us both good."

The world started to spin. I couldn't—I couldn't breathe.

She fell silent as I took a step back. Away from them. Away from *her*. Her next words were the final cut to my heart.

"Leave, Remus."

I felt like I had suddenly succumbed to the war inside me. Utterly lost and empty. I looked to Caius. "Maybe now you will have your wish and never see me again."

He didn't respond and looked away.

Blood still trickled down my brow as I left, making my way through the Pack forum. I heard people gasp at the sight of me but no one approached. I was the Lone Wolf. And I would continue to brand myself in shame.

I was a man without his sun. A man without his blossoms and thorns.

Spitting blood and saliva, I managed to pull on enough strength to shift into my wolf form. I ran until my lungs burned and blood tore through the pads of my paws. Until the city of Rome disappeared behind dirt roads and hills, and any hope of being part of the Pack again became nothing but withered leaves and starless nights.

FIFTY

Diane

Darkness returned with a vengeance. It continued to unfurl from me, cradling me as if sensing the turmoil in my heart. The constant hums of the shadows were starting to drive me mad.

The Alpha was on his hands and knees, a hand pressed to his chest like the pain in his heart was too much to bear. His teeth clenched as he relived the pain. A wound that had never truly healed was raw once more.

My eyes strayed to the path Remus had disappeared from. The last look on his face before he'd left had cut through me. He must know that I truly cared for him. That I . . . longed for him. I despised the thought of him believing I had only probed into his dark past for the Pack. It was never like that for me. Even when I thought of my duty, I *wanted* to know Remus.

I didn't doubt his feelings for me, even though it had pained me to hear his words. He and I were both hurting. We needed some time alone before facing each other again.

Remus's entire life had been disrupted by the Ram. Anthony had given up on being a pater to him and his sister. My heart broke imagining a younger Remus, completely confused and hurt by his pater's lack of empathy and love toward him.

I couldn't fathom the pain he must have gone through. And Remus had had to bear it alone. Another voice slid through my thoughts. Remus *should've* told someone—my pater, perhaps. My pater, as the Beta wolf, would've fought against Anthony's corruption. Perhaps something could've been done. Perhaps not. This had happened eight years ago; Remus would've been twenty years old at the time. Too young, barely having reached manhood, to understand—emotionally. Though it didn't stop Remus from finding his pater with the intention of killing him. *Would I have done any different?*

His pater held the upper hand as a beloved Alpha to the people, and Remus was supposedly guilty of killing his sister. Anthony had every wolf believe Remus had chosen to abandon his Pack.

There was another thing to consider. Remus and Helena had been silently advocating for the Pack, protecting the integrity of the wolves.

In an odd, twisted way I could see why the daemon king was angry with the gods. He'd wanted his kind to have a home. Wouldn't that justify wanting retaliation? No, it didn't justify the destruction and loss of innocents.

I continued to stare at the empty path, absurdly hoping that Remus would return. I knew I would have the chance to speak with him again, but I felt the need to run after him. Explain. Hold him.

Atticus's hand came to my arm. He pulled me gently, trying to grasp my attention.

"Diane, breathe," he coaxed. "Your power is about to lash out."

I took a deep breath. Suddenly, I felt this overwhelming pain. The hurt for Remus, the pain of Cato's death, the destruction of the Pack haven. Everything. The shadows continued to stretch out from my body, pulsating around me. My control on them was slipping.

I gritted my teeth through the surge of energy. "Don't get near me. I don't know if I can control it."

Marcus inched closer. The ice in his blue eyes softened. "Remus will come back."

My teeth clicked as the shadows whirled, shrinking to bulbs of energy at my palms. I closed my hands and the black wisps slipped through my fingers like water. I looked to Caius, who was being helped up by Drusus.

"I know you're in pain, Alpha," I said. "We are here to support you, always."

Caius's eyes were downcast. The rage seemed to have left him completely drained. "I was a fool. I allowed my emotions to get the best of me."

My chest tightened at the vulnerability. At his sadness. "You have a right to be upset. Remus needed to know the truth, regardless."

Caius lifted his head. His eyes watered and I could see the smears of Remus's blood on his face. "I'm so sorry, Diane."

I smiled sadly, taking a step away from the Alpha and my brothers. I turned toward the wheat fields.

"Where are you going?" Marcus called out

I inhaled the scent of citrus and herbs, still strong even among the bloodshed. A realization settled within me with a dull thud. "I need to do something I should've done long ago."

The wheat strands brushed against my arms and legs. I soon found myself at the entrance of the she-wolves' courtyard. The sound of beating wings made me look up. A white pegasus landed in front of me. Sabina slid off her bonded stallion, taking my hands into hers as she approached me.

My Commanding She-Wolf looked me in the eye. Her own aether hummed through the touch of our palms.

Sabina's eyes softened. "You are ready."

A lone tear slid down my cheek. "I am."

There was a faint curve to her lips. "Then let's celebrate, she-wolf. It is time for your Rite."

There was hardly any ceremony for my Rite. Traditionally, there would be festivals and dinner parties. Residents of the haven would fill the streets with flowers, and the air would be heavy with scented oils. However, it wasn't exactly appropriate to have any of that now, nor did I want all that attention. I requested the she-wolves help the other haven residents with their belongings before we celebrated.

Sabina hosted a small ceremonial festivity for me. Just us and the other she-wolves. We lounged in her courtyard. Settees were strewn across the ivory floor with white plush throws and pillows. The warrior she-wolves had abandoned their fighting leathers. Underneath their dresses and skirts, hitched on their thighs or over their backs, their hidden blades glinted. A warrior she-wolf hardly ever parted from her weapons.

One of the she-wolves played the harp. Music sounded delicately throughout the marble hall, and I tried to drown my feelings and thoughts with lots of wine. My hand wiped at the rivulets that trailed down my chin.

"Oh, dear gods," Sabina *tsked*, pouring me another glass.

I smirked. "You're the best Commander ever," I slurred.

Sabina shook her head, downing a cup of her own. "Keep drinking. It's been a shitty couple of weeks."

My heart felt numb, but I welcomed the warm buzz. Sabina was just as torn up by Cato's death as I was and in need to forget, just for a little while. When we'd returned to the haven from the griffins' kingdom, I'd run to find Cato's body. Before I could, Sabina had found me, nearly knocking me to the ground. Her eyes had been swollen with tears, and she and I held on to each other tightly.

I learned they'd put Cato in his own villa, wrapped up and resting on a platform. His mater and avia—grandmother—had shared the home with him. They would keep his body there for a week before moving forward with the funeral procession.

I needed to complete the Rite before then. As I found myself slipping back into those thoughts, I quickly gulped more wine.

"What?" I asked, knowing Sabina was eyeing me, without having to look up.

"Did you want to see him?"

I shoved my wine cup toward her. "Not yet. I need to do this first. I can't explain it, but something is telling me that the Rite will help me. Does that sound silly?"

The corner of Sabina's lips perked up faintly. "Not at all. I think there is something ingrained in our senses that pushes us to complete the Rite. For some she-wolves, it doesn't happen. They never complete the Rite, and that is okay. But I know that you will find the answers you seek during yours."

I gave her a questioning look, but Sabina's gaze drifted toward the other side of the room. Laelia and Meredith entered the court-yard. Meredith looked healed, bandages were still wrapped around her arms and legs, but at least she was moving again.

She smiled softly when her eyes collided with mine. She nudged Laelia forward, and they moved closer to where Sabina and I sat. My teeth slid over my lip nervously as Laelia stood before me, a hesitant smile on her face. I didn't have to think twice. My feet found the floor and my arms were around her in a heartbeat. I'd missed Laelia's com-pany. I couldn't blame her for her outrage, the cold fear she must have felt at the thought of losing one she loved.

Laelia stiffened for a moment before wrapping her arms around me. She gently tapped my cheek, her face falling. "I'm sorry about Cato. I ... still can't believe it. . . ."

It was all she could say. My throat bobbed, and the burning sen-sation behind my eyes returned. "He was obsessed with you," I said.

She laughed tearfully. "Do you remember when he and Drusus had a bet on who could throw a horseshoe around the spear of Jupiter's statue in the temple? Caius was livid."

"The heathens," Sabina snickered.

My throat cracked at the laugh that escaped my lips. We sobered, a moment of silence in Cato's memory.

Sabina tapped her chest with a fist and burped. "Shall we return to getting absolutely buzzed?"

Meredith groaned. "Gods, yes please."

We brought another settee closer. Despite the tragedies that had happened and everything still to come, the evening spent mingling and getting lost in the wine with my sisters-in-arms was one of the loveliest I'd had in a long time. At one point during the night, Sabina scurried out of the villa. The mischief mixed with tight worry behind her eyes told me she was sneaking away to see Drusus.

Hours later, when light had barely appeared over the mountain ranges, Sabina returned and led me to the edges of the haven. Her fingers were smeared with the kohl she had lined around my eyes. My Commanding She-Wolf stood before me, clasped in a velvet cloak that encased her lithe frame, and held out my sword and dagger to me.

Her expression was serious, save for the gleam of pride within her smoke-gray eyes. "She-wolf, I wish you courage and strength. May you complete your Rite with honor, and return as a Daughter of Mars."

FIFTY-ONE

Diane

All I had was a sword, a dagger, a satchel, and the aether in my veins. Godsdamn the Fates.

Fighting leathers were strapped over my tunic, tight over my chest and thighs but leaving my shoulders bare. My hair was pulled up by a leather band. I ran my fingers over the Egyptian-made ear cuffs, thoughts churning wildly in my head as I began to fully realize that my Rite was about to commence.

How many times had I seen she-wolves returning from the Rite, riding their winged stallions, an extra glow in their kohl-rimmed eyes? Word of what they experienced during the Rite was never shared. It was then, when the she-wolf and her bonded pegasus paid tribute to the temple of Mars, that an otherworldly experience awaited them. Some said it was a prophecy of sorts, a peek into the life the she-wolf would live. In other words, it didn't seem like much to me. I presumed I would pay tribute, offer allegiance to the god of war, and that would be that.

I tightened the satchel over my shoulder. It held dried meat, nuts and berries, and a waterskin. It was only three days' worth of supplies but, if rationed properly, could be stretched to a week. The longest a Rite had been was three weeks. Length of time did not matter, only the heart of the warrior who returned.

A Daughter of Mars. The name called to me like a siren's song, my power ready to claim it. I was prepared to toss my fear into oblivion and finally realize that this was part of who I was.

The green grass shifted in the breeze like rippling water, and the hills rolled toward the canyons. The pegasus were known to venture near the cliffs, where the waters and lands were untouched by man and Olympians alike. The soft crunch of my boots was the only sound aside from the songbirds.

My legs burned after hours of walking and searching. I managed to find shelter in a small cave formed of rocks and boulders among the hills. A small fire now burned at my feet. I hadn't seen the harm of it since the area was absent of daemons and the Order. However, I kept my sword on my thigh, just in case. I leaned my head back against a slab of rock, tossing a strip of dried meat into my mouth.

Soft heat warmed my face as my fingers ran lines down the sleek blade of the sword. I didn't want to wake up without Remus's large arms wrapped around my waist, that sharp jawline grazing my hair.

Sleep was difficult to find, thoughts and grief churning in my head, so I watched the flames slowly dim throughout the night until I could no longer stay awake.

I was on a narrow stretch of land, a canyon to my right with a river at its base. Thank the gods and goddesses it wasn't blistering hot. After days of tracking, I spotted hoofprints and signs of grazing. The pegasus had obviously taken flight as their prints disappeared. My eyes drew up along the canyon's tall wall of gray stone. Mars's temple rested among one of those cliffs. The thought of visiting such a holy place sent a nervous chill through me.

As I tracked the herd, I found myself venturing farther into the woodlands, away from the canyons. I stumbled upon a meadow that crawled up a rocky hillside, and I shielded my eyes from the bright sun.

The pegasus herd had never looked more celestial.

Shades of powder white and dust gray colored their pelts. Powerful wings were folded over their backs, and their large heads ducked down to graze the grass. The aether in my blood sang at the sight. It pulled from me, stretching out toward the herd. Searching, calling for my bonded-to-be.

The pegasuses jerked their heads up, their dark eyes landing on me. I stiffened under their gazes. Honestly, it felt like I was being scrutinized. I reeled my power back, and one by one, the pegasuses returned to their grazing, seeming unaffected by my presence. I was sure they knew who I was. A she-wolf looking for her pegasus. My heart stumbled. Was my bonded pegasus meant to come to me? I was always told that it was the animal who chose. But right now, I felt ignored.

I walked further, the ground beginning to slope upward. Sunlight caught on the shimmer of their wings, like specks of crystal. Pollen danced along the curtains of light, and the only sounds I could hear were their soft snorts and the swooshing of their tails. It was the most at peace I'd felt in a while.

As I moved among the pegasuses, they continued to ignore me. I sighed, arching an eyebrow at a snow-white winged stallion. "Not very interested in me, are you?"

The majestic creature peeked up from its patch of grass. Its nostrils flared, releasing a snort that could've passed for a bored scoff. My lips danced in amusement. "No offense taken."

I released my aether, allowing the energy to flow away from me. It wasn't the dark shadows, but the pure she-wolf-borne power I had summoned my whole life. Invisible aether rippled through the herd, gently caressing the animals. I hoped I would be able to *feel* the bond, whatever that meant. The energy stretched out but still no reaction. Until—right at the far back, just where the rocks crawled up the small hill, a head rose. My breath caught with anticipation as I walked toward the pegasus.

He was male, tall with sinewed strength lining his chest and legs. His pelt was a dove gray, like the wolf fur of a lost brother. The stunning animal watched me, and my power hummed as it made contact with the pegasus. The touch was slight, the faint brush of a feather, and I stiffened as ripples of energy echoed back at me. Coursed through me. It was bright and wholesome, like golden liquid. Warm and inviting. My soul drank in the purity of it.

The pegasus tilted his head and I knew he could feel what I was feeling. Pure, godsgiven aether flowed between us. He was mine, and I was his.

My hand reached for him. "Looks like—"

I reacted on instinct as I felt another presence looming behind the rocks, and I spun around, unsheathing my sword. A large figure bolted out from the rocks toward us. The pegasus jumped back, large wings flaring.

Dark brown wings and lion paws pounded the ground. It was a chimera. This wasn't good. I'd only encountered such a beast one other time, and I'd been with my she-wolves. But not this time. I would have to fight this on my own.

Hunger boiled in its eyes, the hackles of its mane raised. The other pegasuses neighed and shrieked, many of them taking flight. I wanted the pegasus I was bonded to to run, but he didn't. The stubborn winged stallion pawed at the ground with his hoof. He was a fighter.

The chimera roared as the pegasus reared back on its hind legs. There was a horrifying *thump* as his hooves made impact with the chimera's shoulders. The chimera dug its fangs in the pegasus's neck, making the elegant creature unleash a blood curdling scream, tossing his head side to side, attempting to buck the chimera off.

Without having to move a hand, my aether burst out. Invisible whips of power shoved the chimera off the stallion. I sprinted forward and swung my sword in a wide arc. The metal glided against the chimera's thick neck, a line of red following.

The chimera didn't pause, stubborn in its attack. My power exploded from me again, and the chimera tumbled to the ground. I was unsure what had happened to me. The sensation had overcome my senses so naturally that I could do nothing but listen to it. I landed on the pegasus's back, my power careening forward as the stallion charged toward the beast. I'd seen this move countless times from the Daughters of Mars and their pegasuses in the courtyard, so I jumped off the winged horse, my sword raised, and it felt as if I too had done it many times before.

The sleek silver blade sank between the chimera's neck and

shoulder. The animal shuddered, and the pegasus bit down, ripping a chunk of its flesh off. A river of red flew out as I wrenched the sword back. The chimera's body thudded on the ground next to me, and I rolled away, expecting it to launch at me once more. It didn't move.

I looked back at the pegasus. Red streamed his snout and neck where the chimera had dug in its claws and teeth. He shook its silvery mane and padded toward me. Once he drew closer, I noticed the quiver in his legs. But he didn't hesitate nor flinch away; he dipped his head and pressed his snout to me. I forced myself to my feet.

"Careful now," I said.

The pegasus blinked, seeming to digest my words. My hand rummaged through my satchel, and I cursed under my breath. I'd packed some ointments, hadn't I? I found the small canister that Junia had given me and began rubbing the oil onto the pegasus's wounds.

I caressed his neck; his pelt was soft and shiny. "I'm sorry, it's the best I can do."

He turned his head and nudged me closer to his body as if in an embrace, and the aether soared between us once more. He was my bonded pegasus. The one who would join me in battle, walk beside me in life. There was a profound sense of gratitude and peace at the thought, in addition to the adrenaline and excitement from today. I didn't realize I'd been smiling until I found myself leaning my head against him.

"I guess it would be appropriate to name you," I mused, letting my fingers roam through his thick mane. "How do you like . . . Dromos?"

The stallion blinked once more, and his soft breath graze my cheeks. I smiled more broadly. "I'll take that as a yes. Shall we complete this Rite together?"

FIFTY-TWO

Diane

The world dropped from under us as Dromos took to the sky.

"Shit!" I jolted forward, my hands grabbing onto Dromos's mane. I could've sworn he snickered.

Daring a peek below, my eyes widened as the trees grew smaller and smaller. The river below was nothing but a curved line of blue. I'd worn my hair loose today, and it now whipped wildly in the wind. The night of the chimera attack, I hadn't dared ride Dromos, let alone fly with him.

We'd spent the night near a stream underneath a grove of pine trees. After feeding him whatever was left in my satchel, I had curled against his side, his legs folded underneath him. I'd slept in the warmth between his wing, which draped over me, and his powerful body.

Nightmares did not find me that night.

This morning he'd hauled himself to his feet, spread his wings, and cocked his head at me as if to say *well, are you coming?* Aether hummed between us, and he must've sensed what I planned to do today. What an intriguing thing, the bond.

The deep flap of his wings echoed in the silent sky. Today would be the last day of this Rite. A final step before we could return home. I dropped my head back and extended my arms. Wind caressed my ears and neck.

He climbed higher and higher until he was parallel to the canyon's edges. We bent the winds to our will. Something bubbled from my lips, freeing a heaviness from my chest. I was laughing, and it felt good. So good.

Dromos ripped through a low bank of clouds and banked his wings out, holding us midair. The canyons blended into mountains, and the mountains tore through the clouds above.

I leaned forward, stroking Dromos's neck. "Thank you, my sky. I have never felt so free."

The pegasus snorted in response, and I felt a trickle of warmth pass through the bond. Dromos kicked forward as we glided through the peaks. Amid the jagged teeth of stone, sitting on its own plateau, stood a lonely structure. Pearl white pillars were erected along its small entrance. Unblemished limestone with dark arched halls, save for the glows of ember inside.

The temple of the god of war.

Power purred in my veins. The sensation vibrated from Dromos as well. Wings folded over his back as he landed. I slid off him, keeping to his side as we walked. Stone steps led to the entrance. Torches lined each side of the passageway beside each pillar. The fires that burned here never died, a result of a type of aether I didn't understand. Dromos's hooves clopped on the ground, and I found the sounds to be somehow comforting.

The only form of light inside the temple was the fire at the center that crackled in its hearth. The temple wasn't large—an altar stood in the middle of the space, a statue of Mars behind it. The god stood in striking marbled beauty and strength. Dried petals and incense had been scattered across the smooth altar, the offerings of previous she-wolves.

Dromos lingered at the entrance, his snout nudging my back. I rubbed his muzzle and planted a kiss on the large space between his eyes. My boots echoed softly as I neared the altar, my heart pumping even louder. I had been running from this moment for years, and now I was here. And I was ready.

I pulled out a vial of blossom petals I had saved for the offering. There was a light pop when I opened it and I began scattering the petals on the stone surface.

Bowing my head to the god of war, the father of the wolves, whose blood ran heavy in my veins, I began to whisper my prayers. Prayers filled with gratitude, sorrow, hopes, and regrets. Tears welled in my closed eyes, but they didn't fall.

"There is a power inside of me," I whispered. "Another force of energy that has awakened, and I fear its darkness. I fear that I *like* it." The unasked question tolled in my head: *Who am I?*

I opened my eyes. There was silence until a breeze swept through the temple, brushing the petals across the altar. The aether in my body stirred. The fire in the temple flared brighter. Dromos neighed loudly. I felt it then.

Someone or something was here.

I blinked, and a harsh string of curses fell from my lips as I jumped back, my hand landing on the pommel of my blade. A man was leaning against the statue. Strong arms folded over his chest. His *godly* features molded from granite. Dark brown locks hung over his brow, the ends curled at the nape of his neck. Muscles that could've been made out of stone lined his olive complexion, perfect against the bronze armor he wore. His eyes were like burning embers, dipped in amber gold.

The aether in my veins thrummed excitedly, and I couldn't understand why.

A humored expression touched the male's beautiful face. "That sword will do nothing against your god, mortal."

"*My god?*" My eyes darted up to the statue and back to him. The statue was not identical, but with the chiseled planes and details, there was a strong similarity. And I understood why my aether was reacting almost with a sense of . . . familiarity. I fell to my knees, my voice barely audible. "You are Mars."

The smile on his lips widened. "That I am. Hello, Diane."

A hysterical laugh that could've passed as a sob escaped me, and I quickly sobered and dipped my brow to the cool ground.

The sound of his voice was rich, like ancient wood. "Rise, daughter. You and your pegasus showed promise in the bond. This pleases me."

Standing, I sheathed my sword. My legs felt numb. What in the gods' name was happening?

Mars smirked and it oddly reminded me of Remus. He pushed off the statue and made his way across the temple. "Peace, my she-wolf. You've called for me, no?"

The god of war was standing before me. The fact was slowly settling. It was difficult to ignore the deep hums of power that followed his presence, so I almost missed the ink that curved along his shoulders and up his neck. *Our god of war has tattoos.* For whatever the reason, I especially liked that part.

"I guess I did," I managed to say, still wondering whether this was all a dream.

His gold-fire eyes softened. "You wish to know who you are?"

I swallowed. "Yes. There is this other power thriving inside me. Of dark fires and shadows. It feels like I have known this power all my life, as if it's a part of me, but it has only surfaced recently."

Mars nodded, seeming unsurprised. He already knew what I was, and the anticipation was beginning to unnerve me. Mars made his way to Dromos and ran a hand down his snout. Dromos huffed in elation, closing his eyes at the god's touch.

"What do you know of your lineage?" the god of war asked.

"Well, my pater is the Beta wolf," I responded slowly. Confusion pinched my brow at what Mars could be insinuating.

His lips twitched, pulling up at the corners. "And your mater?"

"She was from Egypt, but I know she wasn't born with any aether. My mater was human."

Mars raised a finger, turning from Dromos to me. Wicked silver flames winked in his eyes as he grinned. "Quite the opposite, Diane. I have someone for you to meet."

Darkness yawned. The fire flared once more, like a beacon in a growing sea of mist. Shivers trailed down my spine as the tendrils of shadows yearned to pull from me. A figure stepped out from the wall of shadow.

A tall, athletic frame with dark leathery skin. A black breastplate around the chest, gold linings rimming the armor. The stomach was bare, showing the fine carvings of the abdominal muscles. Armor wrapped around the waist down the legs. An ivory leather piece was tucked into the waistband and hung down between the legs. On the head, a black-gold headdress. The face was that of a jackal, with long pointed ears and a snout. Gold ink was imprinted from the temple down the line of the snout.

My eyes widened. I recognized *him*. His presence. I sensed it when I fell deep in the midst of my shadowed aether. The figure of speckled night was him.

The Egyptian god of the dead, Anubis.

"He likes the theatrics," Mars commented as the jackal god prowled closer.

The corner of Anubis's dark lips curled and peeled back, revealing terrifying teeth. The *god of the dead* was grinning. "I do love to make an entrance, Mars." His voice was pure power.

My legs almost buckled, but Dromos held me up. "Anubis," I breathed.

His onyx eyes, glinting with stars, slid to me. "You've certainly caught my attention, mortal."

Gods. My eyes jumped between the two immortals, speechless. Amusement still lingered in the god of war's expression. He angled his head to the jackal god. "You wanted to be here, are you going to tell her?"

I forced myself to meet Anubis's intimidating gaze. "What does all this have to do with my mater?"

The jackal god's headdress gleamed as he watched me with a measured look for a moment before responding. "The aether in Egypt is no different to that of Rome. The wolves have always been with the jackal-shapeshifters. However, there is so much to discover beyond the sea, beyond the sands, beyond what the wolves know. Your mater came from a long line of warriors. Warriors who have served many kings and queens and continue to do so even now. The aether of the jackal-shapeshifter ran through her veins. *My* blood ran through her veins, as it does through yours."

My heart thundered in my chest as Anubis's words drowned the world around me. My mater was never a human. She'd had the blood of the jackals. The next words rolled slowly off my tongue as I tried to process what I was hearing. "She never exuded any sort of power. I never saw it . . . they never told me."

Starlight winked in the god's onyx eyes. "You are a part of me just as much as you are a part of Mars."

"Incredible power thrives inside you," Mars said. The fiery light in his eyes darkened, the humor disappearing, and I could only imagine what the god of war looked like in true rage. "Incredible but dangerous."

I released a shaky breath. "My power looks awfully like that of the Order's."

Shadows flared from Anubis, anger in his expression. "Whatever that daemon summons is not a part of us. *My* bloodline courses through *you.*"

When I continued to stare dumbly at the god of the dead, his voice turned gentle. "Aether is of pure essence. The only twisted or malicious things of this power are the intentions of the wielders."

Something dark drew over Mars's gaze, his eyes straying to the floor as if deep in thought at the mention of the Ram.

A newfound strength willed to life in my bones. "How come the gods and goddesses have not helped?"

I'd questioned the gods. I should've regretted the words, but I didn't. They were standing before me now, and I only wondered where they'd been this entire time. Anubis didn't move, but there was a softening in his dark, endless eyes. Eyes that could open gateways through the celestial skies.

The god of war sighed in exasperation looking more mortal than ever with such a *human* reaction. "When we banished the Ram and his kind, we had to withdraw our ability to interact with the mortal realm."

I almost scoffed. Almost. "Seems a convenient excuse for someone with unimaginable power."

The corner of Mars's lips tipped upward. But it was a sad smile. "I'm sorry, young one. Even the gods are bound by laws of nature. That is why aether exists. As well as our powers that lay within our mortal bloodlines. There must be balance, and aether should only be used for great, wondrous things, or it could be abused for the darkest of desires. You have the power of two gods in your veins. Though it may only be droplets passed on by generations, it is still power, and you decide what to do with it. No Order can define that for you."

Something tugged within me. Choice. *Liberum arbitrium.* Free will. That is what it all came down to, no? The Ram's decision to find his kind a new home. My decision to suppress the shadowed aether. To postpone the Rite. Remus's decision to seek vengeance. His decision to embrace the power he'd found and return to the Pack.

"I do have a question," I whispered. My eyes jumped from Anubis to Mars. "The Ram. He's trying to find a home for his kind. Isn't it cruel to shut his people out of our realm? Can they not find a home here?"

The air *growled* as Mars's expression darkened further. Fire the color of the moon flickered across his gaze, and he turned to face the view of the mountains. "The gods may have made a mistake in banishing a whole species, but the daemons weren't fit for this world. Trust that they are living good and fruitful lives in the realm they currently reside in. But the Ram was angry with us. He accused the gods of undermining him. We told him he and his followers could join the rest of his kind in the other realm. For whatever reason, he became obsessed with this mortal realm. A part of me suspects it was purely out of pride that he wanted to stay. We banished him and his armies to a dark corner of the Underworld, to a prison realm where he wouldn't be able to hurt anyone. All those years ago, I hoped we had done enough. For this, our failed attempt to leash the Ram angers and saddens me to the very essence of my being. I want to intervene, but the laws of nature forbid it."

The god of war now faced me, pinning me with a serious look. "Which makes me wonder how, in all the years this realm has existed, a mortal managed to gain more power than they were born with."

Understanding dawned. "Remus?"

"Remus," his voice hummed. "I have plans to meet with that one. He managed to take something that wasn't his to take."

Fear ensnared my chest at the god of war's tone. "Please, don't hurt him," I pleaded. "He didn't mean to take anything. It was only a means to survive."

Mars watched me for a beat, considering and calculating. "Relax, little one. Unfortunately, I can't intervene on his current state of power either. Not while he lives. Though I must admit, I am relieved he managed to obtain some of my power. You will need every help you can get against the Ram."

"The forces that are rallying against you will be strong, and you need to trust in yourselves as well as each other if you wish to see victory," Anubis advised.

Trusting Remus was as easy as breathing. I'd leave my life in his calloused hands. It was trusting in myself that gave me pause, but now my origins had come to light. Questions still plagued my mind, about my mater and who she truly was, but my fears had been eased. These dark shadows were not the source of an evil force.

I looked up to see Anubis gazing at me as if he already knew the direction of my thoughts. The god of the dead was so tall, I had to tip my head back to see his face. "My young one, do not fear who you are. Darkness has a reputation of being something to avoid, but it can also be solace, a place of trust and intimacy. Bend the darkness to your will, Diane, and you will never fear it."

I felt his words through my bones. Tears welled in my eyes as I stared at the god of the dead. I could've sworn realms of stars and pale moons shone in that gaze. Anubis leaned down, and his snout lightly touched the top of my head as if in reassurance.

"Thank you," I whispered.

Dark clouds rose softly from the corners of the temple. Anubis's eyes twinkled as he took a step back. My body felt empty as the god's empowering presence got further away. Darkness billowed, completely enveloping Anubis. Just as quickly as the shadows had come, they left, spiraling into nothingness, leaving an empty space in the temple. The god of the dead had returned to his godly realm.

My eyes slid to Mars, who was again staring out at the temple's entrance. His voice wrapped around me, and I found the sound comforting. "When aether and this mortal realm were young, I used to wander amongst these lands. Out of curiosity mainly. A lot of the gods and goddesses did so back then. One fateful day," he chuckled at the words, his voice melting like warm honey, "I met a human woman, and I fell in love. The god of war had become lovesick."

Warmth skittered across my chest. "I've heard the story. It was how the wolves were born."

He turned his head to me. The smile on his face was that of a man in love. "She and I now roam the golden plains together. Love is what began the wolves' line, and love will be what saves them too."

I wondered what he meant by that. Mars cracked a smirk at the questioning look on my face. He winked at me, and the wickedly handsome god vanished in a blink. The gods' presence had brought a profound warmth. With them gone, the air felt cool, less easy to breathe in, and the world less bright. It was like a veil had been ripped from my eyes. I gasped and stumbled a few steps, my hand finding Dromos's muzzle. The pegasus neighed softly, pulling me out of my stupor. I turned to him, running my hands through the loose hairs that rested over his brow.

The tears that had been welling in my eyes finally fell. Each clear droplet touched the temple's floor. Tears of heartache turned to somber joy as I found solace.

It was time to go home.

FIFTY-THREE

Remus

Blossoms had managed to penetrate through the weeds. Some had scaled along the ivory walls. The colors of dandelion and pale wine spotted the villa grounds. Beauty had found its way in the heart of an abandoned house.

I made my way up the stone steps from the private beach. Sand was wedged between the toes of my bare feet. I had been spending every day on the same sands where I'd spent my childhood. My mater had lounged in the small boat as Helena and I ventured out into the waters. I was in my family's villa. I'd returned home.

When I'd left Rome, I didn't know where I was going until I found myself padding up the steps of my old home. I'd shifted back into my human body, my low howl of pain twisted into a groan. I had gripped the sides of the front doors as the weight of all that had occurred crashed over me.

The villa had been robbed and plundered. Chairs and tables were splintered across the floor. Broken vases and other pottery. Some rugs and fine pieces were missing, primarily the jewelry my mater had owned and Anthony's weaponry. An ache had lanced through my chest as I wandered through the empty villa.

I spent the remaining week cleaning my old home. Tossing out the broken furniture and sweeping up the shattered pottery pieces. I lit the torches in the villa to ward off any other potential robberies.

The people in the nearby town knew who had lived here before and they would know who had returned.

At the top of the steps, I now stood in the dirt courtyard that had been used for training. Helena and I'd enjoyed fighting, except for when Anthony would become involved. Now it was home to wild-flowers and weeds.

I stepped into the villa and found myself ahead of Helena's room. I'd been avoiding it. I'd managed to enter my parents' room, but un-surprisingly, I hadn't found any secret notes or journal entries about my pater conspiring with the Ram.

With the tip of my finger, I pushed Helena's door open.

My sister's room had also been raided. Her sheets were spilled over the edges of the bed. The rugs and blankets had been taken. I only hoped that they had been given to someone in dire need—or if they'd been sold, that the person deserved to keep whatever sum they'd earned from it. My nose wrinkled at the thick layer of dust that covered the surfaces.

I had avoided her room, as I didn't want to see just memories. She should be here with me. I would have still been a part of the Pack, she would still be with Caius. And I could've introduced her to Diane.

My thoughts wandered to Diane. I hadn't stopped thinking of her. The last image of her pained expression was burned in my mem-ory. I hadn't wanted to leave, but I knew I'd needed to. Counting the days, I suspected Cato's funeral would be held soon. I wished I could be there for her, for Drusus, but some time away was necessary, es-pecially after that godsawful fight.

I had laid myself bare, torn down my walls, and had revealed the truths that had haunted me for so long. I'd known Caius would hate me, and why wouldn't he? My fingers went to my lips. The bruising had faded, but I still felt pinches of pain at my ribs.

He needed time too, I could understand that, but time was not our friend. War was at our doorstep. The Ram's army was already marching from the southern lands to where Aurelius held the current frontline. I knew I needed to return, lend my power to help defeat the Ram, and then return to the life of the Lone Wolf.

If we managed to rid this realm of daemons, I was unsure of what I would do next. My entire adult life had revolved around the Order and daemons. Around hunting them. I would imagine there would still be many followers to dispose of but that wouldn't be forever. What then? Perhaps I could still appeal to the griffin king then.

I felt lost. I snatched one of the surviving clay vases and hauled it against the wall. My body sagged against the door, and I slid to the floor, my empty gaze fixing on nothing. I'd killed her. I knew my mind had been tricked, but the blood on my hands haunted me nonetheless. Tormented me since that night. Damn the Fates and the gods and every cursed realm.

I stayed on the floor, broken, watching the starlight seep into my sister's room. The sickening sensation hadn't found me again since I'd confessed everything to Caius. Truth be told, I felt better than I'd had in a long time, but now, a hollowness had replaced the anger. I let my thoughts fade and be lost into the quiet night.

FIFTY-FOUR

Diane

Twinkling torchlights bounced throughout the expanse of trees and villas. The scent of lemon landed on my tongue as the haven grounds appeared before us, and I heard the faint sound of music. A harp and other string instruments. Masses of people held torches and candles. Petals rained over the grounds, and I began to laugh.

It was my welcome home.

Standing at the head of the haven were my brothers. Dressed in their finest tunics, swords strapped to their hips, their eyes brightened upon seeing me. Sabina and Laelia stood among them with wide grins. Caius was also behind them, and I was pleasantly surprised to see him there. I searched for someone else and fought the twang of disappointment. My pater wasn't here. I knew he wouldn't be; he was leading armies, waiting for the rest of us to arrive.

Dromos landed, and even before my feet had touched the ground, Drusus knocked into me. He held me in a tight hug, and I felt Marcus and Atticus joining in behind him.

Sabina shouted from where she stood. "Your wolves planned this welcome party."

I gasped, pulling back to look at my brothers. My heart tightened. "You did?"

Marcus smiled, his curls tousled over his brow. "You deserved a welcome from your Rite."

Atticus sauntered forward. The flicker of amber light kissed his cheekbones. "Daughter of Mars, welcome back."

"Oh, dear gods." Drusus gasped in awe, his wide eyes drawn to Dromos, who lingered behind me.

My lips curved, meeting each of their gazes. "Brothers, there's someone I want you to meet."

An earthy spice tinged the air. Wisps of smoke from the candles danced up toward the sky as the priests burned frankincense. Torches lined the pathway to the sarcophagus. Olympians walked up the green hill, passing the marbled tombs. Night painted the hills in its dark shade as the firelight flickered like stars.

Cato would be laid to rest tonight. I hadn't had the opportunity to participate in the viewing processions prior to the funeral, but I knew Cato would understand. His body had been washed and donned in his finest attire. A wreath of gold and white blossoms crowned his head, and two coins rested on his eyes to pay the ferryman on his journey to the afterworld.

Felix and I helped Cato's mater and grandmother with the cleaning and preparation of Cato's body. They admitted they had wanted to wait for me to return from the Rite before the funeral. I felt honored and relieved.

My heart had broken for Felix. He and Cato had kept their relationship a secret, not wanting to draw attention to themselves, and I could see the pain in his eyes from the loss of his beloved. Felix stood beside me now, tears lingering along his thick eyelashes. He was smaller than most of the male wolves. Thin, with sharp cheekbones and more delicate feminine features and curly black hair.

I tried to imagine Cato, a tall burly wolf, embracing tiny Felix. Cato's face bright with adoration and love. I smiled softly at the thought.

Caius had paid his respects to Cato's family, offering them security and advice on financial support. Caius always went above and beyond to ensure the families and loved ones would be taken care of following the passing of one of his warriors.

The black cloak brushed against the back of my legs. All the wolves and she-wolves wore similar attire. Some of the males had arrived in their wolf forms and kept to the edges of the pathway, their animal eyes glittering in the dark.

Black kohl ringed my eyes, covering the redness from the tears. Obsidian jewels crowned my head, and a black dress clung to my hips and breasts. I wished Remus were here. I knew he would've wanted to be, but Cato's body could not be left out any longer.

There were many wolves who would've wanted to be present but couldn't be. The legions that my pater led had been stalling the daemon forces. From what Caius had told me, our numbers were straining, and the remainder of our forces back home needed to join them immediately.

We stopped in front of the sarcophagus. Cato's body rested inside. A carver had etched figures of wolves along the face of the tomb. There were six wolves under a sky of stars. It represented us. I was just as much a wolf as the others, and seeing me depicted as such warmed my heart. Remus had also been included in the carvings. He hadn't had as long a friendship with Cato as the others, but Cato had adored Remus. He'd seen him for who he was and not by his title of Lone Wolf.

The priests continued their procession. Caius spread petals over Cato's tomb. It was tradition among the wolves for the Alpha to spread petals as a farewell and to wish the departed safe travels toward the golden plains. Cato's mater and avia were next, murmuring their love and goodbyes. Atticus, Drusus and Marcus filed after them. I heard Marcus sniffle, and red began to tint the corners of his eyes and the tip of his nose. Felix and I held hands as we said our final goodbyes.

This would be an ache that would never truly wane. I would forever and always hold the memories of Cato close to my heart.

I stepped away from Felix to allow him a moment, and I caught some of his words. "Rest, my love."

After the funeral was concluded, we walked back to the villas.

It was then that the horns were blown, and a deep thunder rolled through the hills. Not thunder, but the sound of marching hooves.

The minotaur army had arrived.

Wolves stalked through the haven. Horses were strapped to carts, and wagons had been filled with food and supplies. Healers prepared to mount some of the wolves and horses. Dawn brushed its soft light through the groves, sunlight pouring over the sleeping city of Rome in the distance.

A white wolf stood at the head of the Pack, puffs of air billowing out from its snout. Caius lifted his head and howled, followed by the rest of the Pack. The song filled the sky, touched the clouds, reached for the gods above.

The minotaur army stood amongst the wolves. I could see King Cain and Prince Theon near the front with the Alpha.

Marcus, in his wolf form, nudged my head. *"Join us soon."*

I nodded as I patted the brown wolf's head. I wouldn't join the armies yet; I was first going to retrieve Remus. My gaze turned to Drusus. "Do you know where he might be?"

The gray wolf's tail brushed the leaves from the ground. *"He would've gone to the place he hasn't visited in the time since he became the Lone Wolf. The one place before his innocence was stripped from him."*

The villa of his childhood. I recalled Remus's story of how he used to play in the ocean with his sister, his mater always there with them. My heart pulled with a flurry of emotions, heartache and maybe some lingering frustration and sadness at the thought of seeing him again.

"Bring him home," Drusus said.

FIFTY-FIVE

Diane

The villa stood upon a hill, hidden by olive trees, and faced the shimmering sea. The structure was smaller than most Roman houses, but it still looked elegant despite how long it had been abandoned.

Dromos stayed back as I entered the villa's grounds. Pillars at the entrance led to a quaint courtyard, where wild shrubbery had taken hold of the marble and limestone. In the center of it was a fountain with a statue of Minerva, the goddess of war and wisdom. I stepped through the doors into the main living space of the villa, and on the other side was another set of open, dark wooden doors to the back courtyard.

My black gown swept over the smooth floor, the same one from the procession. As tradition, we would wear mourning black for a week. I had removed the kohl and jewels, and a blade was hitched at my thigh. My sword and armor were packed and strapped to Dromos.

I felt Remus's presence before I even saw him. Pine and ocean. Power and dominance. Remus was shirtless, exercising with his blade in the small courtyard. Sweat glistened along the thick muscle of his sun-kissed skin. His dark hair was tied back into its usual knot with a leather band. His long legs shifted gracefully as he sparred with an imaginary opponent. The sun and ocean behind him.

I watched from the steps of the villa, and I was held captive by the movements of his powerful body. Remus twisted around and froze when he saw me.

His lips slowly parted, chest fighting for breath as he stared. I was pinned under his gaze. Tongues of heat and anticipation licked the air between us. Being near him again . . . He was like the night, offering his arms of comfort to the stars. The dark to my light.

"Remus," I breathed.

Remus took a step toward me but paused, hesitating. "You found me."

Gods, that voice. My heart hummed at the sound of it. Strong and alluring. A line of heat ran straight down to my core.

"Drusus," I said, as if that were enough of a response.

Remus took a step. And another. My heart skipped a beat, then I was moving as well. I stopped on the last marble step but still had to look up to meet his eyes.

"I've missed you".

He lifted a hand, letting a finger trace along my cheek. "I've missed you, too."

A soft smile touched my lips, my stomach to fluttering.

Remus searched my gaze, his sweat-kissed face etched with worry. "Diane, I'm so sorry. For what I said to you and how I reacted. You have every right to be upset with me."

I shook my head. "I am sorry too. You have to know that I feel terrible for how this all started. But it was all *real*, you have to believe me. I care about you, Remus."

He tilted his head, his expression soft. "I never truly doubted what happened between us. I know it was real, I could feel it with every fiber of my being. What you and I have could never be questioned."

My chest was pounding. "I felt so conflicted and foolish. I was afraid you would hate me."

"Never," he said sternly. "I was the foolish one. I feared you would loathe me when I should've allowed you past my walls, as you did with me."

Hearing him say those words began to lift the heaviness that lingered over my heart. Soothed and healed me. "I haven't stopped thinking of you," I said.

"Nor I you, lotus." A confident resolve came over him as he held my gaze. "I've been torturing myself for so long. Every night, whenever

I closed my eyes, all I saw was my sister's death. The guilt that followed me after I was banished from the Pack . . . I didn't think I deserved anything good. And to speak about the truths of my past became so difficult it was physically sickening. I was lost, Diane. Until you found me."

He leaned closer, our brows almost touching. "It was because of you that I began to find myself again. Your influence. Your patience. Your belief in me. Everything that made you *you*. I found strength in myself, and the ability to tell Caius the truth. For that, I have to thank you. For the support you have shown me."

Remus's words squeezed my heart. Little did he know that he had been saving me too, all this time, empowering me with his constant support. I cupped his cheek, his skin warm under the palm of my hand. "Know that you are *worthy*, Remus. I can see that you have been preventing yourself from healing. You were just as much a victim as Helena, and it is okay to feel the hurt. To let yourself feel it all and grieve. And to forgive yourself."

Something crumpled in his expression. He leaned farther into my touch. A near silent shudder trickled through him. I almost missed it. Several moments of silence passed. Eyes drawn low, his shoulders dropped, and his chest heaved with a deep breath. A release of the chains inside of him.

"Diane," he whispered. *Pleaded.* "It hurts too much."

My heart twisted with pain for him. I could feel his walls breaking, whatever was left of his resolve. "It's okay, Remus. It's okay."

His large arms wrapped around me just as I reached around his neck. He dug his face into the slope of my shoulder as we slid to the ground, clinging to each other on the steps of the villa. His shoulders began to quiver, and I realized he was crying.

Remus broke apart.

He cried out. A tortured sound. His body shook, and I felt tears soak the fabric at my neck. Years of pain were being spilled. The guilt that had rooted itself so deeply was finally being unraveled. And I held onto him. His sorrow pierced through me. My heart broke along with his. Tears of my own tracked my cheeks as I gazed out at the shimmering blue waters. The sun slowly made its descent, flocks of birds soaring toward the orange glow.

And Remus and I began to heal.

———

Stars began to appear above, and the ocean darkened to a nightly blue. Remus had cried in my arms until he had no tears left. He pulled back to face me, and I swept my thumbs under the corners of his eyes. A soft smile touched his lips, and he placed his palms over mine as I held his face.

He was forgiving himself.

He was finding his way.

Remus stood up and briefly disappeared into the villa, returning with an armlet in his hands. "Helena's," was the only thing he said as way of explanation before asking me to wait here and saying he wouldn't be long, that there was something he needed to do. I nodded and watched him walk in the direction of the beach. I was curious as to what he was doing, but I wanted to give him space.

Dromos still lingered close by. He had flown off a few times but never strayed too far. I felt the connection of our bond, and I knew he was safe.

Not long later, Remus came up the steps from the beach. His hair was tousled from the salted wind, and his eyes were brighter than I'd ever seen. And I noticed the way he carried himself. Lighter.

The intensity of his gaze seared me in place, a sudden shift in the air between us. I marveled at how significant he had become to me. This arrogant male who I'd been forced to work with now held such an essential place in my life. I became attuned with every sweep of his eyes, every lilt of his lips, his words and laugh. His strength, not just in battle, but in his heart. How he was a honed blade, as well as a male with a hidden softness. Just *him*. Who he was. This was the male who had done everything he thought right to help the Pack. He was no stereotypical hero, but he was mine. I loved every beautiful, jaded part of him.

I loved him.

Remus's eyes shined. He watched me as if he could read on my face what I had just realized, and I thought I could see a similar emotion reflected in his gaze.

His lips parted. "I see you."

I see you. The first thing he'd said to me back in the catacombs. When I'd held him at sword's point. It felt like a lifetime ago. My lips curved. "When and where you are, then and there I will be."

Remus stilled. The words that left my lips, the proclamation I'd now made back to him, after he'd said it to me when'd finally been reunited, drifted between us, waiting. His eyes searched me as if afraid I wasn't real. Like what I had just said was a dream. And Remus's face glowed with warmth.

"Diane, you have been my strength. Even when you doubted yourself, you still persevered. You have a resilience and power that I have always admired."

He fell to his knees and caught my face in his roughened palms.

"You are the light of my life," Remus whispered. "And I've fallen in love with you."

Silver rimmed my eyes, and my soul felt as if it were on the verge of exploding into stars. The sincerity that blazed in those green eyes! He loved me. Remus, who had been so irritating, sarcastic, and cocky, *so godsdamn broody,* loved me. He was mine. As I was his.

"I've lived a good life," I said, feeling like I was floating, like the sun was embracing me. "I have a loving pater and caring friends, and I am grateful for my upbringing. But no one *saw* me the way you did. Challenged me the way you did. I have come to admire you, be inspired by you. And I feel at home when I am with you. I love you, Remus. I love you so much."

He was no longer the Lone Wolf to me. I didn't care about the title. He was my night, the comfort of the dark, the solace among the stars. Our love had been forged by steel and fire, a story of fangs and shadows.

Remus stared, a soft look in his eyes. He cradled my face like I was something invaluable. He brushed a thumb over my lips as he leaned forward. Slowly. I gasped when his lips melded to mine. We kissed, every emotion that had been roaring between us since we'd met echoing behind our touch.

My hands slid up his bare chest, the smooth feel of his skin hot under my fingers. His tongue parted my lips, the slow glide of it against mine making me shudder. He gently took me in his arms, pushing me to the soft ground at the foot of the villa's steps as he moved on top of me. Remus slid his thigh between my legs, pinning me to the grassy dirt as he loomed over me. His hand went to the back of my head, his lips never leaving mine.

I ran my tongue over his bottom lip, and a groan rumbled at the back of his throat. He broke the kiss and moved along the corner of my jaw and down my neck. Each kiss was a delicious torture.

A heavy sensation grew between my legs, my core aching and begging for more. My body arched and I rolled my hips against his thigh. Remus grunted in approval, and I felt his smile against my neck.

"You need more, lotus?" he murmured.

His hand traveled down my waist to my ass, firmly gripping me. He squeezed tighter when I didn't respond, and a pathetic whimper left me.

"Yes," I breathed.

I moaned as he swept his tongue down my collarbone, and the sound unleashed him. He growled, eyes darting to mine. Bright. Hungry. He hauled me up, flinging my legs around his waist. His lips claimed my mouth, and our tongues clashed as Remus walked up the steps into the villa.

We entered a room, and Remus placed me on the bed sheets. He didn't stop kissing me as he slowly pulled the gown down my shoulders, exposing my breasts to him.

He bent down and wrapped his lips around the tightened bud. I arched at the touch, shivers coursing through me, my hands clawing at the sheets. Remus caught my wrists and dragged my hands above my head. His tongue kept up the torture. Licking, sucking, and nipping at the skin until it felt sore.

His voice was a dark, delicious purr. "Since the night I first tasted you, I knew I wouldn't be able to stop wanting more."

He peered up at me through thick lashes, a devilish smile on his lips. A promise. He pulled the gown further down, ripping the fabric of my undergarments and tossing them away in the growing darkness. His eyes went to the dagger strapped to my thigh. A finger tugged at the leather with a *slap.*

"You're keeping this on," he ordered. A dangerous excitement and lust rushed throughout my body, touching every nerve ending.

Remus slid lower until he was nestled between my legs. With his dark hair and molten eyes, he looked like he could really be a god of war and darkness. I gasped at the slow glide of Remus's tongue on me. My hands gripped at his hair as I rolled my hips and grinded against his mouth. Breathy pants and moans filled the room. I tiptoed toward the precipice of bliss and my legs began to shake. Remus halted just before I could finish.

My growl of frustration at him stopping turned into a gasp as a finger dipped inside me, thrusting in and out. I arched my back trying to feel more of him. Godsdamn him, I wanted—needed all of him inside me. I needed him to fill me.

"You like this, lotus?" He purred, the corner of his lip curved further. "You like me fucking you with my finger?"

With another torturous plunge of a second finger, I groaned, slamming my palm on the bed sheet. "Yes," I said through clenched teeth. "Yes, I do."

A full smile bloomed on Remus's lips. It was the most beautiful and rarest of sights. He continued to fuck me with his fingers, his mouth sucking at my clit.

"Remus," I moaned. My eyes fluttered shut.

There was a growl from him before the intensifying heat finally erupted. My thoughts scrambled, legs quivering, but I was now desperate for more.

"Take off your clothes," I ordered, opening my eyes.

Remus smirked as he shrugged out of his trousers, and I tracked the muscled length of his body. Looking lower, my eyes widened at his hard length. I still couldn't get over how thick and *big* he was. Remus gave a dark chuckle as he gripped himself.

"This cock is yours," he said.

A bolt of heat shot through me. My eyes flitted up to meet his. "I need you," I whispered.

Something other than arousal lit up between us. Remus's hard body leaned over me, and he kissed me deeply, passionately, as he edged himself closer to my needy core. I felt the push of his cock at my entrance, and my legs widened further. His thick length pressed into me, inch by inch. My mouth opened in a silent scream as I struggled to get used to his size. He paused, giving me a moment to adjust, and he trailed scorching kisses along my neck. It didn't take long for the pinches of pain to melt into a languid warmth. We both groaned as he fully sank into me.

Lips at my ear, his voice deepened as he shuddered. "Fuck."

My nails dug into his back as he began to move, his hips finding a rhythm. I threw my head back on the bed, savoring how well he filled me. "Yes, Remus," I moaned. "Harder."

Remus chuckled darkly, pausing for a breath. And he fucked me. He began thrusting hard into me at a delicious pace that had my legs tightening around his waist. Flames of moonlight and silver flickered over his skin, the sensation of his aether humming against my own, and I gasped at the feeling. I dropped the remaining mental barriers and shadows fell from my fingers. Aether thrummed against the walls, alongside my sobs of pleasure.

Remus kissed my neck, teeth grazing my skin. The filthy sound of our bodies meeting as we fucked among the ribbons of our powers echoed in the room. It was all too much, in its own beautiful intense way.

I cried out his name as I came undone. Remus soon followed me, growling and groaning his release. Our power reverberated through our peak, the room lighting in shadow and light, and the walls trembled. We slumped down in the slick sheets, our bodies buzzing. Flame and shadow soon dissipated.

Remus dipped his brow to mine. His eyes brimmed with love and adoration, and so much life. "You are my light," he declared, pressing his lips firmly to mine. "The light to my dark."

FIFTY-SIX

Remus

There were no exact words that could describe it. She saw me in my entirety. Broken and lost. And yet, she had still chosen me. I was still the Lone Wolf. The damning consequences that followed the title would still affect me. But I was not going to let it destroy what was left of me. And I would not let it get in the way of her happiness either.

We were entangled in the sheets, gazing at the stars through the open window of my room. Her fingers ran along the tattoos on my chest and down my arm. She was telling me about her Rite. I could feel myself swell with pride as I listened to her experience of finding her pegasus and visiting Mars' temple and the origin of her shadowed aether.

At the next part of her story I jerked my head toward her. Her face was pressed against my shoulder, a leg draped over mine and her hand on my chest.

"You met the Roman god of war and the Egyptian god of the dead?" My jaw dropped.

Diane grinned, golden eyes glittering with excitement under the starlight. "Can you believe that? I am part jackal, part wolf. These shadows come from the jackal side of me."

"That's incredible, my light. Now you know more about your ancestry. You come from two gods. Not one, but two."

I saw her smile grow at what I'd called her. *My light.* And she was. Diane had been there to help me through my own darkness. She claimed I'd done the same for her, guided her through her own insecurities and fears. Knowing she felt that way had warmed me, though I knew it was nothing compared to what she had done for me.

My light.

"I know how many gods, Remus. I was there." She laughed.

"Are you going to speak to your pater about this?"

Diane sat up, hair splaying down over her breasts, and she chewed on her lip thoughtfully. "I will. He must have known about this, about my mater."

I gently cupped her chin, trying to reassure her. "It will be fine. He loves you, and I could not be prouder of you."

I gazed at her, twirling a strand of her dark hair with my fingers. "Assuming we survive this war, what would you like to do after?"

She looked my way, an angry flash across her eyes telling me she didn't like how I'd phrased the question, but her brow smoothed out as she considered it.

"Egypt," she responded softly. "I would like to visit Egypt. Meet my family there, learn more about my aether."

The corner of my lips lifted as I dragged a thumb over those lush lips. "That sounds like a plan."

Diane's eyes glimmered, winking suns and sands. "With you, of course. If you would like to come with me." Her cheeks suddenly flushed pink. "I know Egypt has not provided the best of memories for you. I would understand if you wished never to set foot there again."

I sat up and wrapped my fingers around her jaw. I pressed my mouth against hers in a harsh kiss and spoke against her lips. "When and where you are, then and there I will be. That is my oath to you, lotus. If you will have me, I will follow you to the ends of this realm. I would fight earth and sky and even the gods themselves for you."

Diane sighed with relief, as if she seriously thought I'd say any different, and wrapped her arms around my neck. She kissed me deeply, and I sank into her touch, raked my hands through her hair.

She pulled back to press another light kiss on my lips before sliding off the bed.

Diane walked—albeit a bit unsteadily—toward the bath chamber. She looked over her shoulder, her black hair brushing the tattooed stars on her back. Her voice turned silk and velvet. "Care for a midnight bath with me?"

I pointed at the thigh strap and weapon on the side table that I had removed at some point during the night. "If I ever say no to that question, feel free to use that dagger on me."

Diane laughed and left to start running the water. I entered the bath chamber moments later to see her at the counter, facing the mirror. Her gaze collided with me through the reflection and I pressed my body against her back, brushing the strands of her hair over her shoulder. Being here, with her, and like this, sent a fire through my veins. Blood rushed through me, and it didn't take long before my hard cock pushed against her ass. Diane, my naughty lotus, pressed herself back against me.

"I've had so many filthy thoughts of what I wanted to do to you," I growled. "I would think about them when I was alone, my hand around my cock."

She shivered, making me smirk. I kissed a trail down her back, slowly going to my knees. "Did you think of me when you touched yourself?"

Diane trembled, breath scattering. I slid a hand between her legs and palmed her, feeling the heat and wetness there.

"Mmm." Her eyes fluttered closed.

My teeth nipped at her ass, and she jerked her eyes open. "Yes," she breathed. "Whenever I touched myself, I thought of you, imagining it was your hand on me. Your tongue. Your lips."

Gods, the image I conjured at that made me even harder. With my other hand, I gently pressed on her lower back till she was bent over the counter.

"Prop your leg up," I instructed.

She obeyed. Her beautiful body was exposed just for me. I licked my fingers and stroked her core. Diane whimpered as I toyed with her. When I replaced my fingers with my mouth, she cursed loudly.

Chuckling against her skin, I murmured. "What a dirty mouth."

She writhed and began to sway her hips as I ravaged her core, as I fucked her with my tongue. Her panting filled the room, but I wanted to hear her scream.

"Please," she begged. "Fuck me, please."

I stood, lips swollen and glistening with her wetness. With my knee, I nudged her legs wider. Diane reached for my hand, placing it around her throat. I couldn't help but growl in approval at what she desired. Her eyes were gleaming with lust and excitement. I kept my other hand on her waist. Diane choked out a gasp as I slammed into her.

"You feel so good, my light," I gritted out, feeling a shudder rack through my body.

I pulled out completely before thrusting back into her. Diane's heady moans had me in a vice-like hold. My pace quickened, and I fucked her with meticulous force. The bottles and toiletries began to topple over, the thuds against the counter causing the mirror to tremble.

My hand around her throat slid up and I pressed two fingers into her mouth. Her lips wrapped around me, sucking me, and moaning around my fingers.

I pushed her down so that her feet were planted on the floor. My hands exploring the skin around her waist. Diane bit her lip as she began to move her hips, forward and backward, sliding my cock in and out of her. I groaned as heat spiraled through my torso. I slapped her ass, hard, then soothed the growing redness with my palm. She cried out and began to increase her pace.

"Look at you," I murmured. "So beautiful when you're being fucked."

Her eyes met mine in the mirror. Mouth parted, panting. "Gods, I can't."

"Yes, you can." I bent to graze my teeth along her shoulder. "Put your hands on the counter."

She leaned forward and braced herself. I fucked her from behind, my hand gliding around her waist to rub her clit. Her body shook, and she clenched around me. Diane shouted and broke apart. I came straight after her, no longer being able to hold myself back.

I eased out of her, cleaned her up, and led her into the bath. The scent of vanilla and blossoms was strong in the chamber. We bathed each other, kissed, and allowed ourselves to enjoy being together. I couldn't help but get lost in the feeling engulfing me.

This sense of true happiness.

———

"Are you sure about this?"

Diane glanced over her shoulder. She was fighting back a laugh. "Are you seriously afraid of a pegasus? A wolf warrior who has fought daemonic creatures and faced the daemon king himself, who has also ridden on griffins, shudders at the sight of a horse with wings?"

I tossed her a dry look before reluctantly meeting Dromos's skeptical stare. "No," I dragged out. "The griffins were fine because they were massive, and I felt like I wouldn't be able to fall that easily. I simply prefer my feet on the ground. Also, I don't think he likes me."

Diane smirked. She ran a hand down the pegasus's snout. I took another tentative step toward them, and the horse's wings flared in warning. I took a deep inhale and bowed my head. I was not foolish enough to think that the pegasus couldn't understand me.

"Pleasure to meet you," I said.

Dromos snorted, ears flicking. He angled his head to the side, as I raised a hand and slowly approached him. It had been some time since I'd been face to face with a pegasus. His coat was soft and the color of a dove's wings.

"Stunning," I murmured in awe.

Dromos's wings expanded, showing the silver and gray of his feathers. I jerked away at the sudden movement, earning a chuckle from Diane.

"Flattery may be the way to Dromos's heart." Diane began stroking the stallion's mane.

I eyed the pegasus warily. "How does the bond work exactly?"

Diane swung a leg over Dromos's back. "It's hard to explain, but it is almost like we can communicate through emotion. It's also just intuition—we can sense each other's wants and understand our intentions."

Hesitantly, I mounted the pegasus and sat behind Diane. "That is a unique bond to have with a creature. I must admit that when I was young, I loved the pegasuses. And when I learned that Helena would have one, and it wouldn't be me, I was furious."

Dromos suddenly pushed off the ground, and I yelped and clung to Diane. She chuckled and twisted around to plant a kiss on my cheek. The act was enough to make me want to grab her waist and pull her to me, but I simply gazed at her, dumbfounded.

She smiled. "This is the first time you spoke about Helena without that dark cloud over your head."

I paused at that. Stunned, and happy that my sister's memory was what it should always have been. Good and pure.

Diane nudged me. "You must tell me more about her."

I felt myself grinning. "She would've liked you."

She leaned against my chest, the length of her hair draping against my arm. I began to twirl it mindlessly between my fingers.

"Both resilient, capable women of literal and figurative power?"

"More like," I tugged on her hair, "overly cocky and stubborn."

Dromos swayed gently from side to side as he drifted on a current, his wings flapping intermittently. The town of my childhood came into view below, and the pegasus's wings fluttered as he landed, his hooves stomping the ground. Bystanders shrieked in excitement at seeing the majestic pegasus and its rider.

Diane patted his mane and beckoned the townspeople closer. "He doesn't bite."

I snorted, sliding from the pegasus. "Sure, he doesn't."

Dromos's tail swooshed and slapped me in the face, and Diane's laughter rang in my ears.

We spent the day in town, Dromos tailing us like a chaperone. Diane's hand clung to my arm as I escorted her through the market stalls. The town was smaller than the other cities we'd been to and miraculously untouched by soldiers and daemons alike.

Diane's fingers ran over bright fabrics and handcrafted pottery. I stopped at a canvas smeared in blue and gold with a glittering depiction of the sirens, my brow furrowing as I recalled what I'd learned in the griffin's library.

Diane had paused to look at an ivory vase with streaks of brown and gray. On the center of it was a carving of Minerva.

I peeked over her shoulder. "Do you like it?"

Diane picked up the vase, sweeping her fingers down the smooth curve. She looked to the female satyr managing the stall.

"Did you make this?" she asked.

The satyr grinned. Trinkets dangled from her dark horns. "Yes, dear. These hands have been molding pottery for half of my life."

I nudged Diane and slipped coin into her hand. "Get it."

As we walked away from the stand, Diane bumped a hip against mine, propping the vase on her side.

"For your home," she said. "I noticed from your mother's belongings that she loved Minerva. I thought it'd be nice to give your home a fresh start."

My feet skidded to a stop. I blinked at her, and she scrunched up her face at my reaction.

She bit her lip in worry. "Did I overstep? I'm so—"

I cut her words off as my hand dove into her hair, and I crushed my mouth to hers. "That is so thoughtful of you, my light. Thank you. It's beautiful." The words brushed against her mouth, and she sighed.

"Are we being selfish?" she asked in a whisper. I knew she was referring to not being with the Pack to prepare for what was to come.

I closed my eyes, my teeth lightly tugging on her bottom lip. "One more night," I murmured. "In the morning, we will head back."

I wanted just another day of this peace before I'd have to face whatever bloodshed on the horizon.

FIFTY-SEVEN

Remus

T he ocean mist rolled along the shore. Thin blankets of a white sheen hung above the water. Leather and armor were clasped onto my body as second skin. What I'd read in the griffins' library had brought me here. The words from the book the dryad had given me echoed in my head.

How does one summon the sirens?

I walked along the shore, water pressing its cold lips around my ankles. The offering I'd left the other night was gone. Helena's armlet.

Begin the summoning with a prayer to the gods of the sea and request an audience. For a week, offer what you believe to be precious. Not of monetary value but by the value of your heart. On the final day, sing to the siren. If they find the offerings and prayers of pure intent, then they shall deem a visit worthy of their time.

It had been a week since I'd come to my family's villa. The first night here I'd waded into the waters, burned incense, and prayed to the gods and goddesses of the sea. And for a week I'd made offerings. Items that symbolized my family and who I was. I had no idea if the writings in that damn book were truth or utter bullshit. But I had to try.

Watching the misty waters, I exhaled through my nostrils in frustration. The salty air smelled good; it always did. Soon I would smell nothing but blood and death. We were meant to leave today, and my aether riled in anticipation.

Parting my lips, I sang the siren's song documented in the book.

The foreign words slipped out smoothly from my tongue. A part of me felt silly singing to nothing. But at the same time, the words felt surreal, dipped in an aether unknown to me. The flames shivered over my skin, and I continued to sing. I could not, for the love of all the gods, sing.

As the last verse ended, I drew out my final offering. The object I'd carried through my years of solitude, my time as a Lone Wolf. The thing I could never seem to part with. My pater—Anthony's—sword. Deep down, I believed I had been yearning for my pater's love and holding onto his sword as a way of coping with the ugly reality that I would never receive it.

"I know you're out there," I called out. "I need your help. *We* need your help."

The waters had stilled, as if they too waited for a response. A voice lovely like forged jewels crept up from the mists, singing the same words I'd been moments ago. The water shifted, lifted up from the sea, and rippled toward me.

A golden-haired siren emerged from the water. Rivulets cascaded over her exposed breasts, and patches of pink scales dotted her pale skin. Her tail curled out from underneath the water's surface, the same iridescent pink as on her body.

Large emerald eyes watched me curiously. "It has been hundreds of years since a mortal has summoned us." Her voice was light, like spring air. "Your offerings made me curious."

I allowed my eyes to shift into those of my wolf as moonlight flames briefly spun around my fingers before flickering out. "As you can see, I am no mere mortal."

Her lips pursed in amusement. "We shall see. Go on, say your piece."

"I'm sure you're aware of what is happening on the dry lands, aren't you?"

She began to inspect her fingernails, a gesture I'd seen Diane make on multiple occasions when she felt she had the upper hand—or at least pretended to. "If you are referring to the imminent invasion of daemons and power-hungry fools, yes. And I have to tell you it might be too late to stop it. The world is already overrun with those. The ocean is not as ignorant as you think."

I began to walk forward, but the siren stopped me with a warning look. I raised my last offering. "Then you know how much we need your help."

The siren watched me carefully, raising her chin almost in challenge. "Ask me what you seek from us?"

"I humbly request the assistance of your protector, one of the gods of the sea. The Leviathan."

Intrigue lit the siren's soft face before she began to chuckle. The sound was so cold and humorless it raised the hairs on my forearms.

She waved a hand in dismissal. "What you are asking is ludicrous."

"If the daemon king wins, what is to say that they won't continue to ravage the other continents. And after those have been destroyed, what's to say they'll stop there? They already have winged daemons so they can attack the griffins. The Ram has *armies* waiting to pierce through our realm, perhaps some of them even have fins."

If the siren was at all horrified at the thought, it didn't show. Her pale face betrayed no emotion, and I started to worry that my attempt had been futile and I'd wasted my time.

The siren brushed her wet hair over a shoulder. "Your speech is repetitive and seems practiced. I guarantee nothing from your request."

I bowed, extending my father's sword toward her. The waters swayed and splashed as her fin propelled her forward. She placed her webbed hands on my father's sword, keen interest flashing in her eyes as she admired the blade.

"I can feel how significant this was to you," she crooned. "I can taste it."

"How?" I asked.

She tilted her head. Her body lifted higher from the water, the scales at her waistline gleaming, and droplets trickled over the blade.

Her pale fingers tapped over her lips as she considered me. "We can sense it. This sword meant something to you, once. Only for it to disappoint you."

I pursed my lips, anger and resentment and other emotions I

couldn't name tumbling through me. "Something like that. I've carried it for so long and now, I am ready to let go."

The siren took the blade, and the weight was lifted from my hands, from my chest. "You intrigue me," she mused. "Best of luck to you, Wolf of the White Flames. I hope I don't have to see you again."

I watched as the siren drifted back into the waters. "You knew who I was."

The siren smirked. "I already said that the ocean is not ignorant."

As she disappeared, the sounds of the ocean waters lapping up the sands returned. Caius had wanted word of my power to spread, knew it would somehow ignite hope amongst mortals. Had it spread this far? Was it truly giving people enough hope to keep going? I couldn't say, but the sirens somehow knew of me. I just hoped what I'd done so far would be enough.

PART III

WOLF OF THE WHITE FLAMES
&
DAUGHTER OF ANUBIS

FIFTY-EIGHT

Diane

The city of Aurorae had once been beautiful.

Its edifices, the domed structures and homes, sat along the sea cliffs as the waves crashed below, attempting to crawl up the rocks. But now, the place was painted with mortal and daemon blood, its white, limestone walls stained with it.

It was fortunate that the residents of Aurorae were far away from here—my pater's forces had ensured their evacuation.

Because this city was now a battlefield.

The Ram's army was reported to be marching north, which caused my pater's forces to use this city as a means to intercept them.. So far, only small battalions of the common daemons had appeared. The real battle had yet to begin.

News stated that Octavius would be leading the human naval armies that were heading our way on Egyptian ships, a battle against Mark Anthony and Queen Cleopatra. And while the humans fought amongst each other, there would be a battle amongst the Olympians. How intriguing.

"I should've told you."

My pater's voice pulled my gaze from the window. I had been waiting for his response. One of the first things I had done since arriving in the city was confronting him about my mater.

It had been over a month since I'd seen him and despite the secrets he'd withheld from me I was happy to be with him again. We had arrived to the city earlier this morning and had been assisting the wolves in cleaning the streets of any stray daemons. And now, it was merely a waiting game until Caius arrived with the Pack's remaining armies. My pater's forces had taken shelter in Aurorae's fort which stood at the peak of the cliffs with a view of the city below.

My pater was settled in the seat beside me in front of the desk of his temporary office. It had belonged to one of the governing officials of the city, who was now miles away from here. Remus lingered by the door, leaning against the frame with his arms folded over his chest. He watched my pater with a hard expression. I realized it was an act of protection; he was ready to defend me if needed. My chest tightened at the thought.

Remus's wary gaze slid to me, immediately softening as he met my eyes. He had offered to give us privacy, but I'd refused. I didn't want to spend any time away from him, not when there was no guarantee of tomorrow. And his presence was a comfort I needed, especially right now.

I watched my pater. Shadows spilled between my fingers. I raised a hand, the dark ink dancing and twirling above it. I had told him of my discoveries about my mater's power, and I'd demanded an explanation.

He drank in the sight of my shadows, no fear or disgust in his gaze. "Your mater and I hadn't initially known of the aether that ran in her veins," he began. "When she was pregnant with you, a man visited us. A jackal-shapeshifter. He turned out to be your mater's uncle. Apparently, he had been searching for her ever since her parents had died, but he'd lost all trace of her. He stayed with us for a time and educated her on her ancestry and the culture of the jackal-shapeshifters."

My pater reached for my hand, the one that was willing the shadows, and took it in his own. "The jackal aether runs differently in each person. Depending on the individual, male or female, it allows them to either shift into a jackal or to control the shadows. And, in the most extreme cases, the power can also remain dormant, waiting to be awoken, hence why your mater had no idea. If her parents had been alive then, perhaps she would've gone through the appropriate training and realized about her aether sooner."

I tried to process all of that. A lineage of Egyptian warriors. Anubis had mentioned as much. I had family across the sea. Family I'd never met. My eyes darted to Remus, who had a look of genuine surprise. He glanced my way and offered me a small, encouraging smile.

I leaned back in my seat, mulling over my pater's words until a thought came to mind. "Wait. My mater never practiced aether. Even after discovering who she was, she never tried learning to control her power?"

Pater shook his head. "No, your mater made the decision to leave her aether dormant. She said that she had gotten through all of her hardships without it, that she was someone with power, even without it."

Pride shone in the depths of his eyes, and I found myself smiling as well. That sounded like my mater, and I shouldn't have been surprised by her decision.

I squeezed his hands. "I thought something was wrong with me, and I was afraid of saying anything about how I could somehow will the shadows."

Heartbreak echoed in my father's gaze. "Of course you didn't say anything. You were afraid, and I should've been there for you. I'm so sorry—I should've told you. Your mater and I had planned to, but then she died, and with the growing tensions between Rome and Egypt, I lost contact with your mater's family. I raised you to be able to defend yourself, and there was no guarantee that your jackal aether would even wake. So I allowed nature to take its course, but I failed to help you when you needed me most."

How easy it would have been to drown in my anger and lash out. To be angry at the past and how differently my childhood could've been, knowing the truth about myself. I had that right, but something inside my chest lifted. The truth had tied that loose end, filling an empty space inside me. And I understood why my parents hadn't told me, even though I didn't agree.

"I am frustrated you or mater never told me, I cannot deny that. But I forgive you. Thank you for telling me now."

The conversation slipped into war preparations, Remus stepping in to assist with the planning. He and I volunteered to take watch on the fort's walls, and once we were done, we left my pater's office.

My thoughts were consumed with the truth about my mater. If anything, it just further confirmed my desire to visit Egypt. I wanted to learn more about the Egyptian side of me, maybe meet some of my family members. Perhaps some had even known my mater and could tell me more about her. I was so distracted by my musings, I didn't realize we'd made it to the wall until I felt a hand wrap around the back of my neck.

Remus tilted my head back until I met those bright, green eyes. "Do you want to talk about it?" he asked.

I took a deep breath. A sense of confidence gradually settled. "No," I said. "No, I feel good." And I meant it.

He pressed his lips against my brow. "I'm glad."

We took our place along the wall. I leaned against the ledge, watching the torchless roads. "Remus, you asked what I wanted to do after the war," I glanced his way, "what about you? What do you want?"

A pensive look swept over his moon-kissed features. He rubbed a hand over his clean jaw. "This wasn't set in stone, but I thought of asking the griffins to stay with them."

That was a surprise. "Really?"

Remus chuckled at whatever he saw on my face and bumped my nose with a finger. "This was when I thought there was no possibility of a future with you."

He moved to my side and I rested my head against him. I thought what a gift this night was. Peace before the storm. A stolen moment under the stars.

"You and I, Remus," I said. "We've been made from loss and heartache, stepped out of the fires of chaos, and been changed for the better. And I am honored to be beside you."

I looked up at him, playfully bumping my hip against him.

He chuckled and responded with a gentle sweep of his lips against my brow, his eyes fluttering closed. I took the moment to relish in the heat of his body. The strength of it. How he always seemed to gravitate toward me as if to protect me as if ready to defend me from anything. As I felt with him.

The cedar, ocean, and masculine scent that always clung to him brushed against my senses. The feel of his hard body lured mine to press against him, my nipples hardening to the touch. I realized we were alone on the wall, and I couldn't help the wicked lustful thoughts that surged through my mind. My hand went to his trousers, palming him.

Remus's chest rumbled with laughter. "Lotus, are you hungry?"

I could only nod, heat already pooling between my legs. I clenched my thighs together to try and ease the growing ache. His eyes ran down my body, a ravenous gleam in them.

He leaned in to kiss me. The touch of his lips melded against mine, our tongues gently sliding over one another. Time stopped, or sped up, I was unsure. I was happy to be lost in him. In the back of my mind, a small voice warned that tomorrows were never guaranteed. That the war was reaching its peak.

The thought caused me to kiss him more forcefully. My arms wrapped around his neck, pushing my breasts against his chest. I *was* becoming more hungry for him. Remus grabbed onto my back, fingers biting through the fighting leathers.

"You are trouble. We are supposed to be on watch." His teeth pulled on my earlobe. "Get inside the watchtower. *Now.*"

We barely made it inside the four-cornered space before Remus flipped me onto my back on the lone table. We stripped just enough for Remus to shove his cock between my legs. I yelped at the feel of him, at his thickness. Gods, I would never get enough of this. He yanked my fighting leathers down enough for his teeth to graze over the swell of my breasts.

He groaned as he began to move his hips. "I love you."

I held onto him, crushing my face against the crook of his neck to muffle my sobs of pleasure as he fucked me senseless. The table skidded along the stone floor, Remus angling himself so my clit would grind against him. Our lips collided as we came, drinking in each other's moans, allowing ourselves this reprieve.

"I love you," I panted.

Remus and I lingered in the tower, unwilling to abandon this moment. His fingers traced the line from my nose to my mouth. We whispered our wishes and desires for after this war, not caring whether or not we would see another tomorrow.

It wasn't until later, when we were back on watch, that Remus stiffened beside me. Dread sank deep in my stomach when I followed his eyeline and saw rows and rows of glowing, blood-red crescent eyes.

Fīfty-Nīne

Remus

The Ram's armies hadn't advanced on us yet.

They were waiting, watching us from the city's borders. Members of the Order were perched on their horses behind their first line of defense.

Aurelius's wolves were already prowling through the city. Some of them had leapt onto the rooftops to keep watch. The sun crawled higher in the sky. The wait was painful-—the silence before the storm.

Diane drew up beside me. Her hair was again pulled back. Black kohl lined her eyes, and a gentle sweep of gold paint across her cheekbones. And then I remembered, the jackals lined their snouts like that as well. She was representing both sides of herself.

"You look beautiful." I slid an arm around her waist, pulling her in for a kiss.

Up close I could see the exhaustion under her eyes, despite the pink that now flushed her cheeks. I didn't think I would ever stop feeling smug at having that effect on her. Diane gestured toward the daemons. "Any movement?"

I shook my head. "Not yet. But I'm sure it'll happen soon."

Her pegasus landed on the walkway behind her. Diane had managed to secure armor for her winged stallion; bronze pieces were clasped over his chest and under his belly, a narrow slip of protection strapped along his brow and snout. Diane and Dromos looked like they'd been summoned by Minerva herself. I could see other soldiers staring at them, equally enamored with how the pair looked side by side.

Diane was truly befitting of her new title as a Daughter of Mars.

A wolf howled.

All those stationed on the wall tensed as the daemon armies began to move toward the city. It almost seemed like the ocean winds had stilled, that the very waves crashing below us had been silenced as a deep hum whispered from the skies.

The air grew heavy, and a dark presence trailed unseen fingers across my shoulders. The soldiers around me shuddered. They had felt it too. The Ram was here. The sound of wings pounded the air as the sentinels soared from the sky. They looked like clouds of insects, hovering above their battalions. At the far end, black smoke rose from the ground. A chill ran down my spine as I recognized the ancient aether. The Ram stepped out from his shadows, his obsidian armor gleaming under the morning light.

I was afraid. Not for me, but for *her*. I looked to Diane just as she turned to me. Our fears echoed between us.

I felt the Ram's eyes on us, and I turned back round. He was watching us; the feeling sickened my stomach, and I fought the urge to place myself in front of Diane. Remove her from his line of sight. She probably wouldn't approve of my overprotective move and would just call me an ass.

The Ram raised a hand and bellowed. The sound was amplified with aether, loud enough to shudder through the walls of the city.

The Beta Wolf came to stand beside us. "Wolves," he commanded. "Shift."

The soldiers who were still in their human forms obeyed. Aether light exploded in all directions as hundreds of wolves marched toward the main street of the city, a straight path to the daemon army.

Aurelius, too, shifted, and a rugged brown-red wolf appeared. I could see the age of the male in the white on his snout. The Beta Wolf's eyes slid to where his daughter stood.

"*Do not advance unless the daemons slip past our line of defense. That is an order.*"

Diane's eyes glistened, but she nodded firmly. "Be safe, Pater."

The wolf seemed to grin before he leapt from the wall, landing among the wolves below. Aurelius lifted his head and howled. A command.

Charge.

The wolves tore through the empty city, others jumping from rooftop to rooftop as the daemons began to race toward them. My blood was pumping with adrenaline, my aether and the instincts of my inner wolf wrestling with anticipation.

And the two armies collided.

The sound of crashing bodies was deafening, and I saw Diane force herself to keep breathing as she watched her pater fight. Daemons screamed, the sounds so high-pitched I gritted my teeth against the noise.

Daemons began to pour out from the wolves' line. I shifted, quickly looking toward Diane. *"Any that I don't get are all yours, lotus."*

She smiled sarcastically, but I caught the amused gleam in her eyes. "So romantic."

I dove into the city. I decided not to use my aether just yet in an attempt to save every sliver of energy. My fangs ripped through the necks of the daemons I came across, killing them one by one until the numbers started thinning out.

I stood in the forum, glaring at where the Ram stood. He slowly cocked his head, and I saw his mouth move from where he was, the words inside my head.

"You were so busy on the ground, you didn't bother to look up."

Blood roared in my ears just as Diane's voice tore through me. "Remus, above you!"

A sentinel rammed into me and we crashed through the wall of a building. Chunks of limestone and brick exploded into plumes of dust as the winged daemon and I rolled along the floor.

Screams rose from outside, and I knew more sentinels had landed. *Diane.* I needed to get back to her. I knew she could handle herself but I had to see it for myself all the same. The first line of daemons had been a distraction so the Ram could set his winged creatures on us, catching us unawares.

Aether flared out from me, throwing the sentinel against the wall. Its wings twitched from the impact, but it didn't slow as it rushed toward me again. I grunted, my nails scraping against the ground. The sentinel matched me in physical strength.

Horns blared in the distance, but I couldn't focus on what it meant as I watched the daemon unhook its aether-limiting chains from its waist. *Shit.*

I tried to back away, but the daemon slammed a fist against my chest. I heard a crack, and air wheezed through my lungs as I stumbled. The sentinel wrapped the chains around my paw, and I could feel the aether shrinking away from me.

I braced myself to lunge for the daemon's neck when its wings were suddenly ripped from its back. The sentinel screamed, lurching backward, the chains loosening from me. A sword had been rammed through the creature's back and was sticking out of its chest. The daemon spasmed for a moment before the blade was yanked free, and it was kicked to the ground.

Caius slammed his sword back into its sheath. Shock tore through me. *He's here. The Pack's armies have arrived.*

I shifted back into my human body, crouching with my hands on my knees as I fought for breath. "The horns," I realized. "It was you."

Caius let out a reluctant and tired laugh. "We arrived in time to wipe out the first line of daemons, both on the ground and in the sky. It's quiet now, but I'm sure it won't be long before the second line advances."

I stood upright and we both seemed unsure of what to do or say next. I opened my mouth, but nothing came out. Caius watched me, his brows slowly pinching. Like he was worried. Uncertain. Then he moved. In three long strides, Caius embraced me.

I staggered back from the force of it, but my arms instinctively wrapped around him as well. I felt an overwhelming sense of *relief,* and something else. Something whole and profound. The feeling was airy and bright, soothing the rough edges of my heart. *Forgiveness.*

I pulled back and looked at my brother as he grabbed the back of my head to press our brows together. "Even while you were gone, and despite the title, you were *always* a part of the Pack. I never forgot you."

My voice came out raw with emotion. "And I never forgot you."

Caius gave me a soft smile. "Now then, shall we prepare for the finale?"

SIXTY

Remus

The Pack's and the minotaurs' armies marched through the city streets. Harpies and the Daughters of Mars had already taken to the skies. Diane was among them. I could see her, her black hair whipping wildly against the wind. I was sure she had a feral grin upon that breath-taking face.

Our separation would only be temporary. Caius wanted us to regroup and for Diane and I to close in on the Ram while the others cleared a path for us.

"What about the griffins?" I asked Caius.

The Alpha was walking ahead of me as we headed toward the front lines. He glanced over his shoulder. "They are on their way. Remember the plan?"

I rolled my shoulders. "Destroy the second line of defense."

The wolves parted ways with us, and I saw three familiar figures, still in their human forms, waiting at the very front of the army. My pace quickened.

Drusus barreled toward me. "It's good to see you, brother." He paused, and he narrowed his eyes on me with suspicion. "You look . . . happy."

I couldn't help but look up to where Diane flew, a shit-eating grin spreading over my face. "I am."

His eyes gleamed. "It's about godsdamn time."

I looked at him now. At my brother. He had *seen* me just as much as Diane had. The Pack had scorned me. Spat on my name. But Drusus hadn't care and had went after me. He'd helped me, even though I was on the hunt for blood, and he hadn't batted an eye.

"Drusus, I have to thank you. For everything. You've sacrificed so much to help me, and I could never have asked for a better male to call my brother."

He said nothing for a lingering moment, and a slow smile spread over his lips. "I would do it all again."

Atticus slid an arm around Drusus's shoulders and fluttered his eyelids with a growing smirk. "How cute."

Marcus beckoned at us, waiting for us to follow. "If you're done professing your love to one another, there's a battle to be won."

Drusus and I responded in unison. "Shut up."

Aether beamed as the others shifted into their wolf forms. Our armies filed through the city and onto the field. While the Ram and all his forces waited on the other side. Except—

"The jackal armies are not here," I growled.

"No." Caius's white wolf dragged out the word. "They are definitely here. But they've yet to make their appearance. It's time, Remus."

The wolves gathered around me in protective stances, bristling and snarling. I extended a hand to the side with my palm facing down. Like with a bowstring, I mentally pulled back the cords of energy. Back and back. And as I slowly swept my hand upward, I released the hold on my aether.

A wall of fire followed. It roared in its silvery light. Fiery gemstones of moonlight devoured the entire second line of daemons. Screams cleaved the air until there was nothing but cinders and ash. The other daemons, including the winged ones, seemed to hesitate.

The armies behind me—wolf, harpy, minotaur—all cheered, the chants reverberating through my chest. *Wolf of the White Flames.*

It was then that I allowed myself to smile. A cruel and defiant grin.

The wall of fire fell, rolling on the grass like waves of water. As soon as the power left my fingertips, I slumped down, panting. A light sheen of sweat beaded my brow.

Marcus whistled. "I suppose training with the she-wolf paid off."

Even in the wake of my obliteration, the Ram's daemons prepared to charge again.

Behind them, trees began to shudder, the ground thundered. And the forest parted, revealing golden armor and khopesh blades.

The jackals were making their entrance.

Unbridled fury awakened every stem of aether within my blood. My power crackled and popped under my skin, readying to attack like a wildcat. Waiting for release.

Caius lifted his head. *"Wolves! It has been an honor to be your Alpha. Look at us now, the Olympian races have united to reclaim our realm. Let us make the Ram regret ever stepping foot into our world."*

The battlefield roared to life. The Roman wolves and the rest of the Olympian forces took to the field or the sky. The gods would lay witness to the chaos. Such immortal beings that had no power in this realm would only be able to watch the utter destruction and death that would be unleashed.

I shifted into my wolf, joining my brothers, running into war's embrace. We were the wolves of Rome. Sons of the god of war. Battle was the air we breathed.

Teeth against steel. Wings against wings. Aether against aether. The taste of blood that gushed between my fangs. The screams of daemons and mortals alike. Death came for all.

But it was the familiar sound of an animal cry and of pierced metal that caused my blood to run cold. To *godsdamn* ice. A battle was ravaging above.

No.

My heart cut in two as I watched Diane and Dromos fall from the sky.

SIXTY-ONE

Diane

The shadows plunged into the throat of the sentinel, burning him from the inside. Its talons had pierced Dromos's wings. The sound of my pegasus's screams punctured something inside my chest as we began to fall. I kept bashing the daemon in the head with the pommel of my sword. The creature's grasp on Dromos slipped enough for me to kick it square in the chest.

The sentinel fell, wings struggling to keep to the air. A black wolf shot up from the ground. Remus snatched the creature by the wing and slammed it to the ground. Its spine must've cracked but the daemon wouldn't have had a chance to escape in any case. Remus pressed a paw over its head until the skull was crushed.

Dromos flapped his wings, seeming strong enough to keep flying, and we banked upward once more. Sweat drenched his dove-gray fur. Frustration slipped into me, and I realized it was from Dromos.

I patted his side. "Get your bearings. We've barely begun."

Dromos veered side to side, guiding me against the barrage of flying daemons. Between my she-wolf aether and the shadows, as well as my sword, I cut through the sentinels. The she-wolves were aware of the daemonic chains that had the ability to nullify the aether of its captive. Some of my warrior sisters had fallen prey to them, the chains somehow finding their way around them, apprehending them enough for the sentinels to give the killing blow.

I vowed I would make their deaths worth it. All the deaths. I promised to make this right. To end it.

I caught sight of Sabina's pegasus, the powder snow of its pelt dotted with black. Sabina was gritting her teeth in exertion, expelling the force of her aether. The power careened toward an oncoming sentinel, splitting it in two.

My Commanding She-Wolf shot me a wild grin and then laughed, almost maniacally. "We are in deep shit, sister."

I laughed in return, bracing my feet on Dromos's back as I stood. Another daemon spun toward us. As it drew closer, I crouched.

Twisting the blade in my hand, I grinned. "Till the bitter end."

The daemon soared in the air, preparing to clash with Dromos. Until Dromos dropped. And I jumped. I glided—or more accurately, fell—past the daemon's back. My sword ran a vicious line along it at the same time. A river of black fell from the cut. And now Dromos was supposed to catch me. Where was he? I tried not to panic while I tumbled toward the earth.

Air was knocked from my chest as I felt an arm catch me. I looked back and met Laelia's eyes, a knowing smile on her lips.

"Your pegasus allowed me the honor," she said.

I barked a laugh, relief mixing with the adrenaline. "My hero."

Laelia helped me back onto Dromos as I saw Sabina dive for another pair of daemons.

A wave of darkness was unfurling below, the jackal-shifters moving amongst the shadows. They were like assassins bounding in the night, slitting throats and stabbing rib cages.

A warning howl. Caius. *Fall back! To the city!*

The armies began to retreat, but there were too many against them. They needed time to draw back.

Dromos sensed my intentions and folded his wings over me. Wind whipped moisture from my eyes as we plummeted closer to the ground. To the space between the two armies. The pegasus snapped out his wings and I stretched out a hand, billowing shadows emerging from my palm. We soared back up into the sky, leaving behind a line of black flames that stopped the Ram's forces from pursuing. I was trying to stall them for as long as possible.

Dromos soared low enough to glide alongside the wolves. Remus and my brothers closed in to run with us. Together. As we would always be.

The Ram eventually managed to penetrate through my power. His own gusts of shadows exploded into the field, chasing after us. Our forces spilled into the city, in the streets and on the rooftops. Soon the daemons and jackals would reach us.

I noticed that the Ram had hardly been using his powers, and I had a sense it was similar to how Remus and I were trying to save our energy.

Aether thrummed again, wild and hungry. It craved the taste of the salt in the air, the sweetness of the grass, and the coppery tang of blood.

I braced myself. I was a Daughters of Mars, blessed with aether from the god of war. Shadows coiled around my arms in preparation, and I grinned as they joined with the aether of my she-wolf.

I was also a daughter of Anubis.

SIXTY-TWO

Remus

R ed mist lingered against the gray light. The sun had risen higher behind the clouds. Buildings and homes were being toppled over. Plumes of smoke and dust twisted through the city streets. I had spotted a horde of daemons as they fought a pack of wolves near a small villa, and the entire home had crumbled to blocks of stone.

It had been a constant onslaught. Battalions of minotaurs and wolves had been forced to withdraw while another team took their place, resuming the bloodshed.

I wasn't sure who was winning. Though, with the jackals fighting alongside creatures of another realm, it didn't seem that the odds were in our favor. Worry tugged at my gut. The griffins had yet to arrive. Something was wrong. Perhaps the Ram had sensed them coming and somehow managed to hold them back. Or done something to them. The worry soon turned into cold fear.

I sprinted toward the city forum to get to the others, but something sharp grazed against my shoulder. A pained sound escaped me at the burn, and I skidded to a stop in time to see an Order rider on its horse galloping toward me. I dipped my head low, clouds of dirt swirled around me as my nostrils flared. The rider prepared to launch another shadowed spear at me when a dark gray wolf lunged, grabbed the human's neck between its fangs, and tossed the limp body aside.

"*I had that,*" I growled.

Drusus's tongue lapped the blood around his muzzle, and he snorted. "*Did you really?*"

The wall of a building exploded, stone rolling onto the road along with a lifeless daemon. Atticus's beige wolf shook the dust from his mane as debris fell around him like powdered snow.

Drusus muttered, "*Show off.*"

Marcus appeared from around a corner, his ears flat to his head, eyes flickering along the rooftops. "*Caius is right behind me,*" he announced. "*And the Ram is perched on one of the dome buildings, attacking from above. He's annihilating our ranks but still won't advance for now.*"

I snarled. "*The bastard is waiting. He still needs Diane and me to open the realms for his other armies. We need him distracted enough so I can send him back to the prison realm.*"

Marcus looked my way. For the first time, I saw panic and fear in those yellow wolf eyes. For me and Diane. Maybe the icy male wasn't so bad after all.

The sound of Caius's roar had me running toward him. There was no thought or hesitation when I heard his call. The other wolves followed, and we scaled the buildings onto the rooftops. Caius was facing a battalion of jackal-shifters.

Jabari and Omari were at the head.

I fought to keep my breathing calm. To not tremble from the mix of anger and dread at the sight of them. *They will not see me fall.*

The group of jackals circled us.

Omari looked excited to see me and ran a tongue over his lips. "Remus, you've come back to play?"

"*Disgusting prick. You will pay for all you've done to him.*" Drusus spat, his hairs bristling as he knelt to a crouch.

Omari only laughed. "You and your wolves took your precious time in rescuing the Lone Wolf. Poor Remus was all alone." He lifted the khopesh and licked the slick blade. "You should've heard his screams."

Drusus snarled, ready to lunge, when Marcus shoved in front of him. His yellow eyes flared with something fierce and dangerous. "*You're the one who killed Cato.*"

Omari spun the pair of weapons in his hands. Gray sunlight blinked with every twist. "At the fort? Oh. The handsome one? *I can't remember*," he leered.

Whatever self-control Marcus was holding onto snapped. He, Drusus and Atticus lunged for them, and the other jackals responded in kind. White flames ignited over my fur. I was a wolf of fire. Jackals that tried to touch me, or came too close, burned.

I plowed through the jackals as Jabari and Omari charged toward me.

"*Remus!*" Drusus's voice was all warning. "*Wait!*"

The world drowned into blurs of chaos. I could only see *them*. Their twisted smiles. Their glittering eyes and all the pain they had caused me.

Omari jumped over me and grabbed onto my back just as Jabari tried to slip past me. My teeth found purchase around Jabari's torso. I held on till the flames flared angrier, and the jackal grunted in pain. Omari, still on top of me despite the inevitable burns, drove a blade into my side. I yelped and tried to shake him off.

Jabari took the opportunity to slash his khopesh up, grazing my muzzle. He managed to free himself, stepping away as Omari's face came into view.

"My favorite plaything. Once the king is done using you, I will request we keep you."

Flashes of me at their mercy sent a fearful shudder through me. No, I would never let that happen again.

Marcus snatched Omari's arm in his jaw, throwing him yards away from us. Omari skidded against the ground, ebony claws scraping at the stone with a chilling screech.

"*I will enjoy killing you.*" Marcus hissed as he prowled to my side.

Omari and Jabari cackled. They steadied their blades. Their tongues ran over bared teeth.

But even they stilled at the sound, almost that of a thunderstorm. It was the crack of snow before the fall of an avalanche, the lightning before a tree splinters into flames.

Dromos soared between the buildings toward us, toward the

jackals, darkness following his wings. Tendrils of shadow clung to Diane, and her eyes were a soulless black. Dark veins crawled along her brow and neck.

She slipped off from Dromos's back like a phantom and landed on the rooftop where we stood as her shadows shrouded the sky. Angry stars flashed within. Jabari and Omari tensed and they watched warily as the blankets of dark mist and twilight stretched and yawned, taking their fellow comrades into their hold.

We couldn't see anything. Neither Diane nor any of the jackals she took. The black plumes thickened, the screams were endless.

Until there was silence.

And Diane stepped out of the smoke.

A warrior born of the gods of war and death.

Flanking her, the darkness took shape—oh gods—the shape of jackal warriors, marching in rows. Made by Diane's hand, the shadowed jackals held their own khopesh blades, and followed their daughter of the dead.

Terrifying. Stunning.

"*Oh my gods,*" Marcus breathed.

Jabari and Omari shifted in place, preparing to attack or flee, I could not tell. Diane didn't give them time to consider. She shouted a command and the shadowed jackals were unleashed. I couldn't count how many there were. They were like rivers of dark flame, spilling from the rooftops onto the streets. Killing and killing.

A pair of her jackals appeared before us, marching—toward the two jackals who had haunted my nightmares. Diane's makeshift jackals were ungodly. Black smoke followed their swift movements, easily seizing Omari and Jabari. One jackal shoved Omari to his knees before Diane.

Her lips twitched, eyes black as night, and she drove a dagger through Omari's chest. She stabbed again and again and again. Her fury resounded with each violent thrust. Omari choked, his body lurching forward as Cato's had when he killed him.

Diane dipped her head, lips hovering at the dying jackal's ear. "This is for Cato, and for Remus."

Omari's eyes widened. The shadowed jackals yanked him back and melted back into shadow as they forced their way through Omari's throat. The jackal finally screamed, begging for mercy. Diane's lips curled up even further as Omari died at her feet.

Seeing him die such a brutal death, I couldn't help but feel a sense of retribution. My lotus had done that.

Marcus shoved a shocked Jabari at my paws. The brown wolf circled us as he eyed the jackal with disgust. *"Finish it. For all the shit he's done to you."*

My lips curled, and I shifted to my human form. I pulled the jackal up by its breastplate and let the flames unfurl from my shoulders. Steam seeped through my lips.

And Jabari's face *paled*. "Your eyes." His voice shook. "They're glowing."

I smiled. This would be my tormentor's last view. This would be a kill I would take joy in.

"How does it feel? To die knowing you were *my* plaything this time?" I drove a blade up his neck. The flames ran up the sword to burn the jackal alive.

Jabari screeched and bucked under my grasp, but I did not let go until his body charred. He went limp, jaw hanging open, stuck in the scream of his death. I dropped the body without a second glance.

It was done. They were gone. And they would never hurt me again.

Diane approached me. Her eyes had returned to gold and the shadows were gone. Even the jackal warriors who'd been ravaging the streets had disappeared.

Her gaze was heated with the excitement of the bloodshed and the power running through her veins. "Did you like my display?" she asked with a vicious smile. "I bet you couldn't do something like that."

I grabbed her, wrapping my arms around her waist. "Cocky as ever."

I kissed her like a depraved man. My tongue pried her mouth open. Clashing, yearning. Bathing in the warm sensation that spread through my chest. Blossoms and blood. *Gods.* A deep, crazed groan rumbled through me as her lips explored mine.

Marcus made a disapproving sound, and Diane broke into a short laugh. My fingers entwined in her hair as her fingers traced along my jaw.

"I'm not going to lie." My voice was roughened. "I am a little jealous I can't do what you just did."

"Needing more lessons?" Diane crooned. "I can't blame you. I am an incredible teacher."

Marcus groaned. *"Both of you need to stop."*

Chorus of beating wings and eagle screams erupted from above. The griffins had finally arrived, and they were picking off members of the Order from the rooftops and taking down the winged daemons. It was a godsdamn relief to see those oversized birds.

King Aquila soared low to speak to Caius. *"I hope you have a plan, Alpha. Those flying bats attacked us on the way here."*

Caius cursed. *"We have to make way for Remus and Diane so they can get to the Ram. It's up to them from there."*

Aquila gave me an appraising look. *"Fates be on your side, Wolf of the White Flames. We will cover for you."*

And they did, the griffins and wolves. A road laced with ruin. Straight to the Ram.

SIXTY-THREE

Diane

I had gone overboard. I could still access my aether, but I felt tired. When I saw the jackals approaching Remus, I had a sense they were the same ones who had tortured him. Used him for their own entertainment. It was why I hadn't hesitated in using some creativity with my aether.

My brothers and the griffins had stayed behind to continue the defense. Dromos now raced up the edifice, where the Ram waited above on a rooftop. He was baiting us, I was sure. But we still needed to face him sooner or later.

Remus's breath kissed the back of my neck. I could hear the urgency in his voice. "Lotus, if anything happens, I need you to know—"

"No," I snapped. "Together. We do this together. Am I clear?"

His arms squeezed around me. Remus bent his head over mine, shielding me from the world for a moment. "I need you to know that I will do everything in my power to ensure you make it. Am *I* clear?"

My eyes stayed ahead as the back of my eyes threatened to burn. "No," I repeated. "You have to promise me, Remus. We do this *together*."

My voice had turned more panicked with every word. Remus was silent. Too long, he was taking too long to respond.

"Yes," he finally responded as he nuzzled my hair. "Together."

We broke onto the roof, and a blast of shadow hurtled toward us, aiming for Dromos. I shouted in panic, but the pegasus was quick enough to dive out of its way. I turned to see Anthony standing farther down on the rooftop. His face was like stone.

Remus and I made our descent and leapt off of Dromos. I urged him to leave through the bond. I could feel his hesitation; he didn't want to leave, but I couldn't risk him. I sent the command, and Dromos flew away from the building's edge, his plea and desperation echoing through me.

The Ram lingered behind Anthony, his eyes burning with intrigue. "I always knew where your aether came from, she-wolf. I recognized it. The taste of stars and sands."

My mind screamed with fury at everything this creature had done, at what he'd cause and what he'd forced us to do. The loss he'd wrought. Remus turned to face me and placed himself in front of me as if shielding me. He looked down, slowly arching a brow. A question in his devilish eyes I could almost hear.

Together, lotus?

I responded by unsheathing my sword. Remus shifted into his wolf, his eyes glowing silver. The black wolf pawed the ground as pale flames roared to life, gilding him in their burning light.

Anthony braced himself for the fight. The Ram grinned as he spoke to Remus's pater. "The Lone Wolf is *mine*."

I moved. My shadows clashed with Anthony's. The kickback of the power was enough to knock me back, and I saw Remus's fiery wolf and the daemon king collide. Horns and fangs ripped into each other. The black wolf latched onto the Ram's hide and the daemon flung his head back and forth, trying to shake Remus off. White flames erupted from the wolf's jaws, billowing out against the Ram. The daemon king roared as its armor began to melt against its skin, gripped Remus by the back of his neck and flung him across the rooftop. The wolf rolled, stopping just before the building's edge. The large beasts clashed again and again, the edifice itself seemed to shake with the weight of their thrashing power.

Anthony and I swung our blades in unison. We made eye contact above our interlocked position, and I swear his green eyes shifted with something, though I couldn't pinpoint what. Our powers crossed once more, but I didn't react quick enough when Anthony attacked. A chain wrapped around my neck, and I felt the shadows weaken.

I struggled against him, clawing and kicking to no avail. Anthony knocked me onto my knees. He grabbed my hair and forced my head up.

Remus roared, the sound filled with unadulterated rage. *"Get your fucking hands off her."*

The black wolf was about to abandon his fight with the Ram to come to me when the daemon leashed him with his aether. The black wolf strained against him, still trying desperately to crawl towards me.

The Ram snapped at Anthony. "Unchain her. I need her power."

Aether returned to me as soon as the chains fell, like fresh water to a thirsty mortal. Barely a moment of reprieve before darkness seeped through the corners of my mind. I gasped. My blood felt like it was boiling. This must've been what Remus had gone through.

The realization only terrorized me further when I saw the Ram doing the same to Remus. The black wolf growled, trying to fight off the violating sensation, but couldn't resist the Ram's power. I saw Remus lift his head, his twisted howls tearing at my heart. The sounds of animal cries turned into the pained sounds of a man. Whatever power the Ram was leeching from Remus was enough to force the wolf to shift back to his human form.

I yelled his name in fear and out of pain, and Anthony's hands on me tightened. His body tensed the moment Remus began to scream.

The daemon king only laughed. His power then lurched further into me, the streams of his aether like fingers as they pried through the crevices of my mind, searching for my power.

"I will destroy you from the inside. The deepest parts of your soul will writhe in agony for the rest of your days."

Those unseen fingers touched the essence of my aethers—both my she-wolf power and the shadows—caressing them like a prized treasure, and latched onto them.

Strings of light and energy pulled from me, piercing into the sky above the Ram. Like that night in the harbor city, in the underground tunnels. The aether taken from me—and from Remus—began to tear the seams of our realm apart.

The portal split open, darkness and red skies inside.

And thousands of crescent eyes on the other side. Waiting.

He'd opened the entryway to his daemon army. The Ram stared at it as if it were the most beautiful sight. My eyes almost rolled back from the pain. *I can't breathe.*

The daemons on the other side of the portal began to shriek and shift excitedly. One winged daemon clawed its way out of the opening. This one was not like the sentinels—it had curved horns like the Ram's, and spikes running down its spine. It flew out from the portal. Then another. And another. My blood ran cold at the sight.

The Ram's voice boomed. "My brothers and sisters, you have been released from the shackles the gods and goddesses wrongly placed on you. Relish in your freedom."

Power was running out of me in violent torrents, and I could do nothing to stop it. I groaned as I felt whatever remaining breaths I had seep from my lungs. My gaze found Remus, his fear-stricken eyes already on me. I tried to mentally resist the Ram's power, but it was like slipping on ice.

I mouthed the words, tears gathering at my eyes: "I love you."

Remus growled and slowly, ever so slowly, began to stand. He was fighting the Ram, his strength enough to get him on his feet.

Anthony was silent as he kept his hold on me, and I couldn't tell if he was watching Remus or the daemons. I gritted my teeth and slammed against the mental walls the Ram had placed over my power.

I had the power of two gods in my blood. I could fight against anything. In my mind, I thrashed like a wild animal, banging against the wall, against the chains.

A sudden bright silver light blinded me. Tongues of flame reached for the sky, disrupting the connection between Remus and the Ram and breaking the rope of aether that tied Remus to the portal. The entryway to the prison realm narrowed, the daemons on the other side frantically trying to pry it open wider and escape.

The sound of the Ram's pained roar was earth-shattering, rattling my very bones, but I couldn't see what was happening between Remus and the daemon king. Anthony's grip on me began to loosen as I felt the Ram's control slip too. My aether rushed back to me, but the portal didn't close. It was still partially open, the daemons on the other side trying to rip through.

I didn't have time to think of what that meant as I kicked off the ground, jabbing an elbow into Anthony's ribcage. He grunted but didn't make a move to grab me again as his gaze lingered on something behind me. I followed his line of sight.

The light. I knew where it was coming from. Recognized it just as my aether did instinctively. Remus. I could see through the blinding light now, just enough to see his face.

There were tears in his eyes. Heartbreak.

And when the light lessened, as Remus pulled his power back, I understood why.

Caius had planted a sword deeply within the Ram's chest. The creature still stood as if fighting the urge to fall. The daemon king was massive, and Caius practically had his feet on him to steady himself. But the Ram had a claw wrapped around Caius's throat and with the other—my heart was cleaved in two—he'd driven a blade through him.

Our Alpha stared into the Ram's eyes, his chest rising and falling, and a moment passed before he pushed himself deeper against the daemon king's blade while simultaneously shoving his sword further into the Ram's chest.

The Ram let out a scream, and more and more of his binds on me began to loosen. Caius had done this. Given us an opportunity. Freed us.

Time slowed as Caius slowly fell from the Ram's grasp, and his eyes stared into the bleak sky. A soft smile came to his lips as if he were staring at something beautiful.

His chest rose once more before it stopped moving.

The Alpha of the Roman wolves was dead.

SIXTY-FOUR

Remus

I stared at him.

At his body. Caius was right there, mere yards away from me, but he would never come back.

Caius was gone.

My senses fell numb.

I had seen him approach. Diane had been struggling against the Ram's power, her aether coursing to the portal. She had told me she loved me, as if in some sort of farewell. Dark resolve had possessed me then.

In the deepest corners of my consciousness, I'd searched, scratching and flailing until I'd found the tether linking me to the Ram's iron-clad grip. The power the daemon king was using was mine to give. Or to take back. I'd pulled against the Ram's hold. Tugging and tugging. I hadn't even been sure if I was accomplishing anything. The Ram's aether was ancient, too experienced and powerful against someone like me.

And that was when I had seen Caius. He had made his way to the rooftop and was creeping closer to the Ram. The Alpha had met my gaze and given me a firm nod. I had shaken my head in warning, pleading with him not to do anything foolish. My eyes had gone frantic.

Don't you dare.

My brother's eyes had softened on me before he faced the daemon king, gripped the pommel of his sword, and charged.

It was in that moment that my power had snapped. My aether still hadn't been completely free but I held enough control over it to cast a bright light in a desperate attempt to help Caius.

I had failed. The moment my light flared out, the Ram had sensed Caius near him, and the two males had met one another in a violent clash of swords while the daemon was blinded by my aether. Despite the madness, Caius had accomplished what he'd sought to do. He had helped to break the binds, and I had felt the connection to the portal snap.

But it was too late to save him. Caius was dead.

Flames as bright as the moon swallowed me whole as I plummeted into my aether's embrace. And I willed it out from me. Every godsdamn drop of power, every tendril of the god of war's silver flames in my blood. I would finish what Caius had started. The Ram had managed to stand back up, the blade still embedded in his chest, but he faltered a step, his attention turning to me and my aether.

I attacked before he could. White fire exploded from my hands. A blast of godly aether tore into the Ram. He stumbled back before columns of his own power shot toward me.

Aether against aether. I strained against the force of it, how it pulled at my very essence. It was too much.

A presence brushed against me. Energy as dark and beautiful as the night.

My light.

My Diane.

She was also free of the daemon king's hold and now joined me, her power entwining with my own. The black, star-kissed vortex mixed with my silver jeweled flames and collided against the Ram's. I felt the shift in the air. The *panic* emanating from the Ram.

In the corner of my eye, I saw Anthony. He was standing there, simply watching the scene unfold, as if unsure what to do. He suddenly started banging his hand against his head. Again and again, he pommeled a fist against his brow. His head jerked up, the look in his eyes bright and . . . angry.

Before I could comprehend what was happening, my pater began to run toward the Ram, crashed into him while the daemon had his focus on me and Diane, and pushed him towards the edge of the building. The Ram's strength wavered, as our combined aether speared through him. A gaping hole appeared through the monster's chest. My pater was within range of our powers, and his mortal body was unable to handle the intensity as he began to burn, his skin turning bright red. It didn't stop him from giving a final push to the daemon king. The monster that had terrorized this realm for far too long fell over the building's edge.

My pater stumbled, straying too close to where the Ram had last stood. His eyes lifted to meet mine and for the first time I saw something that looked like remorse. The sight froze me. Even in the chaos, his voice reached me.

"I'm sorry, son. I tried to resist his influence once I realized what I'd agreed to. But I couldn't free myself and I was forced to create the Order and start this terrible war. I failed you, your sister, and your mater. I hope one day you will forgive me."

He struggled to keep himself on his feet, though his gaze never left mine. I instinctively began to move as if to go to him, reach for him. I saw the life whisk away from his eyes and my pater fell back, disappearing after the Ram.

They were gone. Just like that. I couldn't understand what had just happened. I could only feel disbelief and confusion. Were they truly dead? But with Anthony—my pater's—parting words, I almost felt a sense of sadness. Sadness that I might've had the first and last ever glimpse of what my pater could've been without the Ram's influence. Of his true self before grief changed him.

I couldn't focus on that now. We weren't done. The crack in the sky was still open, and the daemons were trying to push themselves through. Diane and I looked to each other, a silent understanding passing through us, and we aimed our aethers to the portal.

Our powers roared, twisting together as the crack in the sky grew brighter. *Will has a power of its own.* I beckoned the words in my heart. Begged the gods and goddesses. *Save her. Save this place.*

There was a shudder. The jagged lines of the portal began to fall, looking like glimmering ashes. A pulse rippled, deep and malignant, as if the veil between the realms was inhaling, preparing to shatter.

I reached for Diane, abandoning our hold on the aether. My eyes ran over her face, and I caught sight of the edifice's edge behind her.

I kissed her, breathing the words against her mouth. "I love you."

And I pushed her.

The look she gave me—hurt and betrayal. *I would do it again, my light.* A smile touched my lips and a resounding sense of content found me as I faced the world's oblivion.

I saw a brightness: beautiful, like dawn and dusk.

Then I saw nothing.

SIXTY-FIVE

Diane

A moment. A painfully silent moment. Then true pain hit.
He told me we would do this together.
He'd promised.

Remus—

The light of dusk and dawn exploded through the sky. The building began to fall as I did too. This was not real. This could not be.

Dove-gray wings appeared, and Dromos caught me midair. Stray chips of stone scratched my face. But I didn't feel it. I couldn't feel physical pain. I felt *empty*.

Dromos raced away from the collapsing building, and only then did I find the strength to lift my head toward the light and fire above. Remus's name tore at my throat, my hands reaching for nothing. The portal was no longer there.

We crashed to the ground just as the last of the debris nipped at our heels. I was thrown off Dromos's back, and a splitting pain seized the back of my head and legs. My body refused to move. Even though I internally screamed at myself to get up, I was forced to stare at the sky.

I could hear the snarls of the remaining daemons. The Ram may have been gone, but that hadn't stopped his followers. Perhaps this would be my end: mauled by the last daemons on this mortal realm.

My eyelids fluttered and I felt myself weaken but almost didn't believe what I saw. Wisps of silvery light bolted across the sky. Aether, I realized. In the distance I heard roaring, the sound majestic and otherworldly.

I lifted my head, ignoring the blaring pain. A daemon was tearing through the wreckage, its bloodthirsty rage focused on me. I tried to move but only managed to drag my legs up a few inches.

The daemon broke through, but before it could reach me a wolf made of light passed through the daemon, snuffing its life out like a candle.

The light lingered, and my eyes stayed fixed on it as it began to take a different shape. A hand stretched out toward me. Tendrils of silvery light formed limbs and a body. I realized with a pang in my chest that the energy that had killed the daemon was *his* wolf.

Tears ran down my dirt-stained cheeks. Everything around me seemed to pause. "Cato?"

My brother smiled. The warmth of it was enough to cause the energy around him to pulse. "Are you going to get up, sister?"

His voice, something I thought I would never hear again, gave me the strength to stand. My hand slid into his. It felt solid. Cato pulled me into his arms. Gods, I could even smell him, that same scent of lemon and herbs. Like home.

Cato's arms tightened around me as a sob wracked through my chest. "I've missed you."

A broken laugh escaped me. I pulled back and stared at my brother, at his wild hair and eyes, at the life that thrived there. "How?"

Cato ran a hand over my head, mussing my hair. "Remus sent for us."

A jolt of emotion ran through me at his name. "What do you mean?"

His eyes looked at something above my head, and he lifted his chin. "Look."

More shards of light in the shape of wolves ran through the sky, through the battlefield. The spirits of the wolves who had passed before us. Grand in their celestial light as they snuffed the life of the remaining daemons. I couldn't take my eyes off the beautiful sight.

Cato's voice pulled me out of my stupor. "We returned to remove all that does not belong in this realm," he said. "Remus ensured it."

"You are going to leave us again." The words left me in a ragged breath.

My brother's smile turned sad. His hand cupped the back of my head, the light whispering and dancing over the ink on his arms and shoulders. Even in this form, he wore his fighting leathers. A warrior of the afterlife.

"I never truly left you, or our brothers."

I swallowed through the ache threatening to choke me. "And Remus?" I was afraid to ask, to even think of it.

Cato searched the grief in my gaze. The brokenness. He bent to kiss my brow and started to walk past me but paused. "Everything he did was for you. So, you could live."

He smiled once more, and the aether around him turned brighter. "I love you, sister of mine."

Raw emotion spread through me. At the gift of having this opportunity. Of seeing him again. "I love you too. Always will."

With one last look, Cato turned and shifted. The dove-gray wolf ran among the others, taking to the sky and disappearing like a mist of sunlight. The wolves alive on the battleground lifted their snouts and howled as the wolves of the dead saved us—leaving us once more.

We'd survived. Won. We all stood within the wreckage of the city, as if we hadn't fully realized. There were no cheers, only a deep reverence for those who had given their lives to this cause.

Though they were numb, my feet began to move. I felt a warmth press against my side, and I slumped comfortably against it.

"My sweet boy," I murmured, running a hand down Dromos's neck. I was so relieved to see him.

I kept walking, Dromos beside me, as I headed to where I'd last seen Remus. Nothing but rubble was in the streets.

I found Atticus searching through the wreckage, his eyes frantic as he tossed slabs of stone over his shoulders. He hadn't noticed me yet.

"Fuck! Where are you?" he shouted.

"Atticus?"

Atticus's shoulders bunched up before he turned to me. His eyes softened as he pulled me into his arms. His body shook as he battled a sigh of relief. "Gods, we were so worried."

I wrapped my arms around him. "Did you see him?"

Atticus knew of whom I spoke. I felt him smile against my neck, thick emotion in his voice. "Yes, we saw him. It was good to see him one more time." He tipped a finger under my chin as he made me meet his gaze. "Marcus has been searching for you too . . . for both of you."

My heart twisted painfully. Atticus guided me deeper into the center of the debris where the building once stood.

Through the ribbons of smoke, we saw a figure appear. Marcus. In his arms, broken and limp, was Remus. His hair was matted with dirt, and blood streaked his body. He was still. So still. His hand hung loosely to the side as Marcus carried him.

I knew. Whether by instinct, intuition, or by the fucking aether in my blood. I knew that Remus was dead. The pain burned through me, cracking something deep within me. A sob broke from me.

"No," I moaned. I stumbled, Atticus's arms wrapping around me to hold me up as I tried to make my way to Remus on weak legs. "No no no."

Sorrow sliced across Marcus's face. He didn't speak as he gently placed Remus on the ground before me. Atticus let me go, and I practically fell on Remus's body. My hands fisted at the collar of his fighting leathers.

Remus's eyes were open, but the light inside them was gone. How his body had even survived the explosion I was not sure, and I thank the powers of the godlike aether that ran through him. But Remus was no god. He was not impervious to death.

A scream broke out from me. The sorrow crushed whatever

soul I had left into dust. I flinched as a roar tore from somewhere around me.

Harpies, minotaurs, and the other wolves were gathering. Drusus broke through the growing crowd. He halted for a moment, the disbelief turned agony clear on his face as he slowly fell to his knees.

"He can't—" Drusus's voice cracked. Sabina crouched at his side, taking him into her arms as he cried on her shoulders.

"You lied to me," I whispered through the tears, as I stared at Remus.

My fingers ran through his black locks. Skimmed over the planes of his cheeks. Over his lips.

Everything faded as I pressed my brow to Remus's chest. Yearning for a heartbeat that I knew wouldn't come.

SIXTY-SIX

Remus

Tall blades of golden grass stretched before me. Majestic trees towered above. There were mountains in the distance that knew no limit as they pierced through the endless clash between dusk and dawn. I had seen this view before, once, before the aether of silver flames came to me . . .

Where was I?

A voice. Warm and sharp. "Remus?"

I knew that voice. The other part of me. Of my soul. A female stood before me, half hidden by the grass that reached her waist. Her hair was long and black, one side of it braided and pulled back. A familiar set of brown eyes. Eyes that she had gotten from our mater. This couldn't be happening.

"Is it really you?" I breathed.

My twin sister arched an eyebrow, smiled. "Don't be dense. You know it is."

A strangled laugh escaped me. I tried to take a step toward her, but couldn't move. As if I was being held back from stepping any further into this place.

My voice cracked. "Helena."

She reached for my hands, and a gasp pulled from my chest at the feel of her skin. Something like sadness settled in her gaze. "Brother, you've been lost."

I pressed a firm kiss to her knuckles. "I have been," I replied softly. "I felt like I'd failed you."

Her eyes softened, and she tightened her hands around mine. "Not once did you fail me. Do you hear me? I have always loved you and never blamed you for what happened." Something in her expression shattered. "It broke my heart knowing you were in such pain."

My chest tightened. "I've missed you. So much."

Helena stepped into my arms, and a harsh breath fell from my lips. She brushed a light fist against my arm, like she always did when she was alive. "You need to go back."

"Am I dead?"

My sister nodded and pulled back. "Yes and no. A part of you is still tied to the mortal world, clinging to it. I wonder why." She tilted her head, a knowing smile blooming on her face.

Another voice interrupted. Deeper. Thrumming with power. "So, this is the famous Wolf of the White Flames?"

A male with an inconceivably powerful presence surrounding him appeared behind Helena. He had dark brown hair and olive skin, a face carved with familiar features. My power grew restless as I recognized the strum of his aether. The response I'd felt from my desperate pleas. Before I died.

I bowed my head. "Mars."

The god of war watched me with palpable interest. "I heard your call."

Relief skimmed through my chest. "It is done?"

He nodded. "The spirit of the wolves cleaned the realm of the daemons. It was a miracle that I was able to intervene."

"Perhaps it was an act of Fate."

He cocked his head, watching me with a careful expression. "Perhaps."

Silver flickered across Mars's eyes as he narrowed his gaze. "You have a choice, Remus. The power inside you is something a wolf is never born with, but something you called to, and it responded in return. Some of my power is still within you, and it is helping you tether yourself to the mortal plane.. You now have a decision to make.

Stay here among the golden plains with your sister, or have another chance at life. It is your choice, but before you decide, I have a question for you."

I tensed as Mars circled me. Helena waited at my side, but she didn't seem concerned, only intrigued.

The god of war ran a hand over his jaw. That heavy gaze pressed on me with the insurmountable weight of the worlds. "The gods have made mistakes in the past. Those mistakes led to the war on your mortal lands. If I let you walk away from here, will that too turn out to be a mistake? Will this power you now have lead to something that should not be?"

Wolves were not supposed to have the power I carried. I had never asked for this ability, but it had come to me when I needed it. And it had become a part of me.

I met Mars's gaze. "It served its purpose; I no longer need it. Do what you will, but I choose to live."

Mars's lips curved up. His eyes shone and glowed silver. *That is how I must have looked.*

"Disgrace the blessing of my aether given to you, and I will personally see that you regret it." Mars placed a fist over his heart and bowed to me.

My eyes widened and I quickly bowed in return. The god of war acknowledged Helena with a soft smile, before wisping away into nothing. Flickers of aether danced where he stood.

Helena whistled. "Shit . . . don't piss off the god of war, brother."

I nudged her with my shoulder. "Good thing I'm always such a calm, collected male."

She laughed as she squeezed my arm. "Someone wants to see you."

I felt another presence then. His body was now whole and rid of the wound that had killed him. Caius walked through the golden grass, his eyes fixated on Helena. A gentle warmth touched his expression. The creases that had haunted his face had smoothed.

Joy overwhelmed me, and I watched dumbfounded as Caius stepped to Helena's side, his gaze never straying from hers. He lifted a finger to brush a strand of hair away from her face.

My sister's eyes glistened with unshed tears. Her hand raised to cup his cheek, and I noticed the tattooed ink on her ring finger. Husband and wife. Reunited.

Caius's eyes finally slid to me, and he smiled. Warm and bright. "Live, Remus. Be at peace."

My chest constricted to the point of pain. They were here. "Be happy, Caius."

Helena smiled. She wrapped her arms around my shoulders, and I held her tightly to me. All the heartbreak and the haunting nightmares were no more. I felt the strength of her love through her embrace, and I would remember it till the end of my days.

Light emerged from behind me. Ready to take me back. The last thing I saw was Caius taking my sister's hand as they walked back through the golden plains.

SIXTY-SEVEN

Diane

Time slowed. Or sped up. I wasn't sure. My head was still on his chest, my hands still fisted around his fighting leathers. No one dared approach me as I wallowed in my agony.

Then I thought I heard a heartbeat. And another.

I felt the subtle brush of a hand, gently moving the hair from my face. A deep voice I knew so well. "I see you."

I gasped, and I pulled back to see Remus, wide awake, life back in his eyes. He was *alive*. I crashed into him, kissing all over his face. He laughed, the sound melding the broken pieces within me back together.

"You're . . ." I breathed.

He took my face into his large hands, brushing away the tears. His own eyes shone. "I am."

We shakily got to our feet and heard the ruckus of Drusus's laughter. His large body leaned into Sabina, relief making him slump against her. "Godsdamn, Remus. You scared me."

Remus shot him a lopsided smirk. "Must keep you on your toes, brother."

Marcus and Atticus were grinning, coming to help support me and Remus. I even couldn't fathom it. We were standing. We were here. Victorious.

A horn blared in the distance. The distant cry of a soldier. "Warships! Egypt is on her way!"

The group gathered around us cried out in fear and exhaustion. We looked toward the ocean.

Indeed, there were hundreds of warships ramming through the waves toward us.

Marcus cursed. "Octavian and the naval armies are already out at sea. This must be another Egyptian fleet."

I shook my head, trying to fight off the dread. "This is a battle we cannot win."

There was no way we could fight another army. Our forces had been depleted, and most of the survivors were injured and unable to fight. Just when I thought we had a chance at peace. How in the name of the gods could we survive this?

As if in response, the ocean *growled*. Ahead of the fleet, before they could reach us, the water swirled in ever-growing circles before plunging down into the depths as a massive form emerged—a diamond-shaped head with sharply pointed horns, gills along the sides. Its lips curled back over enormous teeth as the beast rose higher, revealing a long neck. Saltwater ran down like crystalline waterfalls along its deep blue scales.

The Leviathan's growls rippled through the waters, rocking the boats.

Remus's breath hitched. "It worked."

"What worked?" I asked.

"The sirens," he replied, eyes wide on the Leviathan. "They heeded my plea. The Leviathan is defending its ocean."

The sea dragon released a shuddering roar. I could see faint arrows being fired from the ships only to bounce off its scales. The Leviathan launched itself upon the ships. Massive claws smashed the boats into pieces. Its horned tail whipped out of the water and thrashed against the wood.

Cheers erupted around us while the Leviathan destroyed the fleet. With nothing but shreds of wood in its wake, the ruler of the seas dove back into the waters. Its tail was the last thing to be seen.

Remus grabbed my hand and held it tight. A breathless laugh escaped me. *Oh my gods.* Drusus boomed a laugh, his hand snatching Sabina at the waist and crushing his lips against hers. The Commanding She-Wolf didn't hesitate as she wrapped her arms around his neck. Atticus's eyes widened, jaw dropping as he propped an arm on Marcus's shoulder, who also stared in shock.

I thanked the gods and goddesses. The Fates. I thanked *us*, our will to survive.

We had done it.

SIXTY-EIGHT

Remus

The clasp of the cloak slipped between my fingers. Even after a week of being bedridden, strength still failed me at times.

The drapes along the balcony rippled softly from the dusk-kissed breeze. The shouts of children playing could be heard outside, together with the subtle sounds of cattle grazing and people meandering through the haven grounds.

Drusus's villa had been quiet. I hadn't seen him much since we'd returned to the haven. Other than making sure I had everything I needed like a damn nursemaid, he'd been spending his days and nights with the Commanding She-Wolf. It was long overdue, and I was happy he was happy.

It wasn't long before we'd received news that Octavian had won the naval battle against Egypt. Word of his valor and sharp wit, especially of a man of such a young age, said he would return an emperor.

I did not know what was to come from here on, but I supposed that was the point of every today.

My fingers trembled as I tried again with the clasp. A weak dart of silver skimmed over my knuckles before a hand wrapped around my own.

"Let me," Diane murmured.

She silently clasped the cloak around my neck. Her wounds had healed well, though she was also feeling a similar sense of weakness. We had been bedridden together. Exhausted and battle-worn. I'd told her about Helena and Caius. And she'd told me of Cato, and I was glad to know my call for help from the wolves' spirits had given her a chance to say goodbye. I had hoped for the same when I'd called on the god of war.

For the first few days we could hardly move, the strain from the extreme use of our aether leaving us weakened. Not to mention my near-death experience. Our friends had visited us often, feeding us and tending to our wounds. Even though we were bedridden, it didn't stop our hands from exploring each other's bodies as soon as we gained a slight bit of energy.

My palms had coursed over her naked stomach down to her core. Diane's constant gasps at my ear stirred the heat in my groin. My hard cock poked at her side as I plunged my fingers in and out of her. We tossed and turned, bodies building a warm sweat. Diane straddled me and rode my fingers. My cock. I nudged her to her hands and knees and feasted on her cunt. But most importantly, every night, every godsdamn night, she was in my arms. Death had almost claimed me, and I could feel her anxieties and fears agitate her while she slept. Her hand always reached for me in her sleep.

"Thank you," I said.

The rough pads of my fingers trailed over the corners of her face. She was draped in black, the buttery soft fabric cinched at her waist and melted against the curve of her hips. Her hair curled slightly down the length of her back.

Diane splayed her calloused hands over my black tunic. "Ready for tonight?"

I shrugged as the door opened and Marcus stepped in. He was also clad in black, the same dark river of cloth draped over his wide shoulders.

The gold-painted sky crowned him like a mighty ruler as he held the door. "Shall we?"

I nodded, grasping Diane's hand as we followed him out into the gilded light. Drusus and Atticus waited in the courtyard, their lips lifting upon seeing us. Sabina stood at Drusus's side, her hands clasped in his. I shot an amused wink at Drusus, and Sabina rolled her eyes.

A crowd greeted us as we exited Drusus's villa. Wolves, she-wolves, harpies, and even the minotaurs and griffins had stayed for tonight. For what needed to be done.

The haven parted for Diane and me and we entered the Pack's meetinghouse. A thrum of respect and awe had been spotlighting the both of us for the past week. The Wolf of the White Flames and the Daughter of Anubis who had saved Rome and the mortal realm. I wondered what songs would come from this.

Side by side, Diane and I walked to the head of the war room where two grand chairs awaited. Aurelius and Sabina took their places beside us as Marcus motioned for us to sit. I slowly lowered myself into the seat, stretching out my legs. Diane placed her hands over the arms of the chair, her chin held high as she watched the room.

I leaned in toward her. My breath tickled the curve of her ear. "You look like a queen."

Diane arched a brow, a wicked glint to her golden eyes. "Are you just noticing that now? Maybe I should question this whole relationship."

"Well, you could've fooled me. When I first met you, you were more the spawn of a daemon than anything."

Diane gasped and swatted my arm, laughing. I chuckled before catching her hand and bringing it to my lips. She tried to pull back, but I kept her hand on my lap as we waited. The remaining forces entered the war room, so many of them that the crowd had to spread out into the main hall.

A horn blared from outside the meetinghouse, and a few in the crowd gasped. Human Roman soldiers marched through, making way for the man who strode in after them. His pale, yellow hair was cropped short. A strong nose sat over a thin set of lips, his eyes too cold and calculating for his youth.

The male's lips curled into a smile, void of warmth. "I'm pleased to have made it in time."

Marcus strode forward to stand before the human, refraining from bowing to the male. "Octavian, your invite here is out of courtesy. You know well that we act outside of the city's jurisdiction."

Octavian nodded, extending an open palm. "Of course, I do not intend to interfere."

I eyed the young emperor. His cold gaze flickered to me, and I allowed the silver behind my eyes to flare. Octavian's jaw twitched, but he held his ground. He knew of me from the days when I'd tampered with Caesar's plans to conquer the wolves. The human knew where his power lay, and it was *not* among us.

Aurelius clasped his hands together. "Pack and fellow allies, we honor Caius tonight. For the vision he had of how the Pack and those who share the same land could unite, especially in a time of need. In the anticipation of his untimely death, Caius had one last request."

My brow pinched in confusion at the words. Aurelius beckoned to Marcus, who was holding a parchment I hadn't noticed.

Marcus's blue eyes went to mine briefly before he began to read aloud. "'In the event of my death, I give my final declaration as Alpha and renounce Remus, son of Anthony, as the Lone Wolf. He is welcomed back to his rightful place among the wolves of Rome. He is now, as he always has been, one of us.'"

I felt the soft squeeze of Diane's hand, and I shifted in my seat. My throat went thick with emotion. For so long I had secretly yearned for this, even when I had been angry and broken. All those years. Caius, even in death, had saved me again.

The feeling was so profound and immeasurable I could only manage a deep bow of my head. Murmurs of agreement and quiet applause strummed through the room.

Marcus rolled the parchment closed, his blue eyes flitting to me. "The other item of this evening is to proclaim our new Alpha."

Sabina and Aurelius turned to me. Their arms crossed over their chest in unison, as if challenging me, and Marcus smiled. "Remus, we ask that you reclaim your title as Alpha."

The crowd now stirred, both in delight and question. Diane sucked in a breath. The announcement washed through the previous overwhelming emotion. All I'd known growing up had been to become one of the most skilled warriors of the wolves, to learn and go into battle and eventually take my pater's place as Alpha. That had always been the calling given to me.

I looked at Diane and saw the genuine support and pride in her eyes. I pressed my lips to her knuckles again before I moved to stand. I had always known what the answer would be if I'd had a choice. It was what I had always wanted.

I stopped before Marcus, the corner of my lips lifting. "I do not accept."

His eyes widened as shock rippled through the room. I looked at Aurelius and Sabina, letting my gaze coast across the crowd. "I am honored to be a part of this Pack again. For as long as I've known, becoming Alpha was always expected of me. However, you have someone amongst you who has shown time and again he is truly worthy of leading the wolves."

I clasped a hand on Marcus's shoulder. "He is your Alpha. Not me."

Aurelius smiled and gave a firm nod. He understood. I was no longer the wolf the Pack had known while I was growing up. The role of Alpha was not meant for me. Marcus taking on this role felt right. Meant to be.

Marcus stared at me like he wasn't sure he'd heard correctly, and I tilted my head. "Your choice, Marcus, but I have seen you amongst the Pack. The dedication and love you have for our kind. You have always had the makings of an Alpha."

He blinked. Once. Twice. Then flashed brilliant teeth. "It would be my honor."

Atticus and Drusus hollered and clapped his back. Shouts and cheers erupted and shook the war room as the Pack welcomed their new Alpha.

Diane watched me with a gentle look. "I'm proud of you."

My smile grew. "I heard they're throwing a feast tonight."

Diane tapped a finger to her lips giving me a curious look. "Oh? Does the Wolf of the White Flames have a desire to drink the night away like last time?"

My expression smoothed, but I still felt a kernel of warmth in my chest. I tapped a finger against her nose. "This time, I will be dancing with you and only you."

I could've sworn stars winked in those golden eyes. "I like the sound of that."

The Pack forum was lined with torches. Music rang throughout the streets. The smell of lemon and thyme floated in the moonlit night. People gathered, laughing, and eating and dancing. A glimpse of life without war, without the daemons, and without the realm's lurking darkness.

Diane wrapped her hands around my arm as we joined the others. Drusus and Sabina were already on the dance floor, mostly kissing rather than dancing. Camilla had dragged Atticus on there as well, shouting for Diane to follow.

Diane tugged at my arm, her hips swaying to the music. "You can't back out now, Wolf."

I drank her in and felt my lips part at the sight. She made me so incredibly happy. I lunged for her, grabbing her waist and her hand, and spun her off her feet. "Never."

She laughed, the sound of summer rain. We danced, we embraced, and we reveled till the dawn kissed the night.

Grateful. I was grateful for this, for my path of healing and love. For those I'd had and still had in my life.

My Pack.

My family.

My light.

EPILOGUE

Diane
One year later . . .

Waves brushed against the sides of the boat. Salt-sprinkled breezes misted over my tongue and face. The sound of the open sea and the flaps of the sail in the wind were a welcome rhythm to go with the excited pounding in my heart.

My fingers brushed against the ring on my finger. Gold roped around a thin band.

Calloused hands slid around my waist, pulling me against a hard chest. I drank in the smell of ocean and cedar as Remus brushed his jaw against my ear.

"Hello, wife," Remus rumbled.

My smile grew. Flutters still stirred in my stomach at the word. It hadn't taken long for me to make the decision. Marriage wasn't absolutely necessary, but this had been my choice. Something I'd wanted to do to represent the love I had for this male.

Rome was long behind us. Business between the Pack and the other Olympians had been strengthening. And Marcus was doing well as Alpha, ensuring that trade and business continued to progress through the realm, realizing Caius's dream.

There were still surviving members of the Order alive and trying to cause havoc, and Marcus had led the hunt against those who still aimed to carry out a rebellion in the Ram's name. Remus had helped the fight for a while before laying his weapons down for this new venture with me.

I rested my head against my husband's chest. "The captain said we will be docking at any moment."

He tucked his chin between my neck and shoulder. His green eyes looked to the sea. "To Egypt."

My grip on his hands tightened, eyes drifting to the matching gold band on his finger. "I hope this time your experience will be better."

He chuckled. "Of that I have no doubt, as I've yet to try their wine."

"You're ridiculous."

"Adorable, you mean."

Warmth blossomed in my chest as I tilted my head to look up at him. "I love you."

Remus brushed his lips against my temple. "And I love you, my lotus."

The gilded ribbons of the setting sun reflected along the water's surface, casting a blinding glow. As the light lifted, figures of what looked like dusted gold teeth bit into the evening sky.

My lips parted as the pyramids emerged from the distance.

The End

ACKNOWLEDGEMENTS

Oh my. What a journey. I am overwhelmed with joy that I have finally written and published a story that has been on my mind for about seven or eight years. I have to mention that I am obsessed with mythology and ancient cultures. I was inspired by the myth of Romulus and Remus. They are the twin demigods that were born from the god of war and were raised by a she-wolf. When I heard this myth I thought, what if we made this fantasy, what if the twins could shift into wolves? And the idea of *Of Fangs and Shadows* was born and developed over the years.

Remus and Diane have done so much for me. It was so much fun getting to know them, to see what their personalities were like, and how they grew throughout the book. I found such a passion in writing, it became a fulfillment to create and make everything I see in my head "come to life."

I must begin my acknowledgements by thanking my parents. My mama and my papa, thank you for always encouraging me to pursue my goals. And thank you for helping me grow my love for books since my childhood. I am a dreamer because of you both. ¡Los quiero mucho!

And to mi amor, my love, I cannot express enough how grateful I am to you. Thank you for always supporting me, for cheering me on even when I was most discouraged. I am so thankful for all you have done for me, especially when you turn on anime to help soothe my soul after a long day. When and where you are, then and there I will be. Te amo.

Thank you to one of my dearest friends who is also my editor, Jen. You were there from the very beginning, from listening to my crazy ideas to all my insecurities and fears. Thank you for helping me. Your encouragement and constructive criticism meant a lot to me and I am ever grateful. Love you!

To the friends I made over Bookstagram, thank you so much. Your support and excitement for this book and my overall goal to become an author never went unnoticed. I am so appreciative of all the help, I could not have made it this far without you all. A million thank yous!

Thank you to the fantastic ARC team who helped me take *Of Fangs and Shadows* off the ground. You are all incredible. Thank you for volunteering and being part of the journey. I truly could not have done this without you.

Family and close friends, I thank you with all my heart for your encouragement and love. For motivating and inspiring me to keep going. I love you all!

And to you, the reader, I cannot express how deeply thankful I am for you. Thank you for reading, I hope our paths cross once again.

MEET THE AUTHOR

Jessica is a graduate of the University of California, Irvine and received her Master's Degree in Business Administration in 2022. She currently works in the healthcare industry. Jessica has always been passionate about writing and has often found herself creating stories ever since childhood. When not writing, she can be found weightlifting, watching anime, or wandering around a bookstore. She currently resides in Southern California with her husband, most likely listening to Epic music in search of creative inspiration. Connect with Jessica by visiting her website:beacons.ai/ book.baddie.